Praise for Sophia Money-Coutts

'Feel-good and enormous fun. It's a delicious, warm, witty book'
Sophie Kinsella

'With laugh-out-loud moments, you'll love this romcom'
Prima

'A laugh-out-loud book… the perfect summer escape'
Lindsey Kelk

'Full-on funny from the first page, filled with Sophia's trademark wit and warmth. A great tonic to the year we've all had'
Zoë Folbigg

'Romcom writer extraordinaire'
OK

'For fans of Jilly Cooper and Bridget Jones'
My Weekly

'I laughed out loud throughout this – no mean feat! This is a sure-fire summer hit!'
Laura Jane Williams

'Heartwarming and fun'
Bella

'A joyful, big-hearted balm of a book from one of my favourite writers. A funny, life- and love-affirming special book'
Cressida McLaughlin

'For fans of Jilly Cooper… warm-hearted, hilarious and romantic'
Best

D1390830

Praise for Sophia Money-Coutts

'It wouldn't be summer without a new romcom from Sophia Money-Coutts'
Red

'Sophia Money-Coutts' writing is sharp and clever, and *Did You Miss Me?* is no exception. Super funny, super witty and so warm. I loved it'
Lia Louis

'Howlingly funny'
Sunday Times

'A laugh-a-minute page-turner, perfect for poolside reading'
HELLO!

'Hilariously relatable. *Did You Miss Me?* feels like a nostalgic treat'
Sophie Cousens

'A beach cocktail in book form'
Metro

'Hilarious and uplifting'
Woman & Home

'An entertaining page-turner… I couldn't stop smiling as I raced through it'
Holly Miller

'Perfect light summer reading'
Evening Standard

'As fun and fizzy as a chilled glass of prosecco… this is the perfect read for your holiday'
Daily Express

Sophia Money-Coutts is a journalist and author who spent five years studying the British aristocracy while working as Features Director at *Tatler.* Prior to that she worked as a writer and an editor for the *Evening Standard* and the *Daily Mail* in London, and *The National* in Abu Dhabi. She's a columnist for the *Sunday Telegraph* called 'Modern Manners' and often appears on radio and television channels, talking about important topics such as Prince Harry's wedding and the etiquette of the threesome. *Looking Out For Love* is her fifth novel.

Also by
Sophia Money-Coutts

The Plus One
What Happens Now?
The Wish List
Did You Miss Me?

LOOKING OUT FOR LOVE

SOPHIA MONEY-COUTTS

ONE PLACE. MANY STORIES

This novel is entirely a work of fiction. The names, characters and incidents portrayed in it are the work of the author's imagination. Any resemblance to actual persons, living or dead, events or localities is entirely coincidental.

HQ
An imprint of HarperCollins*Publishers* Ltd
1 London Bridge Street
London SE1 9GF

www.harpercollins.co.uk

HarperCollins*Publishers*
Macken House, 39/40 Mayor Street Upper,
Dublin 1, D01 C9W8, Ireland

This edition 2023

1
First published in Great Britain by
HQ, an imprint of HarperCollins*Publishers* Ltd 2023

Copyright © Sophia Money-Coutts 2023

Sophia Money-Coutts asserts the moral right to be identified as the author of this work.
A catalogue record for this book is available from the British Library.

ISBN: 978-0-00-846707-4

This book is produced from independently certified FSC™ paper to ensure responsible forest management.

For more information visit: www.harpercollins.co.uk/green

Printed and Bound in the UK using 100% Renewable Electricity at CPI Group (UK) Ltd, Croydon, CR0 4YY

All rights reserved. No part of this publication may be reproduced, stored in a retrieval system, or transmitted, in any form or by any means, electronic, mechanical, photocopying, recording or otherwise, without the prior permission of the publishers.

This book is sold subject to the condition that it shall not, by way of trade or otherwise, be lent, re-sold, hired out or otherwise circulated without the publisher's prior consent in any form of binding or cover other than that in which it is published and without a similar condition including this condition being imposed on the subsequent purchaser.

To our hospitals, and all who work in them.

CHAPTER 1

STELLA SHAKESPEARE LONGED FOR love. She longed for love so much that it felt like a dirty secret, something that she should hide lest her desperation put others off. She wanted all-consuming, can't-think-about-anything-else, can't-even-manage-to-eat kind of love.

What she found beside her in bed that morning was definitely not love.

She lifted her face from the pillow and frowned at the unfamiliar headboard. A studded leather headboard. She didn't remember that from last night.

To the side, she noticed a strange bedside table on which there was a glass of water – full – which would explain why her tongue felt like a boiled owl.

At the sensation of someone stirring under the cover beside her, she looked right at a head of dishevelled black hair she didn't recognise, and a pair of broad, male shoulders.

The stranger made a waking-up groan and Stella looked back to the leather headboard. What sort of man had a leather headboard? Or maybe even pleather. Stella reached her fingers towards it. Yes, pleather. This definitely wasn't love.

'Morning,' came a low drawl.

Seconds later, Stella felt a hand slide along the back of her thigh and over her bottom.

'What time is it?' she asked, ignoring the hand as it snaked up her back. The audacity! He hadn't even looked at her yet.

The hand retracted itself and he raised his head to squint at his watch. His hair was obscuring his face so Stella's eyes slid to the curve of his bicep as he pushed himself back from the mattress. Where had she found this guy? She'd been in the pub, having drinks with Billie, and then Jez had shown up and insisted on taking Billie home, but Stella wanted to stay. It was a Wednesday night. It wasn't *illegal* to stay up past ten on a Wednesday night. So she'd stayed, and chatted to Jack behind the bar for a bit, and then, well, Stella wasn't entirely sure.

'Nearly nine,' he replied.

'Nine! I need to go.' Stella looked down and noticed a black smear the size of a thumbprint on her pillow. 'I've got some mascara on this, sorry.'

She glanced at him and was met with an easy smile.

He was attractive, actually. Thick stubble lined his jaw and his eyes – green, alert, betraying no signs of a hangover – softened as they met hers. He looked as if he could advertise a new line of coffee pods. Stella mirrored his smile as she remembered flashes of the previous night: his body moving above hers, his mouth hot against her neck, his hands running down her arms, holding her, teasing her, the confident way he'd shifted her around, as if she was an instrument he was playing for the pleasure of them both. It had been good, Stella recalled, still smiling. Really good. Maybe she could stay in bed for a few more minutes. She couldn't possibly fall in love with this stranger, but lust was very different to love.

'Don't worry,' he replied, nodding towards the mascara, one side of his mouth curving higher. 'Probably not yours.'

There was a brief pause while Stella digested the implication before she kicked her legs free from the duvet and stood. 'I need to go.'

She scrabbled around on his carpet, peeling up various items of clothes in the gloom. Jeans, T-shirt, sweater, one sock. Every time she bent over, she angled her bottom away from him, towards the shutters. Not her mascara indeed. He might be handsome and attentive in bed but he was also an arsehole. Another one. Stella would have a stern word with herself later. She was never going to find her great love if she continued to behave like this, drifting through London like some sort of arsehole magnet.

Still grinning, he pushed himself up on one arm. 'I was joking! You're welcome to stay. My shift doesn't start for...' he paused and looked at his watch, 'four hours.'

'I don't think so. I think you've had quite enough.' Stella dragged her eyes away from his chest, as muscled as a museum statue, and spotted the missing sock. 'I bet you don't even know my name,' she said, reaching for it.

He laughed. 'You weren't very interested in names last night. What's mine, anyway?'

'I haven't got time to stand here talking about names! I've got an interview.' She scanned his bedroom floor for her knickers.

'It's Sam. And you are?'

'Hardly matters now, does it?' Stella mumbled while squinting at a small dark item at the foot of the bed. One of his socks.

'Here,' Sam said, retrieving a pair of pants from under the duvet and dangling them in the air.

'Thank you.' Stella snatched them and made for the bathroom, only to discover she'd opened a wardrobe door and was facing his shoe rack.

'That way.' He nodded towards another door.

'Yes, OK, thank you,' she snapped, hurrying for it before shutting herself in and reaching for a cabinet above the sink. Please could this man have some sort of painkiller. Paracetamol, Nurofen, morphine, even. Stella's head felt like it might burst.

She peered into the cabinet. There was a can of shaving cream, a tub of hair wax, a few razors, a yellow tube of cream and, beside them, a metallic strip of Nurofen. Only one pill left but one would have to do. Stella tossed it into her mouth and leant over the sink to palm tap water into her mouth. Then she squeezed a globule of Colgate onto her index finger and smeared it around her teeth. She rinsed and stood to inspect her face in the mirror. Not ideal: her eyelids were puffy and faintly purple; her skin dull and dry. And now she had to get to Holborn to convince a legal contact of her father's that she was a responsible, presentable employee who'd make an ideal assistant.

She sighed. What was the population of London? Stella wasn't sure of the exact number but she knew it was a lot. Millions. Millions of men in this city. All right, a few less if she discounted the gay ones and the ones who were too old for her (over forty-five) or too young (under twenty-five). Obviously she also had to ignore the men who sneezed without covering their mouths and the ones who wore pointy shoes. Nor was Stella interested in any adult man who insisted on calling his mother 'Mummy' or the sort of man who gave his car a name. Or his penis, for that matter. But even if she took *all* those men away, there still had to be plenty of others. So how come every man Stella ever met was an asshole?

She sighed again. No time for philosophy; she had to go. Stella ran a finger under each eye to remove the sooty stains of eye-liner, peered back into the cabinet for a moisturiser to inject some colour back into her cheeks and grabbed the yellow tube.

When she emerged from the bathroom, he was still in bed, leaning back against the pleather headboard. Grinning, he ran a hand through his hair, flexing one of his biceps. 'I definitely can't persuade you to stay?'

Stella glanced pointedly at the pillow with the mascara stain before picking up her bag and marching towards his kitchen. 'No thank you, I've got a very important interview.'

'Any chance of a number?' Sam shouted after her.

'If it's meant to be, you'll guess it,' she shouted back, slamming his door behind her. Which is how Stella Shakespeare, thirty-two, set off for her important job interview with Scholl's athlete's foot cream smeared all over her face.

CHAPTER 2

OUTSIDE, STELLA DISCOVERED THAT she was in a part of east London she didn't recognise, and that her phone was dead so she couldn't look up directions. She squinted at a map in a bus stop, which helped her find Aldgate East station, travelled west on the Tube to Holborn and, via the help of another map in another bus stop, finally found the office of Spinks, London's top law firm, where she'd been expected for an interview at 9.30 a.m.

Now it was 10.10 a.m. and she felt sick. The single Nurofen hadn't worked, and she'd sipped a black coffee on the Tube, which was repeating on her. Stella cursed herself for not buying a packet of chewing gum and blew a small acidic belch from the side of her mouth before pressing the buzzer.

At the sound of a click, she pushed through the front door, then a second glass door to find a reception area with two cream sofas, a marble floor and paintings in gold frames on the walls. One of these paintings showed a ship pitching on a stormy sea, the bow pointing skywards on the crest of a foamy wave. That was exactly how her stomach felt, Stella thought: decidedly choppy.

She looked from the painting to a man on one of the sofas who resembled her father: grey hair, pink handkerchief perfectly positioned in his suit pocket, gold signet ring. He was tapping at his phone with an air of urgency, which Stella's father often did too, breaking off from family members to bark into his phone at an employee.

'Can I help you?'

She glanced towards the reception desk, which was staffed by a woman with a severe fringe and a headset.

'Morning, I'm Stella Shakespeare, here to see Gideon Fotheringham?' She smiled before quickly pinching her lips together as she felt another coffee belch rise.

The receptionist blinked at her computer screen. 'Says here the meeting was for nine thirty?'

'It was, but I live in west London and I caught the wrong line from Earl's Court. By accident. It's very easy to do that.'

The receptionist's lips twitched with suspicion.

'Look, Rosemary,' said Stella, taking in her name badge and leaning one forearm on the desk. 'I'm going to level with you. It's been a long morning and I'm not feeling great but I really, *really* need this job, so anything you could do would be appreciated. From one girl to the next, hey?'

Rosemary bent her head back to the computer and, after a small sniff, started tapping. 'Mr Fotheringham is exceptionally busy this morning. I'll have to see whether he has any time.'

'Excuse me, I don't wish to interrupt,' came an aggrieved voice behind them.

Stella turned to look at the man on the sofa and realised he didn't exactly resemble her father, because he had a moustache that drooped over the corners of his mouth, like a fat caterpillar that had become lodged under his nose and died.

He glared at Rosemary and continued, 'I have a ten fifteen with Gideon and I really can't be late.'

'No need to worry, Mr Williams. This...' Rosemary paused and looked at Stella as if trying to work out whether she was a vegetable or mineral, '*lady* might have to wait until he's seen you.'

Stella laid her forehead on her arm. Standing up felt like too much effort. If she didn't get this job, her father would kill her. Well, he'd stop paying off her credit card, which was almost as bad. This was the fifth interview Stella had gone through in two weeks and she was desperate.

'Hello, Mr Fotheringham?' Rosemary said into her headset. 'I've got a Stella Shakespeare to see you... Yes... I know... No, I know... She said she got the wrong train.'

'At Earl's Court, tell him that,' Stella mumbled.

'Fine. No problem, Mr Fotheringham, yes, absolutely, I'll inform her of that, yes.'

Stella looked up hopefully.

'Mr Fotheringham says he hasn't got long because he has to see Mr Williams, but if you don't mind taking the lift to the third floor, he'll see you quickly now.'

'You're a babe, thanks, Rosemary,' Stella replied with relief, before stepping to the side and hitting the lift button.

When it stopped on the third floor, the doors opened to reveal a tall blond man with very red cheeks, mouth wide open as if he was about to shout. But he closed it as soon as he saw Stella.

'Mr Fotheringham?'

'Yes. And you must be Stella?'

'Mmm, yes, I mean. So sorry I'm late. It was... Tube trouble.'

'Not to worry, I understand,' Gideon Fotheringham replied smoothly, beaming at her.

Stella often had this effect on men. Once a golden-haired, green-eyed child, she'd become as beautiful as a Botticelli painting and now attracted glances from both sexes when she walked down the street.

Still almost white-blonde, her long hair was always loose, often tangled and tugged self-consciously over one shoulder, and she had a body other women stared at because they believed life would be much easier if they had it themselves: long legs, a narrow waist and very perky, pillowy breasts that didn't look natural but absolutely were.

Men like Gideon stared at her too, although for completely different reasons.

To be fair, it was partly because of these looks, and her father's limitless credit card, that Stella had seemed to glide through life like a swan on a country lake: beautiful and seemingly unruffled by anything surrounding her. But even swans have their off moments, and more recently Stella felt as if she was drowning, not gliding, as she lurched from one disaster to the next. Running late for an important job interview was merely the latest calamity.

'This way,' Gideon went on, placing a meaty hand between Stella's shoulder blades, propelling her along a corridor. 'I'm so glad you could come and see me. My colleague has just left, very suddenly, so I need a brilliant assistant to help manage things.' He smiled and revealed all his teeth as they stepped into his office. 'Do sit,' he added, gesturing at a chair in front of a mahogany desk covered with photos in silver frames, mostly of himself.

'Thank you,' Stella replied, grateful to sit since the hangover seemed to have weakened her legs.

'So,' he went on, collapsing in a leather chair behind the desk like a sack of flour and flashing the same wide smile. 'I can't recall what legal experience you have?'

'Umm...' Stella paused. She had precisely no legal experience. She had barely any work experience at all.

In the past few years, she'd tried various jobs but failed at every single one.

She'd interned at *Vogue* but been fired after three months when she was found asleep under a clothes rail in the fashion cupboard, wrapped in a very expensive fur coat that had been called in for a photo shoot.

After that she decided to become a yoga instructor, but had to leave her teacher-training course after she slept with the instructor, a bearded man called Marcus with a large tattoo of a dolphin leaping up his back.

Next, Stella borrowed more money from her father and designed a range of artisanal boxer shorts, but failed to sell more than a few pairs to her own family members.

Even though she couldn't cook, she'd then offered to cook for a friend of her mother's who had a large house in Holland Park, but been 'let go' when she burned the spaghetti. Quite hard to burn spaghetti; she'd forgotten about the pan on the hob until all the water had evaporated and the pasta strands turned black.

Not long after that, Stella met Miles St George, handsome heir to a dog-food fortune, and gave up any attempt at developing a career because she'd assumed she would marry him.

'Ummm,' she murmured again as Gideon's eyes dropped to her

chest. 'No, I don't have much legal experience but…' Stella wanted to say that she'd rather lick the sole of her shoe than work for this creepy pervert, but she needed the money. 'I'm a big fan of *Law & Order*.'

This, at least, was true. Since she and Miles had broken up, Stella often found herself lying on the sofa in the afternoon, watching old reruns of the show, trying to distract herself with grisly and improbable murders. The previous week, while watching an episode where the murderer had killed his victim with an ice-cream scoop she'd wondered whether she could do the same to her now ex-boyfriend.

Gideon frowned.

'The TV show? It's American, set in New Yor—'

'I see. I think you'll find it's very different here. Spinks is London's most prestigious law firm, and I head up the family department so we deal mostly with divorces. Very high profile.'

'Right,' said Stella before swallowing quickly at another coffee burp.

'We often see clients at their worst, very distressed at the end of their marriages, which means discretion is paramount, you understand?'

She nodded, trying to concentrate on his words, but her stomach was churning.

Gideon leant forward across the desk and placed his fingertips together. 'Do you, er, have a boyfriend?'

This was one step too far. Stella's stomach kicked, the back of her throat tightened and she looked wildly around for a sign for the bathroom.

But there was no sign, so she reached for a cream wastepaper basket beside his desk and vomited her coffee into it.

CHAPTER 3

TWENTY MINUTES LATER, STELLA left the Spinks office feeling pretty confident she hadn't got the job. After wiping her mouth with her fingers and apologising several times, she'd asked Gideon where the nearest loo was and carried the wastepaper basket with her.

'Please don't tell my father,' she'd begged when she'd returned with the bin, rinsed in the bathroom sink. Gideon murmured that he'd be in touch.

The entire morning had been a shambles. Another disaster. She couldn't even manage an interview for a job as an assistant. What on earth would she do now? What could she do? Nothing. She was good for nothing.

As Stella stood on the stone steps outside the Spinks office, she watched a pigeon peck at a cigarette butt on the pavement and wondered whether the pigeon didn't actually have a better life than she did. At least pigeons didn't have to get jobs.

She was overcome by a desperation to get home for a piece of toast and a cup of sweet tea, but she didn't think they had any bread or fresh milk in the flat. She'd pray to the money gods and chance her card in Nisa.

Except, just as Stella made to turn left from the steps and head towards the Tube station, she was rapped on the arm by a short, very round woman wearing a belted mackintosh and a pair of chunky combat boots. On her head was a golf visor, white curls of hair escaping over the top of it like bed springs. 'Excuse me!'

'I don't have any money,' Stella replied wearily, having lived in London long enough to know that anybody weird enough to approach a stranger (and touch them) was probably after cash. 'I've got no money. And no job.' Her voice went wobbly. 'And I haven't got a boyfriend becau—'

'Shhh, stop it, you ridiculous girl. I don't want your money. And I don't need your employment history or sordid details of your romantic life. What I *do* want to know is if you saw a man who looked like a walrus in there.'

'What?' said Stella, unable to keep up with the short woman's demands.

'In Spinks. In there.' She jabbed a chubby finger at the door. 'That's where you've just come from, isn't it?'

'Mmm,' Stella admitted. This woman was clearly mad. She certainly looked mad; dressed like some sort of park ranger, with small dark eyes twitching above a large nose and that uncontrolled white hair.

'And? Was there a man who looked like a walrus?'

'Er…'

'Come on, think!'

'There was a man with a kind of… walrussy moustache on the sofa, yes.'

'I knew it!' The short woman swung a clenched fist in the air.

'Mr Williams, he was called,' Stella went on, remembering

what Rosemary had called him. 'And he had a suit and a pink handkerchief. And he was wearing a signet ring!'

She smiled like a proud mother. 'Excellent work.'

'Oh,' said Stella, taken aback.

'Look, I've got to get going, but if you really do need employment, I might have something for you.' The short woman reached into her pocket and pulled out a dog-eared business card. 'Always on the lookout for observant types. You can reach me on that number.'

She hurried off before Stella could even ask her what she did. Then she looked at the card in her hand: *Verity Culpepper Ltd.*

How strange. Presumably a lunatic.

Stella dropped the card into her bag and resumed her journey towards the station. She needed that cup of tea and she wanted to wash and remove all traces of the previous evening. Jobless. Heartbroken. Smelling faintly of sick. No wonder Miles had ended things, she thought gloomily.

It had all looked so rosy at the start. Miles was the great love Stella had spent so long waiting for: the rich, well-connected heir to a dog-food fortune. Her parents, naturally, adored him, and his parents – Lord and Lady St George – approved of her. Why wouldn't they? Stella Shakespeare was exactly the kind of woman Miles St George was expected to date: a creamy-skinned English rose from a wealthy family herself, who could ride horses, play tennis and ski – all the key skills Miles was looking for in a wife.

Having met at a mutual friend's engagement party in a Chelsea pub, Stella fell for Miles immediately and, believing herself to be madly in love, started moulding her life around his. She devoted her time to redecorating his flat in Chelsea, followed by the cottage he'd inherited from his grandmother in Gloucestershire. It was astonishing how much time it took to choose wallpaper, Stella solemnly told her best friend, Billie.

It wasn't just redecorating, though. Going out with Miles St George meant a busy schedule of dinner parties, of shooting weekends in the winter, and polo and croquet weekends in the summer. Not long after she'd started dating him, Stella realised she didn't have time for a job, but that was all right because she didn't seem to be very good at working and Miles was bound to propose at some point. After the pair had been together for two years, Stella's mother started emailing her links to wedding dress boutiques, and everybody waited for the big announcement.

Until Miles ended it and everything fell apart. Her parents were furious with her; most of her social life evaporated overnight. She'd thought she'd had plenty of friends until then. Friends she saw at dinners and polo matches or stayed with in the country. Friends who invited her and Miles to Mayfair restaurant openings and exhibition launches. Even though Stella had found some of them very dull, it had been fun and she'd felt part of a gang. Except, as soon as Miles had broken up with her, she'd been kicked out of that gang.

As Stella trudged her way to the Tube station, she was hit by the memory of *that* morning. It still haunted her at least once a day.

Miles had showered, dressed and come to sit on the edge of his bed to kiss her goodbye as usual, before heading into the dog-food headquarters in Marylebone. Still in bed but sensing him nearby, smelling his aftershave, Stella had turned her face towards the ceiling, eyes closed, waiting for a kiss. But when the familiar feeling of his lips on hers hadn't come, she'd opened her eyes to see Miles looking uncomfortable, like a Labrador who'd recently snuck into the hen house.

She'd reached for his hand. 'What is it?'

Miles swallowed and told Stella he 'wasn't sure' he wanted a relationship any more.

'When did you decide that? Last night while we were having sex, or more recently?' Stella replied crossly.

Miles, continuing to look guilty, had stuttered that it had been a 'gradual thing', that he thought it was 'for the best' and could Stella leave his house keys on the hall table? Then he'd kissed her on the head, like a father saying goodbye to his daughter before work, and left.

Stella had got up, got dressed, scraped Miles's toothbrush around the rim of the loo bowl several times and put it back beside the sink, *then* left. Keys on the hall table, just as he'd asked.

Numb, she managed not to cry until Billie – her oldest, truest friend – arrived home to their flat that evening. But she cried, drank and chain-smoked for several weeks afterwards. Six months on, the crying had finally stopped, but not the drinking or smoking. And even now, every time the scene reappeared in her head, Stella felt winded, as if she was back in Miles's bedroom, teetering on the edge of a cliff that he was about to push her off.

She continued to think about Miles every other minute. She carried him around like a heavy burden that pressed on her chest and made her whole body ache. She thought she'd found her great love but she'd been wrong and, to make matters worse, she was broke. She'd continued to use Miles's Uber account for several weeks after the break-up, always ordering the more expensive cars to spite him, but eventually he'd changed his password and Stella had been forced to start taking the Tube, which she found very confusing. She often did get the wrong line through Earl's Court, so she hadn't *exactly* fibbed to the Spinks receptionist. It just hadn't happened that morning.

At the station, Stella stepped back from the sliding doors to let the passengers off before wearily climbing back on and making her way to Notting Hill.

Except, unfortunately, when she got to her local corner shop, her card didn't work, maxed out on the journey.

Stella looked pleadingly at Nigel. She'd been in here a thousand times over the years, buying milk, eggs, bread, packets of cigarettes that she smoked through her sitting room window, bottles of vodka and tonic water, crisps if they had friends coming over, wine and chocolate for Sunday evenings when she and Billie wanted to sit on the sofa and watch a film to distract them from their hangovers.

Nigel shook his head. 'Sorry, love, no exceptions. Even for you.'

'No problem, I'll just starve to death,' Stella said with a dramatic sigh as she walked out, leaving the bread and milk on the counter.

Upstairs, in the flat, she found a bottle of Billie's almond milk and some of her revolting German bread. Not ideal, but it would have to do. Beggars can't be choosers, Stella told herself as she spread Marmite across a slice of toast and spooned three sugars into her mug.

She had a bath, pulled on a clean T-shirt and tracksuit bottoms, got into bed and fell instantly asleep. It wasn't even midday, but she couldn't face another long afternoon by herself on the sofa.

CHAPTER 4

'STELL? YOU HERE?'

Stella lifted her head from her pillow and frowned. What time was it? What day was it?

'Stell?'

'I'm here! Just...' She quickly swung her legs out of bed and started scraping the clothes on her carpet into a pile to disguise the fact she'd been sleeping.

'What you doing?' asked Billie, appearing round the door.

'Tidying!'

'Have you been in bed?'

Stella, still crouched, unpeeling a dirty pair of pants from crumpled jeans, decided not to fib. She never could lie to Billie. 'Yes?'

Billie rolled her eyes.

'It's not my fault! I had a weird morning,' said Stella, dropping the jeans and standing up.

'I'm sure. You were flying by the time we left you in the pub.'

'Mmmm,' Stella mused, unable to add much detail since she couldn't remember what happened after Billie and Jez went home.

'Tell me about it over a cup of tea?'

Stella curled her lip.

'What?'

'Or a glass of wine?'

'We're out. And this arrived for you.' Billie slid a hand around the door to reveal an envelope. She flicked her wrist and threw it like a frisbee so the letter fluttered to the carpet.

Stella eyed it warily. 'Is it a bill?'

'A summons to court, I think.'

'*What?*'

'Kidding. Our smear test results.'

Stella groaned as she crouched for the letter. 'I'd almost prefer a bill.'

'Tea,' ordered Billie before disappearing behind the door.

Stella reached for a jumper and followed her to the kitchen.

Although the flat was home to both of them and they'd lived together for nearly a decade, the place was technically Stella's, bought for her by her father. Ian Shakespeare was a self-made millionaire who'd made his fortune in the retirement business – buying up development plots on the outskirts of various northern towns and building red-brick care homes on them. His first home – Sunset Village – had been built near Rotherham in 1988, and he now had sixty-four of them. Sunset Village Coventry, Sunset Village Plymouth, Sunset Village Southend-on-Sea and so on. According to last year's *Sunday Times* Rich List, he was worth £220m.

He and Stella's mother, Valerie, owned a house in Buckinghamshire and another in Richmond, although Ian spent much of his time driving around England inspecting his business properties while Valerie remained at home in the country, in their large mock-Tudor house just outside Beaconsfield. There, she interspersed trips to the local salon with energetic sessions of tennis, golf, bridge and Pilates.

Ian bought the Notting Hill flat for Stella just before she started a (subsequently aborted) music degree. It was a bright, two-bedroom apartment with high ceilings and tall windows, on a road of pastel-coloured terraced houses with pink magnolia trees that blossomed in front of them every spring, which tourists photographed for Instagram.

Inside, the flat was charmingly chaotic. Visitors stepped from the top-floor landing into a living room that had become increasingly filled with the sort of ephemera that two women in their early thirties collect over the years: a blue bowl from Greece on a side table in which Stella and Billie dropped their keys when they got home; a papier-mâché elephant on the mantelpiece from a trip to Thailand; a ceramic B and S propped up on the highest bookshelf; a large black and white photo of Marilyn Monroe hanging over the sofa, opposite a Banksy print that Billie's anti-monarchist boyfriend had once given her, which Stella hated but had allowed on the wall anyway. It was a chimpanzee wearing a tiara, which was supposed to look like the Queen. Hideous, Stella thought.

The kitchen was little better. Billie was a neat person but, since she went to work all day and Stella did not, she often came home in the evening to find plates covered with crumbs and multiple half-drunk mugs of tea on the table, and the odd knife, smeared with butter and raspberry jam, abandoned on the kitchen counter like a murder weapon.

That evening, Billie moved Stella's toast plate into the sink and filled up the kettle.

'Real tea or fake tea?'

Real tea meant an Earl Grey; fake tea meant one of Billie's strange teabags made from nettle dust or moon juice or whatever new box she'd recently bought from the lady who ran the crystal shop on the Portobello Road.

'Erm...' Stella stood on tiptoes to feel into the wicker crate on top of the fridge. Her hand groped inside it and retrieved a bottle but it was old whisky, as dark as apple juice, and even Stella wasn't that desperate. 'I swear we had another bottle.'

Billie raised an eyebrow.

'What?'

'We drank it last night.'

'Did we?'

'Yep.'

'OK, real tea, please.' Stella slid onto the bench that lined one side of the kitchen table and picked underneath the envelope flap with her index nail.

A month earlier, Stella and Billie had received letters from the Chelsea and Westminster Hospital reminding them that it had been three years since their last cervical screening and they were both due another test. They duly made appointments on the same day and went together, like they did most things in life. As close as sisters, they'd been to school together, moved to London together and lived in the same flat together for the past nine years.

They didn't look alike. Walking along the street together, they seemed a comical pair. Stella was the tall blonde who people stared at, while Billie was short and rounder, with a mass of dark curls that she could never control and a round, freckled face with dimples that had near-permanent residence either side of her mouth.

Their physical differences were underlined by their contrasting characters. While Billie had the sunny, serene disposition of a Swiss milkmaid, Stella was the opposite: rarely calm, often combative.

Stella's list of dislikes was long: the Tube; tourists who dawdled in front of her on the Portobello Road when she wanted to get home; vanilla ice cream because it tasted of nothing; whoever invented Instagram for fuelling her deep sense of insecurity; her brother's wife, Pandora; being single; restaurants that used obscure words or pictures for the loos instead of 'ladies' and 'gentlemen' so she walked into the wrong one; washing up; doing laundry; three per cent phone battery and no charger, and so on and so on. Billie's list was much shorter: bananas and the sound of polystyrene pieces rubbing together.

Still, they had been best friends since they were eleven and so, on a hazy August morning a couple of weeks earlier, they'd visited the hospital's gynaecology department for their check-up. Typically, Billie had been stoical about the test but Stella was hungover that day and complained that she'd rather eat her own toenails than have a doctor poke about inside her with a pipe cleaner.

At the kitchen table, Stella mumbled her letter. '"Dear Miss Shakespeare, thank you for coming to your recent cervical screening. The cells in your cervix looked normal. You will be invited to have your next screening test in the usual three or five years, depending on your age…" Oh, fine, OK. Great.' She made a small cheer and raised one fist in the air. 'A normal vagina! Not a compliment you get every day.'

'More normal than mine.'

'Wait, what?'

Billie nodded at another letter beside the fruit bowl.

Stella reached for it and mumbled again: '"Dear Miss Martin, thank you for coming to your recent cervical screening. The laboratory found some abnormal cells called high grade..."' she paused at a strange word, '"*dyskaryosis* in your sample. This means it is very important that you have a colposcopy to take a closer look at your cervix as soon as possible."'

Underneath that was a date and time for a return appointment.

She looked up. 'I'm sure it's fine. Aren't smear tests often wrong?'

'Wrong?' queried Billie as she poured boiling water into the mugs.

'Misleading. Tricky area to get to.' Stella looked down at the letter and squinted. 'What is a... colposcopy anyway? Sounds like something to do with your bottom.'

'That's a colonoscopy. And I've just googled it, it's like a biopsy. They snip a tiny bit out to test.'

Stella's eyes bulged. 'Of your *vagina*?'

'Technically of my cervix,' Billie replied, stepping across the kitchen to open the fridge.

Stella exhaled and clamped her knees together under the table. 'You don't think they could have got them mixed up? The letters, I mean.'

'I don't think so.'

'When's the appointment?'

'Next week. Hang on, I swear there was some milk left.'

'Finished it earlier, sorry. And I'm coming with you.'

'Black tea it is,' Billie said, reaching for the mugs before sitting down. 'Don't worry, I can manage.'

'You kidding? Course I'm coming. Don't tell me you'd rather take Jez?'

Stella didn't get on with Billie's boyfriend. He was a news reporter for *The Guardian*, who Billie had met six years ago during a poetry reading at the Southbank Centre, where she worked in the fundraising department.

Jez was often dismissive towards Stella, because he believed she represented everything that was wrong with the world: she was privately educated, spoiled, didn't work and had been given a flat in Notting Hill when most of their generation couldn't afford to rent a studio in Zone 6.

It was ironic that Jez blamed her for all this, given that he'd had a very middle-class upbringing himself. He grew up in a detached house in Haslemere. His dad worked in advertising; his mother was a music teacher. He was made to play the French horn until he was fifteen, and his middle name was Albert.

But ever since he'd landed his graduate trainee job at *The Guardian* and worked his way up from there, he'd tried not to be so middle class. Recently, he'd decided he was into grime music and was attempting to grow a mullet.

His embarrassment at his own background was exactly why he resented Stella for hers. 'She should be more aware of her privilege,' he'd complained to Billie, more than once, apparently ignoring his own.

Fine, OK, Stella had been to boarding school, but she didn't think that was the *greatest* crime in the world. So had Billie, although admittedly on a scholarship because her parents could never have afforded it otherwise. Billie's dad ran a pub just outside Harrogate and her mum was a dental assistant.

Stella, meanwhile, thought Jez was patronising and not good enough for her best friend, although deep down she knew that some of Jez's accusations about her were fair. Stella *was* spoiled and untidy, and she did sometimes leave teabags on the kitchen counter instead of transferring them three feet to the compost bin that Jez was always banging on about. 'Why don't you just MARRY the compost bin if you love it so much?' Stella had recently shouted at Jez during an argument about a small pile of orange peel she'd left on the coffee table in the sitting room.

His other irritating habits included but were not limited to: constantly calling the Royal Family scroungers; an obsession with coffee and his 'special cafetière', which nobody else was allowed to touch; using Stella's Netflix account, which confused the algorithm so Netflix started suggesting programmes about Formula One and Nazis, which she had no interest in; and stealing her shampoo in the bathroom (Stella got her own back by using Jez's razor to shave her bikini line).

The trouble was, Jez stayed in the Notting Hill flat almost every night of the week because it was much nicer than the room he rented in Walthamstow. He lived there, essentially, so he and Stella had to spend a lot of time together when the only thing they had in common was their devotion to Billie.

'Come on,' Stella urged, 'this is a girls' thing. We can nip in together, get it all over and done with, and have a coffee afterwards?'

'Might have to play coffee by ear, depending on work,' said Billie, 'but OK, yeah, thanks, you'd be better than Jez. Hang on, though, none of this gets you out of explaining what happened this morning. Where did you even stay, Stell?'

'OK, so I was in the pub, and you guys left at what… ten?'

'Nine.'

'All right. Nine. Ten. Whatever. I had a couple more drinks and then…' Stella concentrated on a patch of table, like a murder inspector puzzling over a crime. 'And then I'm not totally sure.' She spread her hands in front of her. 'But, long story short, I woke up in east London beside a man called Sam.'

'Do we know anything about Sam?'

Stella ran through the details – pleather headboard but surprisingly good in bed, east London, late for her job interview – and Billie listened in silence until the part about throwing up into the wastepaper basket.

'Oh my god, Stell!' Billie covered her mouth with her palm.

'I didn't want to work there anyway,' she replied defensively. 'The guy was a creep. But then I came home and tried to buy some milk downstairs, more milk because I did actually know we needed some, and my card was refused so… yeah… I need to do something about a job.'

Stella's financial situation was unusual: she wasn't exactly facing destitution. Her parents were rich and she lived, rent-free, in Notting Hill. Thanks to the credit card, she had a wardrobe of expensive clothes and had been able to fund a bougie London lifestyle of dinners out, bottles of wine, posh face creams and overpriced spinning classes. She also had a good education and a sharp brain, when she could be bothered to use it.

But until recently, she'd never been encouraged to use it because her parents had old-fashioned ideas about life: Stella's brother, Andrew, was the son who would take over the Sunset Village empire, and Stella would get married. But three months earlier, tiring of supporting a daughter who showed little work ethic and had blown her relationship with a future lord, Ian Shakespeare had ordered Stella to stop relying on his credit card.

Billie blew over the rim of her mug. 'There'll be something. What about the tutoring agency?'

'Never emailed me back.'

'Prostitution?'

This, at least, made Stella laugh before her expression turned glum and she looked down at the letter, picking at the envelope's plastic window. 'Might as well get paid for it, the rate I'm going.'

In the past few months, while trying to get over Miles, Stella had woken up in several strange bedrooms. There'd been a strange bedroom in Fulham: a garret with a sloping roof and a yellowing No Fear poster on the wall, in a bed beside a man who, it turned out, still lived with his parents. This became clear when Stella went downstairs and was beckoned into the kitchen by a lady wearing an apron (his mother), who insisted on making them both eggs on toast. 'Poor Eddy mustn't go to work on an empty stomach,' she'd said reproachfully, as if Stella had married her son overnight and was already failing in her wifely duties.

There'd been another strange bedroom in Knightsbridge that resembled a nightclub – black walls, gold four-poster bed, gold-framed mirror above this bed, black silk sheets. The only thing that wasn't gold or black was a leopard-shaped rug on the black carpet. 'Because I'm a tigerrrrrr,' the bedroom's inhabitant told Stella in the morning, before she rushed out and, unable to work the lift, had hurried down the fire escape stairs.

There'd been more strange bedrooms in south, east, north and west London, briefly exciting at night but depressing in the morning. 'Could this be the one?' she'd think, every time, until she woke up in their bedroom still wearing the previous night's make-up, with a slight ache between her legs, and felt even lonelier than before.

Making her way home from these unfamiliar bedrooms, Stella would often look at couples heading into work together, suited, holding hands. She imagined them brushing their teeth beside one another that morning, grinning in the mirror before getting dressed. On their commute, one would get off at a Tube stop before the other, and they'd kiss briefly before the doors opened and mumble see you laters. They were grown-up, mature relationships, the sort of devoted togetherness that Stella longed for but, in the past six months, had started to wonder whether she'd ever find. Compared to the couples on the Tube, Stella felt like a teenager desperately dreaming about love, sitting and waiting while doodling hearts in her diary. Friends had long teased her for being a 'hopeless' romantic and Stella always shot back that she was 'hopeful' instead. But her reserves of hope were running low.

She'd make pledges to herself – tomorrow she'd try harder, get up earlier, stop looking at Miles's Instagram, not go to the pub and drink vodka to, briefly, smother her sadness. But then tomorrow would arrive and look exactly the same as yesterday. Life for everyone around her seemed to be surging forwards while Stella felt as if she was regressing, and this only intensified her desire to find the sort of love that still seemed to elude her but she saw in others, or onscreen or in books.

'Hey, this weird thing happened though, as I was leaving the interview,' she told Billie, changing the subject.

'Mmmm?'

'This lady came up to me, just as I was leaving.'

Billie frowned. 'Did she work there?'

'Uh-uh, this was outside. On the steps. She just asked me questions about a man I'd seen inside. It was sort of… shady.'

'What d'you mean? What sort of questions?'

'She wanted to know if I'd seen this man in there. And I had. I remembered him because he reminded me of Dad – pink handkerchief in his suit pocket, signet ring, this air of superiority, you know?' Stella looked up at Billie and wrinkled her nose. Billie knew all about Stella's dysfunctional family.

'*And?*'

'And what?'

'What did that man have to do with the lady outside?'

'I don't know. She didn't say.'

'Why didn't you ask?'

'I'd just been sick in a bin, Bill, my small talk wasn't its best.'

'Fair.'

'But then she gave me her business card and said if I ever wanted a job I should give her a ring.'

'What? What does she even do?'

'I don't know! But look…' Stella reached down the bench for her bag and groped around the bottom for the card. 'Here,' she added.

'Verity Culpepper Limited,' said Billie, taking the card and running a finger over it. 'Funny name.' She looked up. 'And you didn't think to ask anything else?'

'No! Like I said, I'd just chucked up my coffee into a bin. What I most wanted to do was get back here and brush my teeth.'

Billie slid the card back across the kitchen table. 'You could give her a ring.' Then a frown crossed her face like a storm cloud.

'What?'

'What if she's the head of a trafficking ring? Or involved in some criminal syndicate? It *was* a law firm.'

'Bill, she must have been in her mid-sixties. And she was wearing a golf visor and a tatty old coat. I've seen more menacing lollipop ladies.'

'You googled it? The business?'

Stella nodded. 'Mmm, but I couldn't find anything. Well, hardly anything. She has a website but it's just a page with a form for people to fill in their details.'

'Call her and find out what she does. But if she suggests meeting anywhere private don't go. Go to a coffee shop.'

'Thank you, PC Billie Martin.'

'Only saying,' Billie replied with a shrug. 'You never know.' She drained her tea. 'I'm making a curry tonight. Jez and I thought we'd watch that panda documentary. Want in?'

Stella squinted up at the kitchen clock. Nearly seven. Early yet. These were the choices she faced: eat tree-bark curry (it would be something like that, because Billie was a committed vegetarian) on the sofa with her and Jez. Or she could go to the pub. Tomorrow she would call that strange woman and suss out whether there was a job or whether she was recruiting for an underground gang. Tomorrow she would start afresh, again. Tonight, she wanted a drink to dissolve her embarrassment about that morning. Just one drink, or two, depending on the generosity of Jack the barman. 'Nah, thanks, might see if anyone's around in the pub.'

'Don't fancy an early night? Eating something with vitamins in it?' Billie was the one who cooked in the flat since Stella was incapable of following a recipe and largely survived on toast.

She shook her head and looked away from her flatmate in case she saw any traces of judgment in her face. Or, worse, pity. 'I won't be late, promise.'

'Stell…'

Stella looked up and took in Billie's uneasy expression. 'What?'

'This isn't meant to sound like a lecture, I get that you're not having an easy time. But being in the pub all the time, and not coming home at night, I just don't…'

'Don't what?'

Billie sighed before answering. 'I don't know if any of this is making you very happy.'

'This sounds quite like a lecture,' Stella replied, pushing her chair back and standing.

'It's not,' Billie said, shaking her head. 'I want to help bu—'

They were interrupted by the sound of a key in the door and, for once, Stella was grateful to see Jez coming through it.

'Jeremy, good evening.' He hated his full name – 'sounds like I belong to a golf club,' he said once – so Stella used it as frequently as she could.

He dropped his bag by the door and took an exaggerated look at his watch. 'Hello, Stella, awake already? Bit early for you, isn't it?'

'I'm heading out.'

'No surprise there. Hi, sweetheart,' said Jez, brushing past her to kiss Billie. 'Brought this back for you, Sal said they sent two copies so she didn't need this one.' He held out a yellow hardback with a cartoon couple on it.

Sal was *The Guardian*'s literary editor, who constantly gave books to Jez, which he'd leave lying open beside the bath, their pages wrinkled.

'The new one! You're my hero, thank you,' said Billie, wrapping her arms around his neck.

'I'll leave you to it,' Stella announced, uncomfortable at feeling like a gooseberry in her own flat.

Billie, pulling back from Jez, looked over apologetically. 'You OK?'

'Mmm, fine.'

'And you're sure you're OK to come to that?'

'To what?'

Billie nodded at the letter on the table.

'Oh, right. Yeah, course. Not like my diary's exactly overflowing at the moment.'

'Hey,' Billie replied with a small smile. 'So what you're saying is you're *wide* open?'

And even though she felt told off, Stella couldn't help but smile back. She might not have a boyfriend or a job, but she had a best friend who could make her laugh with a terrible smear test joke. So that was something.

CHAPTER 5

THE FOLLOWING MORNING, AT least Stella woke up in her own bed. But she had another hangover because she'd stayed in the pub until closing, before returning home and looking up her ex-boyfriend on Instagram.

Pressing her face into her pillow, she groaned. In the pub, after Stella told Jack the barman the wastepaper basket story, he'd given her a vodka tonic on the house. Then another. And another. Jack had a crush on Stella, which she manipulated for free drinks. She appreciated it, but she was never going to sleep with him; Jack talked of little other than Arsenal and had dirty fingernails, which Stella noticed every time he slid another drink across the bar. She couldn't lower herself *that* far.

Anyway, once she'd got home, she'd given in to the urge to look at Miles's profile.

Last night, panic had made Stella's chest feel tight when she saw his most recent picture: one of Miles at a garden table, covered in empty wine bottles and ashtrays, where he appeared to be sticking his tongue into the ear of a thin brunette who was wearing sunglasses and beaming with pleasure. And even though Stella knew that sunglasses helped people who weren't very attractive look much more glamorous than they were in real life, she could tell that this brunette woman was very attractive indeed.

She spent the next half an hour scrolling through Miles's list of followers, and the list of those following him, trying to spot new female names she didn't recognise, squinting at their thumbnail pictures. Stella didn't have a formal degree, but if there was a university that offered a course called Social Media Stalking and How To Identify A Potential Threat, she'd graduate with top marks.

Eventually, she'd narrowed the field down to one: Annabel Longbottom. It had gone midnight by then but Stella lay in bed and googled Annabel, looking her up on LinkedIn, on Facebook and the PR website where she worked.

She moaned into her pillow again. Why did she do it? Always, now, in the mornings, she felt ashamed for stalking him. But she never felt ashamed at the time. It was like an addiction; she wanted to know what Miles was doing; she wanted to know who Annabel was. She scrolled as if it would make her feel better when it only made her feel worse. And then she'd wake up and feel furious with herself.

She glanced sideways at her clock. Past nine. She needed a cup of tea, a couple of painkillers, and then she'd ring that mad woman, Verity Culpepper. Worth checking out, as Billie said. She needed the cash. And, actually, having somewhere to go during the day, so she didn't mope around the flat and look at her ex-boyfriend's Instagram account might not be such a bad idea.

She swung her feet out, picked up a jumper from one of the many strewn across her carpet, and went through to the kitchen. Shit. She'd forgotten again. No milk. Not even any oat milk.

She went back to her bedroom and tipped the little pot she kept on her bedside table out onto her duvet. Out fell hair ties, odd earrings, two silver rings and 17p in coins.

Like many politicians before, Stella wasn't sure of the price of a pint of milk but she suspected it was more than 17p. She tried the junk drawer of old chargers, old keys and painkillers in the kitchen, but this only yielded another 5p piece.

She sighed and put her phone down on the kitchen table. What if she went downstairs? Not to Nigel in the corner shop but to their neighbour in the ground-floor flat beneath them. She always tried to avoid their elderly neighbour, Harold. It wasn't because he was unpleasant or difficult or some sort of hoarder or one of those nuisance neighbours you saw on TV. But this was London, and he was a stranger, even though Stella had lived above him for nine years. Sharing the same building and the same pale-pink front door didn't mean they had to be friends.

She'd barely said more than a few words to him, just the odd 'Hello' or 'Morning!' if she bumped into him on the way in or out. All she really knew was that he was a retired policeman or, to be more accurate, a retired police dog handler, and that his wife had died last summer.

Since then, Stella had tried even harder to avoid him. For instance, if she was ever about to leave the flat but heard Harold's front door open, she would wait until he'd definitely left the building before leaving herself. Stella was too English to have a stilted conversation on the stairs, and the idea of having a conversation with him about being widowed made her feel almost ill. What on earth could she say? 'Hi, Harold, so sorry about your wife! Looks like there's a letter from the council for you here. Have a nice day!'

Billie was better with people. She'd been friendlier with Harold's wife and would often stop to chat if she bumped into him on the stairs. Recently, she'd even taken a slice of a courgette cake downstairs for him – gluten-free, dairy-free cake, which Stella wasn't sure counted as cake at all. Was a cake made from courgette going to add joy to anyone's life?

But now she needed milk.

Stella propped her front door open with a trainer and went downstairs to knock on the door, which immediately made Harold's dog bark.

It was only as his door swung open that Stella noticed the mug that she'd carried down from their kitchen. It had been a present from Jez for her last birthday, clearly panic-bought in a gift shop, and around the front of it ran the words '32 – and still a massive TWAT'.

'Hello,' said Harold, smiling as he stepped back from his door. He was a slight man neatly dressed in collared shirt and pressed trousers, with an enormous pair of square spectacles that made him look like a wise old owl. 'Shhh, Basil, be quiet.' Harold turned to pat his Alsatian on the head, then glanced down at Stella's bare feet. 'Are you all right?'

Stella quickly dropped the mug to her side. 'Yes, er, fine, thank you. I was, er, just wondering if I could borrow some milk?'

'Some milk?' queried Harold. That morning, he'd finally sat down to call the utility companies in order to get Ellen's name taken off the bills, but the effort of calling them, of sitting on hold for so long listening to terrible crackly music, then having to say his wife's name and explain over and over again that she'd died, had left him dazed.

Stella lifted the mug, covering the words with her fingers. 'Yep, if you don't mind, I need a cup of tea and we've run out and…' She trailed off, unwilling to admit that she couldn't go to the shops and buy some.

'Oh, milk,' said Harold, coming to his senses, 'sorry. Come in, follow me.'

Stella looked at her feet and then Harold's carpeted corridor, before following him past several framed photographs of dogs that spanned the walls, and into his kitchen, which smelled of digestive biscuits and Pledge.

'It's so different down here,' she wondered aloud, turning her head to take in the Formica cupboards. It was very tidy: just a small cluster of pill bottles on the countertop and a dog lead curled beside them. There was one side plate and one cup drying beside the sink and, next to the window, hanging from the wall, a small blackboard on which was written Harold's shopping list: bread, tuna, new socks.

He made for his fridge as the large Alsatian yawned and lay down in a yellow rectangle cast by the morning sun on the linoleum. 'Falling apart a bit, but it suits us, doesn't it, Basil? Right, here we go, pass us that.'

Stella held out the mug. 'Sorry for the… it was from my friend's boyfriend, for my birthday. He's an idiot.'

Harold held it up in front of his glasses and laughed. 'I've heard worse.'

He retrieved a small carton of milk from the fridge and poured at least half of it into her mug, then held it back out. 'Are you sure you're all right?'

Stella raised a hand to her face, suddenly conscious that she hadn't looked in a mirror before coming downstairs.

'Mmm, fine, thank you, just need a tea,' she said, holding up the mug. 'I've got a job interview,' she added, feeling a strange impulse to reassure her neighbour that she was a functioning human being.

'Oh, smashing. What's the job?'

'Er, I'm not actually sure.'

'You're not sure?'

'No, not really. This lady came up to me yesterday morning and gave me her card, and I'm going to ring her today.'

Harold narrowed his eyes. As a former policeman, he didn't like the sound of this: a strange woman potentially taking advantage of his dishevelled young neighbour. 'Is it on the phone, this interview? You're not meeting the lady in person?'

Stella shook her head. 'No, I'm going to ring her.'

'Good.'

'That's what Billie said too. You know, my flatmate? She said not to meet her anywhere private.'

'Quite right,' said Harold, relieved that at least one of the girls living above him seemed to have her head screwed on. He felt guilty that he'd never made more of an effort with them but what did he, a 71-year-old man, have in common with a pair of thirty-somethings who seemed to be coming and going at all hours? Although the other one was very kind. Since Ellen had died, she'd even brought down pieces of cake, except the last piece had been made from some sort of root vegetable, so he'd thanked her, then closed the door and fed it to Basil.

'Is that Dusty Springfield?' Stella asked, cocking her head as she heard music float through from the room next door.

'It is indeed,' said Harold. She'd been one of Ellen's favourites, so he'd fished out an old album that morning and put it on her record player to compete against the call centres' hold music.

'Thought so.'

'You like her?'

Stella nodded. 'I like all soul, really.'

She'd grown up listening to soul with her grandfather, not only to Dusty Springfield but also to the likes of Sam Cooke, Etta James, Smokey Robinson and Patti LaBelle. It was an early childhood memory – sitting in the back of her granddad's car while he sang from the front. He'd been a local journalist in Sheffield, but retired by the time Stella started school and insisted that he pick her and Andrew up in the afternoons, that the Shakespeares' nanny didn't have to do it, which suited everyone until he died.

Stella was thirteen when that happened, just a few months before she was sent to Queen Margaret's. She arrived that first term not only with a new tennis racket and a trunk of new uniform, every kilt and scratchy blue jumper name-taped, but also a stack of her grandfather's old tapes. That autumn, between classes, other girls sang Avril Lavigne and muttered Eminem lyrics under their breath as if they were gangsters, while Stella stuck to Ray Charles.

'My wife liked it too.'

A silence fell and Stella stared at the mug of milk. 'Better go,' she said finally, looking up at Harold with a half-smile. 'Thank you.'

Harold waved a hand as Stella turned and made for the front door. 'You're very welcome. Best of luck with that interview.'

'Thanks,' she said again, before pulling the door closed behind her. He seemed so sad, standing in his old-fashioned kitchen with his dog.

Was there any point in looking so hard for that great love if one could be left so lonely in the end?

Stella had spent so long thinking about finding this love that she'd never thought much about what happened after that. In her head, she would simply meet someone and they'd live happily ever after. But the sight of Harold's solitary existence – the single side plate drying up beside the single cup, his modest shopping list, talking to his dog – was unsettling. Perhaps life would be easier if you spent it alone and never even risked a relationship? No heartbreak, no grief.

You're going mad, she told herself as she climbed the stairs. Course it wouldn't be easier. When she finally found her great love, it would make all the dramas until now worthwhile.

And when she got a job, *if* she ever got a job, she also told herself she'd be friendlier towards Harold. Perhaps even make a cake herself and take him down a slice?

No, that was probably too ambitious.

But she'd be able to afford a packet of biscuits, perhaps, and she could share those with him instead.

CHAPTER 6

BACK IN HER OWN kitchen, Stella made a tea and spooned two sugars into it, then put on a bra. It was only a phone interview, but even she realised it was unprofessional to enquire about a job braless. After that, she brushed her teeth and her hair before mulling over whether to file her nails, but knew these were time-delaying tactics.

What was so daunting about a phone call?

It was her lack of confidence. At thirty-two, most people Stella knew talked of promotions and pay rises. They weren't so desperate for money they'd take anything, even an offer from a mad woman on the street. Billie had worked in the fundraising office of the Southbank Centre for six years and now had an assistant. Their schoolfriend Rose was a litigation lawyer who always insisted on paying for lunch if they all went out together; another schoolfriend, Britt, worked for Netflix. It felt embarrassing to be ringing a woman she didn't know, to enquire about a job she knew nothing about, which would presumably be boring and pay nothing.

'Get on with it,' she muttered, picking up the business card and dialling the number.

It rang for so long that she nearly hung up, but after six trills, there came a cough from the other end.

'Hello? Hello, is that Verity?'

'Hang on! Hang on! I'll be with you in a second.'

Then came a noise that sounded very much like a phone being dropped on a hard floor, before a large sigh into the microphone. 'Deary me, what a palaver. Who is it? Are you still there?'

'Er, yes, Verity? I'm still here. It's, er, Stella.'

'Bella?'

'STELLA. Stella Shakespeare. We met yesterday. You gave me your card. Outside Spinks.'

There was a pause while Verity digested this. 'Oh yes, I remember. You were wearing a pink shirt?'

'Yes,' said Stella slowly, trying to remember.

'I remember now. It's all coming back. And you'd seen Mr Williams inside. Nasty piece of work.'

'The man with the moustache?'

'The one who looks like a walrus, quite. And it's not Verity.'

'Sorry?'

'My name. It isn't Verity. It's Marjorie.'

'But it says Verity on your business card?'

'It's a front. Did you know that the name Verity means truth? It comes from the Latin, *veritas*.'

Stella's head began to spin. 'A front for what?'

'Now look,' went on Marjorie, ignoring the question, 'my last one's just left and I need somebody to start right away.'

'Last what?'

'Girl. Or secretary, I should say. Although some people get

upset about that too these days, don't they? I can't keep up. Assistant, that's what you're supposed to say.'

'What do yo—'

'I need someone to come in and answer the phones, mostly, and emails. I hate emails. Nasty impersonal things. Much prefer a phone call, don't you?'

'I'm no—'

'But you may need to help me out with the odd job when I need it.'

'What *is* your job?'

'And I may need you to drive,' went on Marjorie. 'You can drive, can't you?'

'Yep,' Stella replied. This was legally true; she had a licence but no car and she hadn't driven for years.

'Splendid. When can you start? Monday? Oh no, hang on, Monday's no good, I'm in Brighton on a job. Could you come in on Thursday? That would work.'

'Um, yes, I think so. But can I just ask, what is it exactly that you do?'

'Don't worry about that. I'll explain on Monday. No! Not Monday, *Thursday*. You see? This is why I need a secretary. *Not* a secretary! An assistant. Now, come along to 153c Harley Street at nine a.m., it's above the chiropodist.'

Stella felt as if she was being sucked into something that she had no power to stop.

'Can I ask about pay?' she said, trying to reassert control.

'Pay?'

'Mmmm. What's the salary?'

There was another brief silence while Marjorie considered this. 'Let's say £100 as a day rate, in cash.'

Stella frowned. If she was paid £100 a day, then that was… £500 a week. And that meant how much a year? She couldn't do the sum in her head but, given that she had £1.12 in her bank account and she could no longer use the Coutts credit card, it sounded very decent.

'OK,' she replied, trying not to betray too much enthusiasm, 'yes, I think that would be fine.'

'Make sure you have comfortable shoes.'

'*Shoes?*'

'Plimsolls, flats. No heels. I have a fabulous pair of boots from Clarks that have a cushioned sole. Can't go wrong with a cushioned sole.'

'What? Why?'

'You might be on your feet a bit.'

'Sorry, Ver— I mean Marjorie, what exactly will I be doing?' Stella tried again. Answering phones? Driving? On her feet? Was she going to be a delivery driver? She grimaced into her phone at the idea. Being paid £100 a day was good money, but if that was to drive around delivering other people's Amazon deliveries, it would be humiliating to admit as much to friends who were lawyers and worked for Netflix.

'Like I said, mostly answering phones,' went on Marjorie. 'But there may be the odd day when you're more up and about. Nothing to worry about. I'll explain it all next Thursday. Now I really must go. Did you write down the address? 153c Harley Street.'

'Above the chiropodist.'

'Exactly. See you there at nine sharp. Toodle-pip!'

Marjorie hung up and Stella frowned at her phone. That was definitely odd. Wasn't it odd? She expected to feel relief and euphoria; excitement, even, at the fact she had a job. But she mostly felt uneasy. Who was this woman who gave out business cards with the wrong name on them? And why was she so secretive? Was Stella going to be doing something dodgy? Like a drugs mule? Had she been picked off the street by this woman because she didn't look like a criminal and was therefore less likely to get stopped, delivering drugs around London?

She glanced at the clock on her bedside table. 10.15 a.m. She wanted to discuss it with Billie.

I got that job... she texted, *but I'm not sure what it is.* She added several frowning emojis.

Stella's heart beat harder as she frowned at her bedroom floor. Marjorie hadn't looked like a drug dealer but maybe that was the point? Maybe it was all a disguise and she *was* actually a drug baron? Pablo Escobar had looked like a plumber, after all.

The idea quickly became more and more plausible. Marjorie was clearly a drug baron who preyed on innocent young women, gave out business cards with a fake name and persuaded them to drive around town delivering packets of heroin and cocaine, before paying them in cash. What if she was arrested? What if her father's name got dragged into the papers? He'd be furious. Stella pressed a palm to her chest to calm her heart. Was she being hysterical? Or was she being lured into a trap that ended with a spell in prison?

After a few minutes, Billie still hadn't replied. She bit her lower lip and wondered whether she should text her brother and ask his advice, but if she told Andrew then he was bound to alert their parents, and the thought of her mother or, worse, her father calling her up and delivering another lecture was too much to bear. She'd already messed up the Spinks interview and didn't want to involve them in another potential job disaster. She had to prove to them that she could manage perfectly well by herself. Harley Street was a reputable place, so surely this Verity or Marjorie couldn't be doing anything *that* bad? But what if she was involved in illegal activities?

Stella had a brainwave. She'd go back downstairs to ask Harold what he reckoned of the whole business. He was a former policeman, after all. He'd know what to do.

'More milk?' Harold said when he opened his front door to see Stella standing there for the second time that morning.

Stella shook her head. 'No, sorry. It's not that. It's just… the interview.'

'Ah. How did it go?'

She frowned and slid one thumbnail between her teeth before answering. 'It was odd. I got the job…'

'Congratulations!'

'But I think she might be a drug dealer.'

'Oh.' Harold looked startled. 'Why do you think that?' He stood back from the door. 'Do you want to come in and discuss it?'

'You don't mind? I'm not interrupting?'

Harold, who'd just been explaining to a Scottish man in a Glaswegian call centre that Ellen had died six months ago which meant she no longer needed a mobile phone, didn't mind a bit. 'Not at all. Do you fancy another tea?'

'Go on then.'

He made the tea while Stella recalled the phone conversation.

'What's her surname?' he asked, passing her a mug.

'I don't know! I didn't ask. But it's Harley Street, so it can't be that dodgy, can it?'

'Well…' Harold started, before petering off. He did think it sounded a bit odd. In all his years of working in the police dog unit, he'd never heard of an elderly lady running a drug ring. More likely she was running some sort of pirate goods business out of that office. Counterfeit handbags or watches. All sorts of operations were indeed run from private offices on Harley Street, and he didn't want his young neighbour getting involved in all that. But nor did he want to put her off a job if it was legitimate.

'One moment,' he said, lifting a finger in the air.

Harold disappeared into the sitting room and rifled in a drawer, then returned and held out a small black fob towards Stella.

'What is it?'

'Personal alarm. You should have one anyway. Take it with you. Just don't p—'

His words were drowned out as a high-pitched siren filled Harold's flat, which alerted Basil to danger. He came racing through from the sofa to the kitchen, barking.

'Calm down, calm down,' shouted Harold as Stella replaced the pin in the side of the fob.

'Sorry,' she said, once peace was restored.

Basil looked between his master and Stella, confused. That noise told him something was afoot but he couldn't smell anything.

'It's all right, Basil,' Harold told him again, bending over to pat his head. Then he looked up at Stella. 'Take that with you, keep it in your bag.'

Stella felt as if she was in an episode of a crime thriller. 'You think it might be dangerous?'

Harold shrugged. 'Probably not. But it never hurts to be prepared.'

'OK,' she said uncertainly, frowning at the fob. It wasn't like she had many other options, and Harold didn't seem *that* worried.

She sighed and slipped it into her pocket. Accidentally landing a job working for a drug baron was exactly the sort of thing that would happen to her. Other people were normal. They got normal jobs in a normal way and went about their lives normally. But when it came to Stella Shakespeare, there always had to be some sort of drama.

CHAPTER 7

WHAT STELLA HAD BEEN waiting for happened the following Tuesday.

She was sitting at the bar of the Ladbroke, gloomily mulling over her prospects. Her new job was due to start in two days and, having thought about it all weekend, Stella had convinced herself she was going to work for a criminal mastermind and would potentially be in prison before the year was out. She'd seen *Orange is the New Black*. That was the sort of thing that happened to people like her. You accidentally delivered a package of drugs for someone and, before you knew it, were being felt up in the communal shower by a tattooed lifer who was in there for murder. Stella had a tattoo but that was different. It was a small star on her foot, which she got on her gap year in Thailand with Billie.

She was also feeling cheesed off about Miles because she'd looked at his Instagram profile again and seen a new picture of him and Annabel at a polo match. She'd snorted with disgust at the sight. Stella had gone to polo matches with Miles when they were going out, and drank Champagne and trod in the clumps kicked up by the polo ponies at half time. But now that someone else was dating him, she discovered she felt very differently about it. Polo. What a ridiculous game. Golf on horseback.

Worse still, underneath this photo had been several comments from people she'd previously considered friends. *LOVEBIRDS*, said Jules, who was married to one of Miles's best friends. *You guys look cuuuuuuuuute!!!* added Evie, another one of the wives. *She's fit! Punching a bit mate!* added Toby, one of Miles's more stupid rugby-playing mates. Someone else had simply left a string of red heart emojis. And Annabel had liked every single comment, Stella knew, because she'd very carefully looked at the likes for each one while trying not to like them herself. The picture, and its enthusiastic responses, seemed to cement her status as an outcast. Annabel was in; Stella was out.

'Another one?' Jack asked hopefully, nodding at her empty glass.

She closed one eye and squinted at the lone ice cube and slice of lemon. Billie had transferred £150 to tide her over until she started work, but Stella was already down to the last £38, having spent much of it on cigarettes and a birthday lunch for their friend Britt at the weekend where she hadn't meant to drink but then had accidentally managed to sink most of the white wine they ordered.

'Please.' She stretched her arm to nudge the empty glass down Jack's end of the bar.

That was when a man in a navy suit stepped up to the bar and, on turning to look at him, Stella felt an electric shock.

Her father had strong opinions about suits. As a self-made millionaire who'd spent most of his life trying to shake off the embarrassment at being born in an industrial town just outside

Sheffield, Ian Shakespeare had developed these opinions to disguise his humble origins. A man's suit jacket should be double-vented at the back, he'd often told Andrew over the breakfast table. It should have three buttons but the bottom one must never be done up. Suit trousers should be slim cut and the hem should land exactly half an inch above the shoe heel. His tie must always be darker than his shirt.

Having grown up overhearing these proclamations, Stella could tell that the man standing beside her was wearing a very good suit indeed, over a shirt that was undone at the collar, revealing a small triangle of tanned chest.

To be fair, had he been wearing a stained tracksuit and dodgy hat, Stella would have noticed him. When scrutinising a potential conquest, she often judged a man on three attributes: teeth, hair, and whether they'd be able to pick her up in a fireman's lift.

This man was tall, with smiling eyes that matched his sky-blue shirt, a strong, straight nose and curling brown hair that fell across his forehead. He looked like a Greek hero who could throw not just Stella but multiple women over each shoulder.

'I'll get that,' he said, gesturing at her empty glass as Jack retrieved it from the bar. 'And one for me, please.' He looked down at Stella. 'Vodka tonic, correct?'

'Yes, thank you,' Stella replied, noticing that her voice had gone funny.

He looked familiar. Had she seen him on TV? Or in a film? Was he an actor? He sounded commanding and confident enough. She could imagine him galloping across a field in a period drama, hair flopping over his high cheekbones, wearing a pair of fawn breeches and leather riding boots. Perhaps a crop and— Stella stopped herself and tried to remember what she normally did when a man approached her at a bar and bought her a drink.

'I'm Stella,' she said, swivelling on her stool, brushing her knees against his legs.

He didn't reply immediately. Reaching into his breast pocket, he retrieved a silver money clip, peeled off a twenty and handed it over the bar. 'Keep the change.'

Stella glanced at Jack, who cocked one eyebrow before turning back to the till.

'Stella. Stella, Stella,' the stranger repeated, his eyes concentrated on hers.

'That's my name, don't wear it out,' Stella replied before she could stop herself. What was wrong with her? She was *good* at flirting. Flirting was one of her only skills. She could do better than repeat a corny line from a film. 'And you are?'

'Fitz,' he replied, holding out his hand.

Stella stretched her fingers to meet it and felt another crackle between them. She hadn't imagined she'd meet her great love in the Ladbroke on a Tuesday evening but, as people were fond of saying, it often happened when you least expected it. She could feel a kernel of excitement inside her. This man wasn't like any of the others. She was vaguely aware that Jack had put their drinks down on the bar but she couldn't look away from him.

She took a breath to steady herself before speaking again, hoping that her voice wouldn't betray the speed with which her heart was beating. 'I've never met anyone called Fitz.'

'May I?' He pulled out the stool beside hers.

'Sure.'

'It's technically my middle name, Fitzwilliam,' he explained as he sat and extended one leg to rest his foot on the metal bar of her seat. He was wearing expensive shoes, too.

'What's wrong with your first name?'

'It's so preposterous I gave it up when I was eight.'

Stella smiled. He sounded so English, so clipped and proper. She laid one elbow on the bar and angled the rest of her body towards him. 'How preposterous? Tell me.'

'I couldn't possibly.'

'Why?'

He picked up both glasses and handed one to Stella. 'Exceptional to meet you, Miss Stella…?'

'Shakespeare,' she replied, lifting her glass to his. 'But you haven't answered my question. Why can't you tell me your first name?'

He took a sip while Stella gazed at the underside of his jawline and fought the urge to graze it with the back of her fingers.

'It would make you like me less.'

Stella fought astonishment as she watched him take another sip. It was as if she recognised him while simultaneously knowing they'd never met. She'd remember it if they had, surely? 'How do you know I like you? We've only just met.'

'Ah, but sometimes one can simply tell.'

She bent her face to her glass and took another mouthful to hide her expression. There was only a foot of space or so between their faces, but that space felt like a forcefield, as if it was a hot day and the air was shimmering between them. What was happening? Normally, when she met a man, it took longer for Stella to decide whether she wanted to go home with him. A couple of drinks at least. Not this man, Fitz. She felt giddy.

'So, how do you occupy yourself, Stella Shakespeare?'

Her confidence slipped momentarily and she frowned. 'I'm… between roles. My new job starts on Thursday. In, er, sales.'

'I see. And why have I been so fortunate as to find you here on a Tuesday evening?'

'It's actually *my* local. So a better question would be what you're doing in this place?'

His mouth widened in a grin. 'Touché. I was in the area, had a meeting nearby earlier, long day, felt like a drink. Is that acceptable?'

Stella nodded. 'What do you do then, to have meetings in Notting Hill?'

'Security.'

'Security? So you're a… bodyguard?' It made sense. He had the confidence of a man who remained in control at all times, and she could see the muscular thickness of his arms through his jacket.

Fitz smiled and shook his head. 'Not exactly.'

'What then?'

'I have a private security firm. So I could provide you with a bodyguard if you wish, but we mostly work abroad. Asia, the Middle East, the odd project in South America.'

'Doing what?'

'Problem solving,' he replied, before draining his glass. 'Helping those who require our services. And to answer your question, Little Miss Inquisitive, I had a meeting with a client at his house nearby and fancied a drink afterwards.'

She nodded before finishing her own drink and putting it down on the bar beside his to denote they should order another.

'I'm off,' he said, standing up, at which point Stella's spirits plunged to the floor.

What? She didn't often get this wrong. There was chemistry here, a connection. This conversational dance between them was verbal foreplay, the on-court warm-up before they got into the real game. She'd rehearsed this routine hundreds of times. Well, maybe not hundreds. But quite a few times recently, and they always stayed. Stella might not know much about politics or quantum physics or even how to get from Fulham to Sloane Square on the correct Tube line, but she knew when a man was interested in her. And this man was interested. So why wasn't he staying? After years of stares and wolf whistles in the streets, of attracting male attention like a walking honeypot, Stella felt intensely frustrated. This wasn't how it normally worked.

She had to conceal her disappointment, though. Men didn't like needy women, her mother had often told her when younger – not that Valerie Shakespeare was necessarily the woman to take relationship advice from; Stella's parents hadn't slept in the same bedroom for years.

Trying to play it cool, she flicked her hair to one side. 'How sad. I hope you've got something very pressing to do.'

Fitz smiled again and leant down to brush his mouth against her cheek. 'Sadly, I have,' he murmured into her ear, 'otherwise I'd stay here with you.'

So she hadn't got this *entirely* wrong. 'Another time.'

'Indeed,' he said, pulling away from her before freezing briefly, and a frown crossed his forehead. 'Has anyone ever told you you have extraordinary eyes?'

'Yes,' she replied boldly, both because they had and because she wanted him to know that.

Fitz grinned. 'I'm sure they have. Very good to meet you, Stella Shakespeare.'

But before he asked for her number, which was the question Stella was anticipating, he turned and left her stunned on the bar stool. Their interaction hadn't lasted ten minutes but it felt very significant, as if the Earth had hiccupped and everything had settled back down slightly altered.

'You'll catch a fly in that,' said Jack, sliding up to the bar to collect their empty glasses.

She swivelled to face him. 'You seen that guy in here before?'

'Not that I can remember.'

'Don't you think he was intriguing?'

Jack laughed. '"Intriguing"? Very la-di-da.'

'Just different to the usual crowd in here.'

'He's a posh guy in a suit, babe,' said Jack, peeved at Stella's obvious interest. 'Didn't look that different to me. You having another one?'

'Yeah, please,' she replied, because she wanted to remain on her stool and roll the interaction with Fitz around in her head. Her frustration was tinged with the certainty that she would see him again. Somehow, she felt like she would.

'I'll make it a double,' Jack offered glumly, turning to the bottles behind the bar.

Stella pulled out her phone to see if she could find him online and realised she had very little to go on: a shortened first name and a vague description of his job. Imagine if all the frogs until now had simply been leading up to this, she thought as she typed, a chance meeting with a handsome, well-spoken, suited stranger.

Actually, handsome didn't even do Fitz justice. He was more than that. He was magnetic. He was the jolt she'd been waiting for. Although then he'd left, which was disappointing, and entirely predictable given her run of luck lately.

Still, she'd do some online sleuthing and think about how to orchestrate another meeting. Stella had to see him again. She felt as if she *would* see him again. No man had ever made her feel so electric.

CHAPTER 8

NEEDLESS TO SAY, STELLA overslept the following morning, which threatened to make her late for Billie's hospital appointment.

Billie had gone into work as normal and was going to meet Stella there at eleven, except now it was 10.58 and the bus was crawling towards Chelsea more slowly than an asthmatic slug. Stella texted that she might be running a few minutes late *for a very good reason*, but Billie hadn't replied even though the ticks had gone blue.

Bit passive aggressive? Stella loved Billie more than anyone else in the world, certainly more than any member of her family, but since her break-up with Miles, she'd felt twinges of jealousy towards her best friend. It was all right for Billie; she had a boyfriend and a good job. She had parents who she spoke to almost every day. Billie rarely seemed troubled by anything; her life was a drama-free zone.

Until recently, these differences had never bothered Stella; they'd always been a joke, in fact, between them and their shared friends. How could two such radically different characters be so close? Stella never thought about it very hard; their friendship was a constant element in her life, like air or water, and it had been that way since the first term at school.

It had all started on Stella's twelfth birthday, or *their* birthday technically, since she and Billie were both born on 5 November. That year, the year they both turned twelve, they'd only just started at Queen Margaret's but, whereas Billie's parents came down from Harrogate to take her out for dinner, Stella's did not.

She still adored her best friend, obviously, but in the past six months, as Stella's life unravelled, she'd found Billie's calm increasingly unfair. It was a vicious cycle, too, because as Stella's jealousy of her best friend grew, she loathed herself even more. How could she envy the person she loved most? It felt mean and petty, especially today, when Billie was the one stripping off for a doctor to have another poke around her uterus.

Nearly there, Stella texted again as she hurried towards the hospital. She was walking so fast she felt like a middle-aged speed-walker, arms pumping robotically either side of her ribcage. The words 'ELEVEN AM' were written in thick blue biro on her left hand, a temporary tattoo she'd given herself in the pub the previous night to make sure she remembered to get to the Chelsea and Westminster on time.

Then she'd met that intriguing man and forgotten the appointment entirely.

It didn't matter. She was convinced she'd see him again even though her online sleuthing had turned up no results. There was a buzz between them that she hadn't felt with any of the no-hopers from the past six months. Fitz was different: more sophisticated, more intriguing. She'd spent hundreds of evenings in that pub and most had blurred into one, but last night felt like a distinctive, defining experience. It meant something; she just wasn't sure what.

Also, Stella realised happily as she hurried towards the hospital's main entrance, for the first time in months she hadn't gone to sleep thinking about Miles.

She pressed her palms against the revolving glass door and peered through it, trying to spot Billie. No sign.

Instead, she saw another person, a person she wasn't expecting, smiling at her from another section of the revolving door.

It took Stella a few seconds to process who this was. She knew the face, she recognised it from somewhere, but where?

Oh no. Seriously? Now? Here? In the *hospital*?

It was the man she'd woken up beside the morning she'd hurled into the wastepaper basket at Spinks. The one who'd lived in east London. The one with the pleather headboard. What was *he* doing here? Oh Jesus, now he was waving at her. What was wrong with him? Why couldn't they pretend not to know each other? That was the rule after one-night stands: if you happened to bump into that person again, you had to turn around and walk nine hundred miles in the opposite direction.

But now he was going round again in the revolving door, coming back in, following her. Which meant she'd have to talk to him. What a weirdo.

Stella couldn't remember his name. It began with an 'S'. Simon? Stephen? Sebastian?

'Hi,' he said, still smiling, stepping out of the door. 'Fancy seeing you here.'

'Hello. And yes, I've got an appointment and I'm quite late act—'

'Nothing serious, I hope?'

Before Stella could stop herself, because of the awkwardness of the situation, standing here, in the hospital reception area, talking to a man she'd last seen naked whose name she couldn't recall, she replied: 'Don't think so, just an appointment with the gynaecologist.'

He frowned and she rattled on: 'Nothing infectious. And it's not *my* appointment, don't worry, you're safe. It's actually for my friend, a colonoscopy. But like I said, I'm late so I should prob—'

She was interrupted by the shout of her name, so turned her head to see Billie approaching. Thank god.

'Hiya,' Billie said, reaching them, looking expectantly at the man.

'Hey, Bill, sorry, I know I'm late, the bus was slow. This is, er…'

There was a pause while he raised his eyebrows at Stella, waiting for her to go on.

'I'm Sam,' he said eventually, turning his grin to Billie.

'*Sam*,' Billie replied, gently swaying her shoulder against Stella's. 'Hello. You work here?'

It was only then that Stella realised he was wearing a white coat and a blue hospital lanyard around his neck: Dr Sam Ansari.

'Yep, upstairs, paediatrics.'

'Oh wow, you'll go to heaven,' Billie replied.

'Hopefully not quite yet,' he said with another grin.

Stella stood quietly digesting this information. He was a *doctor*? But… but… he didn't seem like a doctor! He'd got drunk with her in the pub. The following morning, he'd joked about the mascara on the pillow. He'd tried to persuade her to stay in bed with him. What was he doing sleeping with strangers when he should be here saving children?

'We need to get going, no?' Stella said, glaring at Billie. She wanted to get away from this man and never see him again. 'Although I need a coffee.'

'Some of us have been here for so long we've already had a coffee,' Billie chided gently.

'I know, I know, I'm sorry.'

'Top tip,' said Sam, 'the café behind the escalators does very good coffee.'

'Cool, thanks. Come on, Stell. Let's go, first floor.'

'Good to see you again, Stella,' Sam offered.

In return, Stella flashed him a grimace and turned to follow Billie. So friendly. So sincere and unawkward. What was *wrong* with him? Clearly, as suspected, the guy was a weirdo. He probably shouldn't even be working with kids.

Once on the escalator, she pretended to be looking at her phone in case Sam was still watching them. But when Billie cleared her throat for a second time she looked up.

'What?'

'Excuse you, don't "what" me. That was Sam? Sam from the other night?'

'Mmmhmm.' Stella looked back to her phone to demonstrate how little she cared.

'Seemed nice.'

She fluttered her lips like a horse. 'Bit full of himself.'

'Stell! Firstly not true. And even if it was, I think doctors who save children are probably allowed to be a bit full of themselves. And secondly, he seemed hot. You didn't say he was hot.'

Stella glanced over her shoulder but Sam was gone, and then the revolving door slid out of view.

'Can we not talk about that morning? I think it gave me PTSD.'

Stella made a mock shudder before the escalator delivered them to the first floor.

'Over there,' said Billie, nodding towards a pair of swing doors with a purple gynaecology sign over them.

'Did you see my message about why I'm late, by the way?' asked Stella, following. 'I think I'm in love.'

Even for Billie, who was unendingly sympathetic to her best friend and listened to every single complaint and grumble, this was a lot to take in before her appointment. 'I did see it but can we discuss it once the doctor's cut out part of my cervix?'

'Yes, sorry, course.'

'Let's get a coffee afterwards and you can tell me everything,' said Billie, guilty at having protested, even very mildly, at Stella's preoccupation with her love life. She knew her friend had been miserable for the past six months, and she'd tried not to judge her drinking or the late nights when Stella came crashing through the door like an elephant looking for a waterhole. Or the nights when she didn't come home at all. Billie understood more than anyone that Stella's obsession with finding The One was only because she wanted to be loved so much after growing up in a family where it was viewed with disdain, as if it was an emotion to be ashamed of. She got it, which is why she loved Stella so fiercely to try and make up for it. This morning, though, she just wanted to get through her appointment before listening to Stella's latest drama.

CHAPTER 9

BILLIE GAVE HER NAME to a receptionist before they sat on a pair of blue chairs. Everything in the waiting room was worn: the parquet floor, the grey paint on the swing doors, which had rubbed off along the bottom, and a nearby vending machine with a piece of paper stuck to it saying 'out of order'. 'Just like this hospital,' someone had written underneath in blue felt-tip. The faint sound of a desk phone ringing mingled with the murmur of other people waiting and, on the wall, was a poster that declared that doctors aimed to see all patients 'within 30 minutes', apologising in advance if this wasn't the case.

A few moments later, a man in a white shirt and grey trousers appeared from a different door and said Billie's name.

'Billie Martin? Hello, I'm Dr Bush, consultant gynaecologist.' He smiled at Billie as Stella dug her teeth into her lower lip. Dr Bush the gynaecologist. She glanced at his lanyard and saw it was true: Steven Bush. Although at least he looked like a doctor: bald; middle-aged; small, round spectacles. Stella couldn't imagine Dr Bush lurking in west London pubs and chatting women up. He seemed the sort of man who had a nice wife at home, Mrs Bush, and perhaps a golden retriever. He probably spent his weekends mowing the lawn and going to th—

'Stell?' said Billie.

'Mmm?'

'You all right?'

Stella shook her head as if her ear had water in it. 'Sorry, miles away.'

'Follow me,' said Dr Bush.

They followed him through to a small room with a desk and with a medical bed pushed up against the back wall. 'Have a seat,' he told them.

He ran through a few details with Billie – full name, birthdate, had she had any abnormal symptoms and so on – while Stella gazed at a poster of a woman's reproductive organs.

'Looks like an alien,' she mused.

Dr Bush stopped talking.

'Sorry, ignore me. Carry on.'

'So,' continued Dr Bush, looking back to Billie, 'like I said, it's a straightforward procedure. Much like a smear, but we use a microscope, which allows us to have a closer look and take a small biopsy from your cervix.'

'Actually,' Stella interrupted, 'can I check something?'

'Yeeees,' Dr Bush said warily because he was a bright man and had already realised that the blonde woman was the more difficult of the two sitting in front of him.

'The letters, they couldn't have been muddled up?'

'Letters?'

'After our smear tests, we both had them here, on the same day, two weeks ago. It seems strange that Billie should be sent a letter saying she's the one with abnormalities when she's been with the same person for six years and is basically a saint and I've, well, slept with half of London.'

'Stell!'

'OK, maybe not half. But a good number of them. So could they?'

'Have been muddled up?' checked Dr Bush. He'd only come on duty half an hour earlier and had already seen a woman who'd asked if she could have become pregnant from a public toilet seat.

'Yes.'

'No.'

'You're sure?'

'Stell…'

'I'm sure.'

'Fine, fine, only wanted to check,' Stella replied.

'Right,' Dr Bush sighed, 'where was I?'

'About the biopsy,' Billie answered.

'Exactly, the biopsy.'

'Will it hurt?'

He smiled sympathetically. 'It shouldn't. Just a small scratch. And some women find they have a small amount of bleeding afterwards, but it shouldn't be more than that.'

'And after that, after the biopsy, when do I get the results?'

Dr Bush tilted his head from side to side. 'Usually a week or so, depending.'

Stella jumped in. 'Depending on what?'

'Depending on what I can see today. Sometimes we can expedite the results. So, if you don't mind undressing your bottom half and jumping up on here…' he spun and tapped the medical bed with a hand, 'I'll have a look. And you're happy for… your friend to stay?' Dr Bush glanced from Billie to Stella.

Billie nodded quickly and stood as Dr Bush pulled a curtain around the bed. Stella remained in her seat, wondering how students decided what line of medicine to go into. Was it nominative determinism? Had Dr Bush been propelled towards that region of the body subliminally? Or was he just fascinated by female anatomy? He didn't look the sort. It must be nice to be married to a man who could talk so knowledgeably about the cervix. If Stella had asked any of the men she'd slept with in the past six months to point out a cervix on a diagram, they'd probably have pointed to her earlobe.

'All good?' Dr Bush asked over the curtain, pulling on a pair of disposable gloves.

'Yep,' Billie replied tensely.

He pulled the curtain back and Stella smiled at her friend, lying on the bed with a paper blanket across her thighs.

'OK then,' said Dr Bush, wheeling himself towards the end of the bed on a stool. 'If you could raise your knees and open them for me, I'll be as gentle as I can.'

If only men were half as considerate before they approached you with their penis, Stella thought, watching him angle a light between Billie's legs.

'You all right?' he checked.

'Mmmhmm.'

'Here we go, I'm going to slide the speculum in. That's it, if you can continue to take deep breaths… that's it… that's it. Sorry, I know it may feel slightly cold.'

'It's OK,' said Billie, eyes staring straight up at the ceiling.

'You're doing brilliantly. Really brilliantly. That's the speculum in place, so what I'm going to do now is use the microscope to have a look and take the biopsy. You should just feel a slight pinch.'

Stella clenched her legs together and held her breath.

'You managing?'

'Yeah, fine, just makes me feel a bit queasy.'

'I meant the patient,' said Dr Bush, glancing over his shoulder at Stella. 'You still with us, Billie?'

'Mmmhmm.'

'You're doing so well. Just a few more seconds and I'm done.' He reached above his head for the light and twisted it slightly. 'Still OK?'

'Mmmhmm.'

'There we go, all done,' said Dr Bush a few moments later, pushing his stool back and sliding a large cotton bud into a test tube. 'You survive that?'

'Just about,' said Stella.

Dr Bush turned and raised his eyebrows.

'Sorry,' Stella mumbled. 'You OK, Bill?'

'Think so.'

'Great stuff. I'll pull this back and you can get dressed.' Dr Bush tugged the curtain around the bed, pulled off his gloves and dropped them in a plastic bin.

Stella gave him a small, polite smile as he sat back at his desk. 'Nice job.' Then, embarrassed, 'I don't mean your job is nice, as in doing this to women all day is nice. I just mean, nice job just now.'

'Stell!' Billie shouted, emerging from behind the curtain.

She sat beside Stella and exhaled with relief. 'Glad that's over.'

Dr Bush tapped at his computer. 'Sorry, I know it's not the most fun you could be having on a Wednesday morning. So I'll send that off and you should hear in about a week.'

'And it looked OK?'

'Couldn't see much. Sometimes, especially when it comes to women who haven't had children, it's often harder to tell. But I'll get the biopsy off this afternoon.'

'Great, OK, thank you.'

'Not at all.'

'Come on,' Stella said, standing up, still keen to talk to Billie about Fitz. It was a good idea, actually, because it would distract Billie from her hospital appointment. 'Big drink after that. Not a *drink* drink,' she added. 'I mean a coffee.'

CHAPTER 10

THEY SAID GOODBYE TO Dr Bush, walked back through the gynaecology department and slid down the escalator.

'You OK?' Stella checked.

'Yep,' Billie said with a small nod.

'All done, proud of you.'

'I hope it's all right.'

'Course it will be. Dr Bush probably does hundreds of these a day.'

'Dr Bush!' replied Billie, scrunching her eyes closed.

'I *know*. I had to stop myself from cackling.'

'Nice man.'

'Mmmm.'

'Come on, then.'

'What?'

Billie stepped off the escalator, followed by Stella. 'Who's this new guy you're in love with?'

'Coffee?' Stella nodded towards the café. 'Let's sit there and I'll spill the beans. I need to eat.'

She ordered coffees and a flapjack, Billie paid, and they found a spare table beside a large potted fern.

'So,' Stella began, 'I was in the pub…'

'As usual.'

'All right, as usual. And I was trying to work out what I'm going to wear for my first day.'

'I'll lend you something.'

Stella paused briefly to consider this. One the one hand, she had nothing practical to wear in an office, and she knew that Billie's sombre work dresses would look awful on her – baggy and ill-fitting. On the other, she didn't have much of a choice; she could hardly go into the office in a pair of denim cut-offs. 'Thanks, let's sort that out tonight. But then this man appeared at the bar.'

'Okaaaay.'

'No, honestly, Bill. It sounds mad, I know, but just looking at him felt like an electric shock up and down my spine.' Stella wiggled her shoulders from side to side in a mock shiver to demonstrate. 'I've *never* felt like that.'

Billie raised her eyebrows.

'What?'

'Never?'

'No! He was different. He was… it was… overwhelming.'

'But who was he?'

'All I know,' Stella went on, through a mouthful of flapjack, 'is that he's called Fitz and he works for some sort of security firm.'

'Like a bouncer?'

'No, that's what I thought too. Or maybe a bodyguard because he has that vibe, like a sort of… dominating vibe. And his arms, Bill! He had the arms of a Viking.'

Billie looked thoughtful. 'Did Vikings have good arms?'

'Yes, obviously. All that dragging antelopes around.'

'OK, OK.' Billie made a spinning motion in the air with her finger. 'Let's not get side-tracked by Vikings and antelopes. What happened?'

'Nothing! That was the annoying thing. We had a drink, he said he had a meeting nearby so that's why he was in the pub, but then he left. After, like, ten minutes.'

'He left after ten minutes and now you're in love with him?'

'I know. It's crazy, even for me. But there was something about him, Bill. It was chemistry, I'm telling you.'

'How hot are we talking?'

'Properly hot. Like, actor hot. Tall, and this amazing hair, dark, and so commanding. He could definitely throw me over his shoulder. And he had these eyes! Eyes that seemed to see right into me.'

Billie shook her head with a smile.

'I know, I get it, classic me. Meets someone for three seconds and is already married to him in my head.'

'Stell…'

'But there was a connection, I swear.'

'What's the deal, though, if you met but then he disappeared?'

'I don't know because he didn't even take my number!' Stella replied loudly. 'I don't know bu—'

She stopped as her phone screen lit up with a message from an unknown number, and she lifted the phone towards her face to unlock it.

Miss Shakespeare, I'd like to see you again soon. Preferably this week. Might you be free for dinner on Saturday? F

'Oh my god, it's him,' she murmured, her stomach flipping like a pancake.

'What? The guy?'

'Yeah,' Stella replied faintly, staring at the words.

'But he didn't take your number?'

'No!' She glanced up with a bewildered expression. 'We talked and then he disappeared. But now he's messaged.' Stella examined the words again and felt a warm surge of certainty. It didn't matter how he'd found her because it was just as she'd thought: this was meant to be.

'I don't get how he's messaged if he didn't take your number. It's definitely him?'

'Yes, look!' Stella held her phone across the table so Billie could read it. She felt giddy at the idea he'd tracked her down. He liked her. He liked her enough to find her.

'Why does he talk like that?'

'Like what?'

'Like he's a character from a period film.'

Stella snatched her phone back. 'It's nice! Actually, it's charm ing.'

'How many drinks had you had?'

'What?'

'Last night.'

'One!'

Billie looked dubious across the table.

'I promise.'

'And are you free on Saturday?'

'Course. And even if I wasn't, even if it was my own funeral on Saturday, I'd make myself free.'

At the sound of a sigh, Stella dragged her eyes from her phone and looked up.

'What?'

Billie pulled her lips into a straight line.

'*What?*'

'Please will you be careful?'

'Yes!' Stella shot back, but with a smile. Not even Billie's serious face, or her tone that sounded a little bit like her mother, could annoy her. Fitz had texted and she was going to see him again. 'What shall I say back to him? Or should I not reply straight away? Should I leave it a few hours?'

Billie sighed a second time. 'Do it now, no games.'

'But what do I say?'

'Just tell him you're free. Or, to put it in his language, "Dear Mr…"?'

'I don't know his surname.'

'Seriously?'

'Stop fussing. People go out with others without knowing their surnames all the time. Sometimes they even sleep with them on the first date, you absolute nonna.'

'OK, OK. In that case,' Billie said, before assuming a posh voice, '"Dear Mr Whoever-You-Are, I would be delighted to accept your kind invitation for the evening of whatever this Saturday is. Yours faithfully, Stella Shakespeare."'

Stella ignored her. 'What about, "Hello, man who moves in mysterious ways, how have you got my number? I am free on Saturday, as it happens." And three dots?' She looked across the table for reassurance.

'Perfect.'

'You sure?'

'I'm sure.'

Stella added the dots and reread the message several times before sending it. Then she quickly placed the phone screen-down (too nervous about his reply to watch for it), and grinned. 'I have a good feeling about this, Bill.'

Billie, who had exactly the opposite, rolled her eyes.

'Hey, what's he doing here?' Stella asked, having glanced across the café and spotted Harold sitting alone at a table, Basil lying at his feet.

Billie followed her gaze. 'Wha— Oh, Mr Vincent.'

'I didn't know dogs were even allowed in hospitals.'

'I hope he's not ill. Shall we go say hi?'

'Definitely not,' Stella said quickly.

'Why not?'

'What if he's here for something embarrassing? What if he's having his prostate checked?'

'So? He doesn't have to tell us about his prostate.'

Stella shook her head. 'I vote we leave him in peace.'

'Honestly, Stell, he's our neighbour, not a dragon.'

'I know, but it feels intrusive.'

The truth was Stella was too preoccupied with thoughts of Fitz to go and chat to Harold. Even though she'd borrowed milk from him the previous week, and even though she'd told herself she'd go back down with a packet of biscuits at some stage, she couldn't think of anything else but Fitz right now. She both wanted and *didn't* want to look at her phone and check for a reply from him. Oh, the agony of a new crush! The fluttering behind her ribs! The light-headedness of it! Stella had forgotten that, when she felt like this about someone, nothing else in the world seemed to matter. Not even impending bankruptcy.

'OK, but I should get going. Geoff will be after me,' said Billie, standing up and pushing her chair back. Geoff was her boss at the Southbank Centre, the director of fundraising, which mostly meant that he took rich, philanthropic donors out for long lunches while Billie stayed in the office.

'You feel up to it?' Stella checked, remembering why they were in hospital.

Billie nodded. 'Mmmhmm, totally fine. See you at home later?'

'Yep, I'm in. And don't worry, it's all going to be fine,' Stella promised, her mood having soared thanks to Fitz's message. Such a small thing; such a powerful effect. 'I know it is.'

CHAPTER 11

STELLA SET FIVE ALARMS on her phone for the following morning and felt proud that she got up after the second one. Previously, she might have left it until the fourth or fifth alarm and gone back to sleep anyway. Not today. She was going to arrive at 153c Harley Street on time, looking extremely professional in a pair of navy trousers and a crisp white shirt. All loaned to her by Billie the night before. The shirt was too big and the trousers too short but actually, Stella thought, standing in front of her bedroom mirror, it didn't look too bad.

Remembering Marjorie's instructions about flat shoes, she slipped on a pair of loafers, fixed a high ponytail and left before Billie had even emerged from her room, which Stella wasn't sure had ever happened before.

It wasn't *only* the prospect of the new job that was putting a spring in her step. It was also the thought of Fitz. He hadn't replied to her message yet, and Stella had carried her phone around with her at home the previous evening as if it was a pacemaker, one eye on the screen at all times in case it lit up. She'd gone to sleep with it lying on her pillow, too, so that any flash of activity would wake her up. She'd longed for this development in her life for so long that the idea of seeing Fitz again made her feel high. And it was this romantic force, the adrenalin of it, that helped propel her from bed that morning. He'd reply any second, and if she could manage her first day in the strange job and not get fired or arrested, she felt like it would be a sign: her run of bad luck was turning around.

She caught the correct Tube from Notting Hill Gate, emerged from Great Portland Street twenty minutes later and bought a coffee to kill time. She only realised this was a bad idea when leaving the coffee shop, because her stomach was already rolling with nerves, and black coffee never helped anybody in that department.

Coffee drained, stomach still spinning, she stood and threw her cup in a nearby bin before processing up Harley Street, scanning the numbers as she passed: 145, 147, 149, 151. They were glossy, lacquered front doors in red, green or blue with smart brass knockers. Several had decorative olive trees in terracotta pots outside them. But when Stella reached 153, her heart sank.

It was the grubbiest door of all, black and dull, the lower half coated with London dust and mud, and the paint peeling around the letter flap. It seemed to be the front door to several offices, so she leant forward to read the various dull bronze plaques beside it.

'The Centre for Infectious Tropical Diseases,' said one.

'London Foot and Nail Centre,' proclaimed another.

'Verity Culpepper Ltd,' said the one beneath that.

'Here goes,' Stella muttered, pressing the bell.

She stood back and waited for the click of the door but nothing came. After a few seconds she pressed the bell again but still nothing. She checked the time – exactly 9 a.m. – and retried the bell.

She sighed and, more in irritation than hope, raised the old door knocker shaped like a lion's head.

'Yooohooooo,' came a strange noise from above her. Stella stepped back and squinted towards the top of the building where Marjorie's head was protruding through a window. 'Bell's broken. I'll buzz you in. Lift's broken too so you have to walk. Third floor!'

Marjorie disappeared and, at the sound of a click, Stella pushed the door with foreboding.

Inside was a hallway that smelled of stale cigarette smoke, so she hurried through it to a staircase covered in a swirling maroon carpet pattern that could only have been designed to hide stains. Filthy, broken bells, broken lifts and stinking; what a dump, Stella thought, as she climbed the stairs. *Vogue* had polished marble floors, orchids and scented candles in its office. This place felt like a crime scene. If she came across a body and a police cordon on the next landing, she'd hardly be surprised.

'You need the money, you need the money, you need the money,' she whispered under her breath with every step.

By the time Stella reached the third floor, her thighs were burning, but just as she reached one arm towards the wall, Marjorie flung back the door.

She looked as extraordinary as Stella remembered: grey curls hanging either side of her face like a mop and that extremely prominent nose beneath a pair of dark, twinkling eyes. If Marjorie had a spirit animal, it was the koala. And she was wearing a dress that appeared to have been made from sackcloth, over the same, enormous pair of combat boots.

'Morning, come in. Come in. Welcome to the madhouse,' she

boomed, standing aside. 'Goodness me, you'll have to get a bit fitter if you're going to work here.'

'I—' Stella tried to remonstrate through heavy breaths but Marjorie swept on.

'That's your desk,' she said, waving at a table underneath a window, covered in old files and a big, boxy, ancient computer. 'I'm in there.' She stuck her thumb towards a smaller office, sectioned off by a glass wall.

'Other things to know: there's a kettle and a fridge.' Marjorie pointed around the corner of her office, 'and the lavatory is that one.' She nodded at a door. 'Hold the flush down after you go. Been on the blink recently.'

'Right,' Stella said uncertainly.

The office looked like a set for a 1960s detective programme: creaking wooden floorboards, a row of grey filing cabinets against one wall, cardboard boxes exploding with paperwork against another wall, a pot plant drooping sadly beside the boxes, and the smell of something unpleasant. Stella wrinkled her nose. Soup? Rotten vegetable? Recently deceased mouse?

'It's the milk,' Marjorie explained. 'Fridge is hit and miss and I forgot to take the milk home on Friday. But I've bought some more, so let's make that your first job.'

'Milk?'

'Making a cup of tea. Very good test, tea,' said Marjorie, eyes narrowing at Stella. 'Tells you a lot about someone.'

'How do you like it?' Stella dropped her bag to the floor and a mushroom cloud of dust motes flew into the air.

'Milk and one sugar. But milk in first. Cooks it that way. Disgusting otherwise. Make one for yourself and we'll get started.'

Marjorie disappeared into her office while Stella located two heavily stained mugs in the cupboard beneath the kettle, fished out two teabags from an old china pot marked 'OPIUM' and dropped a sugar lump into one mug. When she opened the fridge, the smell was so bad she had to hold her breath, so she closed the door quickly and sloshed some milk over the sugar lump. This place was a health hazard.

She carried the mug to the doorway of Marjorie's office.

'Anywhere you can find space,' Marjorie mumbled.

Stella lowered the mug onto a small patch of desk between folders, books, envelopes, a blue vase bursting with pens and rubber bands, a lopsided paper-tray that had lost one leg and was sinking under the weight of documents piled on top of it, and something that looked suspiciously like a dead guinea pig.

'That's my wig,' said Marjorie.

Stella was unsure what to reply. Had she been ill?

'Take a seat,' she added, nodding at an old chair with the stuffing coming out of it.

Stella sat and frowned at a teetering pile of pizza boxes beside her desk.

'Lots of eating on the go in this line of work,' Marjorie said, noticing Stella's puzzled look, before taking a sip of the tea and smacking her lips. 'Very good, the amount of milk is spot on. Can't abide those who make it with too much. Now, what I do here is top secret but I think you'll find it interesting.'

'Okaaay,' replied Stella, glancing towards the door to check that she could run if she needed to.

'They call me the affair hunter.'

'What? What's an aff—'

'A private investigator by trade,' Marjorie sniffed, 'although that's considered an old-fashioned term now. Mostly they call it threat management in the industry. But I think that sounds horribly corporate, and it's really only affairs that I concentrate on. Do you know that over forty per cent of marriages end in divorce? And a good number of those are because someone's been up to no good. Cheating toerags all around us, mark my words,' she said, waggling an index finger at Stella before her face brightened. 'So that's where I come in.'

Stella was too dumbstruck to reply. An affair hunter? What sort of job was that? Could you even call it a job? Oh, this was *absolutely* typical. Her friends worked for Netflix and the Southbank Centre, and here she was sitting in an office that smelled like a cheese factory, listening to the ramblings of a woman who could barely dress herself.

'I've got a couple of cases on the go at the moment, which is fairly usual, although I could be busier,' mused Marjorie, casting her eyes across her desk.

'That morning when I met you,' Stella asked tentatively, 'was that, er, a case?'

Marjorie snapped her head up. 'Eh?'

'Outside the legal office? Outside Spinks?'

'Oh yes, yes, indeed it was. That man…'

'The one with the moustache?'

'The one who looked like a walrus, exactly. His wife called me two weeks ago to say she suspected her husband was having an affair, so I tailed him for a few days.'

'And was he?'

'Was he what?' barked Marjorie.

'Having an affair?'

'Oh yes. Naturally he was, with one of his colleagues. It's often one of their colleagues. Much younger than him, of course. They always are. But while I was watching him, he went to Spinks and that was how I discovered he was about to initiate divorce proceedings. So I informed my client, his wife, a nice lady, Mrs Williams, which meant she had time to find her own lawyer and get her finances in order.'

'Gosh. How did you, er, become one of… I mean, how did you become an affair hunter?'

'I was in the police force for sixteen years. First in south London crime, that was a nasty business. So I requested a transfer to transport but that was even worse. Extremely dull, sifting through people's parking tickets every day, I don't mind telling you.'

'I can imagine,' Stella murmured.

'But I did pick up the odd surveillance trick, and then, well, never mind. Very long story short, the circumstances in my personal life changed and I decided to launch my own detective business, hunting down those who were pouring their treasure into foreign laps, let's say.'

'Huh?'

'It's Shakespeare,' Marjorie explained, pausing for a sip of tea. 'You should know that.'

'No relation,' said Stella, who'd spent a good deal of her life explaining to people that she wasn't a descendant.

'*Othello.* Anyway, that's beside the point. The *point* is the paperwork builds up. I have to write case files for every client, to present what I've found from my investigations, and I need someone to stay on top of those and answer the phone. And occasionally assist me on the odd case. Would you be interested in that?'

Stella's eyes widened. 'In helping with the cases?'

'It wouldn't involve much,' Marjorie replied, flicking her fingers in the air as if swatting a fly. 'Driving around town, sitting in the boot of my car from time to time, watching. I'll give you one of my cameras. Sometimes it makes more sense to have two women on a job. Less suspicious if there are two women sitting in a car chatting away than just one. We might have been out shopping, for all they know. That's why I always keep shopping bags in the back of my car. And the wigs. They come in handy for the odd disguise. That's my fancy-dress box.'

Marjorie nodded at a wooden chest in the corner of her office. The lid was lowered but not closed and the chest was exploding with clothes, the arm of a beige overcoat hanging over its side as if a body had become trapped in there.

Stella's brain felt overloaded with information. Sitting in the boot of a car! Wigs! A fancy-dress box!

'I have a sense for people who will be good at this job. And I suspected that you'd be just that when I met you that day. So, if you haven't got any more questions, I suggest you get installed at your desk as I've got to go in…' she glanced at a small gold watch on her wrist, 'ten minutes. Job in Chelsea. Most of the jobs are in Chelsea. Rich people,' she tutted.

Marjorie stood and gestured to her desk and, as if on autopilot, Stella made her way to it.

'Mmmm,' mused Marjorie, following and frowning at the sight. There must have been forty or fifty bulging folders stacked on it – green folders, yellow folders, blue folders. 'My last girl was terrible at filing. And tea, for that matter. I'd make a start with those, putting them away.' She turned and nodded at the cabinets. 'I should be back by the time you're done, then I'll show you how that thing works.' Marjorie waved at the computer. 'If the phone rings, take a message. You'll find a notepad under there.'

She gestured vaguely at the desk before hurrying to the door. 'See you in a bit.'

And then she'd gone.

Stella glanced around at the gloomy, dusty office space. What a hovel.

She removed a pile of folders from her desk chair and sat, reminding herself that she needed the cash. And at least it wasn't drug dealing, although she absolutely wasn't going to wear a wig from Marjorie's fancy-dress box.

She could do it for a couple of weeks while she tried to find something else. Something less absurd that Stella could tell her friends and family about. Affair hunter indeed. Imagine describing oneself as that. She'd have to be very careful around Marjorie while she was here. The poor woman obviously wasn't quite right.

In the meantime, for £100 a day, she could manage a bit of filing.

Determined to make the best of a less than ideal situation, Stella reached for a lamp beside the computer, only to discover there wasn't a bulb in it.

CHAPTER 12

AN HOUR OR SO later, Stella had filed roughly half the folders into the grey cabinets alphabetically, according to the name written on the sticky white label at the top. But then she picked up a thick blue folder with a label that said 'Brickbat' and curiosity clawed at her. Each folder was stamped with the word 'confidential', but right now Stella was a Verity Culpepper employee, so presumably she was allowed to read them?

She sat down in her rickety chair and opened the folder. It was unlikely to contain state secrets, she told herself; this place was hardly MI5.

According to the first document in the blue folder, a woman called Cynthia Brickbat had contacted Marjorie because she suspected her husband – Cyril Brickbat – was having an affair. Cynthia had several reasons for these suspicions, according to a badly typed statement that contained several typos.

Firstly, Cyril had taken up Pilates. According to Cynthia's statement, this was unusual because Cyril had never expressed any sort of interest in exercise apart from the occasional round of golf with his colleagues and 'the walk to the fridge and back'.

Secondly, around the same time, Cyril had become obsessed

with his weight and started asking Cynthia how many calories were in the dinners she cooked him every night. Apparently, before this, he'd been very partial to her beef cobbler and always ate a Mars bar after dinner on the sofa. But a couple of months ago his Mars bars habit had abruptly stopped in favour of a herbal tea.

Thirdly, the statement went on, when Cynthia recently asked Cyril to take the bins out, he agreed but took his phone with him. Later, when Cyril was in the bath, Cynthia tried to access her husband's phone but discovered that his passcode was no longer her birthdate.

Underneath the statement were several photographs held together with a paperclip. The top one showed a man with his chest puffed out like a cockerel, dressed in very tight Lycra. Cyril, Stella presumed.

She leafed through the photos. They'd been taken in sequence on a residential street: a few of the man strolling down the road, gym bag in hand, before a couple more of him walking up the path to one house and pressing the bell. The next photo showed him glancing over his shoulder, before the photograph under that showed the door being opened by a brunette with eyebrows that looked like they'd been drawn on.

A few more photos showed Cyril stepping over the threshold, then of the closed front door behind him. A yellow highlighter note divided that set of photos from the next, with a handwritten scribble noting that these had been taken an hour later. These showed Cyril leaving the house, and the lady with caterpillar eyebrows blowing him a kiss from the porch.

Stella put down the photos and picked up the next document from the folder, which revealed that, according to the electoral roll, Marjorie had discovered that the house where the photographs had been taken was owned by a couple called Mike and Emma Baldwin, who had lived there for seventeen years. Further printouts of Facebook pages and an Instagram page revealed that Emma Baldwin was a Pilates teacher in Balham, and a picture printed from the studio website revealed she was the woman with the extraordinary eyebrows.

The folder's penultimate document was a single typed page on which Marjorie detailed her findings, confirmed that she'd witnessed Cyril visit the property – 117 Blossom Road – and the date that she'd taken the photos.

Underneath that, an invoice for £950, which was marked 'PAID' with a red stamp.

Stella leant back in her chair and sighed. Poor old Cynthia. Cyril had obviously been having an affair with Emma the Pilates teacher.

She closed the folder, wondering what had happened to Brickbat's marriage, then jumped at the sight of her phone screen lighting up on her desk.

It was him. *Let's meet at Flemings, 8 pm Saturday.*

Stella felt another spark of adrenalin at this. Flemings was a members' club in Knightsbridge, very exclusive and very discreet, and owned by a reclusive Scottish billionaire. Stella knew about the club since Miles's father, Lord St George, was a member, and Miles had been on the waiting list.

She laid her phone on her desk and wondered how long to leave it before replying but she only managed twenty seconds before picking it up again.

Is that an order? she tapped back.

Yes, came the immediate reply. *See you then.*

They were short, unemotional messages but she felt a flare of excitement. Flemings was a serious, grown-up place for a first date, and Stella liked him even more for not suggesting some Chelsea pub or cocktail bar where the loos smelled of drains. She was into the assertive tone of his messages, too, and momentarily imagined his hands running up her thighs, until she heard footsteps outside the office door and jumped to her feet. The folders! She hadn't finished.

She gathered a big pile into her arms and dropped them to the floor so that they were hidden behind her desk. Adopting a studied expression of innocence, she picked up a yellow folder and resumed filing as the door crashed open.

'Hello!' trilled Marjorie. 'How did you get on? Any phone calls?'

'Er, no, no phone calls.'

'Not a single one?'

'No, sorry,' Stella said because the dismay on Marjorie's face made her feel like she should apologise.

'Ah well, can't be helped. Managing those, are you?' Marjorie peered at the desk as she unpicked her duffel coat.

'Mmmhmm.'

'Don't forget the ones on the floor,' she added, nodding at the pile Stella had hidden.

'Course, I was just… sorting them into alphabetical piles.'

'Rule number one, you can't hide anything from a private detective,' Marjorie told her with a wink. 'Now, how about another tea?'

Stella smiled, relieved that she didn't seem to be in trouble. 'Sure.'

A few minutes later, she carried another stained mug into Marjorie's office before loitering in the doorway.

'Um, Marjorie, can I ask you a question?'

'Depends on what the question is,' Marjorie mumbled as she rifled through the papers on her desk. 'I make it a rule never to discuss politics or religion.'

'It's not about either of those.'

'Then try me. Ah! Here it is!' Marjorie sat up and triumphantly held what looked like a black kaleidoscope in the air. 'Been looking for that for ages.'

'What is it?'

'My night-vision lens. Very useful on the odd job when I have to stay up late. But come on, what's this question?'

'How easy is it to track down someone's number if you only know their name?'

Marjorie barked with laughter. 'Ha! Google knows every time you go to the bathroom, young Stella. Getting a number can be done in less than ten seconds by someone who knows how. Child's play. Why do you ask?'

'No reason, just wondering,' Stella replied quickly because even she knew it was unprofessional to discuss one's personal life on the first day in a new job, and she already suspected that, in her line of work, Marjorie couldn't be much of a romantic.

CHAPTER 13

As Stella passed Harold's door the next evening, just after six, she heard the sound of Sam Cooke floating from underneath it.

She paused, then knocked.

A few seconds later, Harold appeared, a tea towel over his shoulder, holding a potato masher. He wasn't an experienced cook; Ellen had always been in charge of that department. But in the past year, he'd discovered the BBC Food website and tried out a few recipes. Tonight, he was attempting fishcakes, though worried the haddock he'd bought from Tesco had gone off. Basil had left the kitchen when he'd opened the packet.

'Stella, hello. Everything all right?'

She nodded. 'Mmm, yes, all good. I just wanted to give you these.'

She reached one arm into her bag and pulled out a packet of shortbread, which she'd bought from a deli on Marylebone High Street.

Just before Stella had left the office, Marjorie had summoned her and rummaged around under her desk. Stella had been quite nervous about what she was going to liberate until Marjorie retrieved a petty cash box and fished out several notes. 'I'll pay you every Friday, if that suits? Good work this week, young Stella, thanks ever so much.'

Stella had consequently bounced down the stairs with the dodgy carpet much more happily than she'd trudged up them, and made straight for the posh deli.

'Shortbread, my favourite!' said Harold. 'But whatever for?'

'Just to say thanks for helping me last week, for the milk, and the advice. And she's not a drug dealer, by the way.'

Harold looked perplexed. 'Who isn't?'

'My new boss. She's not a drug dealer.'

'Your job, of course!' he replied, raising the potato masher in the air like a conductor's baton. 'How was it?'

'Fine, not sure how long I'll be there,' said Stella. 'But you can have your alarm back if you need it?'

Harold shook his head. 'You keep that. You should have one anyhow. So what are you doing if you're not peddling contraband on the streets?'

'Well, she's a… um… she's a private detective.'

On the Tube home, Stella had looked around her at the other commuters who presumably had sensible jobs – women in suits, men leaning forwards over their free newspapers – and decided this was the less embarrassing way to describe her boss. Her *temporary* boss. She'd spent that day finishing the filing before Marjorie had shown her how to access the email inbox on the giant computer. After that, Stella went through it, deleting old emails, cross-referencing them with the files to work out which cases were closed and which were ongoing. And actually, some of the cases were quite interesting. In the past few weeks, Marjorie had tailed one man to the South of France and discovered he was sleeping with his sister-in-law, and followed someone else's wife to the park to find she was having an affair with the dog walker. But still, she could hardly go around telling people that she was working for an affair hunter.

'A private detective, gracious,' said Harold, standing in his doorway. 'I knew a few of those in my time. It's all changed, mind, what with technology.' Then he winced at Stella. 'Actually, if you have a moment, could you help me out with a small matter?'

Stella, high on her exchange with Fitz as well as getting through the first couple of days in that office, had been thinking of the olives and the crisps she'd bought from the posh deli, and the bottle of wine that she knew Billie had put in the fridge. She'd been anticipating that first icy sip while walking from Notting Hill station. But she felt it was mean to say no, especially after Harold been so helpful with job advice.

'Sure.'

'Come in,' he said, standing back.

'What's that smell?' Stella asked, walking towards his kitchen.

'Haddock.'

'Oh.'

'I'm making fishcakes for dinner. You're very welcome to stay if you'd li—'

'No, thank you, my flatmate's got a bottle ready to celebrate.'

'Course,' Harold said, placing the masher on the kitchen counter. 'I won't keep you long, but what it is, well, it's a bit embarrassing. I volunteer in a hospital, you see. At the Chelsea and Westminster.'

Since Ellen had died, days at the hospital had become the highlight of Harold's week. Volunteering had been Ellen's idea, like all the best ones. She'd been in Ward E, for her last three weeks, and Harold came in every day, from early morning until 6 p.m. when visitors were kicked out. He'd spent most of his time sitting in the blue plastic armchair beside her bed, reading the paper aloud. But when he needed a break, he walked down to the ground-floor café.

One afternoon in the queue, he had got chatting to a lady carrying a bird cage covered with paisley cloth. It was a parrot, she told him, an electric-green Amazon parrot called Kermit, and they volunteered every Tuesday in the children's ward. At the mention of his name, Kermit had wolf-whistled from under the cloth, and Harold had been so impressed that he'd gone back upstairs and told Ellen. She'd murmured that Basil and he should do the same. It was prophetic, as if she knew that it would be good for him after she'd gone.

So now they did exactly that.

'That's good of you,' Stella told him, suddenly ashamed that she hadn't said hello to him in the café with Billie.

'Not really,' Harold said, his cheeks turning slightly pink. 'It's the least we can do for the hospital after, well, after everything they did for my wife.'

'Right, yes, of course,' she replied, immediately feeling awkward as well as ashamed.

'And yesterday, in the hospital, I got talking to Johnny,' went on Harold. 'He's one of the lads I read to. Smashing lad. My favourite, although I probably shouldn't say so. Dear me, that does whiff a bit.' He leant across and turned the oven down. 'Anyway, I'm flip-flapping. What it is,' he said, standing up again, 'is that Johnny suggested I join a dating app.'

Stella bit down hard on her lip. She'd been imagining that Harold was going to ask her how to use emojis or how to get his emails on his phone.

'Which dating app?' she managed to say after a few seconds.

'That's what I wanted to ask you. I'm not sure. Johnny said his uncle has met quite a few women on one of them. But I didn't think to ask which one. Not that I want to meet lots of women,' he said hurriedly, 'maybe just the odd one.' He looked panicked again. 'I don't mean *odd* odd. A normal woman, with any luck.'

Stella smiled. 'I think it's a great idea.'

'Do you think so? You think I should give it a whirl?'

'Definitely,' Stella replied, although she wasn't sure where to suggest. Tinder wasn't the right place for Harold. It might put him off dating altogether.

A few weeks after the split from Miles, she and Billie had spent a Thursday night in the flat creating Stella's dating profile for Hinge. Stella hadn't wanted to do this. Could one find their great love on an app? It felt unlikely.

But Billie said it was a step forward, so they'd scrolled through hundreds of pictures of Stella, most of which she hated: Stella in a black bikini top and sarong on holiday in Italy; Stella lying on the grass in Hyde Park one summer evening; Stella dancing at their friend Rose's wedding in a glittering silver dress that made her look like a mermaid; Stella laughing over a mug of tea, taken by Billie on the flat's balcony.

She looked radiant in them all, blonde hair cascading over her shoulders, huge smile, but couldn't see it because her self-confidence was shot. So although Billie created the profile, Stella had never used it, preferring instead to go to the pub and be chatted up there. It felt less depressing.

She'd never thought about people in their seventies dating before and wondered whether a bridge club or a ballroom dancing class might be a better idea. But presumably there *were* older people on dating apps. Why not? She felt briefly despondent at the idea that she might be still hunting for love by that age, but Ellen had been Harold's first great love, and now that she was gone, why shouldn't he try and find another? Perhaps we did have more than one great love in our lives. Perhaps a person could have two or even three. Look at Joan Collins, on husband number five and still going to parties. Perhaps she had a sixth husband in her?

'I'm on one called Hinge,' Stella volunteered. 'Although I don't use it.'

'Hinge?'

'Mmm, Hinge. And there's another called Happn. And Raya. And there's Bumble, which is where women have to make the first move.'

'Goodness.'

'And then there's Thursday, where you can only match on a Thursday, so it's supposed to stop people just scrolling and scrolling, and encourage them to actually chat and meet up instead.'

'Gracious.'

'There are all sorts of others depending on your, er, interests. Like if you're religious, or gay, or into, um, certain things.'

'What things?'

Stella, wishing that she hadn't gone down this route, chewed her lip again before answering. 'Like if you're into dressing up or… larger people. Or uniforms, like police uniforms!'

Harold shook his head. 'No no, I don't think that's for me. But do you think there might be one for more, how do I put it, mature sorts?'

'Probably. They seem to have them for everything. I'll have a look only…' Stella paused and glanced over Harold's shoulder at the kitchen clock, 'I said to Billie I'd be back for a drink. So can you leave it with me and I'll let you know? What's your number? I'll text.'

'Yes, of course, I don't want to keep you. But that would be very kind.'

Harold read out his number and Stella tapped it into her phone. 'OK, on it,' she said, heading for his door. 'Have a good weekend.'

'You too,' Harold said, closing it behind her. Although the truth was, his weekends weren't very different to his weekdays and he had nothing planned for the next two days. That's why this dating app idea was a good one, he told himself, although from what Stella had told him, he'd have to be very careful about which app he picked.

Stella hurried up the stairs to her flat with an unfamiliar sensation of lightness in her chest. She had money in her pocket thanks to Marjorie. She hadn't been fired and the job would do for a bit while she looked for something else. She was seeing Fitz the following evening, and, as she pulled her keys free, she realised she quite liked these interactions with her neighbour. He'd helped her out; now she'd mull over his dating app question. Being friendly with him was probably easier than avoiding him in the hall every time she went out.

'I'm back!' she shouted as she closed the door. 'I've bought supplies. And you'll never guess what just happened downsta— Bill? Hey hey hey, what's up? What is it?'

Billie was in the kitchen, sitting at the table, crying into her hands.

Stella crouched in front of her knees. 'What's happened? Is it Jez? What's he done?

Billie shook her head and gestured towards her phone, then wiped her cheek. 'It was Dr Bush. He just called. I've got to go back in.'

'Oh. OK, how come?'

'They think it's cancer, Stell, cervical cancer.'

'What?' Stella replied faintly, although she'd heard the reply. Her brain just needed time to catch up with her ears. The planet had gone still.

Billie broke the stillness with another sob and Stella reached for her hand. Her fingers were hot and damp. 'Bill, listen to me, what exactly did he say?'

'He wouldn't tell me at first, he said could I come in next week to discuss the results.'

'OK, there we go. He didn't say it was bad, he just said could you come in.'

'Stell, no, listen to me. He said could I come back next week to discuss the results, but if they were fine why would he need to discuss them? So I pleaded and said I couldn't wait all weekend, and it was only when I begged him that he told me it looked like I had early-stage cervical cancer.'

'Why? Why do they think that?'

Billie pulled a hand away to wipe her cheek. 'He said he'd asked the lab to look into the biopsy, after my appointment, because he had concerns. And it's come back showing cancerous cells so I have to go in next week for blood tests, and to talk about treatment. Treatment, Stell!'

'But… but… but could they have been mixed up?'

Billie wiped her cheek again. 'What?'

'The results. Could they have been mixed up? OK, the letters weren't but I bet the results could have been. They must do hundreds every day. Thousands, maybe!'

Billie shook her head.

'But… Bill, there's no way. There can't be. You're thirty-two, and… and… and you don't smoke. Or eat meat! And you eat unpronounceable vegetables and drink milk that has been squeezed from a nut. It doesn't make sense, there's no way,' Stella repeated. 'They'll have to do more tests. These ones are wrong.'

'I don't think they are,' Billie said quietly.

Stella felt wholly inadequate. She wasn't the consoler. Billie did the consoling. Stella wasn't the consoling sort. She never knew what to say. 'OK. OK, OK, well, we'll just see about that. When did Dr Bush ring?'

She sniffed. 'A few minutes ago.'

Billie rarely cried either. Stella was the crier. That had been the pattern since they'd met. The first time it happened was just after they'd started at boarding school, in the attic, where Stella had been sitting with her back on the warm boiler, crying while listening to a soul CD, missing her grandfather. Billie had gone looking for her with a packet of strawberry laces and they'd sat alongside one another with one earpiece each as Stella's tears streamed.

When Stella stopped crying, restored by so many strawberry laces that her tongue stung, the pair went back downstairs to watch *Dawson's Creek*, sitting close together on beanbags in the common room, and every few minutes Stella felt Billie turn and look sideways at her, just checking.

There had been plenty of Stella's tears since. She cried over men; she cried when she had a bad hangover; she cried in films and, in especially unguarded moments when she let it get to her, over her family. But Billie always acted as she had in the boiler room, sitting with Stella until her face was dry. Now she was the one sobbing, Stella felt less calm.

'OK,' she repeated before wishing that she could stop saying OK. 'Have you called your parents?'

'No,' Billie said before letting out a sad, tortured moan. 'How can I ring them and tell them this?'

'I can ring them.'

She shook her head. 'I should.'

'Have you told Jez?'

Billie made another moan. 'No, oh god, I'm so scared, Stell.'

Stella swallowed and reached for Billie's other hand, so she was clasping both of them. 'OK, Bill, listen. Look at me. Bill? Seriously, look at me.'

Billie raised her red eyes.

'This is going to be fine,' Stella said fiercely. '*You* are going to be fine. And do you know why?'

Billie shook her head.

'Because you are the best person I know, and they've obviously found this early, and Dr Bush seemed like a pretty good sort of doctor to me, not that I know much about doctors, clearly. But it will be all right. Bill?'

She'd dropped her head but raised it again at this.

'We've got this,' vowed Stella. 'I promise.'

CHAPTER 14

GUILT HAD NEVER BEEN a familiar emotion to Stella. As a child, she had little to feel guilty about. She breezed through her early years, raised in a large mock-Tudor house in Buckinghamshire with a swimming pool and a pony called Spot. Once she'd met Billie, she breezed through school and exams because she was bright and capable – when she wanted to be. She breezed through her twenties, living in Notting Hill with her best friend, making half-hearted attempts at working while still supported by a credit card covered by her father. She partied, drank, met Miles and presumed she'd settle down with him because getting married was what everyone else seemed to be doing.

Then the breezing stopped. Suddenly Stella Shakespeare was thirty-two and didn't have a plan. That was when the guilt started, rising inside her like the sun every morning. Stella felt guilty that she hadn't tried harder at school, guilty for being so spoiled, guilty that she'd flunked every course or job she'd ever attempted, guilty that she didn't have a career, and guilty that she'd frittered away her twenties. And now she felt an almost overwhelming guilt that she wasn't the one who was ill, that her best friend, the best person she knew, had cervical cancer.

She woke early the next morning and googled statistics in bed, clicking through page after page, scrolling down. The highest cervical cancer rate was in women aged between thirty and thirty-four, she was horrified to read. It was the fourteenth most common cancer in Britain, and it affected white and Black women more than Asian women. Stella clicked another link to read that 21 per cent of cases were caused by smoking, which made her think of the ashtray on the balcony, spilling over with her Camel butts, and feel a renewed wave of guilt. Billie had never smoked a cigarette, not even as a teenager when Stella started having the odd drag to impress boys.

She read on and on, dizzying herself with the terminology as if she'd eventually find a page promising that Billie would be fine, which was what she'd kept telling her the night before.

'You're going be fine,' Stella had insisted multiple times. When Jez arrived home, they'd sat in the sitting room, discussing it while Billie cried on and off and Stella slugged her way through the wine. It hadn't seemed real. Cancer was something that happened to other people.

But now the initial shock had receded, Stella could sense the reality settling in. Billie has cancer. Billie has cancer, she mouthed in her bed, trying out the words. It wasn't just guilt that came with this realisation, either. As she repeated the sentence, again, and then a third time, Stella was hit by a rush of fear that made her chest feel tight.

She squinted at the small text on her phone screen. According to the Cancer Research site, 90 per cent of women who were diagnosed with cervical cancer at Billie's age survived for five years or more. But five years or more was nothing. Five years ago they were twenty-seven; that was the year after Billie met Jez; the summer that she and Billie went to Greece and sunbathed topless on their apartment balcony until they realised a local window cleaner was taking photos of them. That was the year Stella dated a Scottish musician and the year she and Billie decided the flat needed a goldfish, which they christened Alan and who died only a few weeks after they bought him from a dodgy pet shop in Kensal Rise. It felt like yesterday.

Stella dropped her phone, sick of reading numbers, and went through to the kitchen.

'Oh, hey,' she said, surprised to see Billie up, cradling a mug at the table. 'You sleep OK?'

'Yep.'

Stella pointed to the kettle. 'Another one?'

'I'm good.'

She topped up the water and turned to Billie. 'You're going to be fine.'

Billie made a small smile and Stella willed herself to say something more helpful. There had to be something. But what were the right words? If only there was a phrase book for this situation so she could stop offering the same pathetic reassurance.

'You're going to be fine,' Stella repeated, reaching into the cupboard for a mug, 'although I think it's worth checking with the hospital to see if they *have* mix—'

'Stell,' Billie said so sharply that Stella spun around from the counter.

'Mmm?'

'Can we not talk about it?'

'Sure.'

'Jez has been going on about statistics and no-sugar diets all morning. I know he wants to help, but he's actually making it worse, as if he's already assumed it's terminal and I've only got hours left.'

Stella winced at the flippancy. It was so unlike Billie. 'Obviously it's not going to be term—'

'What did I just say? No more. Please. Let's talk about something else. Literally anything else.'

'Is Jez here?'

'Nope, sent him to football early.'

Stella poured her tea and sat opposite Billie.

That kitchen table had witnessed various mornings after. The mornings after Notting Hill carnival weekend, when it was usually covered with half-empty cans of Red Stripe and crusting pots of hummus. Monday mornings, when Jez left it piled high with the weekend newspapers. The mornings after they had friends for dinner, when small wax pools were left in the middle, having dripped from their candlesticks. The morning after Miles broke up with Stella, when three or maybe four empty wine bottles were pushed to one end. The morning after *that*, when Stella sat with her head in her hands, Ian Shakespeare on speaker phone, telling her that she needed to 'do something' with her life and that it wasn't his fault she couldn't 'maintain' a boyfriend, as if Miles was a pot plant that Stella had failed to look after.

But no morning after had felt as significant as this, and the early sun pouring through the windows only made it seem more surreal, strange that it was so lovely outside when it felt bleak in the kitchen.

Stella sighed and blew on her tea. 'OK, so you want to hear about my mad job?'

'That is *exactly* what I want to hear about, tell me everything.'

Stella went into cheering-up mode: she sat at the table and talked about Marjorie being a private detective and her eccentric dress sense, and about the dismal office that smelled of dead mouse and cheese, and the wigs and the overflowing fancy-dress box, and the cases that she'd read about, including Cyril Brickbat and the Pilates teacher, and the dog walker.

Billie smiled, and then laughed, and ended up lying along the bench, doubled over at the idea of Stella's new boss tailing several dogs in the park in disguise. 'Only you would end up working for Miss Marple,' she said through wheezes of laughter.

'I know… I don't think it's for ever. But it'll do for a bit. Hey, also, I asked her about how easy it is to get the number of someone you don't know, and she said very easy if you know how. Like, it could be done in seconds.'

Billie looked confused. 'Oh *him*, your mysterious new stalker. But hang on, isn't tonight the night?'

Stella rubbed invisible circles on the table with her finger. 'Yeah, supposed to be, but obviously I don't have to go and we can lie on the sofa and watch something. Or do whatever you like really.' She looked up. 'I don't want to abandon you.' She'd thought about this while lying in bed. She really, really wanted to see Fitz; it almost felt as if the rest of her life was going to be decided by this one evening. But even Stella knew that her rampaging, overactive, wildly optimistic romantic sensibilities needed to be put to one side for the time being.

'Stop it,' Billie replied firmly. 'If you start talking like Jez I'll have to send you to football too.'

'Bill, I really don't have to go.'

'You're going and I don't want to hear another word about it.'

'OK, but I'm coming to hospital on Mon—'

'NOT ANOTHER WORD!' Billie shouted, closing her eyes and waggling her fingers in her ears. 'But I think you need to be careful tonight,' she added, lowering her hands to her lap.

Stella frowned. 'What d'you mean?'

'You know nothing about this guy, Stell. Take that alarm Harold gave you.'

'He's booked dinner in a nice place. A really nice place. I hardly think I need to take an alar—'

'What place?'

'Flemings? That club in Knightsbridge, you know the one Miles's dad is a member of?'

'Mmmm,' Billie murmured. 'Still, this is how they do it.'

'How who does what?'

'Psychopaths. They lure you in and before you know it I'm looking at a photo of you in the paper and your mum's sobbing on the news.'

'Can dragons sob? I'm not sure they have tear ducts.'

'Seriously! Please just take the alarm.'

'All right, *all right*.'

'What you going to wear?'

Stella sighed dramatically. 'Not sure. I haven't been on a date that I cared about this much for ages.'

'Want to play gladiator?'

It was one of their in-jokes, a game they'd devised as teenagers after watching the Russell Crowe film where the emperor turns his thumb down to signify that the gladiator should be killed. Around the same time, whenever Stella and Billie were dressing up for a party, they'd try on clothes, sticking their hand out and wobbling their thumb at one another, turning it up or down depending on whether they approved of the outfit. Even now, if one of them texted something the other disapproved of or made a lame joke on WhatsApp, the other would send a gif of Joaquin Phoenix in a crown of laurel leaves, his thumb towards the ground.

'Do you feel up to it?'

Billie frowned. 'Hang on, let me just check.' She dropped her head to one side as if trying to hear something. 'Yup, no, my vagina says that's completely fine, I'm allowed.'

'Ha ha.'

'Come on,' Billie added, pushing her chair back. 'Let's go and find something inappropriate for you to wear. I'm thinking borderline illegal.'

In the end, having tried on several dresses, a jumpsuit, a short skirt with a black top, and back into a dress again – by which point Stella's bedroom looked like it had been ransacked by a burglar – they settled on a short strapless black dress so that her blonde hair, loose, could fall over her shoulders. Plus a pair of silver heels and a leather jacket.

Jez scowled over the back of the sofa when she emerged from her bedroom that evening after two hours of preparation. 'Thought it was a date, not a funeral.'

'Wish it was your funeral,' Stella muttered.

'You what?'

'Nothing, nothing. As ever, your input is much appreciated.'

'Ignore him,' said Billie, also on the sofa, draped across Jez. 'You look absurdly hot.'

'Do you think?' Stella asked nervously, fingering the hem of her dress. It was *very* short.

'I do think.'

'What I really want it to say is "bend me across the table and do me immediately, but also maybe marry me".'

Jez snorted. 'You going to bang him on the first date? Actually, hang on, you want to marry him, having not even been on a date yet? That's pretty ambitious, Stella, even for you.'

'I'm not saying I *will* sleep with him, just that I want him to want that.'

'There's a first for everything,' he replied, reaching for the remote control. 'Ow!'

Having slapped his arm, Billie reached for the back of the sofa and pulled herself up. 'Important question: have you got that alarm?'

Stella nodded and lifted a small clutch bag. 'In here.'

'OK, go, have fun.'

'I will.'

'Look forward to seeing you crawl in tomorrow morning, Stella,' Jez added as she opened the door.

Already halfway out, she paused and glanced back at him. 'Jeremy, the only thing that crawls around here is you. Have a nice evening!'

Honestly, Stella thought as she skipped down the stairs, other people's romantic choices were extraordinary.

CHAPTER 15

MOST LONDONERS WOULD WALK past Flemings without knowing it was there. From the pavement, the member's club looked like a private house: one of several on a Knightsbridge street, with windows that revealed nothing to the outside world, and a plain black door.

But this was exactly the point; its members didn't want it to be showy or flash. The club had existed for nearly 140 years, counted several former prime ministers among its ranks, had hushed, dark interiors and a wine list of eighty-three pages. Multibillion business deals were often made with a handshake over lunches that ran into the evening and then to the cigar terrace at the back of the club before being announced in the *Financial Times* several weeks later. Although journalists were forbidden from the club. As were trainers and baseball hats.

It was the perfect place, in other words, for a very intimate, very discreet date.

Stella checked the address on her phone, approached the black door and knocked.

It was opened by a man wearing a white tie and tailcoat. 'Good evening, madam. Welcome to Flemings.'

She stepped into a dimly lit reception room with a fire burning on one side and an antique desk on the other. 'I'm here for dinner with…' Stella faltered because she didn't know Fitz's surname and admitting that felt embarrassing. What if they thought she was a prostitute, called up for the night? A high-class prostitute, admittedly, the sort of subtle, elegant woman you might see sitting at a hotel bar, on the look-out for a rich client. But still, Stella didn't want them thinking *that*.

'She's here for me.'

Stella turned to see Fitz smiling down at her, and the sight was almost overpowering. It was the same, physical reaction she'd felt when she first saw him: an electric thrill that ran the length of her body. 'Hi,' she said nervously.

'Mr Montague, of course,' said a lady in a red dress and lipstick, hurrying out from behind the desk. 'Shall I take your coat?' She stretched a hand towards Stella, who shrugged off her leather jacket.

'The cloakroom,' she ordered, passing it to the man in white tie before turning back to Fitz. 'Your usual table?'

'Please.'

Feeling his eyes on her bare shoulders, Stella deliberately coiled her hair around her neck and followed the lady in the lipstick through another darkened room. She took in the silk wallpaper, the candles flickering on every table, and the thick velvet curtains hanging in front of every window. Even the air smelled expensive – the heavy scent of rose wafting from several large vases, mingling with cigar and wood smoke from the open fire.

The lady pulled out a corner table, which allowed Stella to slide along a velvet bench, then pushed it in as Fitz sat beside her so their knees grazed under the tablecloth.

'Thank you, Julie. And I'm going to guess,' he said, turning to Stella, 'vodka and tonic?'

'Mmm, please.'

'Two of those. Belvedere.'

'I remember, Mr Montague,' said Julie, backing away with a coy smile.

'We meet again,' Fitz said, leaning forward and resting his forearms on the table.

The light from a candle in a silver pot on the table danced between them, and their table was spaced so far from any other that the room felt hushed and intimate, as if she and Fitz were the only people in it.

'Montague. At least now I know your surname.'

'You've got me,' he replied, clapping a hand against his chest. 'You look very beautiful, Miss Shakespeare.'

'Thank you.' A small voice inside her didn't believe this but Stella had spent two hours trying to make it true: two hours of exfoliating, and moisturising, and a hair mask, and hair drying, and so many layers of mascara that her eyelashes swooped up and down above her cheekbones like butterfly wings. 'I still want to know how you got my number, by the way.'

Fitz grinned. 'I can't tell you all my secrets.'

'*Yet*,' she retaliated.

'Yet.'

A waiter appeared and lowered their drinks, along with a silver pot of pistachios.

'Thanks, Luca.'

'You know everyone here?' Stella asked once he'd retreated.

Fitz nodded. 'I stay nearby when I'm in town, and I use this place a lot for work, so, mostly, yes.'

'You don't live in London?'

He lifted his glass in the air. 'To the land we love, and the love we land.'

Stella copied him and took a sip before she lowered her glass. 'What's that?'

'An old soldier's toast.'

'You were in the army?'

He grinned and scooped up several pistachios in his hand. 'So many questions, Miss Shakespeare.'

'I'm intrigued.'

'I can tell.' He paused, unpicking the shells, then threw the nuts back in one go. 'I was in the navy. The SBS.'

She cocked her head and tried not to sound impressed. 'The SAS?'

'No, the SBS.'

'What's that?'

'It means Special Boat Service. It's a unit of the navy.'

'Is it like the SAS?'

Another grin. 'To the uninitiated, yes, although we thought we were better than them. We *were* better than them.'

'Did you go abroad?'

'I did. Some time in Afghan, stint in Libya. A couple of years in Kenya.'

'Doing what?'

He shrugged. 'Depended. Jumping out of helicopters, tailing pirate boats. Trying to storm tankers that had been taken over by pirates.'

'*Pirates?*'

'Somali terrorists.'

'Seriously?'

'Seriously. Until a few years ago when I left to do my own thing.'

'Why?'

'I wanted to be my own boss.'

'So, private security.'

'Private security, exactly.'

'Which means what? I mean, I know you said problem solving but is it…' Stella tailed off and Fitz met her eyes, amused, before reaching for another handful of nuts.

'Is it?'

'Dangerous?'

Fitz laughed, embarrassing her. How was she supposed to understand what he did when he talked in riddles?

He shook his head. 'No, it's not dangerous, it's very simple. My company helps out individuals, businesses, or sometimes governments, with their security needs. Take my Notting Hill client, for example, who I'd just been to see when I met you. He's a rich Frenchman who wants his children to be protected on the way to school and back, and when his family travels abroad. I have people who can do that. Or it's a tanker that needs a team of security on it while it runs back from the Middle East. No problem. Or sometimes, increasingly, it's online security. A Japanese bank is hiring a new CEO. Can we run background checks on him, that sort of thing.'

'So *that's* how you got my number,' Stella mused, recalling what Marjorie had told her. 'You know how to find out… secrets about people?'

'Maybe.'

'OK, but if you don't live in London, where's home?'

'Who says I don't live here?'

'You! You said you stay around the corner.'

'It doesn't mean I don't live here.'

Stella rolled her eyes. 'Oh my god, you're infuriating.'

It felt like a game of cat and mouse: one moment Stella was the mouse, Fitz teasing her; the next, she was the cat, trying to pin him down. But she liked it; she felt more alive sitting here than she had for months.

He smiled again and leant against the banquette, extending one arm along it so his fingers nearly reached her shoulder. 'Now it's my turn with the questions.'

'Uh-oh,' Stella joked, picking up her glass.

'You're Stella Shakespeare.'

'Mmmhmm.'

'And you're thirty-two.'

Her mouth made a circle in surprise. 'How do you know that?'

'My turn, like I said. You're Stella Shakespeare and you're thirty-two. And you live in Notting Hill?'

'Mmmhmm.'

'Alone?'

'With my best friend, Billie.' At this, Stella felt a pang of guilt that she was out while Billie was at home, mulling over the diagnosis. 'She, er…' Then she paused. It wasn't first-date conversation. 'We've lived together for eleven years, we're basically married.'

Fitz raised his eyebrows. 'Lucky Billie. And in that case, what I don't understand is what somebody as… intriguing as you was doing in that pub by yourself?'

'Why shouldn't I be there by myself? You know women are allowed in pubs by themselves these days?'

'Are you mocking me, Miss Shakespeare?'

'I wouldn't dare.'

'In that case, I'll repeat my question. Why were you there by yourself? No boyfriend? No terrible ex-husband?'

Stella smiled. She liked being interrogated by him. She liked his sternness. If he was this bold and frank in conversation, what must he be like in bed? He would presumably know exactly what he wanted to do to her and she'd be completely at his mer— She shook her head briefly and told herself to answer the question. What was the question again? Oh yes. 'My ex and I broke up six months ago,' she replied airily, deciding not to mention that she'd been dumped.

'And nobody since?'

'Nobody like you.'

They held one another's gaze until the lady in the red dress ruined it by appearing beside their table.

'Would you like the menu, Mr Montague?'

Fitz kept his eyes on Stella's for a beat before looking up. 'Yes please, Julie. I'm extremely hungry.' He turned back to Stella. 'You?'

Stella thought she'd never been less hungry in her life. Also, by this point, Fitz's knee was pressing against her thigh and the sensation was so overwhelming that she wasn't sure she could remember how to read.

'Wine?' Fitz asked a few moments later, when they were handed the menus.

'Mmmm,' she replied, trying to understand the words in front of her.

They ordered fish, and Fitz asked for a bottle of wine, before their cat-and-mouse game continued.

'How old are you?' Stella had wondered this on the evening they met. Some years older than her, she'd guessed. Now that they were sitting so close, she could see a few silver hairs running through his curls, and his tanned forehead had two grooves running through it. But this hardly mattered to Stella. Actually, they only made him seem more experienced. More suave.

'Guess.'

Stella rolled her lower lip through her teeth as she thought. 'Forty-two?'

'Close, forty-four. OK, my turn again, how's that new job going?'

'My new jo— Oh, I told you in the pub.'

'You did. In sales?'

Stella pulled a guilty face. 'That wasn't totally true.'

'I could tell.'

'How?'

His eyes scanned hers across the table, as if he could see behind them. 'I'm good at reading people,' he replied after a few seconds. '*Some* people.'

'And you think you can read me?'

'I think I understand you,' he said, leaning forward so his face was only inches away. Stella thought he might lunge, but Fitz grinned and leant back. It felt like another tactic; he was playing with her, luring her in before spinning her out again like a yoyo. 'What's the job?'

'It's on Harley Street,' Stella replied slowly, 'for a woman called Marjorie.'

'Go on,' ordered Fitz, detecting her hesitation.

'She's… a private detective.'

'Intriguing,' he drawled. 'Tell me more.'

'There's not much else to say,' Stella replied, pulling her hair across one shoulder. 'I've only been there for a couple of days and she seems mad.'

'Mad?'

'Eccentric. She has a box of wigs in her office. And the office is chaos. Files and folders everywhere.'

'What sort of cases?'

'Affairs. She specialises in them. It's kind of crazy, the whole thing, working for someone who's genuinely nicknamed "the affair hunter", but I…' Stella paused, embarrassed to admit that she needed the money. 'I'm not sure how long I'll be there. It's just a temporary thing. And I'm not sure my family would approve so…'

'You care what they think?'

'I guess. I wish I didn't, but don't most people mind what their family thinks of them?'

He shrugged. 'Why be most people?'

'What d'you mean?'

'Most people lead very boring lives. They get up at seven a.m. and get home at seven p.m. They think that marriage will make them happy, and when that doesn't work they decide they need a bigger car or a bigger house or another marriage. They do the same thing every day, all of them, playing out the same lives as one another until the grave. Why would you want that?'

Stella puffed out her cheeks. 'Don't sugar-coat it.'

Fitz laughed. 'What I mean is, aim higher. You're better than that, I can tell.'

Stella narrowed her eyes, trying to work out how serious he was being. 'OK, what about yours?'

'My?'

'Your family. What's the story?'

He shrugged. 'No story. We're not very close. I grew up in France, and my father died a few years ago but my mother's still there, in Paris. That's where I have an apartment. That's home.'

'Paris! I've never been.'

It was Fitz's turn to look surprised. 'Don't tell me that ravishingly beautiful, cosmopolitan Stella Shakespeare has never been to Paris?'

Stella shook her head. She'd been on dozens of family holidays when she was a child, and she'd visited various other European cities, but she'd always longed to be taken to Paris by someone she was in love with. She knew it was corny – that the Eiffel Tower would be a let-down, French waiters disdainful and that the Seine would smell like sewage. But still, it was Paris, and Stella wanted to visit it when dizzy with love and behave as if she was in an Audrey Hepburn film.

'Then I'll take you.'

Stella's heart spun with pleasure. 'Deal,' she replied, hoping that she sounded cooler than she felt. 'So you're French?'

'British, but my parents moved when I was small. My father had business there.'

'In what?'

'Mining. Minerals. The mining and the minerals were in Africa; the business was based in Paris.'

'No other siblings?'

'No, *seulement moi.*'

'You're fluent?'

'*Oui, Mademoiselle Shakespeare, et je pense que tu es très charmante.*' He smiled at Stella's expression; 'I find you completely charming.'

'Oh,' she said, as a visible blush spread across her cheeks.

Stella wasn't used to being undone by a man so quickly. Despite her lack of self-confidence, she'd realised the effect she had on men relatively young; at teenage parties, she was always the first girl asked to dance. Later, when her friends cried over boys who didn't text them back, Stella's mobile constantly lit up with messages asking her out. But because it all came so easily to her, it didn't seem special. She wasn't interested in the men she could have by clicking her fingers. She wanted more: more electricity, more promise, more love.

If you discounted the flings, and the one-night romances that were briefly exciting and then very, very unexciting the following morning, she'd fallen in love three times, but each relationship had ended in disaster.

In 2012, when Stella was twenty-three, she was with a Scottish singer called Callum, who she met at a gig in Camden. This was back when The Maccabees and Cold War Kids were around, and Callum's band, Hazardous Material, had been successful despite its terrible name, and even reached number five with their single, 'Plenty More Girls In the Sea'. But Callum's love for drugs soon overtook his love both for music and Stella, and he broke up with her in the summer of 2013, screaming that she was too 'needy' after a gig, when he was high on cocaine and euphoria.

A couple of years later, there was a Greek banker called Nico, who took Stella away for weekends, not to Paris but to Greek islands like Mykonos and Hydra. He'd seemed sweet and kind, and talked of their future children, and he had a nice flat in Knightsbridge because his family were related to the Onassis shipping family, so Stella's parents were extremely keen on him. But after nearly two years, Nico broke up with her, claiming his parents wanted him to marry his Greek cousin.

Then Miles, who Stella met the year that various school-friends started announcing their engagements on Instagram (waving their hand at the camera as if to prove they could count to five), and who she *had* hoped would one day propose to her.

Now Fitz, who felt the most promising of them all.

None of the others had been right for her, she realised, with a peculiar embarrassment at the idea she could ever have believed herself in love with her exes. How could she have slept beside them for so long? Have used pet names for them?

But maybe she could spend the rest of her life with this man? How clever the heart was, she thought while studying his face, to be able to renew itself again and again. Or was it just forgetful?

Stella didn't care either way. She simply knew that Fitz felt like the man she'd been waiting to meet. It wasn't just his looks, although it was admittedly helpful that he had the kind of Hollywood face that could be plastered on the side of a bus. It was his character, too. She liked his teasing sense of humour, his frankness, his ambition and the idea that he didn't want to be like everybody else, even his hint of danger.

It was, of course, very dangerous to fall in love with the *idea* of someone before you got to know them, to build them up and idolise that person based on mere perception, but Stella was convinced that she and Fitz had somehow been brought together deliberately. The universe was working its magic. In the great game of love, everyone got their turn eventually.

Perhaps it was finally hers?

CHAPTER 16

BY THE TIME THEIR plates were cleared, Stella felt relaxed enough to ask a more personal question. 'You've never been married?'

Fitz squinted over the table as if weighing something up.

'You don't have to talk about it if you don't want to. I was just wondering because…' She trailed off, silenced by the intensity of his expression.

'Because?'

'I thought you might have been,' Stella replied with a quick shrug. 'You're older than me, and obviously very successful and not *bad*-looking and…' She went quiet again under his stare, feeling as if she'd stepped into forbidden territory, probing too far into that unknown space that exists between two people when they're on a first date, trying to figure the other out.

Fitz remained silent for a couple of seconds before replying. 'I was married.'

'What happened?'

'She left me. Not her fault. I wasn't around, always posted abroad. When I was home, in Paris, I wasn't much fun to live with.'

'Why?'

He leaned forward to lower his forearms to the table. 'It makes you restless, being in the navy. I can't sit still. Never could. So… take that as a warning, I guess.'

'For what?'

His mouth curled with a smile. 'For this.'

'There's a this?' Stella replied playfully.

'Perhaps,' Fitz replied, his expression amused again. 'But that's enough seriousness for one evening. Drink at the bar?'

'Sure.'

He stood, pulled the table back for her and told a hovering waiter that they were going upstairs.

'Of course, sir. Follow me, madam.'

As she turned away, Stella felt his hand briefly brush her back and flinched as if static had passed between them.

'Can I go to the bathroom?' she said, glancing over her shoulder as they reached the staircase.

'That way,' Fitz instructed, nodding towards a door behind the desk.

They were the kind of loos you found in expensive hotels, each cubicle with its own marble basin and a neat pyramid of rolled hand towels. Stella hitched up her dress and sat, considering her options. She'd told Jez she wasn't going to sleep with Fitz, but that determination had begun to crumble the second she saw him. She'd had a hypnotic evening with a man she liked very much, and she wasn't going to be judged by anyone. Especially someone with hair as silly as Jez's.

Also, Stella had held out with Miles and only slept with him after their fifth date. Or was it the sixth? She frowned. After two vodka and tonics and several glasses of wine, she was fuzzy on the dates. Whatever. She didn't care about Miles now and she could sleep with Fitz tonight if she felt like it. Stella nodded at herself in the mirror.

Except when she got back to the club's reception area, Fitz was standing beside the fireplace and frowning at his phone, annoyance contorting his face.

'Everything OK?'

He looked up and grimaced. 'I'm so sorry to do this but I have to go.'

'*Now?*' This sounded more high-pitched than Stella intended.

'Believe me, I wish it were otherwise. But there's a work situation I can't ignore.'

'On a Saturday?'

'Forgive me, I will make it up to you,' Fitz replied, pressing his palms together. 'But I have to deal with this.'

'What is it?'

He shook his head. 'Just a situation with one of my guys in Hong Kong. I'd stay here if I possibly could but you wouldn't have my undivided attention and…' he pocketed his phone, 'I very much want to give you that because it's the least you deserve.'

Stella felt the same tumbling sense of disappointment that she had when he'd left the pub. Did he like her? She'd been so certain this time that she was right about their connection. You could fake orgasms but you couldn't fake chemistry. It was *here*, she could swear on it, but now the only thing she could do was hide her frustration at him leaving again. 'That's a shame.'

'It is,' Fitz replied before glancing over her head. 'Julie, can you let my driver know he's taking Miss Shakespeare home?'

'Of course.' Julie picked up the desk phone. 'And will you be needing another car, Mr Montague?'

'No, that's all right, thank you.'

'I'm fine, I can get a cab,' protested Stella, although quite feebly because the idea of a free ride to Notting Hill was very small compensation for the evening ending early.

'And allow a stranger to drive you home? I don't think so,' Fitz replied, reaching for her hand, rubbing his thumb against the back of her fingers. Even that, the lightest brush of his skin against hers, made her shiver. But just as Stella dared to hope again that he might be about to kiss her, Julie was by their side.

'Here we go.' She held out Stella's leather jacket. 'And Mr Montague, your car will be here in two minutes.'

'Thank you, Julie,' Fitz said smoothly as he took the jacket from her and held it for Stella. 'See you soon.'

Stella stepped down to the pavement and, at the sound of the door closing, found herself spun around, encircled by Fitz's arms. 'I am very, very sorry about this,' he murmured.

She blinked, now so close to him that she could see each individual stubble hair lining his jaw. 'That's OK.'

Fitz dropped one hand to the small of Stella's back and pulled her closer before pushing his fingers through her hair. 'It's not OK for me.'

He moved his mouth towards hers, and Stella felt every hair on her body stand to attention. But the effect was all too brief because, just as she braced herself for the sensation of a kiss, Fitz tilted his face and whispered in her ear, 'That was an immensely enjoyable evening, Miss Shakespeare.' Then he stepped back and gestured to a large black Mercedes.

'This is Victor,' said Fitz, opening the passenger door. 'He'll get you back safely, won't you, Victor?'

Dazed by the speed of the past few moments, Stella could only blink at the front window where a man with a thick neck and driver's cap sat behind the wheel. 'Course I will. Where we going, madam?'

'Er, Notting Hill... thank you... Amberley Gardens.'

As she lowered herself into the car, Fitz caught her fingers. 'We'll do this again soon.'

Stella smiled at that thought as he closed the door. She liked him. She *really* liked him, and his disappearing acts only made her crave him more because she was so unused to being treated like this by a man. Any man.

'Number forty-four,' she told Victor before falling back against the leather seat.

The only good thing about going home alone was that she could be very smug when she saw Jez.

CHAPTER 17

THE NEXT MORNING, STELLA went to the kitchen to find Jez and Billie were already at the table having breakfast, sifting through the newspapers.

'Hi, babe,' said Billie.

Jez pointedly leant over in his chair and craned his neck as if he was trying to see behind Stella.

'He's not here,' she said, pushing up her dressing gown sleeves and reaching for the kettle. 'Told you I wouldn't sleep with him last night.'

Jez grunted and returned to *The Observer*.

'How you feeling?' Stella asked Billie, leaning on the kitchen counter. She could still sense a lurking guilt for leaving her on the sofa the previous evening.

'Fine. Exactly the same. But forget me. How was it? Is he a weirdo?'

Stella smiled and shook her head. 'No, not a weirdo. And it was amazing, Bill. He's just… I don't even know how to describe it. He's really, properly great. He asked me so many questions, and actually listened. You know how you can be talking to some guys, and they're sort of half-listening but really they're just trying to imagine what you look like naked?'

Jez grunted again as Billie nodded.

'He's not like that. He's different.'

'Everyone thinks that in the beginning,' said Jez, raising his eyes from the paper.

Stella had become so used to the sight of Jez lounging around the flat, taking up the whole sofa, carping on and on about the compost bin, leaving newspapers in every room, that the irritation had worn down. Instead of a sharp pain like a paper cut or treading on a drawing pin, having Jez around had become a dull ache, like a hangover or indigestion. But every now and then he said something so patronising that Stella fantasised about creating a *Home Alone* trap as revenge. Nothing fatal. Perhaps just electrocuting him via a door handle, or blowtorching his stupid, trendy haircut.

'I'm not sure that's true,' Stella replied coolly, 'because I remember you being as much of a dick six years ago as you are now.'

'Guys, come on, it's too early,' said Billie, swiping Jez's newspaper with the back of her fingers. 'So did you kiss him?'

'Seriously?' Jez groaned. 'While we're eating?'

'If you don't like it, you can go next door. Do you want any omelette, Stell? There's more.'

Stella moved to the table and reached for the milk. 'I'm good. And no, we didn't even do that! I thought he was about to kiss me, just as we were leaving, but then… nothing. He just said we'd do it again soon. But when is "soon"? Does he mean soon like next week or soon next month, because if it's next month I might go mad waiting to see him.'

'OK, OK, wait a minute,' Billie went on. 'If he's not a weirdo, who is he?'

Stella rested her chin on her fist. 'OK, so I found out his surname, it's Montague, and he has his own business, a security business, and he was in the army. Actually, no, not the army, the navy. The… SBS?'

'The SBS?' asked Jez, looking up.

'Mmm.'

'That's pretty serious. Is he ripped?'

Stella nodded.

Jez frowned. 'What's he do now?'

'He has his own private security business.'

'Ha! That means arms.'

'*What?*'

'Arms dealing. They call it private security, a nifty term that covers all sorts of skulduggery,' Jez said, glancing between Billie and Stella. 'But mostly it means arms dealing. All these guys who leave the army. Or the navy. They make contacts while serving, and then realise they can make more cash by going private. Dozens of them have sprung up. We did a big piece on it. I'll send you the link.' He paused and looked sideways at Stella. 'Did he serve abroad?'

'Er, yeah. Afghanistan, he said, and Kenya.'

Jez nodded. 'Exactly. Guarantee you it's arms, shipping them to contacts wherever he served.' He turned back to his paper and muttered into it. 'Classic you.'

'Excuse you, what do you mean, "classic me"?'

'Nothing,' Jez replied without taking his eyes off the page. 'Only that it's very typical for you to be dating a billionaire arms dealer. I'd die of shock if you ever brought back someone normal, like a plumber or an accountant.'

Stella had actually slept with an accountant called Thomas two months earlier but she didn't want to remind Jez about that particular encounter now.

'He's a billionaire?' Billie went on, eyes widening at Stella.

'No! At least, I don't think so. I mean he seems successful, but I don't think he's a *billionaire*. Or sells guns, Jeremy. He talked about helping rich people protect their kids, and protecting tankers.'

'Course. He'll do that too. He's hardly going to sit down for dinner and admit that he flogs MAG 58s to the Saudis. But it's a front for the arms side of the business. I'm telling you that's what he does.'

'OK, OK, you two,' said Billie, stepping in. 'I'm sure he isn't doing that. What was his surname again?'

'Montague. Fitz Montague.'

'I'll get the defence editor to look him up in the office,' said Jez.

'Don't do that,' warned Stella. 'And anyway he won't find much because I've already looked.'

'Because he's an arms dealer. You're shagging an arms dealer.'

'I'm not shagging him.'

'And he's not an arms dealer,' added Billie. 'When you seeing him again?'

'Not sure,' said Stella, deciding she wouldn't mention the fact that he'd had to leave very suddenly for work reasons last night.

'Have you heard from him?'

She shook her head. 'Do you think I should text to say thank you for dinner?' After months of leaving various bedrooms and hoping never to hear from their occupants, it was strange to feel like a lovesick teenager, pining for a message. For Stella, the diehard romantic who woke up every morning wondering whether she'd meet the man she was going to marry that day, she was almost as excited by Fitz as she was the game itself.

'Yeah, why not?'

Stella wasn't sure. Billie had never had to date much. She'd had one boyfriend at university, a nerdy engineering student called Gerry, and met Jez not long after they moved to London. 'I'll think about it.'

'What you doing today? Fancy a walk? We thought we'd go round the Serpentine.'

Stella squinted through the kitchen window. It was one of those perfect September mornings: a clear sky, with sunlight falling on leaves that were just starting to turn brown as if tea-stained from the edges. 'You feel up to it?'

Billie rolled her eyes. 'Not you too.'

'What d'you mean?'

She looked pointedly between Jez and Stella. 'Only that if you both keep talking to me like an invalid I might move out and leave you here together.'

'You wouldn't dare,' Stella said quickly as Jez shuddered.

'I would dare, but I'm fine. I'm going to be fine.'

'I know,' Stella replied lightly, 'I'm only fussing because I love you.'

'Me too!' Jez added as if the amount they loved Billie was a competition in which he and Stella were competing for first prize.

'Anyway, Stell, this walk, fancy it?'

'I wish I could but…' she paused to let out a dramatic groan, 'it's Hubie's birthday party.'

Hubie was Stella's three-year-old nephew, the youngest member of the Shakespeare family, and a golden-curled, two-foot tyrant. He was worshipped as if he was a very small medieval king, and he acted accordingly. If Hubie woke in the morning and nobody came to his room in under thirty seconds, he screamed. If he was told to sit at the table but there wasn't a boiled egg in his dinosaur egg cup already in front of him, he screamed. If he was asked to wear something he didn't want to, he screamed. If he was put in the bath without his dinosaur sponges, he screamed.

'Course,' said Billie. 'Is it the full tribe?'

'Yup. Speaking of which, did you chat to your parents?' Stella asked to shift the conversation off her own family.

'Yeah. Mum said they'd get on a train and come down but I told them there wasn't any point. I'll see Dr Bush tomorrow and then I'll know more.'

'We'll know more,' corrected Jez, putting a hand over Billie's. 'What time's the appointment? I'll meet you there.'

'No need. I've taken the day off,' said Jez, looking triumphantly at Stella. 'It's all sorted.'

'But thanks, babe,' Billie added with a sympathetic smile. 'I'll call as soon as we're done, promise.'

CHAPTER 18

ANDREW, STELLA'S OLDER BROTHER, lived in a five-bedroom house in Chelsea on a street lined with neat hedges and Range Rovers. Since he worked for the family business and was being groomed to take over, he could afford to live there. That afternoon, however, Andrew's Range Rover had been moved down the road to make way for a lorry. 'Furry Friends Petting Zoo,' large blue letters said on one side of the lorry, above a cartoon sheep.

And it was as Stella lifted the metal latch on Andrew's front gate that she heard a loud and unpleasant noise: the sound of twenty-three small children screaming.

Their nanny opened the door. Lina was a twenty-eight-year-old Romanian who'd worked there since Hubie was born (short for Hubert, which Andrew and Pandora had inexplicably called their first child). She had pale skin, bushy eyebrows, a thick accent and an extremely dry sense of humour. Pandora and Andrew were terrified by Lina's brusqueness but Hubie adored her, so she stayed.

'Hey, Lina,' Stella said, 'how's it going?'

'The noises are making me want to kill my own self,' Lina replied, standing aside in the hallway. 'You see them in the garden.'

Stella walked through the kitchen, past a mountain of presents on the table, and through the sliding doors outside. Andrew paid a former Buckingham Palace gardener to come twice a week, which meant it looked like a show garden you might see at the Chelsea Flower Show: flowerbeds bursting with colour, a lawn so clipped you could play tennis on it and, in the middle of the grass, a pond with a granite mermaid leaping from its centre, spitting a jet of water into the air.

Stella saw her mother, her sister-in-law Pandora, and Pandora's sister, Emily, all gathered around a table. Stella couldn't bear Emily because every time they met, she would tap her watch and ask when Stella was going to get married, as if getting married was some sort of afternoon game show.

Andrew was further down the garden with the children, who were screaming because the owner of the petting zoo had draped a python over his shoulders.

'Where's the evil overload?' Stella asked, circling the table.

She meant her father. Stella had a difficult relationship with both her parents, but especially with Ian Shakespeare. He was a tall man who resembled a Roman bust: white hair, long nose, sneering expression. But he wasn't just physically imposing. He was also loud, dominating the conversation and talking over others if he didn't like what they said, constantly interrupting. And he expected the same deference from his family that he expected from his employees, which is why staff in every Sunset Village across the country whispered that he was a bully and most of his family felt uneasy in his presence.

A self-made millionaire who'd decided early in life to shed his working-class roots, Ian valued money and status over emotion or anything revolting like hugging his own family. That he ran a business specialising in care was very ironic. Until recently, he'd only supported Stella financially to compensate for his lack of involvement in her life, and his pride and vanity had been rewarded by the idea that his daughter was dating the son of a lord. But when Miles ended his relationship with Stella, Ian had taken it as a personal snub and announced he was cutting his daughter off. Stella's mother hadn't protested because she'd been married to Ian for nearly forty years and had learned that doing what her husband said was the easiest way through life.

'Don't call your father that, please,' her mother murmured, tilting her face upwards to offer a powdered cheek. 'You look tired. Are you still smoking? Why don't I make you an appointment with Angelika?'

Angelika was a Greek facialist, one of a large team of people Valerie employed to hide every wrinkle, chipped talon and grey hair. There was also a yoga teacher to keep her supple and a plastic surgeon who had given Valerie her first two facelifts, and who she was going to see soon to discuss a further neck lift. Valerie Shakespeare was sixty-two in real life but around forty in her head.

'No thanks, Mum. I don't want gorilla semen anywhere near my face,' Stella replied, sitting and glancing towards the end of the garden where Jacob, the owner of the petting zoo, was putting the python back in his cage. Another member of his team was leading a small boy on a Shetland pony up and down the grass.

'Don't be vulgar,' Valerie replied with a tut. 'It's *bull* semen. It isn't from a gorilla. How would one even extract gorilla semen? They're very endangered these days.'

'How do they extract bull semen, Mum? Actually, don't answer that.'

'Why are we discussing animal semen at my son's birthday party?' interrupted Pandora. 'Stella, would you like a drink?' She waved at a bottle of Champagne in the middle of the table.

It was always the most expensive Champagne at Andrew and Pandora's house to accompany the expensive meals, normally ordered in from an expensive restaurant. Despite having a huge kitchen with a professional oven and a fridge that could comfortably store several human bodies, the only person who ever cooked anything was Lina. Pandora seemed to think that offering home-made food would be letting the side down, so it was always ordered in. She was a former fashion PR, very determined, who'd met Andrew in a Fulham wine bar and decided that, although he was slightly chubby and balding, a millionaire's son would do very nicely. Andrew, unused to being chased by women, was flattered. They were married within a year; Hubie arrived the year after that.

'Yes please,' Stella replied, reaching for the bottle. 'Whose idea was the zoo?'

'Help yourself. And Andrew's, obviously.'

'That llama's eating your roses,' Stella added.

'It's an alpaca.'

'What's the difference?'

Pandora sighed. 'I don't know but we paid for an alpaca.'

'Hubie's having a lovely time, which is the main thing,' added Valerie.

From the other side of the table, Emily exhaled loudly while frowning at her phone. 'It's so hard! Sugar Beach has a brilliant kid's club but the Rooneys go to Sandy Lane and apparently the breakfasts there are fabulous. Did you know they have their own waffle chef?' She looked up. 'Oh, hello, Stella. We're going to the Caribbean for Christmas but I can't decide which hotel to book. How are you? Are you engaged yet?'

'Not that I know of. But as always, Emily, when I have any news, you'll be the first to know.' Stella tipped back her glass and swallowed a large mouthful of Champagne.

'Tick tock, tick tock,' Emily replied with an irritating smile.

She just had to put up with an hour of this, Stella told herself. One hour, then she could go home.

'Hiya, sis.' Andrew appeared at the table. 'You look good.'

'Thanks.' Stella smiled up at her brother, her one ally in the family. Andrew was a human Labrador: affable, enthusiastic, generous and never bad-tempered. 'Great party. I like the llama.'

'Alpaca,' snapped Pandora.

'I think everyone's having a good time,' Andrew replied before squinting towards the kitchen. 'Any sign of Dad?'

'We'd know if he was here,' Stella muttered.

Their father was always late to family events, if he made it at all.

'We've got to cut the cake at three,' Pandora added nervously, looking at her watch.

'He'll be here,' Andrew said to reassure everyone, including himself, before taking a seat next to Stella and reaching for the Champagne. 'So, how's the love life, sis?'

'Very kindly, Emily's already enquired about this but I'm afraid there isn't much to report.' On the way to the party, Stella had decided not to mention Fitz. It would only invite questions and she felt a lurking fear that talking about him would jinx any further developments.

Emily rapped her pink nails on the table. 'It'll happen when you least expect it.'

People often said that, as if you might stumble across your great love in the Co-Op while picking up a box of tampons.

'It'll need to happen soon, darling, if you want one of those,' Valerie added, nodding towards the children.

Stella watched as a small boy squatted beside a rose bush and stuck his little fist into the mud. A few moments later, with a delighted expression, he pulled out a worm and lifted it towards his mouth.

'Lancelot, no!' shrieked Emily, standing up and running towards him. 'Lancelot, do not eat that!'

'You're not getting any younger, darling,' Valerie breezed on. 'What about egg freezing? I was reading a piece about it in the paper last week, and they said women really should consider it before they're thirty-five.'

'That's true,' added Pandora, her head moving up and down like a nodding dog. 'One of my friends did it but she was thirty-six, and she got hardly any eggs at all.'

'You see, Stella?' said Valerie. 'Why don't we give you egg freezing for your birthday this year?'

Fortunately, the discussion was halted by a loud cry of hello from the glass doors: Ian Shakespeare had arrived.

Andrew leapt to his feet. 'Dad! Hi! Sit, have a drink. Or would you prefer a beer? How was the meeting?'

'Fine, fine,' Ian replied, sauntering down the lawn and taking the chair at the head of the table like a politician arriving late at a summit. 'Hello, team. How are we all?'

'You remember my sister, Emily?' Pandora asked, as Emily returned to the table, clutching a screaming Lancelot in her arms.

'Course I do, Emily, hello, good to have you here,' Ian said as if it was his own house. 'Thanks, son,' he added as Andrew placed a bottle of beer down in front of him. 'Kids having a good time? What's that llama doing in the flowerbed?'

'They're having a terrific time,' replied Andrew, who had learned to be affable at all times as a child precisely because his father was the opposite.

'We might do the cake in a minute, Ian,' said Pandora, 'because the children are being collec—'

'Hold your horses. Let me get through this first,' Ian replied, reaching for the bottle and meeting Stella's eyes. 'Ah, my youngest. Here for a free lunch?'

'Hi, Dad,' Stella replied coolly. 'And no. I'm here to celebrate Hubie's birthday, much like everyone else in this family who managed to arrive on time.'

'Busy morning with work. Someone's got to pay for all this,' Ian replied, lifting his glass. He took a sip. 'Talking of which, what happened to that job at Spinks I got you? I never heard from Gideon.'

Stella offered a silent prayer of thanks that the story of the wastepaper bin hadn't reached him. 'You didn't get me a job. You got me an interview. And it didn't work out. But I happen to have found something else, so I don't need your help, thank you very much.'

Valerie looked as if Stella had just announced she was running for prime minister. 'Darling! You've got a *job*?'

'Yes, Mum. No need to sound so surpris—'

'What is this job?' interrupted Ian.

'I'm… assisting someone on Harley Street,' Stella replied carefully.

Valerie had a very detailed knowledge of Harley Street because she was often there for various medical appointments – for her Botox, for her thread veins, for her colonic irrigations. 'Where on Harley Street?'

'Er, towards the top.'

'Great news, sis,' Andrew chipped in, 'What's the business?'

Stella thought quickly. 'Selling wigs.' Telling them what Marjorie actually did would only invite ridicule.

'*Pigs?*' Ian asked, eyes bulging.

'Wigs.'

He grunted. 'Doesn't sound like much of a business to me.'

'What sort of wigs?' asked Valerie, with a confused expression.

'Just… wigs for medical patients, that sort of thing.'

'That's terrific, Stell. Proud of you,' went on Andrew, lifting his Champagne flute.

'Actually, we have a little announcement of our own, don't we?' said Pandora, who didn't like the attention being away from her for too long. She swept her eyes around the table to make sure everyone was listening and smiled, revealing her pearly veneers. 'I'm going to get fat again!'

'Another mini Shakespeare coming in the spring,' added Andrew.

Valerie let out a shriek of joy; Emily clapped her hands; Ian nodded approvingly.

'Good work, son.'

'Thanks, Dad. Appreciated.'

'Congrats, guys. How's Hubie taking the news?' asked Stella, glancing towards the end of the garden where Hubie was shaking his head at the owner of the petting zoo. Having pulled another child from the Shetland pony, he was refusing to get off and give anyone else a turn.

'We're pretty sure he'll try and kill it the second we get home from hospital.'

'Andrew!' snapped Pandora. 'He'll be fine. I'm reading a parenting book by an American expert who says it's very important to talk to children as if they're grown-ups. So every day, I tell Hubie that he's going to have a little brother or sister, and I really do think he understands.'

'He's three years old, sweetheart. He barely understands when he wets himself.'

'Andrew, please,' interrupted Valerie, holding a hand in the air. 'Hubie will cope. This is very wonderful news. One more grandchild at least.'

Stella sighed.

'Don't roll your eyes at me, darling. I'm just saying you should think about it. Ian… Ian? I was just saying before you arrived, don't you think we should give Stella a round of egg freezing for her next birthday present?'

Ian looked suspicious. 'What does it cost?'

'A few thousand,' Valerie replied airily. 'But well worth it, Ian darling, if we want to have any more grandchildren in the future.'

'Excuse me,' said Pandora, stroking her stomach.

'Sorry, Pandora, I don't mean you. But I do worry that Stella's leaving it too late and unless she finds someone soon her ovaries will have shut up shop. Closed for good. Gone out of business and retired.'

'Thanks, Mum,' mumbled Stella, feeling a familiar wave of

insecurity. Somehow, no matter what else was going on in the world – it could have been war, plague or a surprising and tragic celebrity death – their family always ended up discussing Stella as if she was an embarrassing problem they needed to solve.

Valerie carried on. 'Have you tried those, you know, what do they call them?'

Stella raised her eyebrows. 'Vibrators?'

'Must you be so crude at Hubie's birthday? No, you know, those things where people meet online?'

'Dating apps,' interjected Emily. 'My friend Fenella just got married to a man she met on Tinder. He's very bald and Fenella said she nearly swiped past him, but it turns out he's a banker for Goldman Sachs. Honestly, the diamond on her engagement ring is the size of a satsuma.'

'There you go,' cried Valerie, clapping her hands together. 'He sounds *lovely*.'

'Andrew, what about Patrick?' Pandora said, tapping her fingers on the table.

Andrew frowned.

'Hasn't his wife just left him?' Pandora glanced around the rest of the table as she explained. 'Patrick's one of Andrew's golfing buddies. I don't know the details but apparently there was trouble in the bedroom department and I think his wife has gone off with someone else, so he is now single, if that's any good?' She looked brightly towards Stella.

'Well, he's definitely worth a tr—'

'No!' Stella interrupted before Valerie could continue. 'No. Just no. Stop it. Can everyone stop it? Why do we have to have this conversation every time?'

'Darling, we're only trying to hel—'

'I don't need any help! I *am* seeing someone, as it happens, so can we try and get through just one family occasion where you don't all talk about me like a yoghurt with a sell-by date?'

'Darling! Why didn't you tell us before? Is it a man?'

'Yes, it's a man but that's all I'm going to say.' Stella already regretted blurting this fact out, but she had to do something to end their tiresome efforts at matchmaking.

'Well, well, well. A job and a new boyfriend,' Ian remarked from the head of the table with a smirk. 'Wonders will never cease.'

'He's not my boyfriend,' Stella said, shooting her father a withering look, 'but he's very charming and clever and successful. So I don't need dating help from anyone else. Pandora, please pass my apologies on to Patrick.'

'I hope he's good enough, sis,' added Andrew. 'When are we going to mee—'

They were interrupted by the sound of a blood-curdling howl from the bottom of the garden. The owner of the petting zoo had taken matters into his own hands by plucking Hubie off the Shetland pony, whereupon Stella's nephew had flung himself to the lawn and was now bellowing into it, kicking his little legs up and down, having a violent tantrum.

'Oh, my poor darling Hubie,' said Pandora, already halfway out of her seat to rescue him. 'We really must cut his cake.'

CHAPTER 19

STELLA DECIDED TO WALK home from her brother's house. It wasn't so far from Chelsea to Notting Hill and, as always after spending time with her family, she needed to decompress.

Did other people leave family gatherings feeling this exhausted? Billie didn't seem to. Whenever she returned from Yorkshire, she glowed. She'd burst through the flat door, carrying eggs from the chickens and potatoes from her parents' vegetable patch, telling Stella that they missed her and that she'd have to come north next time. The only eggs that Ian and Valerie Shakespeare seemed to be interested in were frozen ones.

As Stella walked along a street of pastel-coloured houses, she checked her phone and saw a message from Fitz.

Once again, I'm incredibly sorry for interrupting our evening. How's your week looking? I'd like to see you almost immediately.

Instantly, all thoughts about her family evaporated and her mood soared. He'd messaged! She'd see him this week! 'Immediately'. Stella's stomach rolled at the commanding tone.

She mulled over her reply for the rest of her walk and hurried up the stairs when she arrived home, both anxious to check in with

Billie and keen to sit on the sofa with her phone, composing the perfect text to Fitz. When should she suggest? Offering Tuesday felt too keen but Thursday felt too far away. She could suggest they me—

Her train of thought was interrupted by Harold's door swinging open. 'Stella, good evening.'

'Hiya, Harold,' she replied before remembering that she'd promised to send him dating app recommendations. 'I'm so sorry I haven't got back to you about the, er, question you asked me. I've been researching it, and I've got some suggestions, but I just wanted to, um, make sure they were the right ones.'

'No need,' Harold replied proudly, 'I've found an app and I've downloaded it already, but what I did wonder is whether you could help me with my profile. Do you have a moment?'

What Stella most wanted to do was get upstairs but Harold looked so eager that she couldn't refuse. 'OK… sure.'

'Excellent,' he said, spinning around and hurrying back towards his kitchen.

She followed. The air smelled of eggs.

'Kedgeree,' Harold explained before she could ask. 'Thought I'd have a crack at it for dinner. Now, here we go. I've got as far as downloading the app, and I've got a profile name and I've answered my questions, but I'm having a spot of bother with the pictures.'

Stella stood beside him and peered at his phone screen. 'What's it called?'

'Hmm?'

'The app. Which one is it?'

'Silver Singles. I read some reviews of Tinder, on the app store, but I wasn't sure it was for me. What's catfishing?'

'Never mind. Let's have a look at your profile.'

Harold handed his phone over.

'I've called myself Basil1951,' he went on, 'because I thought that might be better, more anonymous than using my real name. And Basil doesn't mind, do you?'

Basil thumped his tail in the dog bed.

'All right,' Stella mused, 'and these are your answers?'

'Yes.' Harold had found it hard to come up with replies initially, but now he was very pleased with his answers.

Stella bit her lip as she read them. Harold had listed his hobbies as 'walking the dog, amateur cooking and hospital volunteering'; his favourite TV show was *Eggheads* and his favourite ice-cream flavour was rum and raisin.

'I've come a cropper with the pictures. They need three photos but I can't seem to get them to work.'

'What do you mean?'

'I can't get them to fit, in the little boxes. Look.' He took his phone back and tapped at it so a close-up photograph of his nose appeared.

'Give it here. All you have to do is this.' Stella slid her fingers together on the screen so the picture shrank, revealing a smaller Harold, with his arm around a smiling woman. 'Oh. I'm not sure you should put up a picture with another woman. Unless that's your sister. But even then I'd avoid it. Have you got any by yourself? Or what about with Basil?'

'That's Ellen in that one,' Harold replied, nodding at the screen.

'We were on holiday in Lisbon. Just a year or so before the cancer got her.'

Stella winced. 'I'm so sorry… and, also, I'm so sorry I've never said anything before now. About Ellen, I mean. That I'm so sorry.'

'That's quite all right. Nobody knows what to say with these things and we had a good run, she and I. Now, another picture. Good point. Let's have a look.'

Harold took his phone back, tapped and produced another one of himself, alone, grinning underneath a woolly hat.

'Much better, but you still need two more.'

'Don't you worry. Now that I've got the hang of this thing I can manage.'

'Sure? Only I said I'd be back to hang with Billie.'

'I'll be right as rain. Thank you, that's ever so kind.' Harold pocketed his phone. 'How is she? I haven't chatted to her for a while.'

'Billie?' Stella paused, unsure what to say. She didn't want to lie to Harold, but equally it wasn't her news to share. 'She's, er, well, she's, er, she's all right. Sort of. She's got to go into hospital next week for a follow-up. Nothing too major. Just, um, to talk about some treatment.'

Concern flooded Harold's face. 'Goodness. To the Chelsea and Westminster?'

Stella swallowed, feeling uncomfortable that she'd already said too much. 'Yep. I'm—'

They were interrupted by the sound of Harold's door buzzer and he looked briefly puzzled before clapping a hand to his forehead. 'The cricket! I'm so sorry, Stella, I quite forgot, I've got a friend coming over to watch the Test.'

'I'll get out of your way,' Stella said, grateful for the excuse to leave. 'But you'll definitely manage with the photos?'

'Absolutely.' Harold nodded as they walked back down his hall corridor and he pressed the button on his intercom. 'Come on up.'

He opened the door for Stella. 'I do hope Billie's all right.'

'She will be,' Stella said with deliberate confidence as he opened his front door. But as she turned to step through it, she was met by a familiar sight – and a powerful sense of déjà-vu.

'Hello,' Sam said with a laugh. 'Are you stalking me?'

Stella couldn't believe it. What was he *doing* here? Why was he behind every door in London? And how dare he ask her what she was doing in her own house? Well, Harold's house, but close enough. It felt as if a higher power was punishing her for having a one-night stand. A good one-night stand, if she was honest. Much better than some of the others. But still, he was a one-night stand and the point was they were supposed to be exactly that: one night. They weren't called one-night-and-behind-every-door-afterwards stands, were they? Stella shook her head and told herself to stop thinking about one-night stands on Harold's doorstep.

'I live here. I mean, not *here* here. Upstairs. And I might ask you the same question.'

'Got it.' Sam laughed again, and ran a hand through his hair. 'Weird. I came over to watch the cricket with Harold.'

Stella knew nothing about cricket and cared even less. 'How do you even know each other?'

'From hospital. Harold's one of our volunteers.'

'Do you two know each other, then?' Harold asked.

'No,' said Stella.

'Yes,' said Sam.

'Sort of,' Stella admitted.

'We met the other day,' Sam explained.

'What a coincidence!' Harold said, grinning.

Classic, Stella thought: she'd now slept with so many men across London that she'd managed to find one who was friends with her neighbour.

'Stella's been helping me out with a very important matter,' Harold went on.

Oh god, please no, thought Stella. The one thing more awkward than bumping into this man again was the idea that they would all now discuss Harold's dating profile.

Sam frowned. 'What's that then?'

'My dating app profile. I found one, it's called Silver Singles. And she's been helping me with choosing the right pictures. She's been ever so helpful.'

Stella leant an arm on the wall to steady herself.

'Sam showed me his dating profile last week,' Harold said, turning back to her, 'on a different app, and I have to say if I was a young woman I'd be jumpi—'

'Thanks, Harold,' Sam said quickly. 'Not sure we need a group discussion about my profile. Hey, are you all right?'

Stella pushed herself upright from the wall. 'Yes. No. I mean, yes. It's just I had my nephew's birthday party today, and it's time for me to go home.' The events of the afternoon and another awkward run-in with Sam had left her feeling like she'd just run a marathon. In clogs. Without any water.

'Sure,' Sam replied, 'but good to see you. Also, is your friend OK?'

'What fr— Oh. Billie,' she said, recalling the first time she'd bumped into Sam. 'Er, yep, think so. Or at least she will be.'

'Good.'

'All right, I'm off,' she said, desperate to get away. 'Enjoy the cricket.'

'Yes, come along, young man,' Harold instructed Sam. 'Play starts in ten minutes and I've made us kedgeree for dinner.'

'I can smell it. Nice to see you again, Stella.'

CHAPTER 20

STELLA GROPED THE BEDROOM carpet for her phone to silence the alarm the next morning, then squinted at the screen through one eye. Having replied to Fitz and suggested Wednesday evening, she was hoping to see a message from him. But the only text on her screen was from her mother.

Darling, here's Angelika's number. Please ring her and make an appointment. My treat. Once jowls start forming they really are impossible to get rid of X

Bigger things to worry about, Stella reminded herself on the Tube into work, thinking of Billie and her appointment.

When she arrived, she found the door to the office ajar, wedged by a black trainer.

Seconds later, Marjorie charged from her office like a horse from its stable and Stella jumped with shock. Her hair! The grey curls were gone, replaced by a sleek blonde mane, thick strands falling either side of her shoulders.

'Morning. I've got to be out for the next couple of hours

but I have a task I'd like you to get on with.' She narrowed her eyes at Stella. 'What's the matter?'

'Nothing. Nothing. Just your hair. It's different. It's nice!'

'Don't be ridiculous, this isn't *my* hair. It's one of my wigs. Nasty, synthetic stuff but needs must. Now listen, I need you to do some digging for me.'

'Sure,' Stella replied.

'Get a pen and a notepad.'

Stella moved around her desk and pulled open various drawers bulging with old notepads, broken pens, stubby pencils and an inexplicable number of ketchup sachets, until she found an unstained notebook and pen that worked.

'Ready? I need you to ring up a hotel in Cornwall called The Trebetherwick and get the receipts for a customer called Christopher Winman.'

'*Win*man,' said Stella.

'Exactly.'

'OK, so I ring them and ask for his receipts to be emailed over?'

'No, no, no,' Marjorie replied, shaking her head so the blunt ends of her wig swayed around her shoulders. 'You can't just ring them and demand his receipts. You could be anyone.'

'I am anyone,' replied Stella, confused.

'Quite, so you need to come up with a cover story.'

'A *cover* story?'

'To get them to send you the receipts. Say you're his secretary.'

'What if Mr Winman doesn't have a secretary?'

'They won't know that! Little bit of artistic licence. Weren't you ever in a play at school?'

Stella had been in plenty of plays, usually the lead since the drama teachers always wanted someone pretty to play the main part. 'Yes. I was Alice in *Alice in Wonderland*, and Cinderella, and Sandy in *Grease*, and Bel—'

'There you go,' interrupted Marjorie. 'You'll be fine. Deploy those acting skills for me. He was staying there last week, from...' she paused looked at her phone, 'Thursday to Saturday.'

'Not with his wife, I'm guessing?'

'No indeed, not with his wife,' thundered Marjorie. 'His wife says he was away on a business trip in Plymouth but I've discovered he was staying at The Trebetherwick instead, which is a very expensive hotel in Cornwall. So unless our Mr Winman is a fisherman and he was on fishing business, I fail to see what he could possibly have been doing down there.'

'Other than an affair?'

'Other than an affair. And I know he's not a fisherman because-his wife says he works in insurance. But we need the receipts to prove it. Or at least to prove that he was there with someone else. So, an Oscar-winning performance, please. I'll be back in a bit.'

Half an hour later, Stella had made herself a cup of tea, googled the number of the hotel and was sitting at her desk, rehearsing what she would say in her head. It was one simple little job. Please could she not fluff this up? She wasn't an *absolute* moron.

Stella dialled the number.

'Good morning, The Trebetherwick Hotel. Gwen speaking, how may I help you?'

'Er, hello.' She cleared her throat. 'Gwen, good morning. I wonder if you can help me?'

'Sure,' went on Gwen. She had a young, tinkly voice that gave Stella more confidence. She didn't sound like a battleaxe.

'Last week, my boss… er… Mr Winman, stayed with you at the hotel, and I'm after a copy of his receipt. He's lost it, you see… and we need it for accounting purposes.'

'Not a problem,' Gwen replied, and Stella heard the tap of a keyboard. 'Do you have the dates he was with us?'

'I do. It was last Thursday to Saturday, so the eighth to the tenth.'

'And what did you say his name was?'

'Mr Winman, Christopher Winman.'

'Eighth to the tenth… eighth to the tenth,' Gwen mumbled while Stella held her breath. 'Oh yes, here we go. The Lobster Pot Suite, two nights. I remember. Did Mrs Winman get her hair tongs back safely?'

'Hair tongs?'

'I put them in the post but it can be a bit hit or miss from down here.'

Stella thought quickly. 'Right, course, the hair tongs. And I'm not sure. Can I triple-check which address you sent them to?'

'Mmm, let me see. Yes, here we go. It was 29a Cintra Park, London SE19 2LQ.'

Stella scribbled the address down on the notepad. 'That's extremely kind, thank you. I'll check with Mrs Winman that she got them.'

'Of course. Now, where d'you want these receipts sending?'

Stella gave her the email address, one of several nondescript addresses Marjorie had set up, which filtered back to the old computer on her desk.

'Great, that's all done then,' Gwen said happily.

'Thanks so much for your help.'

Stella hung up quickly and looked at her inbox, where a new email had just arrived.

According to the attached receipt, in two nights Mr Winman had spent money like a lottery winner: three bottles of Champagne, two dinners in the hotel restaurant at nearly £400 a pop, in-room massages, full English breakfasts, several miscellaneous bar charges and a car park fee plus the suite for two nights came to a grand total of £2,236.

Stella whistled at her desk. Poor Mrs Winman. This was pretty damning evidence. But she also felt a sense of satisfaction; Marjorie had tasked her with this job and she'd managed it. She looked at the address Gwen had given her and began googling Christopher Winman to see whether she could tell he was a cheater from his face.

She was still on his company website, inspecting the team photos, trying to deduce whether any of the women who worked there looked like they used hair tongs, when Marjorie returned an hour later.

'Any developments?' she asked, dropping her wig on Stella's desk.

'Yes, I've got the receipts,' Stella replied proudly.

'I knew you could do it.'

'Oh, and there's something else. He definitely *was* down there with someone, a woman, because they ordered all sorts like Champagne and massages. And when I spoke to the receptionist, she mentioned that he'd been there with a Mrs Winman and asked if she'd got her hair tongs back.'

'Hair tongs?' asked Marjorie, scratching at her scalp with her fingers.

'She must have left her tongs there, whoever it was, his mistress. So I asked where they sent the hair tongs to, and she gave me an address. It's a London address, in Crystal Palace, look.' Stella held up the notepad.

Marjorie pulled her fingers away from her head and clapped her hands. 'Excellent work,' she said as Stella watched several flakes of dandruff catch the morning sunshine and float towards the floorboards. 'Could you add those notes and the address to the case file?'

'Course,' she replied, feeling an unusual glow of satisfaction at such praise. 'How was your morning?'

Another flap of Marjorie's hand. 'Waste of time. Any calls or messages?'

'Nope,' said Stella before she remembered her own phone. She'd been so absorbed with Mr Winman she hadn't even looked at it.

She scrabbled in her bag and her heart leapt in her chest: he'd messaged.

I can't do Wednesday evening, alas. But how about a drink tonight?

Stella frowned at her screen. She couldn't do tonight really because she'd promised Billie she'd come straight home to discuss her appointment.

I can't, sorry. Tomorrow evening?

'Good news?' Marjorie asked, still hovering over her desk as a smile spread across Stella's face.

'Um, yes. It's, well, never mind…'

'A love interest?' Marjorie's eyes narrowed. Twenty-three years in the business had given her a sense for these things.

'Maybe. It's, well, it's early days.'

Her boss grunted.

'Have you ever been married?' Stella asked, emboldened by Marjorie's question about her own personal life.

'Yes. It was like a five-year illness: extremely uncomfortable and it gave me chronic indigestion.'

'Oh,' said Stella as her phone flashed with another message from Fitz.

What about lunch today? Can I steal you away for that?

'And then he took off with our neighbour,' went on Marjorie.

'Blimey,' Stella replied as her fingers crept back towards her mobile.

'Which is when I decided to leave the police force and set up this place, become an affair hunter.'

'Right,' said Stella, starting to wish she hadn't asked the question. Marjorie's nostrils were flaring.

Not sure I can take lunch. Thursday evening?

'Because I'll be damned if I'm going to let people get away with their monstrous behaviour.'

You must be allowed to take lunch? Tell that wig-wearing boss of yours that lunch is a human right.

Stella quickly reached for her phone and turned it face-down on her desk.

'So keep your wits about you,' went on Marjorie. 'Don't trust any of them, is my motto.'

'But surely you can trust *some* of them?' On a day like today, when Stella's heart was singing with the attention from Fitz, this didn't sound very romantic to her.

Marjorie picked up her wig and grunted again. 'Most men are like Kleenex, in my opinion: soft, wet and entirely disposable. Now, where's that tea?'

'On it,' Stella said, pushing her chair back. 'And, er, Marjorie, is there any chance I can go out for lunch today?'

'Lunch?' Marjorie asked from her office doorway, as if she'd never heard of it, which Stella knew to be untrue since her office bin was still overflowing with pizza boxes and empty doughnut bags.

'Mmm, I won't be long. Just for a quick sandwich with… a friend.'

'Oh, *lunch*, yes, course. Why not, given your hair tong triumph. Well done, young Stella. You're a natural.'

CHAPTER 21

FITZ HAD ASKED HER to meet him in a French brasserie just off Harley Street. Stella walked there, self-consciously tugging her fingers through her hair, annoyed that she hadn't known she was going to see him when she got dressed in one of Billie's wraparound work dresses that morning. She felt like a middle-aged librarian.

Pushing open the restaurant door, she was struck by the smell of butter and garlic, and smiled at a hovering waiter with a napkin over his forearm. 'Hi, I'm having lunch with Fi—' But then Stella paused, because she'd spotted Fitz at a table, shirtsleeves rolled up, tapping at his phone. 'I'm having lunch with him.'

'Miss Shakespeare?'

'Yes,' she replied, surprised.

'Follow me please, mademoiselle.'

Stella followed him to the table. 'Hi,' she said shyly when she was standing over it.

Fitz looked up and his face broke into a wide smile. 'Hello,' he replied, standing up to greet her. She leant in and brushed her cheek against his, arching her back at the sensation of Fitz's hand on her shoulder blade.

'How did he know who I was?' she asked when she pulled herself back and they sat.

'The waiter? Very simple. I told him to keep an eye out for a woman who was going to make every other man in here jealous of me.'

'You're ridiculous,' Stella said, laughing.

'I am, occasionally. But in this case it's true. Look…' Fitz gestured around the restaurant where other diners sat picking through plates of rotisserie chicken and green salad, looking at their companions in a bored way, as if they were discussing the stock market or the weather. 'I'm sorry for being demanding about today but I had to see you again.'

Stella pressed her lips together, trying not to give away the intensity of her pleasure. 'You *had* to?'

He was almost absurdly handsome in a pale blue shirt and a blue silk tie (which she knew was expensive because her father also had very strong opinions about ties), and sitting opposite him so suddenly, hearing him say he needed to see her, felt almost too good to be true.

'I did. But I know you're on a time limit so let's order…' Fitz waved at the waiter who hurried over.

'*D'accord, mon frère*, we have to order with tragic speed since my friend here needs to get back to work, so Miss Shakespeare, what would you like?'

'Er…' She glanced down at the menu, entirely disinterested in food since any hunger had been replaced by her stomach fluttering. Somehow, Fitz's low, husky voice was even more seductive in French. 'Niçoise salad, please.'

Fitz ordered a steak and leant over the table.

'I'm delighted that I've persuaded you out during business hours. Tell me, what developments in the world of private detectives?'

She smiled. 'I'll have you know it's been a busy morning. I had to ring a hotel and get hold of some receipts.'

'Very cloak and dagger. Whose receipts?'

'The husband of a client, who told her he was staying in one hotel but it turns out he was staying in another, and had ordered Champagne and massages and so on. So Marjorie thinks he was actually there with his mistress,' Stella said before quickly raising her fingers, covering her lips with them.

Fitz frowned. 'Problem?'

'I should probably be more discreet. Client confidentiality.'

'I can assure you I'm very discreet.'

She met his grin. 'I'm sure. Anyway, how about you?'

'Me?'

'Work issues solved? Whatever the problem was on Saturday?'

'All fine,' Fitz replied smoothly.

Stella waited for him to elaborate but he didn't.

'What?' he asked when she didn't reply.

She shrugged. 'I'm just intrigued.'

'By me?'

'By your job.' She leant forward and lowered her voice. 'Are you an arms dealer?'

Fitz dropped his head back and laughed. 'Who told you that?'

Stella wondered how much to divulge. That morning, not long after Marjorie had returned to the office, Jez sent her the *Guardian* article he'd mentioned, in a patronising one-line email: *Pretty sure this is what your boyfriend's up to.*

'Guns for hire', the article was headlined, and it described how the private security business had boomed in the past two decades because of foreign wars.

> *Nuclear war threats, earthquakes, immigration crises, fresh rumblings from Eastern Europe. They all trigger the same effect in the corporate world: a phone call to a private security firm to plot a plan.*
>
> *The multibillion-dollar industry involves providing soldiers for hire to companies and governments around the world to protect important people and assets from criminals and terrorists.*

Stella read it twice before replying to Jez, pointing out that he didn't know Fitz was an arms dealer and that, according to the article, running a private security company wasn't illegal.

She looked quizzically across the table at Fitz. 'My flatmate's boyfriend works for *The Guardian*, and I happened to mention you and your work in private security. And he said private security means arms dealing.'

'Your flatmate's boyfriend sounds intense,' Fitz replied, lifting his glass to take a sip of San Pellegrino.

'He is.'

'Does he live with you too?'

'Uh-uh, you're not getting out of it that easily. Is he right? Is it dodgy?'

'Would it matter?'

Stella wrinkled her nose. In truth she wasn't sure. She thought that it probably should matter. Billie would say it mattered. But the truth was she was already hooked on him, and his air of mystery only intrigued her more. 'I don't know.'

'You're safe. It's not. Horus is a wholly legitimate security business, based here but which just so happens to sends me to strange parts of the globe. And arms dealing is a dangerous game I don't play.'

'But you do play some games?'

Fitz brushed his fingers against the back of hers and she felt flames inside her. 'Some games, yes.'

Their food arrived and Stella pushed flakes of tuna around her plate as they talked, aware that she needed to leave soon.

'How come you sound so English if you grew up in France?'

'I went to an international school in the Alps so there were all sorts of us kicking about – the children of diplomats, from military families, of those like my father who lived in France for business.'

'But you must have a British passport, if you were in the army?'

Fitz nodded. 'Navy, and yes. I'm British, born here. I just choose to spend a lot of my time elsewhere, and France is where my mother still lives and where I'm happiest. You'll see when I take you.'

He grinned but Stella hadn't finished with her questions. 'OK, so if home is Paris and you spend your life on a plane, how much time are you in London?'

She hoped she sounded casual, but she wanted to work out how often Fitz was here and therefore how often she might be able to see him. If this was even a *thing.* She glanced around her at the other diners. For all they knew, she and Fitz could simply be another pair of work contacts having a catch-up between meetings. Except that whenever Fitz touched her – her hand, her knee under the table – Stella jumped as if his fingers were static. And nobody she'd ever worked with had done that, although to be fair she did have very little office experience.

'A bit. I've got to go away tonight but I'll be back in a couple of days. Any other questions, Miss Shakespeare?'

'Yes, one. Where are you going?'

'The Gulf. Abu Dhabi. But I'm never away for very long.' One side of his mouth lifted in a smile. 'Life would be very boring if we stayed in one place the whole time, would it not?'

Fitz's sense of adventure was one of the aspects Stella liked about him. He was more travelled, and therefore seemed more sophisticated and worldly, than anyone she'd ever met. But it also meant that he was in control of when they saw one another, and Stella wasn't used to being so out of control with a man.

She sighed and glanced at his wrist. If felt like five seconds, but nearly an hour had gone. 'I have to get back.'

'To the dragon?'

'I'm starting to like her, I think. It's... more interesting than I thought it might be.'

'But you're not going to do this job for ever?' Fitz asked with a brief frown.

'No, course not. But it's fine for now, while I work out what I want to do.'

'Do you know what that is?'

'What I want to do for ever?'

Fitz nodded.

'Not sure.'

'Don't waste it,' he said with an odd look, almost tender.

She frowned and dared to reach across the table for his hand. 'You OK?'

Fitz nodded and his face cleared. 'Yes. This has improved my day immeasurably,' he told her before leaning across the table and brushing his lips against hers.

'Mine too.'

He paid and they left, Fitz following Stella outside to where his car was waiting.

'I'll message,' he promised before briefly kissing her again.

It didn't even feel like she walked back to the office; it felt like she floated.

CHAPTER 22

AFTER WORK, STELLA AND Billie discussed that morning's hospital appointment, sitting together on their balcony. It was their favourite spot, especially during summer evenings when the pair dragged out cushions and rugs from the sofa and sat with a bottle, talking about everything and nothing while the sun fell behind the houses across the street.

'So Dr Bush gave me two options,' said Billie as she leant back against the wall.

Stella reached for the wine. 'Tell me.'

'The first option is chemoradiation,' Billie said tentatively because the word felt strange. 'Which means radiotherapy every week, every day actually, and one session of chemotherapy a week on top.'

'What's the second option?'

'The second option is to do a round of egg freezing before the treatment, otherwise the chemo might mean that I can't…' Billie trailed off, unable to finish the sentence.

Stella reached across and put one hand over hers.

'It was the only time I cried, when he asked how important my fertility was,' Billie continued.

'It is important to you, right?' Stella asked gently.

Billie nodded as a single tear slid down her cheek. Plenty of women didn't have children these days, she knew, and Jez occasionally muttered that it was 'immoral' for people to have children because of the planet. But, for a moment, being asked this question felt like Billie's entire purpose was being challenged.

She and Stella had talked about having children as they grew up in the way that young women do, thinking vaguely ahead to a time in the future when they assumed that life would look very different. But what had been a simple, automatic assumption at school that they'd definitely have children had become more complicated as they got older. They still wanted children, but when? Or was there never a 'right' moment and you just had to do it?

'So the second option, right?' Stella asked, squeezing Billie's fingers.

Billie wiped her cheek with her other hand. 'I guess.'

'Mum was talking to me about egg freezing on Sunday, weirdly. Threatening to give it to me for my birthday present.'

'Seriously?'

'She's worrying about grandchildren. Andrew and Pandora are…' Stella was about to tell Billie that they were having another baby but it dawned on her that this might be insensitive.

'Are?'

'They're all for it. Freezing, I mean. Lots of discussion about my love life yesterday. You know, the usual… Anyway, sorry, so you freeze your eggs, then radiotherapy.' Stella paused and exhaled. 'I'm sorry, Bill, I wish it was me.'

Billie nudged her shoulder. 'Don't be mad.'

Stella watched a commuter on a bike pedal along the street beneath them. 'How long does freezing eggs take?' she asked once the cyclist had turned at the end of the road.

'Two or three weeks.'

'Delaying the radiation doesn't matter?

Billie shook her head. 'It's fine, apparently. Dr Bush said a few weeks won't necessarily make that much difference.'

'Did he say…' Stella paused, unsure how to ask the next question.

'Mmmm?'

'Did he say, like… you know how he said it was early, when he called you. Did he say *how* early?' She'd googled this again at work that afternoon, while Marjorie was shut in her office on the phone, and read strange phrases like 'invasive carcinoma', 'highly aggressive' and 'survival rates' until she felt almost dizzy.

'Yep. I'm 1B, apparently.'

Stella swallowed. 'What's that?' She almost added that it sounded like a primary school class and then, again, decided against it.

'Early. And it's small, he says. Like, five millimetres.'

Stella tried to imagine five millimetres. About the length of a grain of rice? 'OK, that's… good. So you freeze and then you start treatment. And how long does that take?'

'If I start freezing next week – Dr Bush said they could – then apparently chemoradiation takes another four weeks.'

'So around six weeks altogether? OK. And how are you feeling? I know it's a stupid question but I'm going to keep asking.'

Billie shrugged. 'I guess it's like the best scenario possible. It's early, Dr Bush is on it.'

'I still can't get over his name.'

'I kno—'

She was interrupted by a squawk as Stella's phone, lying beside her on the tiles, flashed with a message.

'What? Who is it?'

'It's Fitz!'

Thank you for your company at lunch today, Miss Shakespeare. If you happen to be free on Thursday evening, could I reserve you again? I'm not sure I want to go away before seeing you.

'What's it say?'

Stella read the message aloud.

'Why does he call you Miss Shakespeare? And why does he talk like that? And hang on, sorry, you had lunch with him?'

'It was last-minute. He suggested dinner but obviously I said I couldn't because I wanted to see you. So I said what about tomorrow but he couldn't do that, and then he asked about lunch.'

'Where did you go?'

'This French place near Harley Street. And what d'you mean about him talking like that?'

Billie put on a hoity-toity voice: '"Could I reserve you again?" What a weird way of putting it, like you're a restaurant table.'

'It's just a thing he does. He's sort of… very English. Although technically he grew up in France.'

'OK, so what happened today?'

'Nothing happened but…' Stella turned her head and grinned bashfully at Billie. 'I really like him. He's just… different.'

'You said that before. But different how?'

Stella twisted her mouth into a knot and thought. 'He makes me feel like life could be bigger.'

'What d'you mean?'

'Like, when I was going out with Miles, it was fun and we went to parties and the polo and the racing and it was this constant parade of socialising, right?'

Billie nodded. She hadn't been a fan of Miles. Although she and Stella agreed on many things, they had the opposite taste in men. Stella had always gone for men who were obviously attractive – good-looking, ambitious sorts who often tried to mask their insecurities with a swagger and an arrogance that she found almost irresistible. Billie had grown up with parents who were devoted and good to one another, and had always known that qualities like honesty, kindness and trust were probably better, in the long run, than a man who couldn't walk past a single shop window without looking at his reflection.

'But if I think about it now, it was all very… narrow,' Stella went on. 'Such a narrow world. It was the same people, and the same places. It was so *small* somehow. But Fitz doesn't care about all that, about who you're friends with or where you're seen. He's got this… confidence.'

'Stell…'

She turned her head and frowned, detecting Billie's serious voice. 'What?'

'You're going to be careful, right?'

'Yes! I'm a big girl. Don't worry. Anyway, we're supposed to be talking about you.' Stella put her phone down, ignoring the urge to reply to him. 'Did you speak to your parents today?'

'Mmm, I might go up and see them this weekend. Try and do

something normal. Go home, sleep, see the dogs…' Billie trailed off as Stella's phone lit up with another message.

Stella tried to resist it.

'Go on, read it. Honestly, it's fine.'

'Sorry, sorry, sorry.' Stella made a guilty face and reached for the phone. Except it wasn't Fitz. It was an unknown number.

Hey Stella, good to see you again (again). I hope this isn't interfering, but Harold gave me your number because he mentioned your friend was coming back to the hospital, so I just wanted to check in and say if she needs any advice then please let me know. I'm in most days so just shout if I can help. Atb, Sam

'What the hell?'

'What is it?' Billie asked, craning her neck to look at the screen.

'It's that doctor. Sam.'

'Huh? I don't get it. What does he mean, "again again"? How does he know about me? And how does he know Harold?'

Stella sighed. 'From hospital. Harold volunteers there. That's why we saw him the other day. And it turns out he's mates with Sam, which is why I bumped into him in the hallway last night. He'd come over to watch the cricket. I wouldn't mind opening a door he didn't miraculously appear behind one day. And I didn't actually *tell* Harold about your diagnosis. He just asked after you, and I said you were having some treatment but that it would all be fine, because it will, but obviously he's let this slip to Sam. Sorry.'

Billie stretched her legs towards the railings. 'I don't mind. Did you say what it was?'

Stella shook her head. 'Course not.'

'I don't think I'd mind that, either,' Billie said, a note of weariness to her voice. 'It'd save me from having to repeat it over and over.'

'Have you told Geoff?'

'Yeah, thought it was better to get it out of the way. But it's strange saying the word cancer over and over again when it applies to you. When I called him, it was like I had to make a joke about it.' She waggled jazz hands in the air. 'Surprise, Geoff, I've got cancer! It was like I had to manage his feelings as well as mine.'

Stella wasn't sure what to reply to this. It was unusual, feeling awkward during a conversation with Billie. They talked about every aspect of their lives, all the time, but there didn't seem to be big enough words, or comforting enough words, to talk about her diagnosis. 'You don't have to manage anyone's feelings,' she offered eventually, wishing that she could think of something more helpful.

Billie sighed and stared at the rooftops. 'I can't talk about it any more. What are you going to reply to Sam?'

'Sam?' Stella asked blankly.

Billie nodded at her phone. 'The doctor?'

'Oh, *him*. Nothing. It's none of his business.'

'Why not? I don't mind if you do reply. It's a nice message. And what if you bump into him again with Harold?'

'Then we'll have to consider moving flats. But I do need to reply to Fitz. What do I say?'

'What was his message again?'

Stella reread his WhatsApp aloud.

'Are you free on Thursday?'

'Course I am!'

'Fine. Reply about Thursday but you also have to send something back to Sam.'

'What? Why?'

'Because he seems like a considerate human being who talks properly?'

Stella rolled her eyes. 'You didn't see his pleather headboard.'

'Oh, a pleather headboard, I'm so sorry, I didn't realise that was now a criminal offence.'

'It *should* be. OK, what if I go back to Fitz saying "can't wait" with three dots and a winky face? Or no winky face? Christ!' Stella threw her hands into the air. 'Romeo and Juliet didn't have this problem.'

'Romeo and Juliet died because a letter went astray, so I'm not sure they had communication much easier. But that's enough help from me, I'm going to make dinner.' Billie stood and brushed down her legs.

'No no, I'm making it. Hang on, I'm coming.' Stella decided against the emoji – Fitz didn't seem the emoji type – and sent the message before reaching for the railings and pulling herself up.

Just three days until she saw him again.

CHAPTER 23

LATER THAT WEEK, STELLA found herself in a dimly lit bar. It was in the basement of Rakes, a small hotel in Kensington that had the same number of stars as The Ritz and The Dorchester but prided itself on being less flashy. It was where American celebrities often stayed when they were visiting London with a new lover and wanted to go unnoticed by photographers.

If there were any celebrities in that evening, Stella wouldn't have been able to see them. The lamps were turned low and waiters moved between tables like shadows. Stella sat waiting for Fitz, trying to work out how to arrange her legs. She tucked her right leg underneath her on the sofa, then retracted it and crossed them, before changing her mind again and sliding her shin back underneath her thigh. She was wearing a backless jumpsuit, which meant she was also braless, and although Stella's breasts were as pert as a Titian painting, she worried that her nipples would point south if she slumped.

'Sorry I'm late,' Fitz said, appearing over her. He leant down to graze his cheek against hers. 'You look ravishing.'

'Thank you,' she replied, adrenalin flooding her body at the sight of him.

In truth, getting ready for this evening had been a nightmare. She'd had to cart her jumpsuit, her make-up bag and her heels into the office, and wait for Marjorie to leave before changing in the small, cramped loo, which had a tiny mirror and bad lighting. Lucky it was dark in the bar since she'd screwed up her eyeliner and had to make it right with her finger. She'd wanted to look like an avenger: black jumpsuit, feline eyes, towering black heels. As she'd left the office, kohl smeared around her face, she'd felt more like a chimney sweep.

Fitz shrugged off his suit jacket and tossed it on the sofa arm before sitting. 'The usual?'

'Yep, please,' she said, feeling a warm glow of pleasure at the idea that they had a usual.

'Two vodka tonics. Doubles,' Fitz said to a nearby waiter before swivelling to face her. 'How has your week developed? What happened with the case of the missing hair tongs?'

'You have a good memory,' Stella replied, pleased that he'd remembered the details of their conversation.

'I do, but tell me. How does the story end?'

She leant back against the sofa so her bare shoulder grazed his forearm. 'Well, my boss—'

'The dragon?'

'She's not really,' Stella said. 'She went to the address, to the flat where the hotel had sent the hair tongs, and she sat outside it for hours. And eventually the client's husband arrived, so she took photos of him, which was all the evidence that was needed.'

'Caught red-handed.'

Stella nodded. 'Pretty much.'

Fitz leant back as the waiter reappeared and lowered their

drinks. 'I'm impressed, Miss Shakespeare. Looks like I'll have to watch my back.'

Stella smiled, suddenly bashful. 'It wasn't that hard but… yeah, it was… satisfying.'

It had been, too. After her stake-out, Marjorie wrote up her case report, which included the receipts and the photographs outside the Crystal Palace flat, and Mrs Winman had been so grateful that a bottle of Champagne had arrived in the office that morning.

Clients often sent presents, Marjorie explained, because they were so grateful for evidence that they weren't going mad, that their paranoia about their partner had been justified. Then she'd given the bottle of Champagne to Stella and congratulated her on solving her first job. So although Stella still wasn't sure that she'd stay permanently in the Harley Street office, she'd decided she could probably manage a few more weeks.

Her breathing quickened as Fitz's fingers trailed up her spine to the nape of her neck. His hand might as well have been between her legs. 'Anyway, I don't really want to discuss my boss right now.'

He grinned. 'In that case, what shall we discuss?'

'How was your trip?'

'Trip?' Fitz frowned.

'Yeah, to… Abu Dhabi, right?'

His face cleared. 'Oh that. Fine, fine. Hot but fine.'

Stella smiled as his fingers continued circling the back of her neck. 'You seem to like dark bars.'

'I like *this* bar because it's convenient.'

'For what?'

'For the office. I stay upstairs when I'm here.'

Stella tilted her head. 'If you have an office here, why not have a place?'

'In London?'

She nodded.

'Too permanent. I have my place in Paris. I don't need two homes. And like I said, this place is convenient.'

'Does it ever get too much?'

'Too much?'

'Tiring? Being away all the time?'

'Sometimes it does. I'm not much looking forward to going to the States next week.'

'Why?'

Fitz picked up his glass and drained the last finger of vodka. 'Because it'll be humid as hell over there and I'll miss you.'

'Oh,' Stella replied, taken aback by his honesty.

'One of my faults,' Fitz went on, 'or one of my many faults, I should say, is that I get bored quickly. Too quickly. So that's why I do what I do, always travelling, rarely in the same place for very long. But perhaps there's a point when I might tire of that.'

'Tire of travelling?'

'Maybe. Or maybe it takes meeting someone new to make you realise what matters.' He held her gaze and for a few moments Stella felt as if their surroundings had blurred, that it was only them in the bar.

'Another one?' he asked, breaking the spell.

'Mmm, sure.'

'Or…' Fitz began as his fingers dropped to the jumpsuit's knot at the top of Stella's back. He'd heard her breath change. 'We could have one upstairs?'

'Upstairs?'

'In my room. But would you like to eat first? Are you hungry?'

One side of her mouth lifted in a suggestive grin. 'For food? Not so much.'

Fitz matched Stella's smile. 'Excellent. Shall we?'

CHAPTER 24

A LIFT FROM THE bar carried them to the sixth floor, where they stepped into a corridor with carpet so thick it felt like sponge and Fitz guided her towards his suite.

It was the most seductive hotel room Stella had ever seen. The walls were dark red, with velvet curtains already closed and, she noticed, a bottle of Champagne in an ice bucket beside a desk. Paintings of orchids hung around them and a vase exploding with white lilies sat on a lacquered Chinese chest. But the bed was the most impressive sight of all: a four-poster with red silk cascading from its roof, separated into four bunches and gathered around each bedpost, tied with rope. It looked theatrical, like a stage.

Stella thought of the more depressing bedrooms she'd slept in during the past six months and smiled as she stepped out of her heels.

'Something amusing?' Fitz asked, reaching for the bottle.

'Do you always stay in this room?'

'Always at this hotel. Not always in this room. But I thought tonight…'

Stella laughed. 'You assumed I was a sure thing?'

'I didn't assume anything. I hoped. I've found myself dwelling on this moment quite a bit in the past few days.'

'This moment?'

Fitz put down the bottle. Then he started removing his cufflinks, and Stella's heart thudded.

Having pushed up each sleeve, slowly and deliberately, he stepped towards her, pinning Stella against a bedpost. 'This moment,' he said, cradling her head with one hand and lowering his lips to hers.

She pressed her mouth back and, as his tongue found hers, she moaned. He tasted of vodka and smelled of soap. 'This moment I've thought about a lot,' he said, moving his mouth to her neck.

'Me too,' she whispered.

He dropped his hand to the curve of her back and pulled her towards him. For Stella, the sensation was, all at once, too much and yet not enough, but just as she curled her fingers under the collar of his shirt, he took a step back.

A frown flickered across her face, making Fitz laugh.

'What?' she demanded crossly.

He picked up his glass and took a sip. 'You look furious.'

'Well…' Stella stopped, her chest rising to catch her breath. Just when she thought she knew what was going on, he'd confuse her.

'Undo that,' he ordered with a nod, his expression more serious.

'This?' She raised her hand to the knot behind her neck.

He nodded again, so she tugged at a loose end of black material and let the top slide to her waist. It left her standing half naked, nipples as hard as marbles, breath held in her chest again.

'Now sit.'

Stella lowered herself to the edge of the bed. It was a rare moment where she felt as bewitching as she looked, her insecurities melting as Fitz's eyes roamed over her body, like he was a painter trying to decide where to start.

Eventually, he moved closer and pushed her thighs apart. Dropping to his knees between them, he looked up. 'I've thought about this moment too.'

She lowered her face to meet his, but he dodged it and cupped one of her breasts, teasing her, rolling a thumb over her nipple, before taking it in his mouth and flicking his tongue back and forth.

Stella groaned and arched her hips forward, making Fitz briefly look up before his mouth moved to her other nipple, sucking, flicking, making her thrust her pelvis forward while he lightly traced his thumb up and down her crotch.

But then he stopped and stood.

'What *now*?'

'Take it all off.'

'But you're not ev—'

'Off.'

Stella stood and reached for her zip. Undoing it, the jumpsuit slithered to the floor and she stepped free, now covered only by a pair of very small lace pants.

'Your body,' he said quietly, shaking his head, so Stella made a small smile.

He moved forwards faster this time, like a prowling creature, so suddenly Stella was pushed to her back, Fitz above her. Then he started kissing down her body, shifting himself lower and lower, grazing his stubble against her collar bone, the hollow between her breasts, and her stomach. It was slow, so agonisingly slow. She glanced up to see Fitz's arms tense under his shirt either side of her torso, but gasped and dropped her head again when his mouth shifted to her inner thigh.

It was enthralling in the very real sense of the word. Stella was in thrall, bewitched by him. She'd never slept with anyone so in control, so precise – and so agonizingly slow. Every part of her felt as if it was melting.

He concentrated on one thigh, then the other, pressing his lips against her delicate skin, higher and higher until Stella felt his mouth reach the lace.

And then… nothing.

Stella looked up to see Fitz on his feet, pulling his shirt off. His chest was dark, sculpted by clear lines of muscle, and her eyes slid to his belly button where a faint line of hair trailed south.

'But do you know the moment I thought most about?' he asked, standing at the foot of the bed. His voice was now almost a growl.

She rolled her head from side to side as he undid his belt and pulled it free from his trousers. He dropped those, along with his briefs, and finally Stella could see all of him, silhouetted at the foot of the bed.

'This one.'

He leant over her, his fingers grasping each hip, and tugged her knickers down. Then he dropped between her knees so his tongue was on her, pressing inside her, and then out, running over Stella's clitoris, up and down, as she ground herself into the mattress. And as the waves of heat inside her grew, it felt as if he was opening her up with his tongue, peeling back another layer of her.

Nails digging into her palms, Stella made a low, moaning noise as she came, his tongue pushing into her again and again until she couldn't bear it any more, and pressed her fingers to his face. He smiled over her stomach and shifted higher, so she could reach down and feel his erection with her hand. Fitz groaned at that, satisfyingly, so Stella licked her thumb and ran it over the tip, sliding it around and around until he moved back on top of her. 'Do I need to think abou—'

She shook her head, anticipating his question, not wanting to delay the moment any longer.

'My turn. Do you know what moment I've thought about?' she whispered.

'What?'

'This one,' she said as she felt him push between her legs and slid into her with a groan, as if he was unburdening himself.

She ran her nails down his back as he rocked backwards and forwards, tensing herself around him to make him groan again and again. It was the first time Stella felt like she had the upper hand.

He came with another moan, holding a fistful of her hair, his face hot against her neck.

It was only then, staring at the canopy ceiling over his shoulder, that Stella wondered whether she should have held out longer. But she already liked him. More than liked him. She'd known that long before coming to his room, or even arriving at the bar downstairs that evening. If she was really honest, she'd known that in the pub, the first time they met. This had somehow felt inevitable, so why should she hold out against something that felt so very, very good?

CHAPTER 25

WHEN SHE WOKE THE next morning, it was still dark because of the thick, velvet curtains, but Stella could see a thin sliver of daylight behind them.

She rolled over and smiled sleepily at the sight: Fitz, lying on his stomach, one arm bent above his head.

Stella traced her fingers lightly over his shoulder blades and down his back. It was a good back – wide, smooth, hard. For once, she felt no urge to leap out of bed and find her pants before scurrying away. This was much better than waking up in the bedroom of a man and discovering that he still lived with his mother.

Fitz stirred and turned to face her. 'Good morning, and may I just say what an absolute pleasure it is to find you here.'

She smiled shyly. 'You may.'

'Did you sleep well?'

'I slept like a baby. Although isn't that a funny expression, given that babies scream all night?'

He smiled and dropped his hand to her hip, sliding it to the small of her back. 'I like you very much, Miss Shakespeare. You make me laugh.'

'I like you too,' she said before kissing his chest. 'I'm glad you found me.'

Fitz frowned. 'Found you?'

'Mmm. Tracked me down, I mean.'

'I had to. How could I possibly go on in life, knowing that you were out there and I might have missed my chance?'

Stella laughed. 'Such melodrama.' She craned her head to look up at his face. 'Had you been to that pub before?'

'Never.'

Pleased, she settled back down beside him; if Fitz had never been to the Ladbroke then theirs was a chance meeting, which confirmed her belief that the universe was behind this. The love gods were, finally, looking favourably on her. 'Lucky,' she murmured.

'Lucky?'

'Mmm. Just that I could have missed you.'

Fitz brushed his lips against her hair. 'I imagine we might have found one another at some point.'

A wide smile broke across Stella's face and she looked up again, elated that he appeared to think the same. But then she caught sight of his watch. 'Hey, what's the time?'

'Time for me to order us breakfast.' Fitz said, glancing at his wrist. 'Just after nine.'

Just after nine, Stella thought to herself, that wasn't so bad. She could lie here for a bit longer, have a leisurely breakfast, perhaps some sort of flaky pastry that she could nibble seductively in a dressing gown like Julia Roberts in *Pretty Woman*, then a shower, she'd change and...

'Oh my god, Marjorie!' she said, eyes widening.

'It's Fitz, but I'm delighted that you're thinking of your boss while in bed with me.'

'No no, I've got to go! I'm late,' Stella protested, reluctantly kicking her legs free from the duvet.

Fitz eyed her through the gloom as she sat and swung her hair over one shoulder. 'You're very beautiful this morning but much too dutiful. Are you sure I can't use any of my dastardly powers to make you stay?'

She glanced at him. Maybe she could. Another twenty minutes? What was the harm, if she was already late?

No, she told herself, standing up. That's what the old Stella would do. This new Stella had to get to work. 'I'm sorry. I have to go. I wish I could stay but…' She stopped. She'd been about to ask when she could see him again but was hit by a bolt of insecurity. Was that too presumptuous? He'd mentioned Paris last night, which suggested he wanted to see her again, but what if that was just pillow talk?

'We'll see one another soon,' Fitz said as if reading her thoughts. 'I've got this trip to America next week but not for long.'

'Oh, OK, cool,' Stella replied, smiling with relief before leaning across the bed and kissing him.

The marble shower was so big that she could stretch out her arms without touching the sides. She used all the shampoo and conditioner so the floor was covered with suds, then mummified herself in three white towels, as soft as cotton wool, before getting dressed.

Optimistically anticipating this scenario yesterday, she'd stashed clean clothes in her bag. While Fitz remained in bed watching her, she tied the jumpsuit back over a bra, then pulled a shirt on over that and knotted it around her waist.

'When are you back from your trip?' she asked as she rough-dried her hair.

'Not sure yet. Maybe Sunday. But I'll let you know. I'll call you.'

'OK,' she said as she slipped her feet into her heels and walked to his side of the bed. 'But now I'm really late, got to go.'

'If your boss gives you hell, I'll speak to her,' Fitz teased.

'What will you say?'

He grinned. 'That her new employee put in a very late, very impressive shift last night and if she needs to be punished, I'll handle it.'

Stella pressed her mouth to his and felt her body respond with longing. 'Something to think about until next time,' she replied, pulling herself away and picking up her bag.

On the walk down Harley Street, she felt like shouting 'Good morning!' at every pigeon she saw. The wait to see him again would be torture, but it would be worth it. And he'd even promised to call. In the dating timeline, everyone knew that calling was a step up from texting; speaking to someone was more intimate than spending hours trying to construct the perfect message. That meant this new romance was a *thing*.

CHAPTER 26

'SORRY,' STELLA SAID, HURRYING past Marjorie's office door before backtracking a few steps. 'I'll put the kettle on.'

Her boss looked up from her desk and squinted suspiciously. 'Good morning, young Stella. Late night?'

'Er, no, no. Just… had to take my flatmate to a doctor's appointment,' Stella fibbed. She would almost certainly go to hell for using Billie as an excuse but she was probably going to hell anyway, given her behaviour in the past few months.

'Oh I am sorry,' Marjorie replied, admonished. 'I do hope nothing serious?'

'Um, no, no, hopefully not. Tea?' Stella made a mental note to tell Marjorie about Billie at a better moment.

'Tea would be smashing, thank you.'

Stella frowned from the doorway. 'You off to play golf?'

It was a reasonable question since Marjorie was wearing her visor, a Pringle jersey and on her desk, beside the keyboard, lay a pair of white gloves.

'Don't be absurd. Do I look like the sort of person who plays golf?'

'Er…'

'Disgusting sport. No, I have it on good authority that a new client's husband is off to play eighteen holes at Sunningdale today. So I'm off for a spot of recording from the clubhouse.'

'Recording?'

'With my magic pen.' Marjorie lifted what appeared to be a black marker pen and waggled it between her fingers. 'Captures video and audio up to a hundred metres. Not bad, eh?'

'In case he says anything interesting?'

'Exactly,' Marjorie replied before a heavy sigh. 'He probably won't say anything interesting. They almost never do. It's a lot of waiting in fancy dress, this job. But you never know. You'll be happy here? Enough to be getting on with?'

'Yep, plenty more invoices to go.' Stella had decided to start chasing invoices two days earlier and was still working her way through them because nobody seemed to have paid their bill for the past three months. She'd casually mentioned the scale of the backlog to Marjorie while carrying through a cup of tea one afternoon, and suggested that if the business had more money coming in, they could pay for a new fridge, or a new computer for Stella since the old one took about half an hour to get going in the morning ('a bit like me,' Marjorie had muttered). Perhaps even a new doorbell.

But her boss had grunted and said paperwork wasn't one of her strong points, so now Stella was determined to chase past clients for the cash and come up with a more efficient system. She was thinking some sort of spreadsheet, not that she knew very much about spreadsheets.

'Good, good, carry on,' Marjorie instructed. 'They want us to catch their cheating husbands but some of them don't like paying for it.'

Stella turned to go before pausing. 'Is it more usually cheating husbands than cheating wives?'

Underneath her visor, Marjorie's mouth puckered. 'Not always, but women are more likely to use a detective.'

'Why?'

'Often their husband's hiding money, so they need me to find it. Or because they're nervous of their husband's behaviour in some way. Usually it's fear that compels a woman to call me.'

'And a man?'

'Anger, or at least a sense of his property, in this case a wife, being stolen by another man.'

Stella exhaled. 'Depressing.'

'You could look at it like that.'

'Or?'

'You could see it as helping people.'

'*Helping?*'

'Indeed,' Marjorie said firmly. 'I've worked on plenty of cases where I've uncovered evidence of an affair but the couple end up sticking together. It forces them to have a conversation for the first time in ten, twenty, thirty years, and they decide their other half slipped up but isn't that bad after all. It improves their relationship, in fact.'

'I guess,' Stella said uncertainly before frowning at her boss. 'Is there ever a way of telling?'

'Telling?'

'I mean, can you tell if someone's going to have an affair?'

'Of course. You merely have to look at them and ask one very simple question.'

'What is it?' asked Stella, feeling as if she was on the precipice of learning one of life's most useful lessons.

'Does that person have a penis?' said Marjorie before wheezing with laughter.

Stella tutted. 'That can't be true. Who are all the men having affairs with? It can't all be with other men. And you said that married women cheat too.'

'They do, they do. Men are statistically more likely to cheat than women but obviously that's not always the case. Why do you ask?'

'It just seems sad, that's all, that so many relationships end up like this.' Right now, flying high on the euphoria of the previous evening – the touch of Fitz's hands, lying in bed with him afterwards and her face on his chest playing on a constant loop in her head – Stella found it almost impossible to imagine how a relationship could disintegrate so far.

Marjorie gazed sympathetically at her young employee. 'If I've learned anything, the trick is to find someone kind.'

'Kind?'

She nodded. 'Looks and charm and being hung like a prize-winning donkey are all very well, but kindness will outlast all of them.'

'Kindness, got it,' Stella said, turning quickly to go and make tea before Marjorie mentioned donkey genitalia again.

CHAPTER 27

HAROLD RACED TO HIS front door as soon as he heard Stella's footsteps.

'Stella, hello, you got a second?'

'Everything all right?'

Harold was moving from foot to foot as if he needed the loo. 'Yes, fine. It's only that I took delivery of rather a large parcel earlier for you and Basil is very interested in it. Very interested indeed.'

Stella frowned, unable to remember ordering anything.

'This way,' said Harold, ushering her into his flat. 'It took a big delivery man to get it this far, to be honest. It weighs a bit but I knew you were both out so I said I'd take it.'

'Yeah, Billie's gone north,' Stella explained, 'home for the weekend.'

Harold's face turned serious. 'I happened to run into her earlier and she told me about her diagnosis.'

'Oh. Right.'

'That poor girl.'

'I know, but it's going to be fine,' Stella said quickly. 'She's in good hands and it's early, so...'

'She is in very good hands. And I told her, and I'll say the same to you, if there's anything I can do, any grocery shopping or help with any trips to the hospital, then you just let me know. You can just pop down or you've got my number and I always have my phone on loud so I hear it.' He patted his pockets and frowned. 'Where have I put it? It might be in the kitchen, or the bathroom—'

'Thank you, Harold,' Stella interrupted. 'That's so kind. We'll let you know.'

'When does her treatment start?'

'Next week.'

'That quickly? Heavens.'

It was actually the egg freezing process that started next week. From Monday, Billie had to inject herself twice a day with hormones, followed by an operation to take out her eggs around two weeks later. After that, four weeks of chemoradiation.

'I'll do it, I can inject you,' Stella had offered, wanting to do something useful, but Billie laughed because they both knew how squeamish Stella was. When they were fifteen and doing a first-aid course, Stella had fainted at the sight of the plastic cadaver that the instructor used to teach them about resuscitation.

'As long as you both know I'm here if you need,' Harold reiterated. 'When Ellen was ill, it was mostly just me and it can get very tiring, all those trips to the hospital and whatnot. You're not the one going through treatment, of course, but, still, it can be difficult. So if you ever need someone to listen, you just let me know.'

She smiled gratefully. 'I will, thank you. Now where's this parcel?'

'It's this one,' Harold said, nudging a large box beside the sofa with his foot.

Stella crouched and wrapped her arms around it. 'Christ, it is heavy. Can I borrow a knife?' She looked up at him. 'Do you mind if I open it here?'

'Not at all,' said Harold, reaching for a kitchen drawer as Basil whined at the box. 'Come on, Basil, away from it, please.'

Having run a knife across the packing tape, Stella found a heavy crate inside, with yellow pieces of straw sticking out between its panels. Plus a bottle of vodka wrapped in a melting iced sleeve, and several lemons. Using the end of the knife, she levered the wooden lid off to find two dozen oysters nestled in the straw.

'Oysters!' cried Harold. 'Well I never. Who's sent you those?'

Stella reached for the box and found a note sellotaped under the address label.

Until I can take you to France, France will have to come to you.
À la prochaine, F

'They're from a, er, friend,' she explained before glancing back to the crate and frowning. She couldn't eat twenty-four oysters by herself. 'What you doing tonight, Harold?'

'Basil and I are going to watch that new police drama on telly, the one with the bearded fella in it.'

Stella grinned up at him. 'Fancy an oyster?'

It took them half an hour to get the oysters open after they watched a YouTube tutorial about the best method. Harold subsequently found a short, stubby knife in the back of his utensil drawer and, holding each oyster in a tea towel, waggled it until one half came free.

Stella, standing beside him, took each oyster, laid it on a plate and squeezed lemon over the top while listening to Harold tell a story about the ward the previous day, where he'd read a Roald Dahl book to an asthmatic seven-year-old, and played chess with Johnny, who didn't understand the rules but insisted on playing anyway.

'Got any ice?' she asked when the final oyster had been shucked.

Harold pointed to the freezer. 'Have a gander in there.'

'Next question: where are your glasses?'

'In here.' He reached for a cupboard above the sink.

Stella dropped a couple of cubes into two tumblers and poured a thick slug of vodka over the top.

'Steady on.'

'Friday night, Harold. Admit, this is much better than a police drama. Didn't you get enough of that when you were working?' She passed him a tumbler and raised hers to meet it. 'Cheers.'

'Cheers,' said Harold, screwing his eyes shut as he swallowed. 'Goodness, it's been a while since I've done that. Shall we eat them next door?'

He carried the oyster plate through to a table in the corner of the living room. 'And what about some Smokey Robinson?'

'Perfect,' said Stella, following with the tumblers and vodka bottle tucked under her arm, and as the honeyed, husky voice of the Motown king floated from Harold's ancient CD player, she thought back to afternoons in her grandfather's car, driving back from school; the companionable ease of it.

They sat and Harold eyed the plate nervously. They were fleshy oysters, fat ones, shiny with brine and lemon. 'They look...'

Stella didn't feel she could exactly say what each oyster looked like. 'I know, but you have to get over that, Harold. They'll be delicious.'

She reached for one, then retracted her hand and pulled her phone from her pocket. 'Actually, can I just...' She took several identical photos of the plate and tossed her mobile on the sofa. She'd send a picture to Fitz later.

'All righty. Here goes,' said Harold, tipping the shell back into his mouth.

'Bottoms up,' said Stella, copying him.

'Not bad,' he said, smacking his lips. 'I might need another one to check.'

'You might need another ten. Can't let them go to waste.'

'Who is this mysterious F, then? Mind if I give one to Basil?'

'Course not.' Stella picked up her vodka. 'And he's, er, just someone I'm seeing.'

'I see. He's keen, then.'

'Why d'you say that?'

Harold waved at the plate. 'He's sent you all this. I sent Ellen a bunch of sunflowers once, but your friend...?'

'Fitz.'

'Your friend Fitz has outdone that, I'd say. Pity though.'

'What is?' Stella tipped back another shell.

'I was hoping that you and Sam might... you know.'

After Sam had come over last week, Harold had decided to play Cupid and pushed Stella's telephone number on him, urging him to get in touch about Billie. Why not? Stella was helping him with his romantic aspirations; he could do the same for her.

Stella shook her head. 'Sorry, Harold. He seems great, but not my type.'

Harold sighed. He didn't know what young people wanted these days. Sam was a handsome doctor who liked cricket. If he was a young woman, well, that was quite hard to imagine, but he would have thought Sam was an ideal catch.

'How about you?' Stella asked. 'How's the love life?'

He leant back in his chair and frowned at the ceiling.

'Confusing, to be quite honest,' he admitted eventually. He dropped his chin and frowned at Stella. 'I liked one profile.'

'On whatsitcalled?'

'Silver Singles, yes.'

'OK, and…'

'She's called Meredith, and she says she likes gardening and Japanese food, and I believe she has four grandchildren.'

'Lovely. So you've been messaging?'

Harold looked as if Stella had just asked whether they'd slept together. 'Messaging? No. Good heavens, no. Well, that's not entirely true. I did send her one message, saying hello and asking if she was having a nice day.'

'And?'

'And nothing yet. I'm waiting for her to reply.'

'What? How long ago was that?'

'Five days.'

'Harold! You can't just like one person and wait for five days for them to reply. Move on,' Stella told him airily, loosening another oyster with her fork. 'Like someone else.'

Another spasm of horror crossed Harold's face. 'I can't do that.'

'Why not?

'I can't like another woman. What would Meredith think?'

'It's not like that. Firstly, she won't know, and secondly, it's a numbers game.'

'A *numbers* game?'

'Online dating. You have to like lots of people, lots of women, I mean, to find the one. If we only liked one person at a time we'd all die of old ag— It'd take decades.'

'I'm not sure it's for me,' Harold replied, shaking his head. 'I got very lucky with my Ellen and I'm not sure I can be that lucky again. Or want to be, truthfully.'

'Did you know straight away when you met her? That you loved her?'

His hand hovered over the plate. 'I did, the second I saw her at the school gates. She was a grown-up,' he added quickly, 'she wasn't a schoolgirl. She taught music in Nottingham, where I was training with the dogs. And I saw her after school one day, getting on her bicycle, and it was a certainty. Our life would be together.' He paused again and chuckled. 'She used to tell it differently.'

'How?'

'She said no the first time I asked her out. And the second. And the third. It was only the fourth time that she relented. Worn down, she used to say.'

'Why did she say no to begin with?'

'It was the dogs that were the problem. She wasn't keen. And I was a year into training by then so I didn't want to go back. But I won her over in the end, and then she loved them, didn't she, Basil?'

Basil was dozing on the sofa, having decided oysters weren't for him.

'Although she would never have let you up there. Sloppy habits, lad.'

'Did you have children?'

Harold shook his head. 'No, wasn't to be. So we had the dogs.'

Stella wanted to say something comforting. 'Dogs are better than babies, based on some of my friends' babies.'

Harold smiled. 'You like this Fitz character, then?'

'Yeah, think so.'

'Is he the best person in the room?'

Stella tilted her head. 'What do you mean?'

'It's something Ellen used to say to her pupils, the older ones anyway, if they were being mucked around by someone. You have to believe that you're with the best person in the room. The person you're with might not be for everyone, and they'll have faults because we all do, but when you walk into a room with them, you need to believe that they're the best person there.'

Stella nodded slowly. 'It's quite early, but I think he might be the most impressive man I've ever met. Present company excepted.'

'You hold on to him then, pet. If he's sending you this sort of spread, I'd say he's a good one.'

'I hope so. Last one?'

They took a final oyster, leaving the plate covered in discarded shells, and Stella raised hers in the air. 'Cheers, Harold.'

'Cheers,' he said, lifting his oyster to meet it. 'What are we toasting?'

Stella frowned, uncertain.

'How about to love?' Harold suggested, since by this point he'd had rather too much vodka. 'To love and all its magical ways.'

'Perfect,' she replied, 'to love and all its magical ways.'

CHAPTER 28

'COFFEE?' STELLA SUGGESTED AS they stood in the hospital entrance.

Billie shook her head. It was her first day of radiotherapy and she couldn't imagine keeping anything down.

'OK, let's go up.' Stella linked her arm through her friend's, leading her to the escalator, and from there to the radiotherapy department on the second floor.

It was busy already even though it wasn't quite nine. 'Take a seat,' instructed a nurse from behind the reception desk, and Stella was struck by how normally she said it, as if this was a post office and the nurse had told them to join the queue with their parcel.

'You all right?' she checked once they'd found two spare seats. Nobody around them was talking much so the only noises were the swing of the reception door and squeaking footsteps on the rubber floor as others arrived and announced themselves to the nurse.

Billie nodded and Stella glanced around the waiting room. Most people were in pairs, although there was one elderly man in the corner alone, a crumpled plastic bag of belongings at his feet.

Closer by, another couple, possibly mother and daughter, leafed through a magazine together. Sensing Stella's gaze, the older woman looked up. She was wearing a patterned headscarf, knotted like a bandana, and her eyes softened as they met Stella's.

Stella smiled quickly back, embarrassed to have been caught staring, and pulled out her phone. She was hoping, as always, to see a message from Fitz, but the screen was blank so she sighed and slipped it back into her bag.

'When you next seeing him?' Billie asked because she could interpret Stella's sighs like a foreign language.

'Dinner on Wednesday.'

'And when are we going to meet him, huh?' Billie leant sideways and buffeted Stella's shoulder with her own.

The 'we' in this sentence made Stella nervous. She wanted Billie to meet Fitz because she knew they'd get on. Fitz was charming, clever and he talked about real things. Only the previous week, Fitz had told Stella about a podcast he'd recently listened to about a specific type of organism found in the Atlantic that scientists believed could solve the climate crisis. He was cultured and knowledgeable, unlike previous conquests of Stella's who would almost certainly have confused an organism with an orgasm.

But Stella *was* worried about introducing Fitz to Jez, because she was nervous about what he might say to him or reveal about her.

She'd seen Fitz several times in the past few weeks, usually dinner, after which Victor would drive them back to Rakes. It never felt enough time, but Fitz was negotiating a deal with a security firm based in Washington, so she knew she had to be patient. She'd rather have five minutes in his company than five hours in anyone else's. When they weren't together, he messaged and called when he could, and there was talk of going to Paris for a weekend in December. Fitz wanted her to see the trees that lit up Place Vendôme.

She'd never been interested in science at school. As an adult, however, she was fascinated in the chemistry that she felt between her and Fitz. What was this magnetic pull? If Stella was near him, she wanted a part of her to be touching him constantly – his arm, his thigh, his mouth. But what made her so physically drawn to him and physically repulsed by, say, the man who'd sneezed on her hair on the Jubilee line the previous week? What was that alchemy?

He was the first thing Stella thought about when she woke, and the last thing at night, and she dreamed about him too, which must have meant her brain was consumed by him even when she was asleep. She mentioned his name every other sentence; she played embarrassing, romantic playlists on Spotify; she read his messages over and over and over again, even when they only said *Come to the hotel at 7*, and she'd started reading copies of *The Guardian*, which Jez left lying around the flat, so she could impress him with her understanding of the news.

'I want you to meet him,' Stella told Billie.

'But?'

'What?'

'I could sense a but.'

'No but. I just don't know when because he's away so much.'

Billie looked at her. 'Are you in lust or love with him?'

Opposite them, a grey-haired man in a blazer glanced over his paper.

Stella bit her lower lip while she considered the question. The truth was she wasn't entirely sure. She thought part of her might have fallen in love with Fitz the night they first met, in the pub. But she'd been wrong about love before and she couldn't face the idea of getting it wrong again, so she didn't want to admit the strength of her feelings to anyone, not even Billie. Because what if Fitz disappeared? It was all rosy now but what if something went wrong?

'I don't know,' she replied carefully. 'How come?'

'Just wondering. Do you realise you haven't mentioned Miles once recently?'

'Oh yeahhhhh.' A smile spread across Stella's face. She'd hadn't looked up his Instagram profile for ages either. 'What?' she added, as Billie frowned.

'Nothing.'

Stella felt a flash of annoyance. Recently, there had been a few times where Billie seemed lukewarm towards Fitz, questioning his job and his dating history, even though they hadn't met. Stella understood that her best friend was protective, but it still annoyed her. Billie didn't need to be so hostile towards Fitz.

'Would it matter if I did love him?' she replied defensively. 'You fell in love with Jez pretty quickly.'

'I'm just looking out for you.'

'I know, but you and him have been together for, like, six years?'

'Seven next month.'

'Seven, there we go. It's all right for you.'

Billie gestured wearily around the waiting room. 'Stell…'

Stella felt an instant wave of shame. The previous week, she'd come home from work to find Billie crying on the sofa. She'd finished her egg freezing treatment, but was still bloated with hormones, as swollen as a water balloon. 'It's not just this bit,' Billie had told her, clutching a small ball of damp tissue, 'it's everything that comes after it. I'm all at sea, Stell.'

What she meant by everything that came after it was the chemoradiation, which was starting that morning. That was the very reason she was back in hospital. It was a demanding schedule: every Monday to Friday for four weeks, Billie had to come to the radiology department to be blasted for fifteen minutes. In addition, every Friday morning she'd have to sit on a chemotherapy drip for several hours. It amounted to twenty sessions of radiotherapy and four sessions of chemotherapy. Dr Bush had warned that she'd feel tired, sick, emotional and that the effects were cumulative, so she'd likely be exhausted by the end of it.

Stella and Jez had divided up the dates so one of them could accompany her to every appointment. Jez had warned Stella in one of his emails that she needed to be on time for these appointments, and she'd promised she would be. Actually, his reprimand hadn't even annoyed her because an unofficial truce had broken out between them. Billie's situation so outweighed any bickering about the royal family or hair in the shower plughole that, for the time being, their war had quietened. It was the one upside to Billie's diagnosis, Stella had reflected one evening when she was astonishingly unbothered to find Jez's dirty socks on the coffee table.

'Sorry,' Stella said quickly, still hot with embarrassment at the idea she'd implied Billie was luckier than her simply because she had a long-term boyfriend. 'I didn't mean it like that.'

'What did you mean it like?'

'I'm sorry,' she repeated, taken aback by her friend's tone. Billie was never normally so sharp. All Stella meant was that Billie probably couldn't remember the anxiety of falling for someone, of wondering if they were falling back, of the fear that they might not reply to the next text message, of the fear that it might simply end any second.

They sat in silence for a few moments, Stella feeling guilty, trying to work out how to make it better. She looked up as a male name was called and a nurse helped the old man with his plastic bag to his feet, before he shuffled after her through a pair of swinging doors.

'What about our birthday?' she said eventually.

Billie frowned. 'Are we doing that? I don't know if… I'm just not sure how I'll be feeling.'

It was an annual tradition. After leaving school, where Billie and Stella had shared their birthday every year by going to the York Pizza Express with Billie's parents, they'd continued to celebrate by throwing a joint party in the flat every November. It was on the fifth, so they always invited a gaggle of friends and family over to watch the Hyde Park fireworks from the balcony, before continuing the party indoors.

Stella was usually in charge of the drinks, Billie made hot dogs, and it tended to go on until late. Very late. One year, the final stragglers only left when it was light and tourists carrying coffees were starting to walk past the balcony on their way to Portobello Market.

'We don't have to if you don't want to.'

'It's not that I don't want to. It's more that I…' Billie trailed off again. 'I can't tell how tired I'll be.'

'I get it. Let's have a year off. It's not like thirty-three is a major milestone. We can always make it twice as big next year, right?'

'Yeah,' Billie replied faintly, 'although what if I don't get to nex—'

'Nope. Don't want to hear it. Next year we're going to have the biggest party our flat has ever seen. Champagne, cake, everybody we know, maybe a mariachi band and it'll go on for *days*. Next year, Bill, we're going to have our own fucking festival!'

On the row of seats facing them, the grey-haired man with the newspaper cleared his throat.

'Sorry,' Stella muttered.

'Ok, let's do something this year. But maybe quite small?'

'You sure?'

Billie nodded.

'Why don't we play it by ear? And if you don't feel strong enough, we can cancel it on the day. Nobody would mind that. And I'll organise everything. You don't have to even think about it. And then I'll invite Fitz so you can meet him. Good plan?' Stell stuck her thumb out in front of her and waggled it sideways.

Billie smiled weakly and pointed her thumb towards the ceiling's fluorescent lighting.

A few moments later, at the sound of her name being called, they looked up to see a nurse with a clipboard scanning the purple seats.

Billie stood. 'That's me.'

Stella followed her towards the nurse, who shook her head. 'Patient only for the next part, I'm afraid.'

'You OK with that?' Stella asked, frowning at her friend.

'Yep, fine. See you out here when I'm done?'

Stella wrapped her in a hug and mumbled into her hair. 'See you out here, love you.'

She sat in the same seat once Billie had vanished. But reaching for her phone, she noticed her hand was shaking. As if observing a curiosity in a museum, Stella watched her own fingers wobble in the air for a few seconds before dropping her hand to her thigh, overcome by rush of fear that made her feel cold, then hot, and then cold again.

What if Billie wasn't here next year?

She raised her hand to the base of her throat and swallowed. She needed to do more to help. She *had* to do more to help. But she couldn't even find the right words to talk to her best friend at the moment. What are the right words to comfort someone who's sick when nobody, not even the doctors, can say what the outcome of that sickness will be?

Stella glanced at the woman in the patterned headscarf and lifted her phone again, suddenly realising exactly who she could talk to.

She scrolled back through her WhatsApps and was unable to find his name at first, before realising she hadn't saved it, so he was just a number.

She cringed as she reread his message, which was actually very kind, and mumbled half-sentences to herself as she worked out what to say.

Eventually, Stella settled on something contrite but short and to the point. It was the sort of message someone might send to a colleague asking for advice. Most importantly, she needed him to know that they absolutely weren't going to sleep together again. *Sam, hello. So sorry I never replied to this. I wasn't sure what to say at the time, but Billie's started radiotherapy and it would be useful to speak to someone who knows about it. Would you be free for a coffee this week?*

CHAPTER 29

TWO MORNINGS LATER, STELLA hovered in front of the hospital café, feeling oddly nervous. She had nothing to feel nervous about, she told herself, she was simply asking a friend for advice. Except he wasn't her friend. He was someone she'd slept with and run away from, before bumping into him, twice, and then ignoring his message in the hope that she'd never see him again. She cringed. It had been a mean, childish response to his generosity, and she'd felt even worse when he'd come back to her message simply saying no problem and suggesting they met in the coffee shop on Wednesday.

So now here she was, fiddling with her bag strap, waiting.

'Stella, hi.'

She swivelled and pushed the fronds of a large green pot plant away from her face to see Sam behind it in his doctor's coat. 'Sorry I'm late. Drama upstairs.'

Stella imagined a small child on a dialysis machine and felt guilty. 'Sorry, we can do this another time if you need to be on duty?'

Sam shook his head. 'No! Not my drama. One of the nurses has just been dumped so I was doing some consoling. Or trying to.' He grinned ruefully at her and gestured towards the coffee counter. 'Shall we?'

They stepped up to the till, which was manned by a large lady, almost as round as she was tall, wearing a very tight orange polo shirt branded with the coffee shop logo.

'Morning, Janine,' said Sam.

'Look, here he is, Dr Handsome,' Janine replied with a wide grin and a wink at Stella. She leaned forwards and settled her breasts on top of the glass display cabinet.

'What are you having?' Sam asked.

'Er, black coffee. But let me, it's the least I can do.'

'Staff get a discount,' Sam said, waving her purse away before turning back to the till. 'Two black coffees please, Janine.'

'And will you be having anything *sweet* with that, Dr Sam?' she asked, with another encouraging smile.

Jesus Christ, Janine, Stella wanted to tell her, you're serving cappuccinos to hospital visitors, not doling out piña coladas in a strip joint.

'Stella?'

'I'm good, thanks. Just the coffee.'

Once they'd collected their coffee and found a spare table, Stella smiled at him. 'Think you've got a fan there.'

Sam looked over his shoulder. 'Oh, Janine, yes. I once retrieved a piece of Lego from her son's nose and now it feels like I'm going to spend the rest of my life paying for it.'

Stella laughed and had a sip of coffee. 'Thanks for this. And also I'm sorry.'

'For what?' Sam asked as he tugged his lanyard off and laid it on the table. It left a tuft of dark hair sticking up above his ear.

He was so boyish, Stella thought. How could he be a doctor? 'For meeting me. And for not replying to your message before now. It's just been… a strange few weeks. And I was a bit of a mess when we, you know…'

Sam leant over the table and said in a pantomime whisper: 'What? When we *did* it?'

'Honestly, how are you a doctor?' Stella asked, shaking her head. 'How are you allowed to be in charge of actual lives?'

'Well,' Sam replied, his face becoming serious, 'if I tell you a secret, promise you'll keep it between us?'

'Of course.'

'I bought my certificates off eBay.'

Stella snorted with laughter.

'Listen. Don't worry about not replying to my message. I get it. Everyone's got shit going on in their lives. And I didn't want to add to your load, only to say I was here to help if you need.'

She picked at the side of her paper cup with her thumbnail. 'I just don't know what to say to her, to Billie.'

'Where is she with treatment?'

Stella explained the whole story: Billie's smear test, the colposcopy, the test results, the treatment plan, her egg freezing treatment and that she'd started radiotherapy.

Sam listened, nodding, occasionally asking the odd question about which doctor she'd seen, and how long they'd said she'd need to be treated for.

'OK,' he said when she'd finished. 'Do you want the good news or the bad news?'

Stella's stomach cramped. 'What do you mean bad news?'

He rested his forearms on the table. 'Listen, a doctor's job isn't to sugar-coat things. From what you've told me, they've found this early, and the treatment schedule sounds pretty standard.'

'Is that the good news?'

'Some of it. I'm a paediatrician not a gynaecological oncologist, and this isn't my area of expertise, but if this is how they're treating her then it hasn't spread.'

'OK, what's the bad news?'

Sam turned his palms upwards. 'Cancer's never good news. She's young but she'll get tired, very tired. The diagnosis is one thing, and the course of treatment can be physically very gruelling, so physically gruelling that people often tend to focus on that, rather than the mental effects. But just watch her, because she may decline a bit even after the treatment has finished, and it can take a while to recover from that.'

'How long?'

'Depends on the patient. Sometimes weeks, sometimes months. And she might be unaffected. But I wanted to warn you because you don't finish a schedule like this and feel healed immediately.'

'Sure, that makes sense,' Stella said, nodding. 'But what do I say to her? I seem to say the wrong things all the time. Like I constantly tell her she's going to be fine but I don't know that. And it sounds so feeble. I want to say more helpful things, *be* more helpful. But I don't know how.'

He shrugged. 'Why not just tell her that?'

'That I don't know what to say?'

'Sure. It's honest, and in my experience what patients most want in this situation is honesty. Tell Billie that you're sometimes not sure what to say, or how best to help, but that you're here for whenever she needs. She'll know that's true. *I* can see that's true. Why would you be sitting here with me otherwise?'

Stella nodded slowly.

'Look, sometimes people are so worried about what to say in this scenario that they say nothing,' Sam went on. 'I see it all the time with the families on my ward; some of them are literally unable to talk about why they're here. It's too frightening. But if you face it head on, accept it and try to communicate,' he paused and tapped his temple with his fingers, 'it can take some of that anxiety away. And then, with any luck, Billie can be honest back, won't be so worried about upsetting you or trying to hide her own fears.'

It hadn't occurred to Stella that Billie might be worrying about what she should or shouldn't say. She thought back to when Billie had murmured that she didn't know if she'd be here for their next birthday and she'd instantly shut her down.

'I hope it helps. It's tough, all this, really tough. But I can tell you she's being looked after by the best.'

'I know, it seems it. And I take it back, by the way.'

'Take what back?'

'I can see how you're good at this, at being a doctor.'

Stella meant it. She could see how comforting he'd be to an anxious parent. He might look disarmingly young, and he had a sense of humour that suggested he'd be more suited to late-night shifts in a men's comedy club, but underneath that was a more serious person.

'Thank you. I try.'

She tilted her head. 'How come you wanted to go into medicine?'

'I'm the son of two Pakistani doctors, so it was either that or accountancy, and my brother became an accountant.' He leant forwards across the table again and stuck his thumb over his shoulder towards the coffee shop. 'Also, why wouldn't you want to go into medicine when the perks are so good?'

Stella laughed and drained her coffee, then looked at her phone and realised Billie would nearly be finishing upstairs. 'I better go.'

'Any time, seriously. You've got my number.'

'I have,' she replied, standing and immediately feeling awkward about how to say goodbye. She lifted a hand in a lame wave.

'I'd give you a hug but I think Janine would get jealous,' Sam said as he pulled his lanyard back over his head. 'Keep me posted.'

'I will.'

Stella felt a wave of relief. That hadn't been awkward at all, she thought, as she slid upwards towards the radiology department. In fact, it had been doubly useful; she'd cleared the air with Sam and she'd been reassured that other people felt tongue-tied in these situations too, that it wasn't simply her being useless, incapable of saying anything helpful. Now she knew what to say, she'd be a better friend.

CHAPTER 30

LATER THAT AFTERNOON, WHILE Stella was frowning at an invoice, she got a message from Fitz.

Sorry darling, can't make dinner as I have to be on calls with America all evening. But I should be done by around ten if you want to come to the hotel then?

Stella always wanted to see Fitz, but going to a hotel that late felt a bit, well, cheap. She liked Rakes. She could hardly complain about staying in a hotel where the lobby smelled of expensive candles and the sheets were changed daily. Plus, it still felt thrilling to arrive there and ride the lift up to his room. But in the past couple of weeks, she'd started to long for a night with Fitz that felt more real and less like a scene from a seedy TV drama. She wanted to do things normal couples did. She wanted to go to a shop with him and hold hands in the aisles as they picked out ingredients for dinner. She wanted him to see her home. She wanted to wake up next to him in her own bed. What she did not want was to be summoned to the hotel late at night.

'Stella?' came a shout from Marjorie's office.

She dropped her phone, pushed her chair back and walked over.

'Can you look up a business called, hang on, I just had it here... it's called Neptune Investments.'

'Sure.'

'What's the matter?' Marjorie asked, glancing up from her desk. Then her face darkened. 'Is it Billie?'

A couple of weeks earlier, Stella had told her boss about Billie's diagnosis and Marjorie had been instantly supportive, telling her to take time off whenever she needed. Stella was grateful, and liked the agency even more. She felt like she was making a difference, too; she was on top of the paperwork, she'd organised the purchase and delivery of a new fridge, got the loo handle fixed and taken several of Marjorie's wigs to a wig cleaner she'd found online, based just off Oxford Street, because some of them smelled. Now that Stella had settled into it and was handed a roll of notes every Friday, she didn't want to leave. Obviously she couldn't work as an assistant to an affair hunter *forever*, but for right now, with so much else going on, it was fine, especially with Marjorie being so understanding.

'No no, it's not Billie. She's OK. So far so good, anyway,' Stella replied, thinking back to earlier that morning in hospital when Billie had emerged from her third radio treatment insisting that she felt fine.

'What is it, then? Come on, I've warned you, you can't hide anything from me.'

'No big deal,' she said in a falsely cheery tone. 'I was supposed to be having dinner with Fitz tonight, that's all, but doesn't look like I am.'

Marjorie's eyes narrowed across her desk like a sniper. 'Why?'

'Work. He's busy with a deal at the moment.'

Her boss looked back to her computer with a grunt. 'Did you get the name of that company?'

'Neptune Investments.'

'Can you have a hunt around the internet – old newspaper articles, that sort of thing – and gather everything you can find on Calvin Ferrari.'

'Is that a car?'

'No, it is an Italian banker.'

'Who is he?'

'He's married to an Italian lady, Mrs Ferrari, who called me yesterday saying she suspects her husband is having an affair.'

'Why?'

'Oh, the usual. Coming home late at night, clearly after drinking, they haven't slept together for months and so on.'

'Months! When they're *married*?'

Marjorie laughed and shook her head. 'Young Stella, so much to learn. I have some clients who haven't slept together for years. Decades, sometimes.'

Stella felt a pang of pity for such people. She couldn't imagine climbing into bed next to Fitz for months on end, not wanting to touch him. But then she thought of her own parents and wrinkled her nose. She didn't think they'd had sex for years. How did that even happen? How did a couple go from addiction to one another, being consumed by the other person every second of every day, to the point where getting into bed with them every night felt awkward, like accidentally brushing up against a stranger on the Tube?

'Poor Mrs Ferrari,' she sighed, 'but I'm on it. Do you want another tea?'

'Excellent idea.' Marjorie picked up her empty mug and held it out. 'And Stella?'

'Mmm?'

'If this chap of yours continues to make a nuisance of himself, put him on to me. I am only too delighted to give the male species a kick up the derrière when required.'

Stella smiled. 'He's a good one really.'

She turned to go and then stopped, clutching Marjorie's favourite mug, its insides stained as brown as a puddle. 'Do you really never want to meet anyone again?'

Marjorie blinked over the top of her spectacles. '*Meet* someone?'

'As in a man.'

'Pffffft! No thank you. The only man I need in my life is the Domino's man. And occasionally the plumber.'

As Stella flicked the kettle on, she felt a pang of pity for her boss. It didn't sound very cosy, spending every evening alone on the sofa with a pizza box. Even if it was a stuffed crust. That's when the thought occurred to her: Harold.

It made sense! Harold was a few years older than Marjorie, but they were both former coppers, and both on their own. They must have plenty in common.

Stella frowned as she fished a dirty teaspoon from the sink, uncertain whether they'd actually fancy one another. Marjorie was a large, messy, domineering woman, a female haystack; Harold was a slight, tidy man who Stella only ever saw dressed in pressed trousers and collared shirts. But still, opposites attract, don't they?

As the water boiled, she congratulated herself on coming

up with such a plan. It was perfect. Genius, even. Harold and Marjorie could be together before the year was out. Except then Marjorie might move into the flat beneath hers and it would be weird to be living so close to her boss. But perhaps by then she might have found a different job, so it wouldn't matter so much.

It was an excellent idea, Stella decided, as she carried the mug of tea into Marjorie's office.

The only question was how to go about putting it into practice.

Back at her own desk, Stella picked up her phone and pouted at Fitz's message for a few moments. If she said no, she'd sulk and feel sad for the rest of the day. But if she said yes, she felt like she was giving in. His work schedule always dictated when they saw one another, and she'd never complained because she knew he was busy, but at times like this Stella felt frustrated, entirely at his beck and call. Then she'd remind herself what Fitz had told her over their first dinner: that his wife had left him because he'd been away so much. She had to be more patient than that.

OK, see you later xxx, she tapped back. Seeing Fitz, even for a short while, was much better than not seeing him at all.

CHAPTER 31

BY 10.17 THAT NIGHT, Stella was glad that she'd come to the hotel. She'd arrived, waved at David behind the reception desk and gone straight up to Fitz's room in the lift.

He'd opened the door and wordlessly reached for her, wrapping one arm around Stella's back and pulling her into him. They'd kissed, increasingly frantically, and fallen on the bed together, where Fitz had quickly removed every piece of her clothing. As they'd carried on kissing, his hands had roamed across her body, down to between her legs, and it had only taken a minute before Stella felt herself climax, groaning into his mouth as she did. Then she'd climbed on top of him, relishing – for a moment – the power of having Fitz underneath her, inside her, rocking underneath her until he came, with a roar, gripping Stella's hips to keep her in place above him.

'Good evening, Miss Shakespeare,' he said huskily into her ear as Stella lowered herself, her chest lying on his, her thighs either side of him.

She glanced at the clock on his bedside table: 10.17 p.m.

'Hi,' she whispered back with a small laugh. Then she pushed herself up. 'Glad I came?'

Fitz's blue eyes crinkled. 'Delighted.'

She dropped her head for another kiss before moving to lie beside him.

'I'm sorry it's late,' Fitz said, lifting one arm so she could move herself underneath it. He ran his fingers through her hair. 'It won't always be like this.'

'That's OK, I get you're busy.' If he'd said it wouldn't always be like this, that implied he was thinking about the future. He'd never said as much before and it felt like a small but significant step forward. 'How's the deal?'

'A bloody nightmare,' he replied, turning his head to press his mouth against her temple. 'But it'll be done eventually. How's your week been?'

Stella circled her nails around his chest. 'It's been… weird. Billie started her radiation on Monday.'

'How's she feeling?'

'All right, but it's only been three sessions. I think it's cumulative, so she may be less all right in a week.'

'She'll be fine,' Fitz murmured, brushing his lips against her head again. 'Life is light and dark for everyone at different times.'

'That's very philosophical.' Stella lifted her head and frowned. She'd observed this with him; he'd have sudden moments of introspection and come out with something very serious before snapping out of it again as if he'd been in a trance.

Fitz gave her a strange look, almost wistful. 'Trust me, if I've learned anything in this life, it's that it's always changing. Nothing stays the same. The trick is never to get too comfortable because as soon as you do it'll change again.'

'You OK?'

He nodded, squeezing her into him. 'I'm fine, tired. Long week. And I… well, I missed you.'

It was the most affectionate thing he'd ever said to her. 'I missed you too,' she replied, enjoying the feel of the words as they left her mouth. She kissed his shoulder and laid her head down. 'How come we never talk about your friends?'

'My friends?'

'Yeah, you know, they're people we choose to hang out with every now and then. The people who we like but we're not actually related to.'

'I'll get you back for that.'

'Promises promises. But answer me.'

Stella felt Fitz shrug underneath her. 'Mostly for the very simple reason that I don't have that many. A few from the navy but they're scattered all over the world. And there's the odd client who's become more of a friend. But I'm a lone ranger. And I've got you.'

'So there's nobody you'd ring if you'd, say, had a bad day and fancied a drink? Nobody you'd ring up to grumble and just… chat about life?'

He didn't reply so she lifted her head to frown at him.

'Men aren't like women.'

Stella rolled her eyes. 'Duh, I've worked that out after nearly thirty-three years on this planet.'

'I don't need that many others in my life. I go back to Paris to see my mother maybe once or twice a year. But otherwise…'

'Otherwise?'

'I only need you,' Fitz said with the smile that made his eyes soften.

'Oh I see,' she said, arching her chest against him. 'Is this how you negotiate with your clients? Charming them into deals with you?'

'It is exactly. You've discovered my dark secret.'

Stella smiled then suddenly felt nervous. She had a specific question to ask him, but was anxious because she'd always waited for him to make their next date. 'Are you free on Friday evening?'

'Friday? Might be. Why?'

'I wondered if you wanted to come stay at mine?'

Depending on how she felt after her first chemo session, Billie was going home to Yorkshire for the weekend with Jez. She was determined to go, she'd told Stella. Her parents had offered to come down but Billie wanted to go north, to her old bedroom, to her ramshackle home just outside Harrogate where chickens roamed outside and the Martins' three cats patrolled inside.

'You could come stay… I'll cook… We'd have the place to ourselves…'

Fitz gave her a doubtful smile. 'Can you cook?'

'Oi!' She poked his ribs with her right index finger 'Yes. Sort of. I mean no, not very well, but I will for you.'

'In which case, I would love to and I accept.'

'Actually?'

'Yes!' Fitz replied, laughing. 'Why so surprised?'

Stella waggled her head from side to side. 'I just thought you might be busy with work, or away.'

'I'm there,' he promised as he sat up and swung his legs out of bed.

He closed himself in the bathroom and Stella settled back against the pillow. Asking him over hadn't been so hard. And now they'd have a real night together, at her flat, like a normal couple. Her forehead creased as she wondered what to cook. She'd ask Billie for ideas.

She rolled over and reached for a glass of water on his bedside table and the flash of his phone caught her eye.

'Hey, Fitz?' Stella said loudly, reaching for his mobile. 'Your phone's ringing.'

It stopped just as he reappeared from the bathroom.

She held it out to him. 'Five missed calls. Jeez. I hope it isn't a drama. Who's C?'

Fitz took the phone and glared at the screen. 'It's my assistant, Carol. Must be something to do with the Americans.'

'You need to ring back?'

He glanced at the clock. 'No. She'll have to wait until the morning.' Still standing, he tapped at his phone before turning it off and laying it on his bedside table.

'Is Carol the sort of sexy assistant who wears pencil skirts and hold-ups?' Stella teased as she felt a tiny flicker of jealousy at the thought of another woman in Fitz's life.

Fitz laughed and slid back under the sheet. 'Hardly. She's a fifty-something battleaxe who looks like a toad, and if she owns a pencil skirt and hold-ups I most definitely do not want to see her in them. But she runs my life with the precision of a military general. Although she knows better than to interrupt when what I most want to do right now is this.'

He ran one hand over Stella's right hip, along her ribcage and to her nipple, which instantly hardened in response.

She gasped as Fitz moved his mouth to her breast and smiled to herself, pleased that – on this occasion at least – he'd put her before work.

CHAPTER 32

'BILL, CAN I TALK to you about something?' Stella asked the following evening.

They were side by side on the sofa, heads back against the cushions, both wearing white sheet masks. Stella had bought one for herself on the way home as preparation for her night with Fitz in the flat, and thrown another one into her basket for Billie, thinking it might be nice to do something normal together. Jez was working late on a story in his office. A new BBC comedy about drag queens was on the TV.

'Obviously,' Billie replied. She turned and frowned at Stella, although Stella couldn't actually see that she was frowning because of the ghostly face mask. 'Why do you sound so serious? What's wrong?'

'Nothing. But I wanted to say…' Stella paused and readjusted the sheet mask. 'I wanted to say there have been a few moments recently where I've felt like I don't know how to help.'

'What do you mean?'

'We talk all the time, right, but at the moment I feel like nothing I say is enough, like it's inadequate for what you're going through. I try to imagine it sometimes, how you feel, but I can't.

So, because I'm uncomfortable, I end up saying stupid things, like asking how you are all the time or telling you it's going to be fine, because I literally can't find the words big enough to say anything that feels helpful. But I wish I could.'

'Stell...'

'I suppose all I can say is I'm here. I'm *really* here, even though I may say stupid things or make silly jokes or get tongue-tied and say nothing at all. I'm here.'

'I know you are. Believe me, I know.' Billie paused. 'I guess it's the same with me.'

'How come?'

'Sometimes, I don't know what to say to you. Or anyone.'

'That's what Sam said,' Stella replied unthinkingly.

'What? What's Sam got to do with this?'

Stella bit her lip before making a spitting noise. The sheet mask did not taste good. 'OK, so I met up with him in hospital to ask his advice. And he said I should tell you exactly what I felt, and that you might be feeling the same.'

'Did you now?' Billie said, smiling so that the mask wrinkled around her eyes.

'Yes, but never mind him. You don't know what to say either?'

'I think of the worst thing that could happen, like this treatment doesn't work. It's in my head constantly, that "what if" feeling. But I also feel like I can't tell anyone that because I don't want Mum and Dad to worry more, or you. Or Jez. So I keep it inside and sometimes it feels like I can't breathe.' Billie pressed her hands to her heart. 'It's not like any fear I've ever felt before. People worry about things all the time, right? Like money or their kids or their job. But somewhere you always know, or hope at least, for a time when those worries will be OK. You know that there will be a time beyond them. But with this… with this there might not be a time beyond it because that's the whole point. I might just not be here. I want to be an old lady, Stell,' she pushed on, her voice wavering. 'I really want to be an old lady. But what if I can't be that?'

Stella turned and wrapped her arms around Billie's shoulders. 'Bill. I'm sorry this is happening to you. I wish it was me. I want you to be an old lady. I want us both to be old ladies. Ones who smell of talcum powder and mints and drink too much sherry.'

Billie made a noise that was half sob, half laugh. She pulled back and wiped her nose with the back of her hand. 'I want that, I want that so much.'

'Then you just have to believe it. *We* have to believe it.'

Billie nodded. 'Tomorrow, when I'm having my first chemo, I have to visualise a warm light around the tumour, or imagine tiny little Pac-Man characters chasing the cancer cells and eating them… It's stupid but some people online said it helps.'

'It's not stupid! You have to believe it; otherwise it won't work. I'll imagine tiny little Pac-Mans running around inside you. Two people imagining are much better than one.'

'Thank you.'

'Don't say thank you. This is literally my job. I don't mean like it's a chore, obviously. But I mean you're the thing I most want to fix. Not fix! See? Oh god, it all comes out wrong.'

'Not that wrong. My cheeks are starting to feel a bit tight, by the way. How much longer have we got left with these masks?'

'Er…' Stella looked at her phone. 'Another five minutes.'

'Can we get back to you seeing Sam in the hospital?'

'Wasn't a big deal,' Stella said, shrugging. 'I felt bad that I never replied to his message, so I went back to him, we had a coffee, he gave me this advice.'

'Aaaaand?'

'And nothing. He's great, he saves children for a job. I get it, he's right up your street. But he's not my type, Bill.'

'I know,' sighed Billie, 'I just thought there was something about Sam.'

'What, when you met him for three seconds that day in the hospital?'

'Yes! He had a nice face.'

Stella laughed. 'You say that about everyone.'

'He did though! Nice smile, honest eyes.'

'Sounds like *you* fancy Sam. Shall I invite him to our birthday party?'

'Yes! Definitely do that, definitely invite him.'

'Bill, obviously Sam is not coming to our birthday party.'

'All right. But have you asked Fitz?'

'Nope, that's tomorrow's job. He's coming here for the night.'

'WHAT?' Billie said loudly, just as they both heard the key in the door and Jez appeared from behind it.

'Couple of questions,' he said, frowning. 'Bill, what are you shouting about and what on earth is that on your faces?'

'It's a hyaluronic mask and nobody's shouting, Jeremy. We're just discussing our birthday party.'

'Actually, Stella was just saying she's having Fitz over tomorrow,' Billie explained as Jez leant over the back of the sofa and kissed her head.

'That's a shame. Sneaking in the arms dealer so we miss him.'

Stella rolled her eyes. Jez insisted on still calling him that, even though she'd told him Fitz had answered all her questions on that topic. 'I'm not sneaking him in! I've had to *persuade* him so I can sleep in my own bed. Anyway, it would be pretty awkward if we were all here for the first time, queuing for the bathroom in the morning.'

'Especially given what you do in there,' chipped in Jez, returning from the kitchen with a beer.

'Watch it,' Stella said, throwing a cushion at him. Happily, since their recent truce had broken out, these jibes had come less frequently.

'OK, but you have to ask him to the party. I really, *really* want to meet him,' Billie insisted.

'Promise,' replied Stella, sticking her thumb in the air.

CHAPTER 33

STELLA'S FRIDAY AFTERNOON DRAGGED as she spent most of it transcribing a conversation that Marjorie had recorded on her special pen in a Mayfair hotel the previous lunchtime. It was between Mr Ferrari, the husband of the Italian lady who suspected he was having an affair, and one of his business colleagues.

The recording was mostly unremarkable. Against a backdrop of bar chatter and the chink of glasses, the men discussed the gas markets, the Italian football league, the weather and whether the colleague's son should go to university in Britain or America.

It was only towards the end of the lunch, after Mr Ferrari ordered two whiskies, that they got on to the subject of sex, although it was the colleague who talked about his affair. He appeared to be sleeping with someone from the office who'd sent her knickers to him via the internal post system. Mr Ferrari didn't mention anyone other than his wife.

Stella also put a call through to Marjorie from a woman who was in love with her personal trainer but suspected he was sleeping with his other clients.

'Want me to start a case file?' Stella asked when Marjorie appeared from her office after the call.

'No, I didn't take it.'

'Why?'

'There are some cases where I advise the client not to waste their money. That woman,' she went on, crunching a cereal bar loudly between her teeth, 'is past the point of no return.'

'What do you mean?' said Stella, watching her lunch disappear. She'd been too excited by Fitz coming to stay that night to manage a sandwich and so had bought a cereal bar from the newsagent instead.

'I could spend the next week or so watching the personal trainer,' went on Marjorie. 'He's a twenty-four-year-old from California so it wouldn't be the toughest surveillance gig I've ever faced. But I might not find anything. Perhaps the women he's sleeping with aren't in town or he's having a week off. Whatever. The trouble is, as I told her, if she's already suspicious this early into a relationship, then she's got a problem. And they're not married, so better to draw a line under it now. Call it a day.'

'I guess,' Stella said uncertainly.

'I say that to every client,' Marjorie continued. 'If you go looking for dirt, you'll find something. Could be a porn habit. Could be they're talking to an ex. But unless you're prepared to find something out, don't search for it.'

'Did you go looking? Is that how you found out about your ex-husband?'

Marjorie tutted. 'My first inkling was when I found a footprint on the inside of the car windscreen.'

'Wow.'

'The second clue was when a condom wrapper turned up in the washing machine.'

Stella wrinkled her face. 'Gross. Did you confront him?'

'Not exactly. I tailed him when he said he was off to karate. He left in his kit but drove down our road and turned into the next one, where she lived. So I climbed through the garden window and found them at it on the sofa together. I'll give you a bloody karate chop, I told him.'

'Are they still together now?'

'I don't know and I care even less,' Marjorie said, wiping the crumbs from around her mouth.

'Actually, that reminds me. What are you doing on November fifth?'

'No idea. Why?'

'Because Billie and I are throwing our birthday party and you'd be very welcome.'

Marjorie wasn't used to being asked to parties and she was momentarily confused. 'Me? Come to your birthday? Are you sure?'

'Yes. I do the drinks and Billie does the hot dogs, although I'm in charge of those too this year.'

'Quite right. How's she feeling?'

'Not sure, although it was her first chemo session today and I haven't heard from her. But we're doing the party because her treatment will be over by then, so please come and meet her.'

'How thoughtful, I'll be there with knobs on, thank you. Now, how's that Mr Ferrari transcription getting on?'

'Almost there,' Stella sighed before returning to her desk and seeing a message from Fitz that he'd be at the flat by seven. Perfect. She could leave the office, go to the posh fish shop and buy the ingredients for a recipe she'd found online for prawn linguine. How hard could prawn pasta be? Like pesto pasta, just with prawns in it.

After work, along with the fresh pasta, the prawns, the parmesan and the parsley, she dropped a tub of black olives into her basket in the deli, along with a bottle of Italian wine. She also stopped at the florists on the corner and bought three stems of hydrangeas, the colour of sapphires.

Once in the flat, Stella opened the wine, stuck the hydrangeas in a vase, showered, shaved, then fished through the clothes that she'd rammed into the drawer under her bed for her leather skirt and grey T-shirt.

She tipped the olives into a small green pot that Billie had bought on a summer holiday in Zakynthos, turned the living room lights down, lit a candle and then selected her favourite soul playlist. And as Sam Cooke started singing from the speaker on the bookshelf, she stepped back to survey her efforts. Not bad.

In the kitchen, she opened the recipe on her phone and read it while muttering under her breath. 'One onion… two cloves of garlic… fry… Oh shit, red pepper flakes.' She'd forgotten those. Stella ran her fingers across the spice rack but there weren't any. Never mind. She poured herself a glass of wine.

Next, the recipe told her to clean the prawns, so Stella tore away their damp paper and tipped them on to a chopping board. She made a noise of disgust as she cut off a head and used the tip of the knife to peel away its dark vein. One down, eleven to go. She concentrated so hard on the prawns, on making sure they were spotless, that she didn't notice the time until she looked up – 7.16 p.m.

She washed the prawn juice off her hands and checked her

phone. One message from Billie, finally. Stella had called her three times that afternoon to check in after her chemo appointment but she hadn't picked up.

Chemo pretty weird but am home, lying on the sofa. Mum treating me as if I've just got back from war. Sorry (but also not sorry) that I'm not there to hear you make the walls shake tonight. Ring you tomorrow xxxx

Stella sent her a string of red hearts before turning her thoughts back to Fitz. Could she message, asking where he was, or would that make her sound like a cross housewife? She decided to leave it until half past.

Fifteen minutes later, she sent him a message before pouring herself another glass of wine and chopping the onion in the kitchen, opening her eyes as wide as she could to stop her mascara from running.

At eight, there was still no sign and Stella decided to ring but his phone was switched off. She reread his previous message to check she hadn't misread it but no, he definitely said he'd be there by seven.

By this point, Stella was feeling distinctly buzzed. She ate an olive and leant back on the counter. Rakes. She could call Rakes and see if he was there.

'Good evening, Rakes Hotel, how can I help?'

'Hello, it's er, Stella Shakespeare here. I stay in the hotel sometimes with Fitz Montague?'

'Good evening madam, how can I be of assistance?'

'I was calling to see if he was there. Mr Montague, I mean.'

A nervous chuckle. 'I'm afraid I'm not allowed to give out guest information, madam.'

'Fine… OK… In that case could you connect me to Mr Montague's room?'

'His room, madam?'

'Mmm, I understand that you can't tell me if he's there, but could you possibly connect me to his room?'

There was a pause at the other end of the line and Stella heard the tapping of a keyboard. 'I'm afraid we don't have any records of a Mr Montague staying with us tonight, madam.'

'For god's sake.' Stella hung up and inhaled deeply through her nose. It was now nearly 8.20 p.m. Perhaps it was London traffic? Perhaps he'd got stuck on a call? But it was still weird not to let her know, and rude, actually, when she was cooking him dinner. She tried to remember his secretary's name, the one who he'd said was a battleaxe but very efficient. Catherine? Camilla? No, Carol, that was it. Carol would presumably know what had happened. But she didn't even know how to track her down.

Opening a new webpage on her phone, Stella tapped Horus into the search bar and had another look on the website in case there was a telephone number, but no luck. Just the black home page and a generic email address.

Telling herself to calm down, that nothing could have happened to him, she turned back to the chopped onion and garlic and slid them into a frying pan. Sloshing olive oil over the top, she lit the gas and reached for a wooden spoon.

Then a more disturbing thought occurred to her: what if Fitz was ghosting her? What if he was becoming bored, just as Miles had, and everything that she'd felt so hopeful about turned to dust? Perhaps he wasn't going to show up tonight and this was his way of letting her down? Fitz was busy with work; maybe a relationship was too much on top of that. And she'd pushed for him to come and stay here, but perhaps it had been too early for him?

As Stella stood there, stirring, obsessing, she felt her chest tighten as if someone was pulling a thick belt around it.

She inhaled again, through her mouth, but found that she couldn't take in much air and her lungs felt like they were shrinking, which made her feel more panicked still.

Stepping sideways, she leant over the kitchen sink as the sensation gripped her entire torso, then her neck, and she sucked for breath like a sprinter. Glancing down, she noticed that her thighs were shaking, barely able to hold her up; the counter was taking most of her weight. Gripping the side of the sink with her fingers, she lowered herself to the floor while taking shallow breaths. An allergic reaction? The wine? The olive? Placing two fingers on her left wrist, she felt a pulse beating quickly through her veins. Very quickly.

Stella pressed the same fingers to her cheek. Hot. Maybe she just needed a glass of water.

It took all her strength to heave herself up again, whereupon she drank directly from the tap, trying to alternate mouthfuls of water with breathing.

She wished Billie was there. What if it was an allergy and her chest became more and more crushed until she passed out? People did die, didn't they, from bee stings or sniffing a peanut? Perhaps Billie would find her, on Sunday evening, lying stiff on the kitchen floor surrounded by expensive prawns that, by then, would also have started to smell.

This vision did nothing to alleviate Stella's symptoms, and she started gulping harder as her lungs felt as if they were filling up with water. She felt dizzy and the floor appeared to be much further away than usual.

She glanced at her front door and decided that was the sensible solution. Groping her way there, she supported herself with every piece of furniture in the way – a kitchen chair, the back of the sofa, the bookshelf. Carefully, she opened the door, felt her way down the banisters and knocked on Harold's door.

CHAPTER 34

'STELLA, HELLO, WHAT A lov— Good grief, what's going on?'

She put a hand on his doorway. 'I think I'm… I'm…' she gasped for breath, 'having an allergic reaction. My chest is all tight and I'm very hot.'

'Heavens. Come in.' Harold ushered her into his living room and helped her to the sofa.

Stella sat and leant forward, her elbows on her knees, her head dropped.

'I'm going to ring an ambulance.'

She lifted her face. 'No! I don't need an ambulance.'

'You're the colour of a post box.'

'Am I? Oh god,' she groaned, lowering her head again. 'Please don't call an ambulance, I've got a date coming for dinner.'

'What have you eaten?'

'An olive.'

'An olive! I didn't know anyone could be allergic to olives.'

Stella made a circle with her mouth and exhaled slowly through it. The crush on her chest seemed to be loosening. She could breathe more deeply. She glanced up to see Harold tapping at his phone.

'Don't call an ambulance. Please don't. I'm fine, I'm feeling a bit better act—'

'Hello?' Harold said into his phone. 'Hello? Can you hear me? It's a very faint line, I can't really hear…'

She leant back against the sofa and sighed as he moved next door to the kitchen. Her T-shirt was damp with sweat and her hands were mottled.

Maybe an ambulance wasn't such a bad call, just to check she wasn't going to die. She felt bad about wasting NHS time but, hopefully, they could give her a once-over and she could go back upstairs.

She glanced at a clock hanging above Harold's table. Shit, it was nearly nine, and she didn't have her phone on her, so if Fitz was trying to call then she wouldn't know and… Stella's chest started tightening again so she sat up straight and inhaled through her mouth. In and out. In and out. In and out.

'It's all right,' Harold announced, returning from the kitchen, 'I've spoken to Sam and he says don't bother with an ambulance because it'll take too long. He's coming over now.'

'What?' shrieked Stella, forgetting to slow her breathing. 'I don't need Sam.'

'He was in a pub round the corner and says he'll be here any second. You just sit tight. Are you all right? CAN YOU HEAR ME?'

She winced. 'Yes, Harold, I haven't gone deaf.'

'How many fingers am I holding up?'

'Four. I haven't gone blind either.'

'Just checking.'

Stella felt her pulse; it seemed slower. But she remained on the sofa, leaning over her thighs, breathing deeply. Whenever her thoughts flickered back to Fitz, her chest constricted so she pushed him away and concentrated on Basil's face. He was lying on the carpet, front legs stretched forward, ears pricked with concern.

'I'll put the kettle on,' said Harold.

The buzzer went.

'That'll be Sam. That was quick. Basil, stay guard.'

Stella stood up, her legs still shaking, and glanced behind her at a mirror over the sofa.

She looked awful: damp skin, flushed cheeks and a shiny chin. She wiped the sheen with her fingers but, having stood up too quickly, felt dizzy and had to lower herself again.

She curled into the foetal position on the sofa. Tonight was supposed to be perfect, and this situation was the exact opposite.

'Hiya, how we doing?'

She opened her eyes to see Sam very close, crouching beside the sofa, and smiled weakly. 'Having a really top Friday night. You?'

'She can still make jokes. That's a good sign. Do you mind if I take your pulse?' He reached for her right wrist. 'Harold said something about an olive?'

'I'm not sure if it was the olive. I was cooking upstairs because someo— A friend is coming over for dinner. And then it was like someone was standing on my chest, like a heavy boot pressing down here, almost like I was choking.' Stella splayed one hand across her chest, fingertips at the base of her throat.

'And you've never felt anything like this before?'

She shook her head, and then remembered her shaky hand in the hospital earlier in the week, on the first day she'd taken Billie in for her radiotherapy. 'I had this weird, wobbly hand a few days ago. In the hospital, while I was waiting for Bill. But it was early, so I assumed I just needed a coffee.'

'Have you drunk alcohol tonight?'

'Not much,' she said quickly.

Sam continued gazing at her, his fingers encircling her wrist.

'Like two glasses. Three maybe. Only because Fitz… I mean, that's who's coming for dinner, my friend… only because he was late so I was having a drink while I cooked.'

'What you making?'

'Linguine with prawns.'

'Lucky man,' Sam said with a grin before his face became more serious. 'And have you eaten anything else today that could have caused this?'

She rolled her head from side to side. 'Nope. I only had some toast this morning, and then half a cereal bar for lunch.'

'Nothing else? That's it?'

'And a few coffees.'

'How many coffees today?'

'Um, like three or four?'

'OK,' Sam replied, nodding and squinting at her wrist as if he was trying to see her heartbeat as well as feel it.

She lay listening to Harold make tea in the kitchen. It was strangely calming, having Sam there, his hand against hers. He hadn't even taken off his jacket, beneath which was a white T-shirt that she couldn't help noticing was pulled taut across the muscles of his chest. He looked less like a doctor and more like the man she'd met in the pub that evening before she went home with him. Her eyes ran along the neckline of his T-shirt and she remembered waking up beside him that day, his arms, the way he'd tried to persuade her to stay in bed with him.

'How are you feeling now?'

'Better,' she said quickly, dispelling thoughts about Sam's chest. 'My breathing's better.'

'How long did you struggle for breath?'

'A few minutes, maybe?'

Harold hurried through from the kitchen, holding out a purple device that resembled a small stun gun. 'I've found this, if it's any good?'

'What is it?' asked Sam.

'Basil's thermometer. I just thought, perhaps, it would be useful? It's a rectal thermometer but I've given it a rinse and I think, if you pop it under your arm…'

Stella quickly interrupted. 'Harold, I'm going to stop you there. I'm not putting Basil's bottom thermometer anywhere near me. I don't feel *that* bad.'

Sam laughed, followed by Harold, followed, eventually, by Stella. Hearing this, Basil padded through from the kitchen and barked.

'Shh, behave yourself,' Harold told him before glancing back to Stella. 'You sound better.'

'I feel better. It's so weird, I don't think it can have been the olive.'

Sam shook his head. 'I suspect it was an anxiety attack.'

'Like a panic attack?'

'Essentially. They can come on very suddenly but disappear quickly too. Your heart-rate's back down, your breathing's calmer. If it was an allergic reaction, you'd take longer to show signs of improvement.'

'But why?'

Sam tilted his head. 'Variety of factors usually. You haven't eaten very much today but you've had a lot of caffeine. Have you felt particularly anxious?'

'Not really.'

This wasn't true. Stella had felt anxious all day about this evening, about making sure it was perfect for Fitz.

'It might be subconscious,' he went on, 'which would be entirely understandable. Your best friend's going through cancer treatment, you're looking after her and working at the same time.'

'I don't *feel* stressed, though. I'm not the one who's ill.'

'Sometimes stresses like these can be running under the surface and it just takes a trigger to set them off.' Sam's eyes scanned her face as if searching for a clue. 'I think you need to take it easy. Rest this weekend. Cut back on the coffee if you can. And if it happens again, or you feel your hand shaking, stop whatever you're doing immediately and breathe. Inhale for five, hold it for five, then exhale for five. And keep counting until you can sense it subsiding.'

'Or call you and get you to come over from the pub.'

'Or that,' Sam replied with a smile.

'I'm sorry to ruin your night. I hope you weren't on a hot date?' Stella didn't mean to say it but the words slipped out before she could stop them.

'No, just after-work drinks with a couple of colleagues,' he replied, making her feel even sillier.

'Anyone fancy a tea?' asked Harold, reappearing from the kitchen. 'Or something stronger? I've got some beer in the fridge if you fancy it?'

But before Sam or Stella could answer, there came the high-pitched wail of an alarm.

Harold tutted and stepped towards the window, pushing the curtain back and looking out into the street. 'Must be someone's ca—'

'Oh my god, the onions!' Stella shrieked, pushing herself up. 'I forgot, I left them on upstairs and…' She let herself through Harold's front door and attacked the stairs two at a time, but the smell of burned onions reached her before she got to the top.

CHAPTER 35

INSIDE THE FLAT, THE air was smoky and the contents of the frying pan were unidentifiable; black, charred remains of something that might once have been a vegetable.

Stella groaned as she turned off the hob and dropped the pan in the sink, causing another plume of smoke to shoot towards the ceiling.

She flung back the kitchen window and reached for a tea towel to flap at the wailing smoke alarm, only to see Sam reaching up to reset it.

Lifting her hands to her face, she groaned into them; a panic attack, the suggestion that she use an Alsatian's rectal thermometer, a fire alarm, burned dinner. The evening had been a disaster.

'Stella?' Sam asked.

'I'm fine,' she sighed, dropping her hands. 'It's just that a panic attack followed by a near fire wasn't the Friday I had planned.'

Stella stepped towards the speaker and picked up her phone. She'd presumed, after all the drama, that there would be a message or missed call from Fitz. But still nothing.

'So long as you're all right,' Harold said solemnly. 'I might go back down for that beer. Sam? Unless you're heading back to the pub?'

'I'll take a beer. And Stella,' he added, turning to face her, 'you need to drink some water and eat something.'

'I will, although… actually…' She glanced behind her at the kitchen counter. It looked like a tragic still life: empty wine glass, raw prawns sitting in their damp paper. 'Do you guys fancy dinner? I mean, you don't have to. It's just that I've got the ingredients… and I don't want to waste them.'

Sam frowned. 'Is your friend not coming over?'

'Not sure, but doesn't matter. It's the least I can do to make up for ruining your night.'

'Yeah, why not, then? Harold?'

'I'd like that very much. I've never been up here before,' Harold added, looking around at the living room. 'First let me go and fetch those beers.'

'Great,' replied Stella. 'I'll just, er, get going.' She moved to the kitchen and frowned at the frying pan.

'You know what? You sit, I'll do this,' Sam said, following her. 'Amazing place you have.'

'Apart from the smell of burned vegetable, you mean?'

'Especially with that,' he said, grinning at her as he dropped his jacket on the back of a chair.

'You can cook *and* save children's lives?'

'Mostly it's a ready meal when I get back from hospital, but yes, it has been known. My mum taught me. Said no son of hers was going to grow up without being able to look after himself.'

'I'm impressed,' Stella said, lowering herself to the bench behind the table. 'You close to her?'

'You got another onion?'

'Probably.' She leant forwards to peer in the fruit bowl where an onion was hiding under a banana. 'Here you go.'

Sam caught it and turned back to the chopping board. 'I'm close to her but she's back home so I don't see her that much.'

'Where is home?'

'Whitechapel, but Mum's in Karachi. I don't remember much of it. We moved here when I was three.'

'How come?'

He glanced up. 'My dad was worried about security. And he had family here so, yeah, we moved.'

'And then your mum moved back?'

'Yeah,' he said, slicing the onion, 'when our dad died, a couple of years ago, to be near her sister. But my bro and I stayed here.'

Stella was about to ask how often he saw her when Harold reappeared with a Lidl bag. 'I brought a few bottles. Lie down, Basil.'

Sam slid the onion into a clean pan and crushed a clove of garlic, then filled another saucepan with hot water.

Harold opened the beers while Stella put Billie Holiday back on, then opened WhatsApp.

She started typing beneath her last message to Fitz, sent over an hour ago.

Assume you're not going to make it. Had a panic attack but my neighbour called a doctor so fine now. Call whenever you feel like it.

Her finger hovered over the arrow. If she sent this, it would be a turning point. Until tonight, she'd played it cool, rarely texting Fitz first, always waiting for him to call her, always letting him decide when they saw one another. She'd never complained when he got caught up with work, or said that she wished they could spend more than one or two nights a week together. She was scared to demonstrate that she was more into this relationship than he was, but if she sent this message, she would be doing just that: revealing a more vulnerable part of herself.

Holding her finger down on the delete key, she watched every word vanish and placed her phone back down on the table.

'Has your young man stood you up?' asked Harold.

'Don't know.' Stella glanced at Sam's back as he stood at the hob, dropping the prawns into the pan. 'He works long hours… and travels all the time. And he's got this deal on at the moment in America so he's flying there a lot.' She frowned at her phone and wondered if he'd been suddenly called to Washington.

'I wouldn't worry,' Harold offered. 'Did you know, you're five times more likely to be killed by a falling pigeon than in a plane crash? I read that the other day.'

Sam quickly changed the subject. 'How's your love life going, Harold?'

Harold updated them on Silver Singles. He still hadn't heard back from Meredith but he had liked a further three women. 'And one of them, Hilary, seems very nice. She's keen on origami and she's invited me to her club.'

'An origami club?' Stella asked.

'Yes, in Chiswick. And I've looked it up and I can get there on the number seven bus.'

'Are you sure an origami club isn't code?' said Sam, grinning over his shoulder.

Harold looked confused. 'For what?'

'Never mind. Bowls, Stella?'

'In that cupboard.' Stella pointed at it before remembering her plan. 'Harold, are you free on the fifth of November?'

'I 'spect so. Why?'

'It's my birthday party. Mine and Billie's. Joint. We share the same day so you're invited. And Sam, you should come, if you're free?' she added more shyly. She knew she'd told Billie he absolutely wasn't invited, but now he was here it felt impolite not to.

'If I'm not on duty then I'd love to.'

'What do I have to wear?' Harold asked suspiciously. 'I haven't been to a party for a while.'

'Nothing special. Although maybe a nice shirt? And shoes. And potentially a little haircut beforehand?'

His hands flew to his head. 'What's wrong with my hair?'

'Nothing. It's just nice to get dressed up every now and then, isn't it?'

'How's Billie?' Harold asked, keen to stop discussing his hair.

'So far, not bad. She's gone home to Yorkshire for the weekend. But she didn't seem especially tired. Fingers crossed, I guess. I talked to her, Sam, by the way, about everything, and it helped. So… thanks, again.'

'Very welcome,' he said, reaching for a pair of tongs before draping nests of linguine into each bowl. Carefully, he shared the prawns between them and drizzled the remaining oil over the top.

Stella got up to dim the lights and retrieve the wine bottle.

'You feeling all right?' Sam asked as he placed the bowls down on the table, watching her pour a glass.

'Mmmhmm. And cheers.'

The men clinked their beer bottles against Stella's glass and they picked up their forks.

It was the perfect bowl of pasta, just as Stella had hoped before she bungled it herself. The prawns tasted as if they'd leapt from Sicilian waters earlier that day; each strand of linguine was coated in shiny, briny oil and pale shavings of parmesan.

'I'd pay for this if I was given it in a restaurant,' said Harold.

'Excellent, that'll be twenty quid, please,' Sam replied.

'Cheeky sod. And how about you?'

'What about me?'

'I'm talking romance here, Sam. What's happened with that nice nurse?'

'What nurse?' asked Stella, her fork pausing in the air.

'She's called Maddy,' went on Harold, 'and she works on the ward and she's ever so pretty, so I sai—'

Sam cut him off. 'Just someone at work. But I've been pretty busy lately so I haven't had much time to think about dating.'

'You lot these days,' Harold went on as he speared a prawn. 'When I was a lad, we didn't think about it, we just did it. I met Ellen, we started going out, we got married. There was none of this, oh I'm not sure if she's the right one or, oh there isn't much… what d'you call it?'

'Chemistry?' ventured Stella.

'That's it. Chemistry. You all seem to think that love has to be this great thunderbolt from the sky. But love, real love, isn't like that. It's not all electricity and butterflies, you two.'

Stella glanced at Sam, conscious of having such an intimate conversation in front of him. But she asked the question anyway. 'What is it, then?'

Harold frowned at his pasta before looking up. 'Ellen used to leave me these notes in my lunch, back when I was still working. Not every day, but once or twice a week. Mostly they'd be practical, things like "remember the dentist later" or "pick up milk on the way home", but now and then they'd be more…'

'Romantic?' suggested Stella.

'Exactly. More romantic. They'd say that she loved me or that she was glad she'd married me. They were only little notes but they always made my day. What I'm trying to say is, it's the little things like that. That's what I reckon love is.'

Stella blinked quickly as she felt her eyes well up, and Sam cleared his throat. 'What's your lady friend in Chiswick called again?'

'Hilary?'

'Hilary. When are you seeing Hilary?'

'Wednesday at origami club.'

'You'll have to keep us posted,' added Stella, 'as the situation *unfolds*.' She smiled at Sam, who laughed and shook his head.

Harold's mouth fell open like a trapdoor. 'What's so funny?'

'Unfolds,' explained Sam. 'Origami gag.'

'Oh honestly. It's like having dinner with a pair of children.'

They carried on chatting until the beers were finished, as was the bottle of wine, and Basil made a small whine from underneath the table.

'That's my cue,' said Harold. 'Time for his evening constitutional on his favourite lamppost.'

'He has a favourite?'

'He does indeed,' he told Stella. 'It's the one outside number sixty-three. The woman who lives there shooed him away from her steps once and Basil's never forgotten it. Come on then, boy.'

He stood up and glanced around the kitchen, which was untidy with saucepans, chopping boards, smeary bowls, empty beer bottles and curled pieces of garlic peel that had floated to the floor. 'I don't like to leave all this.'

'It's all right, I'll help,' Sam offered, reaching across the table for the bowls. 'You go and pee on that lamppost.'

Harold chuckled because he was three beers down. 'I don't do that myself, Sam, but thank you. If you're sure?'

'I'm sure, go,' added Stella, 'and thanks for everything.'

'Thank *you* for a very entertaining evening. Right, where are my keys?' Harold picked up his jacket, patted its pocket for the reassuring jangle, and he and Basil made their way out. 'Toodle-pip,' he added as he closed the front door.

Sam and Stella looked at one another and laughed.

'He's the sweetest man.'

'He really is,' Sam replied. 'The kids love him.'

'I can imagine. Sad that he never had any of his own.'

Sam looked thoughtful for a second before replying. 'Maybe. But not everyone has to lead the same kind of life, do they?'

'What d'you mean?'

He shrugged. 'Is a life more valuable if you have kids or don't have kids, or you get married or you don't get married?'

'You don't want kids?'

'Uh-uh. I'm not saying that. I just mean not everyone has to do the same as everyone else. There are nearly eight billion people on this planet. Eight billion! And we can't all work to the same timetable, to the same template. Imagine how boring that would be.'

Stella grinned. 'Calm down, Plato.'

'Fair. Three beers and I roll out something that sounds like a motivational caption on Instagram. All right, come on, let's tidy up. You need an early night.' He stood and carried the stack of bowls to the sink.

She grinned at the sight and shook her head to herself. What a weird evening. But somehow, not a total disaster. True, she'd had a panic attack and nearly burned the flat down, and she'd ended up having dinner with her geriatric neighbour and a former one-night stand she barely knew. And Fitz still hadn't arrived. Or messaged. Or called. But somehow, despite all that, she'd had a good time. Sam was easy to talk to. Good company. She didn't have to pretend to be anything with him or worry about saying the wrong thing. He was relaxing. That was the word. He was *relaxing* to be around.

'I'll wash, you dry,' he said, holding out a tea towel.

'Deal.' Stella stood and reached for it, taking in Sam's green eyes, the stubble lining his jawline and the curve of his lower lip, thinking back to the feel of his hands entwined with hers, of his mouth pressed against her neck—

Her thoughts were interrupted by the door buzzer.

'Hang on, sorry,' Stella said, dropping the tea towel as if it was radioactive, suddenly awkward. It felt as if she was being pulled from one world into another.

She went to the door and spoke into the intercom. 'Hello? Oh it's you. Hi, top one, that's OK, come up.'

CHAPTER 36

THEY HEARD FITZ BEFORE they saw him.

'You didn't tell me you lived in an *attic*,' he boomed, coming up the stairs. 'And no lift. But I'm so sorry, forgive me, I am an unspeakably unworthy human being. My phone battery ran out and— Good heavens, something smells good, and I feel very bad that I…'

He stepped through the door and kissed the top of Stella's head before looking across to the kitchen where Sam was hovering by the sink. 'Hello. I don't know you.'

'This is Sam, he's a doctor.'

Fitz frowned. 'A doctor? I didn't know doctors did house calls these days?'

'We don't as a rule,' Sam countered.

'He came over, very kindly,' Stella quickly interjected, 'because he's a friend of Harold's and I had a panic attack.'

'Who's Harold?'

She clenched and unclenched her jaw. 'He's the neighbour, downstairs. I've mentioned him before.'

'Why on earth did you have a panic attack?'

'We can talk about that later. But I went downstairs to Harold for help, and he called Sam, who came over to check on me. And they stayed for dinner because I didn't want all this to go to waste.'

Fitz made a guilty face. 'I'm very sorry I wasn't here. I got stuck with work and lost track of time, but look I've brought some excellent wine so let's have a drink.' He swung an overnight bag from his shoulder and pulled out two bottles.

'I'm going to g—' started Sam from the sink.

'I don't need wine, Fitz, but you could have called.' Stella didn't want to make a scene or be difficult. Her mother had always warned her not to be difficult but Fitz was over three hours late and he hadn't even bothered to ring. 'I couldn't get hold of you, so I called the hotel, and then I thought about calling your office, or trying to get hold of Carol…'

Fitz frowned. 'Carol?'

'Your secretary?'

'Right.'

'I assumed she'd know where you were, but then I realised I didn't even have a number for your office and it was so late by then tha—'

'Stella, I'm so sorry,' said Fitz, making the same guilty face, pulling his mouth wide in a grimace. 'I was dealing with the Americans all evening, and like I said, I lost track of time, and my phone ran out of juice so I couldn't get hold of you, so I thought it was better to simply head over.'

'I'm gonna head off,' Sam tried again.

'There's no food left,' Stella told Fitz.

'That's quite all right. I'll be very happy with a glass of this. It's been a monstrous day.'

'I'm sorry,' Stella said, feeling a small shard of guilt. She didn't want to make his day worse. 'Look, here, I'll get a glass.' She gestured towards the kitchen and reached for one of the bottles.

'I'll leave you to it,' Sam attempted for the third time.

'You don't have to,' Stella protested, although quite weakly because this was an awkward situation. In the doorway of the kitchen was Fitz, in a long navy overcoat, shirt loosened around his neck, hair tousled. And although part of Stella was cross that he'd been so late and, actually, not even that apologetic, another part of her felt relief to see him finally here, standing in her flat. As soon as she'd seen him, despite her annoyance, she'd felt the familiar pull, a longing to touch him.

But on the other side was Sam, still beside the sink, holding the washing-up brush. And he'd only come over this evening because of her, and she'd had a nice time with him, and then there'd been that moment with the tea towel that, well, Stella found quite confusing, to be honest. Why was she thinking erotic thoughts about Sam as he'd passed her a tea towel? Was that normal?

But now Sam clearly felt like he was intruding.

'I should get back, I'm on shift tomorrow,' Sam said, drying his hands on the towel. 'Thank you for dinner, and have an early night,' he replied with a sympathetic smile, before glancing towards Fitz, 'Stella's had a stressful day too.'

'My poor darling,' Fitz said, stepping up behind her and sliding one arm around her waist.

'Thank you for rescuing me, and for cooking. Hang on, I'll show you out.'

'No need, all good, don't worry. See you soon, I guess. And early night, right?'

Stella nodded. 'Yep, and thank you again.'

Sam picked up his jacket, waved a hand and walked back through the sitting room, closing the door behind him.

Stella sighed, emotionally drained.

'Just us,' said Fitz, relaxing his arm and spinning Stella around to face him. 'Tell me, what's this panic attack?'

'I'm just tired, and stressed about Billie because it was her first chemo session today. And I was worried because I hadn't heard from you and I didn't know how to fi—'

Fitz silenced her with a kiss. 'I'm sorry, I should have called to tell you. But you never need to worry about me. It's one benefit of fighting through wars. There's always been worse. More importantly, how is Billie?'

'OK, I think. Said I'd ring her tomorrow.'

'Good,' he replied briskly. 'Now, so far, all I've seen in this flat is the kitchen and, very briefly, the sitting room. But what I want to know is, where's your bedroom?'

'I thought you wanted a drink?'

'I did, but now I've decided I want to take you to bed to make up for being so abominably late.'

Stella was torn. Taking her to bed straight away felt too easy, as if Fitz thought he could smooth the evening over with sex. It wasn't a *wholly* unfair suggestion because he really was very good at it.

But if she said no, she was making a point about being peeved by his lateness, not having sex, and that definitely felt like the less good alternative.

'I'll show you,' Stella told him, taking his hand and telling herself to get over it. He'd apologised, it was one time, no big deal.

Except later, while Fitz slept, she still couldn't shake the feeling that she'd diminished herself. It was a familiar feeling to Stella – she'd felt it countless times in the previous few months, lying in strange beds next to strange men. But she'd never before felt it with him. In fact, up until this evening, she'd felt lifted by him, as if some of his innate confidence was rubbing off on her. But now she felt smaller, less secure, more like she had before she met him: anxious not only about their relationship but about everything else – her job, her family, what she was going to do with her life and whether she'd die alone, a grey-haired old spinster who went to the hairdresser once a week because that was the only time anybody touched her.

Then she remembered Sam's instructions about an early night, rolled over, and eventually her breathing slowed and she fell asleep.

CHAPTER 37

EXCEPT AFTER THAT EVENING, and for the next few days, Stella felt unsettled by Fitz.

She couldn't put her finger on it but it was as if their relationship had shifted. If you could even call it a relationship, she thought, sitting at her desk, blinking at her phone. The morning after the prawn disaster, she'd hoped they might lie in, get up slowly, go for a walk and buy croissants together like other couples on Saturday mornings. Instead, Fitz had woken up very early and said he had to leave because he had a work meeting in Marylebone.

'On a Saturday?' Stella had asked, trying not to sound petulant.

He'd grimaced and apologised and said it was the nature of his job, and kissed her on the head before slipping away again. And since then, nothing.

All she needed was one message. Just the sight of his name appearing on her screen and her mood would lighten. Had it been too early? Did she ruin the sexy hotel fantasy by letting him see too much of her life? Had he looked inside her bathroom cabinet and seen her packet of Rennie?

Negative thoughts swirled around Stella's head like storm clouds. She longed for love but the process felt more complicated than she'd imagined. In the best moments, like when Fitz had sent the oysters or messaged saying he missed her, Stella felt as if she could fight a tiger in a boxing ring, wearing a blindfold, with one arm behind her back. But at more insecure moments like today, falling in love felt like going temporarily insane.

She glanced towards Marjorie's office. Maybe she was right: it was better to avoid men altogether.

As if telepathic, the door flung back and her boss appeared, flustered. 'Stella, are you doing anything tonight?'

'I'm supposed to be in with Bill—'

'Because I need you to go to the Red Carnation Hotel tonight to meet Mr Ferrari as a honeytrap. My model agency's let me down. Jacinta's sick, so they tell me, and they can't provide another model at such short notice. But you'd do just as well.'

'A *honeytrap*? What do you mean?'

Marjorie sighed. 'Occasionally, I use models as honeytraps. That is, I send a beautiful woman, or man, for that matter, to see how a target responds to them. To see if they can be… persuaded.'

'You set them up?'

'Precisely, I set them up.'

'And you want me to set up Mr Ferrari?'

'I wouldn't ask if I didn't have to. But I know he's going to be at this hotel tonight.'

'How do you know?'

'Because I've been tailing him for a week. And he goes there, after work, at around seven every evening.'

'And does what?'

Marjorie waggled a finger at Stella. 'Aha. That's where you come in.'

'You want me to go to this hotel.'

'The Red Carnation, yes.'

'The Red Carnation, and talk to Mr Ferrari about what exactly?'

She lifted a shoulder with deliberate nonchalance. 'Just… flirt with him. Suss him out. See if he's… amenable.'

'Amenable to what?' asked Stella, narrowing her eyes.

'To sleeping with you, obviously. But don't actually sleep with him.'

'Marjorie, is this even legal?'

'Yes yes yes. Stop fussing. It's all perfectly above board. But you'll need to record it, so I'll give you the pen.'

'But I don't look like a honeytrap.' Stella gestured at herself. That morning, she'd pulled on a white T-shirt and a pair of black cigarette trousers, along with her heeled ankle boots. 'I look like a waiter.'

'Nonsense. You're a ravishing young woman who could pull off anything if you just put your mind to it. Take something from the fancy-dress box, although most of it will be far too big for you. And you might do something about your hair. Give it a brush.'

Rich coming from you, Stella thought, raising a hand to her hair defensively. Then her phone lit up with a message. *Do you fancy the new series of I Found The Gown tonight? I'm a bit tired so leaving office now xxxx*

'Stella?' snapped Marjorie, 'Do you think you can manage it?'

Stella slid her thumbnail between her teeth. It was Billie's second week of treatment, so she wanted to be there for her, but she'd have to text and explain that Marjorie needed her for an important job that involved flirting with a strange Italian man. She felt guilty about this but she could hardly say no to one evening of overtime, given that she was taking various mornings off to accompany Billie to hospital.

She bent over and checked that Harold's alarm was still in her bag. 'OK,' she said reluctantly, 'although I'm not sure I'll pull it off.' She'd make it up to Billie by sending a grovelling voice note saying they could watch *I Found The Gown* the following night, and that she'd buy them a takeaway. Safer that than attempting to cook again.

'Don't be defeatist,' Marjorie replied, standing over her desk, nostrils flaring like a general who'd just ordered his troops into battle. 'I have every faith. Now, have you got a pen? Write this down. I'm going to give you very specific instructions.'

CHAPTER 38

A FEW HOURS LATER, just before seven that evening, Stella duly arrived at The Red Carnation. It was on a narrow Mayfair side street, had dirty windows and a red awning that hung over the main entrance like a tattered battle flag. It didn't look like the sort of hotel to take anyone you wanted to impress.

The lobby was empty and smelled of stale cigarettes. She could hear the tinkling of a piano, so followed the sound until she reached a dark bar where a pianist was playing to a very small handful of punters. The barman – greasy, thinning hair combed over his scalp, multiple chins, waistcoat buttons bursting – brightened as she approached. 'All right, darlin', what do you fancy?'

'Um…' Stella wondered whether she should stick to water but feared it would make her less convincing as a honeytrap. And she could do with calming her nerves. 'Vodka and tonic, please.'

'I'll make it a double.'

'No thank you.'

It was too late; the barman was already at the upturned vodka bottle.

He winked and slid the glass across the bar. Stella ignored the wink, took it and turned back to the tables.

The pianist, in a white jacket and red sequin bow tie, launched into a terrible rendition of 'All By Myself', which only made the place more depressing. Stella wasn't sure why anyone would want to come and hang out here every night. Unless you were trying to hide something. Or some*one*.

Squinting at the back of one head, Stella decided it looked most like Mr Ferrari's. She could tell by the ears, having looked at a photo on his company website: he was a balding man with rectangular spectacles hooked over ears like mug handles. He didn't look much like a lothario, Stella had remarked to Marjorie, who replied that they never did.

She left the bar and sat at the table beside him before reaching into her bag and fumbling for the recording pen. Marjorie had taught her how to position it correctly, making Stella practise over and over again that afternoon. She could put the pen on the table in front of her, but according to Marjorie that would be too obvious in a bar. Instead, Stella had to hook the pen lid over the side of her bag, twisting the top so the recording began.

That done, she reached into her pocket for a lone pearl earring, plucked from Marjorie's fancy-dress, before sitting back and flicking her wrist as if throwing a frisbee.

The earring bounced across the carpet like a marble and came to a stop in front of Mr Ferrari's table.

Stella held her breath for a few moments, waiting for him to move. But Mr Ferrari hadn't noticed the earring. His head remained determinedly staring at the pianist, who was working his way through another chorus of 'All By Myself'.

She silently cursed the piano bar's gloom and had a slug of her drink. The earring had landed on the carpet just three feet in front of Mr Ferrari's table and yet he remained oblivious.

'Excuse me,' she said, in a loud whisper, leaning towards him. 'Would you mind picking up my earring?'

Mr Ferrari slowly turned. His thin face looked very sad in real life, and he had the sad eyes of a bloodhound. 'Your earring?'

'Yes, I'm so sorry, I dropped it,' whispered Stella, pointing towards the carpet.

Mr Ferrari leant forward and stretched to pick it up.

'Thank you, I'm very grateful,' she said huskily, attempting to dazzle him with her widest smile, before flicking her hair off one shoulder. She was hoping Mr Ferrari would watch but he'd already turned back to the pianist.

'Fancy another, Calvin?' the barman asked.

Mr Ferrari glanced at his tumbler as if astonished to find it empty and nodded.

The pianist started playing the chords of 'Somewhere Over the Rainbow' very slowly with his eyes closed, and Stella's heart sank further. This place was more depressing than a funeral parlour.

'Do you come here often?' she whispered towards Mr Ferrari's table.

He turned to look at her again. 'Every night,' he said forlornly.

'Oh,' replied Stella, who hadn't expected him to admit as much this early. 'How come? For the cheerful ambience?'

But Mr Ferrari didn't even smile. 'Because I can be by myself here.'

That seemed surprising too, Stella thought. But if he was

having an affair, he was hardly going to admit to it immediately. She simply had to probe. '*Completely* by yourself?'

Mr Ferrari nodded.

'But why?'

'Don't we all need that sometimes?'

Stella pressed her lips together. She felt like a police interrogator, faced with a tricky suspect who was giving away nothing. 'So you're always entirely by yourself here?'

The barman returned with another tumbler of whisky and a large ice cube.

'*Grazie*, Thomas.'

'No problem, guv. You still all good, sweetheart?'

She wished the large barman would stop interrupting when she was on such important business. 'Perfectly,' she snapped.

Mr Ferrari rotated his glass on the table. 'I am always alone here, but I'm afraid I am also married, so if you are looking for company then you will have to try elsewhere.'

'Oh no no! I'm not looking for that. I'm just…' Stella sighed and reached for her vodka. She was failing her mission, not even capable of standing in for a dumb model.

'Why are you here, may I ask?' Mr Ferrari went on. 'What is someone as beautiful and young as you doing in a bar like this on a Tuesday evening?'

'Er, like you, just needed time by myself,' she fibbed.

'At your age? You should be out breaking hearts at your age. You should be in love.' Mr Ferrari's bloodhound eyes turned wistful.

Stella thought quickly. She could continue being a honeytrap, albeit a bad one, and see if she could squeeze any more information from Mr Ferrari. Or she could be herself and see if that got her any further. She had an instinct about him. He wasn't lying, she would swear on it.

'How do you know if you're in love?' she asked him, deciding to be herself. 'Because sometimes I think I am but, other times, I'm not so sure. It's confusing.'

'Ah yes, sometimes it can be confusing. But it is good to be in love.'

Mr Ferrari said this so sadly Stella decided to press him. 'Are you not in love with your wife, then?'

'I am. I love her more than life itself but…'

'There's someone else?' she asked hopefully.

'No! No, there is no one else.' He looked shocked at the suggestion and took a large mouthful of whisky to recover. 'Although, in actual fact, that is not true. There *was* someone else.'

Bingo, thought Stella, glancing down to look at her bag to check the pen was still in place. See? She didn't need to be a honeytrap to do this job; she could winkle out secrets simply by being herself.

'We had a daughter, Isabella and I. But she died. So now I come here to think about her.'

Stella's pride evaporated like steam and she felt her throat tighten. 'I'm so sorry,' she whispered.

Mr Ferrari spun his glass on the table again. 'Thank you.'

'How old was she, if you don't mind talking about her?'

He looked up and smiled, but smiling looked like an effort, as if his muscles had forgotten how to do it. 'No, no, it is nice, because my wife, she cannot talk about her. Our only child and she can't even say her name.'

'What was it?'

'Luisa. She was twenty-seven, and a beautiful young woman.'

'What was she like? You don't have to tell me. But if you *do* want to talk about her, then…'

'She was entirely good, and sweet. And she loved dancing because she was musical. Very musical.'

'Better than this guy?' Stella stuck her thumb towards the pianist and Mr Ferrari laughed softly.

'Yes, better than him. But he is not so bad some days. And she had it all ahead of her.' He turned to squint at Stella. 'Who is this man who maybe has your heart? Is he good?'

'I think so.' Then her face fell. 'But I'm not sure he likes me as much. That's the problem.'

'Pffff! I am sure that cannot be true.'

Stella shrugged.

'How long have you been with him?'

She wrinkled her nose. 'I'm not sure I can say that I'm with him exactly, but we've been sort of seeing one another for a few weeks.'

Mr Ferrari turned his palms in the air. 'A few weeks is not nothing. Why do you not talk to him?'

'About love?'

Mr Ferrari shrugged. 'It doesn't have to be about love. But about your emotions, about this confusion.'

Stella thought she might be sick. 'About how I *feel*?'

'Yes! Is that so bad? Why are you English always so scared of telling somebody what you are thinking, like it is some sort of crime?'

'It's not that it's a crime, it's just…' She paused and inhaled.

'I like him very much, and I think I could love him, but I don't know how he feels and it's making me doubt everything.'

'OK,' Mr Ferrari went on, calmly laying his palms on the table. 'The next time you see this man, this…?'

'He's called Fitz.'

'The next time you see this Mr Fitz you have to talk to him. Not about the weather or all these things that you English people like talking about. But about how you feel here.' Mr Ferrari pressed one hand to his chest before continuing. 'Someone as beautiful as you, Miss…?'

'Stella.'

'Someone as beautiful as you, Miss Stella. I think he will want to know. And you cannot waste time, you know. It can all go, very quickly. You think you have for ever with someone like my Luisa and then, one day, you don't.'

Stella thought of Billie and swallowing suddenly became harder. 'Have you told your wife you love her?' she asked quietly, scared of talking any louder in case her voice wobbled.

Mr Ferrari's face drooped. 'No. No, not for some time.'

'You see, I think *she'd* like to know.'

'You do?' He looked surprised.

'Look, I'll cut you a deal. If you go home tonight and tell your wife you love her, I'll talk to Fitz about how I feel when I next see him.'

Mr Ferrari smiled. 'You are good, I think, like my Luisa.'

Stella felt another stab of guilt about the pen recording in her bag. She would delete this entire conversation when she got home. 'Not always.'

'No person can always be good. But you have a good heart, I can tell. And OK, Miss Stella, you have a deal.'

She stuck her hand out and they shook as the barman loped towards them. 'Another round?'

Stella noticed his eyes trying to peer down her shirt.

'Not tonight, Thomas, thank you. We have business to be doing. Just the bill. Both bills, please.'

'No, please don't,' protested Stella, 'I can pay for mine.'

Mr Ferrari shook his head and pulled a card from his wallet. 'Definitely not. It was a pleasure to meet you. And thank you.'

'For what?'

'For reminding me of her. Of Luisa.'

Stella smiled sadly back, moved by how obviously he'd loved and still loved her. She didn't know that sort of fatherly love, she thought, as she stood from the table, but she was going to find another version of it. If the journey there was confusing, it would be worth it in the end.

CHAPTER 39

'LET ME GET THIS straight, Mr Ferrari is not having an affair?' Marjorie asked from behind her desk the following morning.

'He is not.'

'He goes to that ghastly hotel to think about his daughter?'

'Yes.'

Marjorie sighed. 'I'm not sure what's more depressing: an affair or a dead daughter.'

Stella wondered whether it was Marjorie's lack of sensitivity that put off men from approaching her. Either that or the extravagant wigs. Today, she was wearing a wig of tumbling blonde curls that made her look like an ageing mermaid.

'But hopefully he went home and told his wife that he loved her, and all will be fine.'

Marjorie frowned. 'How do you know he did that?'

'Call it intuition, and he seemed like a nice guy.'

Marjorie tutted. 'Young Stella, I keep warning you. How can you tell a man is lying?'

'Dunno.'

'His lips are moving.'

Stella rolled her eyes. 'You and your cynicism.'

'Thirty years in this business, I'm telling you. Now, can you type up an invoice for Mrs Ferrari? I'm off to Knightsbridge for Lord and Lady Cavendish.'

This was a new case they'd taken on the previous week: Lady Cavendish was a sixty-something aristocrat who lived in a large Leicestershire pile with her husband, Lord Cavendish, and they believed their eldest son Mungo was dating someone unsuitable.

Lady Cavendish had called Marjorie and subsequently commissioned her to follow Mungo's girlfriend, a Swedish model called Astrid, to dig up whatever dirt she could find. From the sound of the Cavendish family, Stella believed Astrid should avoid marrying Mungo at all costs.

'No problem,' Stella replied before returning to her desk and seeing both a missed call from Fitz and a message from Sam on her phone: *Just checking in. How's the patient (Billie) and how is the pyromaniac (you)?*

She smiled and quickly tapped a reply. *Both good, thank you. If medicine doesn't work out, you should consider a career getting heckled as a stand-up.*

She was glad he'd messaged. She'd felt awkward about how the night ended. But now Sam's message cleared the air. And it was kind of him to check in. He *was* kind. A decent, kind man who she'd misunderstood at the start when she woke up in his bed and... Well, never mind. Stella shook her head. She didn't need to go into all that again. Now they could be good pals.

She hit the green button to listen to Fitz's voicemail. Because she hadn't heard from him since the weekend either, she suspected he was going to tell her they needed 'to talk'. She couldn't pinpoint exactly what had happened between her and Fitz, but four days of silence meant something was up.

She held her breath as she waited for the message to begin.

'Hello, Miss Shakespeare. On the off-chance that you're around tonight, I've got a table at Café Cornelia at seven. Let me know if you can't make it. It's been a nightmarish week but the thought of seeing you cheers me immensely.'

Stella glanced at Marjorie's office door before calling him back but it went to voicemail.

She hung up and rolled her lower lip through her teeth. Fitz sounded normal, nothing to worry about. Her irritation at the fact he'd been so quiet for four days vanished under the weight of her relief. And Café Cornelia! It was the newest, hottest restaurant in east London, recently reviewed by the *Sunday Times* whose critic had said he'd 'sell his own mother' for the chance to go back. The waiting list was said to be almost six months long and, when you finally did get in, apparently it was like eating at the Oscars because every other table was occupied by celebrities.

The only problem was that she'd promised Billie she'd be in to watch *I Found The Gown* and order a takeaway to make up for working last night, but the thought of turning Fitz down was *impossible*. He'd been so silent, and she'd worried that she'd done something wrong, but now he'd popped up again, and if Stella said no to tonight, she didn't know when she'd see him after that. It could be a week, and a week felt so long it might as well be a year. Plus, Fitz getting in touch now, the morning after her conversation with Mr Ferrari, felt like a sign. She'd said she'd talk to him about how she felt and now she could.

She knew that Billie would understand because this happened with friendships every now and then when you start seeing someone. Plus, Stella was taking Billie to hospital the following morning for her radio session. She might even appreciate an evening without her, Stella told herself.

She picked up her phone and recorded a voice note for Billie.

'Hey, babe, would you mind if I saw Fitz tonight? He's said he's around, and I quite want to see him because, well, I've been feeling a bit weird about him this week and also I want to talk to him about how I… Actually, long story, never mind, I'll tell you tomorrow. I feel bad flaking again but can I make it up to you tomorrow? I'll see you in the morning anyway. I'm guessing it's nine a.m. as usual? Love you.'

She recorded another for Fitz. 'Hello, old person who leaves voicemails instead of voice notes. I can do tonight, as it happens. And I can't believe you've got a table there. That's amazing, so I'll see you there at seven.'

She put her phone down as Marjorie's door opened.

'I'm off to chase this Swede,' she said with a toss of her wig. 'I should be back in time but if not here's a set of keys.'

'For me?' Stella said, as a keyring with several keys on it flew through the air and landed on her desk, narrowly missing her nose.

'No, for your invisible friend. *Yes* for you. If I'm not back in time, are you capable of locking up?'

Stella nodded. 'Yep, course, all under control. Oh, but is there a burglar alarm?'

'It hasn't worked for five years but by all means have a go,' Marjorie told her as she moved towards the door and waved over her shoulder.

Stella dropped the keys into her handbag so she didn't immediately lose them. Then her eyes slid back to her phone, watching it all over again for a reply from Fitz, but the only thing that rang that afternoon was her desk phone.

Usually clients got in touch via the online enquiry form, having been recommended Marjorie's services by a former client (a discreet word-of-mouth system operated when it came to this sort of work). But occasionally, if they were really desperate, they rang instead.

'Hello, Verity Culpepper, how can I help?' Stella said, cradling the phone against her shoulder.

'Hello, is that Verity?' asked an anxious male voice.

'No, it's Stella, her assistant.'

'Oh, I… I… I was hoping to speak to Verity, if she's around?'

'She's out for the afternoon. Can I take a message?'

An exasperated yowl came down the phone, the sort of noise a cat made if you stepped on its tail. 'I think she's having an affair,' the man went on helplessly, 'and I don't know what to do.'

'Umm…' Stella began, wishing that Marjorie was here. She'd normally put a call like this through to her office. But perhaps she could handle this one? She'd handled Mr Ferrari, after all.

'I might be able to help,' Stella ventured, trying to sound more confident. 'Can I start by taking a few details down?'

The man hesitated. 'What do you need to know? I've never done this sort of thing before.'

'Why don't we start with your name?'

'It's Gerald. Gerald Bartholomew.'

'OK, Mr Bartholomew,' Stella said, repeating it back while she wrote it down. 'And your wife's name?'

'Perdita.'

'And how long have you been married?'

'Nearly sixteen years.'

'Nearly sixteen years! I can't imagine being with anyone for near— Well, never mind,' Stella said quickly, realising she was getting off the point. 'And can I ask why you suspect she might be having an affair?'

'It's…' Gerald paused and sighed.

'I'm only taking notes. You can tell me as much or as little as you like.'

'Thank you, you're ever so kind. It's awfully strange doing something like this.'

'I know.'

'The thing is, I would never have believed Perdy was capable of such a thing. But she's been acting so out of character recently that I don't know what to think any more. She travels a lot, you see, for her job. She's an architect.'

'Right.'

'But she's been away more than usual recently.'

'I see,' mumbled Stella, trying to listen and write simultaneously, 'and you suspect something because?'

'It's a slightly delicate matter.'

'Of course.'

'But when she emerged from the bathroom last week, I saw that she didn't have any, you know, down there.'

Stella's pen paused on the page. 'Do you mean, er, hair? Like… pubic hair?' She grimaced at the office ceiling.

'Exactly,' said Gerald with relief. 'That's exactly what I mean. And I wouldn't have worried so much. Actually, I found it quite exciting at first…'

'Rrrrright,' Stella said slowly, hoping that he wasn't going to elaborate.

'But then I found a hotel receipt in her bag.'

'A receipt?'

'For a dinner and a night in London when she told me she was going to a conference in Bristol.'

'OK, which hotel?'

'We don't live in London, you see.'

'Mmm, OK.'

'We used to live in London. In Fulham, if you know it? Well, more Putney really, but Perdy always used to insist we call it Fulham.'

'Which hotel?' she tried again.

'It's called Rakes.'

Her fingers tightened around the phone. 'Rakes? In South Kensington?'

'Yes, I think so. I have it here… hang on… yes, it's on a road called Roland Gardens.'

'Can I just ask how old your wife is?'

'She's forty-three.'

'And you said she's an architect – does she practise under your married name?' Stella checked, pressing her phone to her shoulder and typing 'perdita bartholomew architect' into Google. Rakes. The coincidence made her uneasy, as if she could have passed his wife in the reception or lift without even knowing it.

'Yes.'

Stella clicked on Google images and saw a severe-looking woman with Snow White skin and a sharp black bob.

'Have you asked your wife about any of this?'

'No, I haven't. We have two children, you see, and I want to make sure before I say anything.'

'OK, what I'll do is pass this on to my boss when she's back and she'll be in touch. Can I just take your number?'

Gerald read his number out twice and they said goodbye.

Stella spent the rest of the afternoon researching Perdita Bartholomew, reading her LinkedIn and Facebook profiles, and scrolling through the various property projects she'd worked on. She became so consumed by web pages about Perdita Bartholomew, in fact, that she didn't even notice that Billie hadn't replied to her voice note.

CHAPTER 40

'WHAT'S THE OCCASION?' STELLA asked.

She was sitting in Café Cornelia, opposite Fitz, who'd just ordered a bottle of Ruinart Blanc de Blanc Champagne, which, Stella knew from her father's opinions on the subject, was deemed to be the most delicious of all Champagnes.

The restaurant was packed and waiters were hurrying back and forth from the kitchen with the urgency of A&E nurses, hardly able to keep up with demand. It was also deafening, with a background soundtrack of popping corks and the noisy, excited hubbub of many people rammed into a relatively small, industrial space with concrete walls and floor. Instead of water glasses, each table was laid with jam jars, and to save paper waste there were no menus so Stella and Fitz had been instructed to take a photo of the blackboard menu leaning on the reception desk when they arrived.

'The occasion is seeing you,' Fitz boomed back, 'but also because the deal is inching closer to being finalised.'

'Congratulations!' she said even louder.

Fitz pulled his chair in closer and leant across the table. 'Listen, I know I've been rubbish this week,' he said, extending his hand towards Stella, avoiding the jam jars. 'And I'm sorry…' He stopped and ran his spare hand through his hair. 'I'm going to do better.'

She smiled and opened her mouth to reply but couldn't find the words.

'What is it?' Fitz replied, his blue eyes narrowing with concern.

Stella pinched her lips together, nervous. She'd locked up the office, double-checked the door was locked, and mentally practised how to begin this conversation the whole way there.

'Fitz, can I have a word about something?'

It was the sort of thing one colleague said to another.

'Look, Fitz, I need to get something off my chest.'

Too aggressive.

'Fitz, what's going on with us?'

No. This wasn't an American high-school film.

She'd then turned the wrong way when she came out of the station and got lost, but once she finally reached the restaurant and pushed her way to the table, she'd decided she'd simply wait for the right moment over dinner and discuss it then.

'What? Tell me, otherwise there may be consequences later.' Fitz let go of Stella's hand and dropped his under the table, running it over her thigh.

'Are we just about sex?' she blurted just as the waitress reappeared at their table with the bottle of Champagne and two glasses.

Stella's cheeks instantly turned hot and she stared at her lap, musing that she should have waited until later when it was just them.

Nervously, she raised her head to gauge Fitz's reaction.

'Superb, thank you so much.' Having tasted the Champagne,

he smacked his lips together and smiled at the waitress. He wasn't even looking at Stella.

As her glass was poured, she noticed the waitress had the word HOPE tattooed across her knuckles. 'What's it say on your other hand?' Stella asked to alleviate her discomfort.

The waitress put down the bottle and held her fists together; LESS was inked across her left knuckles. She grinned, topped up Fitz's glass and left them.

'You hungry?' he asked. 'Let's order because the kitchen looks frantic.'

Was she *hungry*? She'd just asked a serious question about their relationship and he was wondering if she was hungry?

'Er, sure,' Stella murmured while trying to process what else to say.

They picked up their phones and studied the menu they'd both photographed. Pickled fennel, roasted cauliflower, Cornish trout with hispi cabbage. The words swam meaninglessly before her eyes. Stella felt stupid. Whatever this was with Fitz had started to feel like a pantomime relationship. Not even a relationship. More like a *situationship*: a floating, undefinable thing that made her feel anxious, desperate to cling on to him but constantly nervous about saying or doing the wrong thing. What had been exciting and thrilling at the start suddenly felt wobbly, as if it could snap at any moment. Stella held her breath and stared down at her plate as she felt her eyes sting.

One tear fell into her lap, followed by another.

'Stella?' Fitz stretched his hand towards her again as she wiped her cheeks and looked up. 'Whoa. What's the matter?'

'Nothing, I'm being an idiot.'

'You hate the Champagne?' he joked, squeezing her fingers.

She shook her head, unable to laugh. 'It's just…'

'I know what it is,' Fitz interrupted, his voice softening. 'It's not just about sex, and I'm sorry if I've given you that impression.'

Stella wiped her cheek and frowned across the table.

'It's just that admitting to anything else, admitting that I might feel more, well, it doesn't come easy to me. It never has.'

'It's OK.'

'It's not OK. I don't want to upset you when…' Fitz pulled his hand back and shifted in his seat. 'Stella, listen, you mean the world to me. I haven't felt like this about someone for a long time. For years, if I'm honest. And I didn't think I would again…' He stopped and frowned briefly. 'Do you remember our first dinner?'

'At Flemings?'

'Exactly, when I said that I could be restless? That I couldn't sit still?'

Stella remembered every line of that conversation. 'You said it was a warning?'

Fitz nodded. 'I did. But if it helps… being with you is the least restless I've felt for some time.'

She couldn't help but laugh.

'What's so funny?'

'That's like the wooden spoon prize! Saying at least I don't make you feel restless.'

Fitz grinned. 'I didn't mean it like that. You make me feel much, *much* more than restless.'

'You're confusing,' Stella said, slowly shaking her head from side to side.

'But worth it, right?'

She gave him a small smile.

'I just need some time but I do promise it's not just about sex.' Fitz leant forward again and lowered his voice. 'Although I spend a disproportionate amount of my life thinking about sex with you at the moment.' He leant back and placed his palms flat on the table. 'Once this deal is over, life will be calmer. Let's go away. Let's go to Paris. I would very much like to spend more time with you, proper time, instead of late-night glimpses in hotels.'

'I'd like that too,' Stella said quietly.

'Then we will, I promise. You've been immensely patient and I'm sorry, again, to have upset that. That's the very last thing I want.'

She made the same, small smile as Fitz reached for her hand. It felt like the passing of a storm: they'd been in choppy waters but now the sea had calmed and the sun was coming out.

It was only after the roasted cauliflower, the squid, the Cornish trout, the ribeye with smoked anchovy butter *and* a plate of five different cheeses that Fitz asked about Stella's day and she remembered the phone call from Gerald Bartholomew. She explained the details to Fitz and reached for her phone to show her a photo of Perdita. 'You haven't seen her around the hotel, have you? I want to prove to Marjorie that I can do more.'

He took her mobile and frowned at the screen. 'I don't think so. But you need to be careful of these dodgy men who seduce women in hotel rooms.' He grinned and passed the phone back. 'Can't trust any of us.'

CHAPTER 41

STELLA MEANT TO SET her phone alarm. But when she and Fitz got back to the hotel after dinner, they had the sort of sex that would give her flashbacks on the Tube: limbs sliding over one another, his eyes millimetres from hers as he moved inside her, his hands cupping, holding and squeezing every part of her body.

And afterwards, his arm wrapped around her, they'd played one of those fantasy games that couples sometimes do before real life gets in the way, discussing where they wanted to live together when they grew old.

In the hills of Provence, Stella suggested; a small village where old women walked to the boulangerie with their string bags every morning. Fitz said that France was home for him already and he wanted somewhere more exotic.

A beach shack in Mozambique, he'd countered, where they could live off barbecued fish and lie in bed listening to the sea every night. Stella said they'd get bored.

A skyscraper apartment in Tokyo; a Swiss chalet for the winter; a pretty dacha in a Russian forest? Fitz and Stella murmured increasingly extravagant options at one another until their words slowed and they fell asleep.

The upside was that she felt happy again, her confidence in Fitz restored by his hints of a future.

The bad news was that she forgot to set her alarm and didn't wake until just after ten the next morning, by which point Fitz had already left for a meeting.

'Fuck,' she said, seeing five missed calls from Billie.

'Fuck,' she said again, seeing the time.

'Fuck,' she repeated, getting out of bed and looking for her pants. Why was it always pants that were lost? What did they do overnight? Did they grow legs and move?

Pants discovered at the end of the bed, she attempted to pull them on as she pressed Billie's name on her recent call list. If the curtains hadn't been drawn, it would have made a comic display for the office across the street: Stella, hopping on one leg, attempting to hook a pair of pink knickers over her left foot while clutching her mobile to her right ear.

Billie didn't pick up.

'Fuck!' Stella shouted before throwing her phone on the bed and pulling on the rest of her clothes.

She swore again when she saw her face in the bathroom, and a further time when she attempted to layer more mascara over yesterday's mascara and stabbed herself in the right eye.

'Fuck, fuck, fuck,' she said as she grabbed her earrings from the bedside table, slung her handbag over her shoulder and headed for the door.

As she did, Stella noticed that Fitz's overnight bag was still lying on the floor. He hadn't mentioned staying another night but she presumed he must be, or coming back after his meeting to check out.

Quickly, she leant over the desk and reached for the hotel notepad to scribble a note.

Miss you already, Fitz Montague PS You have a sensational bottom, she scribbled, adding a kiss, and folding the piece of paper into quarters before crouching to tuck the note into the bag's side pocket.

Just before she pushed herself up, a luggage label on the handle caught her eye. It was for a place called Sugar Beach, which sounded familiar. But St Lucia? She thought Fitz had been in Washington. Presumably it was old? Stella stuck her lower lip out while thinking before reminding herself that she needed to get hold of Billie, and into the office. She smiled at the thought of him finding it, smiled at the sense that this at *last* felt like a relationship where she didn't have to worry about saying the wrong thing and could leave silly little notes like this for him as a surprise, then hurried into the rest of the day.

CHAPTER 42

STELLA KNEW THERE WAS no point in going to the hospital. Billie would have been finished before she was even awake. She called a further four times on her way into the office but Billie didn't pick up.

'Sorry, was at hospital,' she fibbed, passing Marjorie's door when she arrived.

She called Billie again while the kettle boiled and once more from her desk, but still no answer, so she resorted to a garbled, hushed voice note from behind her computer screen.

'Morning, I'm so so sorry. So so so so sorry. I hope you're OK. I've come into the office and am feeling super guilty. I will be back as soon as I can escape here tonight and I'll get dinner. I'm sorry, forgive me for being the worst friend ever. Fitz and I talked and I… No, never mind, update you later. I hope you feel all right. I'm so so sorry. Forgive me? I love you.'

After that, Stella stuck her head into Marjorie's office, told her about the call with Gerald Bartholomew and started a case file for him. She typed up Marjorie's findings from her mission the previous afternoon, tailing Astrid the Swedish model around Knightsbridge. It had been one of those long days,

Marjorie said wearily, when she'd resorted to using a Shewee in her car.

'Your what?'

'From time to time, when I'm on a job, I can't stop surveillance in case I miss something, so I have a yellow plastic Shewee that I position very carefully in the back of the car an—'

'That's enough, I get it.'

'It's a much less glamorous business than they make out on television, detective work. Will you email me Mr Bartholomew's number?'

When Stella still hadn't heard from Billie by lunchtime, she resorted to texting Jez, confessing to oversleeping that morning and missing her appointment.

She didn't hear anything from either all afternoon. For once, she was longing for a message from Billie but only heard from Fitz, who sent a photo of the note she'd slipped into his bag along with a message.

My bottom and I very much enjoyed last night. And bear with me on the emotional front. I'll get there. I want to prove how special you are to me. I just need time X

By the time Stella got to the top of her street that evening, she'd rehearsed an apology speech in her head. She was sorry she'd missed the appointment, she was a terrible friend, but she'd also been worrying about Fitz and what was going on with them, but now she'd talked to him and felt better about it, she was absolutely there for Billie. She'd be more supportive and never, ever late for hospital again.

Except when she opened the front door, the flat was dark, and she'd assumed Billie would be home by now.

'Bill?'

Stella dropped the bags on the living room floor and said her name again. 'Bill?'

She reached for the lamp beside the sofa and saw that her bedroom door was closed.

'Bill?' she asked more quietly, standing outside it. 'Billie?'

Stella pushed the door open. It was dark in there too, but the light from the corridor cast a shadow over the bed, and she could see Billie lying in it.

'Bill?'

There was a muffled sob.

'Hey,' Stella whispered, lowering herself to the carpet. 'What's up?'

The only reply was another muffled noise. 'Bill…' She reached her hand towards the mattress.

'*Don't*, Stell.'

Stella frowned and tried to see Billie more clearly through the gloom, but the duvet was pulled high and she could mostly see hair. 'Don't what? Can I put this on? I can't see.'

She flicked on the bedside light as Billie pushed her hair away from her face. Her eyes were red and swollen; her cheeks red and damp.

'Bill, I'm so sorry. I totally fucked up but I di—'

'I don't care,' she replied through a blocked nose. 'I don't care what happened last night. Or this morning. Where were you?'

Stella's eyes sank to the carpet. 'I'm so sorry,' she repeated, scratching at a loose strand of wool. 'I didn't hear my alarm, and by the time I woke up it was alrea—'

'You can't say sorry every time and make it better,' Billie interrupted, notes of desperation and exhaustion in her voice. 'It doesn't work like that.'

'I know, I'm sorry. I mean, this time I really am sorry.'

'It's every time, Stell. You're supposed to be my best friend.'

She opened her mouth to reply but Billie carried on. 'You're the person who knows me better than anyone, better than Jez, even. I love you. Sometimes I think I love you more than Jez, and Mum and Dad. And I need you at the moment. I really *really* need you, but you're not here.'

'I am here, and I'm sorry. Fuck, I wish I could stop saying sorry. But listen, I'm so sorry about this morning. And last night. I've just been worrying about Fitz and caught up with that.'

'I'm sick, Stell,' Billie said forcefully. She pushed herself up on one elbow, exhaling with the effort. The cumulative effect of the radiotherapy had started wearing her out, just as Dr Bush had said it would. At the hospital that morning, after her treatment, the idea of getting home by herself had seemed like a marathon because even getting to the entrance felt like wading through a bog. 'I'm properly sick. And I'm tired. And scared. So scared. And my back hurts. And my skin hurts. But he's all you can think about. All you can talk about.'

'Bill, I'm so sorry. Fuck! OK, listen—'

'Life isn't only about romance, or fancy hotels and oysters. There are other relationships to think about. *You* have other relationships in your life, although I know you don't think they're as important. But they are important, Stell! Other people have real, actual stuff going on in their lives, dramas that don't revolve around whether or not someone's texted them in the past twenty-four hours.'

Stella felt a surge of anger. Of course she realised that. She wasn't a total idiot. 'Is this about money?'

Billie pushed a damp piece of hair off her forehead and opened her mouth in shock, staring as if she'd been slapped.

Stella felt instantly ashamed. Never in her life had they discussed the material difference between them: that Stella's father was a millionaire and Billie's parents ran a pub near Harrogate. It had never mattered. But because she was sitting on the carpet in her own flat, feeling as if she was being told off, she'd lashed out using the only weapon she could think of. 'Ignore me.'

'No! Stell, see, this is what I'm talking about. You don't get it. You always think it's about *you*, your love life or your latest drama, and now even your family's money. Which it's not, by the way. I can't believe you'd think that. The planet doesn't revolve around *you* and whether you have a boyfriend or not. Life is so much bigger than that but you're missing it. Life is about all sorts of love but it's like you only care about one of them, as if romantic love is all there is.'

'I'm sorry,' Stella urged. She and Billie had never had a row like this. In the twenty-one years they'd known one another, they'd occasionally snapped at one another or bickered. Most often at the end of a night out when Billie wanted to go home and Stella, invariably, wanted to carry on. But they'd never shouted at one another or reduced the other to tears, unless they were tears of laughter. This was uncharted territory for them and Stella started to cry. 'I know it's not about me, I do, I promise.'

She reached for the mattress again, pressing her hands against its side as if she was begging Billie. 'I know I say this all the time, but I am sorry. This time I'm really, really sorry. For everything. For being the worst friend, for not being here, for saying stupid things, and doing stupid things, but mostly…' Stella stopped and raised her fingers to her cheeks to wipe them, 'I'm so sorry that you're going through this, Bill. I'd give anything for it to be me, for me to have this… thing. I'd give… I'd give… I'd give up everything. I'd give up Fitz. I'd give up falling in love ever again.'

'That's not true.'

'I would!' Stella raised herself to her knees. 'Honestly, I would. Anything. I hate that you're going through this. I hate myself for not being there. And I'll do anything, anything, to help. Tell me, Bill. Please tell me.'

Billie pulled her hands free of the duvet to take Stella's. 'That's the thing. I don't want to tell you.'

Stella frowned at their fingers knotted together. What could she do? Buying a pot of fresh pesto and a chocolate bar for dinner seemed a feeble apology. 'I'll be there for every appointment you need from now on, I swear. And I'm going to throw you the birthday party to end all birthday parties.'

Billie lowered herself down to the mattress. 'I don't know about the party any more, Stell. I'm not sure I'm feeling like celebrating. My last session's the week before.'

'We can play it by ear. I can always cancel it on the day. And you don't have to do a single thing. It just feels like there's more reason than ever to do it this year. But only a small party. Good plan?' Stella held her thumb out sideways.

Billie sighed before very slowly angling her thumb towards the ceiling.

Later, after Stella had cooked and carried two bowls of pasta through to Billie's room where they watched several episodes of a new murder series on her laptop (although Billie barely ate), and once they were both in their own beds, she texted Sam.

Hey, sorry to bother you, but Billie's suddenly not feeling great. The radiotherapy's kicked in so she's tired, and not eating much. I'm trying to think of what else I can do. Is there anything else?

Sam's reply came straight back, *Hey Shakespeare. No bother. Sorry to hear that. How much longer does her treatment go on?*

Stella tapped out, *Another week but I wish I could do something. I feel so useless.*

You're not useless. Anything soft to wear is good, if her skin is affected? It tends to be localised pain with radio but she might be sore. Anything natural that will help her sleep is useful too. Like lavender oil. And some patients like pastilles called Queasy Drops. I give them to the kids sometimes. They can help.

Amazing. Thanks.

NP. How are you holding up?

Stella blinked at her phone screen for a few moments before replying, touched that he'd asked.

I'm fine. Thanks again. Hope you're still on for the party? November 5th.

Totally. Actually, been meaning to ask you, can I bring someone?

Stella let her phone fall flat on her chest. Bring someone? To her birthday? It was supposed to be a party to cheer Billie up, not a dating opportunity for Sam. Had the man never heard of a restaurant? And who was this 'someone', anyway? Where had he met her? She scowled at the idea before reminding herself that, only hours earlier, after her conversation with Billie, she'd determined to be less selfish. Of course Sam could bring a date to her birthday party, and Stella would be extremely civil to her.

Sure. See you then, and thanks again xxx

Any time X

CHAPTER 43

WHILE BILLIE LAY DOWN for her radiotherapy session the next morning, Stella sat two floors beneath her in the hospital café, typing a to-do list.

First was organise the birthday party: *email everyone to remind them of their address; order the sausages, the paper cups and the napkins. Buy Billie's birthday present*, Stella typed. *Decorations*, she added. She wanted the flat to look more celebratory than ever: balloons, paper chains, party poppers. Party hats? Stella frowned while considering it before adding them to the list. This was going to be their best ever birthday party. She would also email Billie's mum to check she was making her famous parkin.

Helen Martin had baked this cake for Billie's birthday every year since she was one. It was a thick, stodgy sponge, as dark as rye bread but sweetened with black treacle. Every year at school, when Billie's parents arrived at Queen Margaret's with the parkin in a Tupperware, Bob reminded his daughter that it was proper working-class fare, made to keep exhausted workers toiling during the Industrial Revolution. And before they went out for Billie and Stella's birthday dinner, Bob would proudly carry the Tupperware to the boarding-house kitchen, where it sat beside the more extravagant cakes sent by Stella's parents.

After the first year, when they'd sent the tennis racket with marzipan balls, there was a Disney castle complete with sparklers that burned from the turrets. The year after that came a stack of multicoloured cupcakes; the following year was a rainbow cake covered in hundreds and thousands, which had spilled with Smarties when Stella cut into the middle. They were the sort of cakes that sat in the windows of fancy bakeries, ordered by Stella's mother to make up for the fact that her parents never came to visit on her birthday like the Martins. But while their friends would coo over Stella's cake and lick the cream frosting off their fingers, Stella had always preferred the parkin.

Fitz? Stella wrote at the bottom of the list, because although she'd mentioned the party a couple of weeks earlier, she hadn't pressed him. But that was before their conversation about their relationship, before he'd reassured her about their future. So presumably he would come, although she should probably mention it again so tha—

Her thoughts were interrupted by a phone call from an ominous number: her father's office.

Stella's finger hovered over the green button. Could she bear it? He only ever called when she'd done something wrong. But she also knew that, when it came to her father, it was usually best to get whatever he wanted out of the way.

'Stella?'

'Hi, Dad. How are you?' Stella concentrated on a small patch of table in front of her, stained with a coffee ring.

'I've just had a message from Coutts, saying there's been unusual activity on one of my credit cards. Is that you?'

'No! I haven't touched that card for weeks. I told you, I've got that job. Which is going very well, thank you for asking. But anyway, there can't be any unusual activity because I haven't used that card. So it must be someone else. Mum's probably bought herself a new nose.'

Her father grunted down the phone.

'Anything else?'

'No. I'll ring them and find out what it is. But no more spending, please.'

'Dad, I told you I haven't used it.'

He grunted again.

'Funny timing, actually. I'm just planning my birthday party. Can Billie and I expect the pleasure of your company this year? Andrew and Pandora are coming.'

Once or twice, Stella's parents had swung by the flat for the party, but usually they claimed they were on the way to have dinner somewhere, or going to the opera (which they loathed but went to so they could boast to other people that they'd been to the opera), and could only stay for ten minutes.

'When is it?'

Stella ground her teeth. 'The same date as always, that's the thing with birthdays. November fifth.'

'You'll have to ask your mother, she's in charge of the diary.'

'Sure.'

'Need to go. Better go and sort out your spending.'

'You do that,' Stella said crisply before hanging up.

As always after any interaction with her father, she felt dejected.

She'd got a job, she was supporting herself, and yet he still saw her as a problem. Unusual activity? There couldn't be. She hadn't even *tried* to use that card since she'd started working for Marjorie. She sighed as a shadow fell over her phone.

'Good morning,' said Harold.

'Oh, hiya. Hello, Basil.' Stella stretched to scratch between the Alsatian's ears. 'How are you guys?'

'We're very chipper. About to report for duty upstairs. You here with Billie?'

'Mmm, she's in radio. Nearly finished the second week.'

Worry creased Harold's forehead. 'How is she?'

'Tired. And not eating. But…' Stella reached down and tapped the leg of her chair. 'Touch wood. One more week after this and then done.'

'Basil and I will touch every tree we see on the way home for luck.'

Stella smiled. 'How are you, anyway? How did your date with Hilary go?'

Harold's face darkened. 'I'm not sure Hilary and I are the right fit. I went to origami club last week, and it was very pleasant to begin with. It's in a church in Chiswick, not far from the river, and everyone sits at different tables, and there was a big tea urn and plates of biscuits…'

'OK.'

'So I sat down beside Hilary and she was teaching me the basics. How to do one of those birds, you know the type? They look more like dinosaurs than birds to me, but what do I know. Anyway, so she was teaching me how to make one of those…'

'Mmmhmm,' murmured Stella, glancing at the time on her

phone. Harold's anecdotes could take some time and Billie would be finished in five minutes.

'But then *somebody...*' Harold glared down at Basil, 'decided to eat another member's frog.'

'A frog?'

'An origami frog. Apparently frogs are very difficult. Much harder than a bird. And, well, the long and the short of it is that we were asked to leave.'

'You were kicked out of origami club?' Stella asked, trying not to laugh.

'Indeed we were. And now Hilary isn't returning my messages.'

'Forget Hilary. You're coming on the fifth still? For our birthday party?'

'Absolutely. And I was wondering, it's been a while since I went to a party, but can I bring something? I'm getting much better with my cooking. What about a cake?'

'The cake's covered, but thank you.'

'Course it is. Not to worry.'

He looked so crestfallen that Stella tried to think of something else. 'But some canapés might be useful?'

'Canapés?' Harold repeated as if he'd never heard the word.

'Mmm, nothing fancy. Like, cheese straws?'

'Cheese straws? I'm not sure how to make those, but I'll have a look on BBC Food. It's ever such a good website.'

'Sounds great, thanks, Harold. But I should be going to get Billie.'

'Righty-oh. We shall escort you to the second floor. Come on, Basil.'

They set off together, patients and visitors staring at the sight of a large Alsatian smoothly gliding upwards on the escalator.

Upstairs, Stella waved them off and made her way to the radiotherapy waiting room. Billie appeared a few minutes later, pale, quiet and so tired that she said she was going to go home. 'But I can get an Uber, Stell. You don't have to come the whole way back.'

Stella ignored this and, on the escalator back down, ordered an Uber for them. Then, once home, she made Billie a peppermint tea and carried her duvet and a pillow into the sitting room, so she could lie on the sofa and watch daytime television.

'Back later, call me if you need anything?' she told Billie. '*Anything*, I mean it.'

'Will do, thank you. And Stell?'

'Yeah?' Stella turned from the front door.

'Love you.'

Stella smiled back, feeling a fresh wave of love for her friend, small and pallid, tucked up on the sofa. 'Love you too.'

A message from her father came through on the bus into work. *Spoke to Coutts. No recent transactions on the card so that triggered the alarm. They were concerned at the lack of activity. Their mistake.*

Stella turned her phone screen-down in her lap. She was lucky in so many ways, she knew, but sometimes all she wished was that her family was normal, that her father was proud of her, and her mother was less obsessed with skincare, and they all hung out together more often and laughed and talked and hugged like some sort of intolerably happy family in a gravy advert. Still, she sighed, you can't have it all in life, can you?

CHAPTER 44

OVER THE NEXT TWO weeks, Stella was a more devoted nurse than Florence Nightingale. She stayed in with Billie almost every night, lying on the sofa or Billie's bed to watch bad Netflix series; she woke up on time every morning it was her turn to do the hospital run; she did Billie's laundry even though she found handling Jez's briefs fully repulsive. She googled 'food for cancer patients' and spent a good deal of her salary in the deli, buying organic spinach, kale, carrots, walnuts and apples, filling the fridge until it looked like a farm shop. She also spent too much at the florist, making sure that there was a vase of something cheerful in Billie's room: pink tulips for a few days, next a bunch of purple stocks.

Except none of it seemed to help and Stella watched her friend wilt, increasingly exhausted by the daily timetable of hospital treatments. Walking to the bathroom was too much for Billie on some days, and she'd developed a red rash that looked like severe sunburn on her stomach from the radiation. She had almost no appetite in the days after chemotherapy, and her mass of curls had started thinning so she'd started wearing one of Jez's football beanies.

On the Saturday after Billie's penultimate chemo session,

Stella was sitting cross-legged on the end of her bed, debating whether to cancel seeing Fitz. He'd got back from another trip to Washington that afternoon, and asked if she'd mind meeting him at the Rakes reception at six thirty sharp. Stella was intrigued about why he'd given her such strict instructions but she didn't mind since Marjorie hadn't cracked the Bartholomew case and she wanted to hang out in the hotel on the off chance she'd see Perdita. But she still wasn't sure she should abandon Billie when Jez was on a stag do in Brighton.

'I'll be fine, go on, see him,' Billie urged. Her duvet was pulled up to her chin so she looked like a sick child.

Stella frowned. Dating, she and Billie had often discussed in the past, was like a video game. You started at level one and had to progress from there, passing various obstacles, jumping through hoops, with each level getting more dangerous than the last because there was more to lose and you might be sent back down to the beginning. And although she hadn't seen Fitz since the previous week, they'd messaged plenty, most mornings when they woke and evenings before going to sleep. It felt like they'd gone up another level since their conversation in Café Cornelia, and she was desperate to see him, but she felt guilty about leaving the flat.

'Go!' Billie repeated. 'One of us should have sex at least.'

'What d'you mean?'

Billie grimaced. 'Jez and I haven't done it for six weeks, not since before my egg freezing. So six weeks and three days now.'

She rolled over onto one side and stared at the wall. 'It's like that whole area has become so medicated, like it doesn't belong to me but to the nurses and the doctors and the radiologists. I can't imagine my body being normal ever again, but what if Jez gets fed up and leaves me?' Billie turned her head and looked at Stella, her eyes wide with worry.

'Firstly, you will feel like it again at some point, but there's no rush. Look at this like a kind of holiday from sex, a holiday from having to do it even when you're really tired or you've eaten too much or Jez has bad breath and you wish you could just go to sleep.'

Billie smiled but didn't reply.

'OK, bad joke,' Stella said before hurrying on. 'Secondly, Jez is never going to leave you, and if he *did* I would stun him to death with Marjorie's taser.'

Billie laughed softly and Stella felt relieved. She could still reach her.

'Please go tonight. Go and see him. I'll be fine, I just want to sleep.'

'But what if you need something?'

'I won't need anything. Hey, has he told you whether he's coming to the party yet?'

'He said it depends on his work, but I hope so. Also, did I mention that Sam was coming with a date?' Stella looked down at the cushion covering her lap. For some reason discussing Sam's date aloud made her feel uncomfortable, as if it was an unpleasant subject like verrucas or the state of British politics.

'Excuse me, no, you did not,' Billie replied, trying to push herself up. '*Who?*'

'Lie down. And he didn't say. Just asked if he could bring someone.'

'And you said yes?'

'Obviously. Why not?'

Billie moved her mouth around in thought and dropped her head back against the pillows. 'Have you told Fitz he's coming?'

'No. Why would I do that? It was a one-night thing, Bill. I've had cups of tea that have lasted longer.'

'Well, what an evening of romance it'll be. You and Fitz, Harold and Marjorie, Sam and whoever his date is. It's perfect.'

'For what?'

Billie smiled as if she had a secret. 'For our birthday. It'll be perfect.'

'OK, but you have to tell me if you don't feel up to it. And that goes for tonight, too. I could easily stay in, and cook the chic—'

Billie rolled her head from side to side. 'No, I don't want any more cooking from you, thank you very much. I want you to go and have a truly sordid night in bed.'

'Deal,' Stella replied, standing up from the bed and grinning. 'I'll go but keep my phone on loud all evening. So if you need *anything* you call me.'

'Promise.'

'If you want another glass of water or you're too hot or you feel sick, you'll definitely ring? I can come straight back.'

'Yes! I've told you.' Billie managed a smile over the edge of her duvet cover. 'Go!'

Stella showered and pulled on a pair of jeans and a lacy shirt before sticking her head back into Billie's bedroom to say goodbye.

She'd fallen asleep. She was trying to conceal how ill she felt, Stella knew. But she could tell how much Billie had faded from the small things, like asking for a glass of water or to turn the bedroom light off when she wanted to sleep, even though the switch was almost within her reach. Stella felt a sudden rush of protectiveness as she realised that the light inside Billie had dimmed too. It was the most powerful surge of love she could remember, a physical jolt that ran from her heart to her feet and back. Billie had to get better, but what if…? No, it was unthinkable. Stella blinked to clear her eyes and set off for Rakes.

CHAPTER 45

FITZ WAS LEANING ON the reception desk when Stella arrived, glaring at the marble floor and waving one hand in the air as he talked into his mobile. No suit, he was wearing a white T-shirt over a pair of tracksuit pants. She smiled. It was like seeing a politician in a hoody. Except no politician could be nearly as attractive as him. He'd get her vote if he was.

As Stella approached, his expression changed and he grinned and held up two fingers. 'Two seconds,' he mouthed before resuming his conversation. 'I've got to go, I'll ring you tomorrow, yes… Yes, yes, no, yes, all right, yes, we'll sort it tomorrow.'

He hung up. 'Hello, Miss Shakespeare.'

'Hi.' She leant in to kiss him. 'All OK? That sounded stressful. And you look different.'

'I dress down for flights, and it was only Carol being tiresome. But everything has improved dramatically in the last ten seconds.'

Stella frowned, confused.

'Because you've arrived.'

'Oh, I get it.' She smiled and ran her hand over his shoulder, leaning in to kiss him again. 'How was the trip? You tired?'

'Very, but I'll live.' Then he looked more concerned. 'Are you all right?'

'Me? Yeah. How come?'

His eyes roamed her face. 'You look exhausted.'

'Thanks very much.'

He reached for her hand. 'What I mean is that, although you look tired, you are still exceptionally beautiful, like a green-eyed—'

'Monster?'

'I was going for temptress.'

Stella grinned. 'Better. And I'm OK, it's just Billie.'

'How is she?'

'She can hardly get out of bed after chemo, and she gets hot and can't eat. I wish I could do more.'

'I imagine you're doing plenty, but this is exactly why I've organised a surprise.'

'A surprise?'

Fitz held one finger up and turned to the receptionist, a new woman who Stella didn't recognise. 'We're ready if the room is?'

'I'll just check for you, Mr Montague.' She picked up a phone and dialled, then waited a few moments. 'Hello, I just wanted to see if the Cardinal Suite is ready for Mr and Mrs Montague? OK, sure, no problem, I'll let them know.'

She hung up and smiled. 'It's ready.'

'Thank you so much. And just for reference, this ravishing creature is not my wife.'

'Oh, I'm so sorry,' she said, her cheeks reddening. 'I th—'

'Not to worry, and thank you very much,' Fitz told her before putting one arm around Stella's back, guiding her towards the lift.

The Cardinal Suite was the same room Stella and Fitz had

stayed in the first time they slept together, but when he opened the door on the top floor this time, Stella was met by the sight of two adjacent massage beds set up between the foot of the four-poster and the desk. The heavy velvet curtains were drawn and small tealights flickered on the bedside tables.

She turned to Fitz with an astonished grin.

'Now, what we need to do is strip off,' he instructed, 'then lie down and two very small but surprisingly strong women will be along shortly to beat the hell out of us.'

Smiling, Stella narrowed her eyes at him. 'How do you know they're very small and strong?'

'I've had massages here before.'

'Have you had a *couples'* massage here before?' She felt momentarily sick at the idea of Fitz doing this with another woman.

'No! Course not.' He leant forward and brushed her hair with his lips. 'I merely thought, as you've been stressed recently, you could do with one of these.'

'I could do with one of these. It's… well, it's very thoughtful.'

In the two months that Stella had been seeing Fitz, there'd been plenty of restaurants and Champagne and expensive wine. But to her, this felt like the most meaningful demonstration of affection. Stella was so touched she wrapped her arms around his back and pressed her cheek to his chest. 'Thank you.' Then she looked up. 'And a couples' massage, huh? Does that imply that, you know, we're…'

Fitz grinned. 'Maybe. But come on, clothes off please, Miss Shakespeare, before our tormenters arrive.'

They stripped to their underwear and lay down, Stella laughing as she tried to tug the towel over the back of her legs, before there was a quiet knock on the door.

'Come in,' Fitz ordered, and Stella lifted her head to see two women – quite small, as he said, and in white spa uniforms – take up position either side of their massage beds.

'How would you like the pressure?' asked Stella's masseuse in a whispery voice.

'Er, quite hard?' she replied, failing to suppress another giggle.

'Miss Shakespeare, is that a dirty joke?' Fitz said from the bed beside her. 'I'd like mine very hard indeed, please.'

She laughed again but was silenced by the sensation of hot flannels on her feet.

Stella had never had a couples' massage before. Until her father had forbidden the use of his credit card, on days when Stella was suffering an especially bad hangover, she'd been a keen visitor to the spa around the corner from her flat but had never seen the point of having a massage *with* someone. What was so romantic about lying side by side being pummelled by different people?

But now, lying in the suite, as her legs were squeezed, as she caught wafts of lavender oil and heard the occasional moan from Fitz, she started to understand. There *was* something suggestive about this, about the knowledge that, a foot or so away, Fitz was almost naked and oiled, getting pleasure from being stroked himself. Although not too much pleasure, Stella hoped.

She only woke up when she felt her feet being wiped by hot flannels again, and heard Fitz groan as he stretched his arms over his head.

'Thank you very much,' he said, sitting up. Reaching for his tracksuit pants, he retrieved his wallet, fished out two notes and held them towards the masseuses. 'That was wonderful.'

'It was,' echoed Stella, who felt so warm and cocooned on her bed, swathed in towels and blankets, that she thought she might simply stay there for ever. Grow old and die in that massage bed.

Except a couple of minutes later, once the two small but almost unbelievably strong women had let themselves out and she'd heard the soft click of the hotel door, Stella was suddenly much less sleepy because Fitz bent over her bed, scooped one arm under her knees and another under her back, and carried her to the four-poster, where they spent the next twenty-four minutes soaking the clean, crisp expensive sheets with oil.

Now she understood the point of a couples' massage, Stella thought, as Fitz's fingers ran up her inner thigh and she shivered. It was as if her senses were heightened, as if an hour of massage had primed her body for this, for sliding over him, around him and under him. She didn't want to think of her masseuse as a fluffer exactly, but she'd worked some sort of magic.

'Oh my god, Fitz. Oh my god, oh my god, oh my god,' Stella moaned into his neck as she came harder than she could remember, and waves of hot pleasure swept from the arch of her feet to her cheeks and back. Fitz came almost simultaneously too, groaning into her ear, which gave her a kick. To her, it seemed to signify that they were drawing closer.

It was only afterwards, as Stella lay in his arms, that she decided it was the moment to broach the birthday party. It was always easier to talk to him when they were naked, as if by removing his clothes it removed a layer of his defence. 'So… do you think you can come, next Friday?'

'Next Friday?'

Her fingers lightly slapped his chest. 'My birthday party. And Billie's.'

'Course, I knew that.'

'Sure,' she replied with another small slap.

'I should think it's possible.'

'You're not going away between then and now?'

'I might need to go back to DC for a meeting but I'd rather not.'

'And there's one other teeny-tiny thing,' she added, lifting her head to give him a pantomime grimace.

Fitz frowned.

'My parents are coming. And my brother. *And* his wife Pandora, who has all the intelligence of a teaspoon.' She rested her head back on his shoulder. 'Actually, I think teaspoons might be cleverer.'

'Happy families,' Fitz muttered into her hair.

'It won't be. If they even come, Dad will make it about him, Mum will tell me I need to start using eye cream or drink more water. Andrew, my brother, he's lovely and will be excited about meeting you, and Pandora will talk on and on and *on* about their son. Just a warning.'

'What's their son called?'

'Hubie. He's like a very small dictator, and he's not coming but if you ask Pandora anything about him she will explode with pride.'

'And Hubie is how old?'

'Just three.'

Stella felt Fitz nod above her head.

'Do you want children?' She hadn't meant to ask this because she didn't want him thinking there were implications to her question, but it slipped out.

'Very much,' he replied.

'Huh.'

'Surprised?'

Stella pursed her mouth. 'I guess I just didn't know.'

'I've always wanted them. But it's not that easy.'

He sounded so serious that she raised her head. 'What do you mean?'

'What I mean is…' Fitz's eyes met hers and they gazed at one another. 'Life can be complicated, Miss Shakespeare.'

'I know, but what does that have to do with having children?'

'Only that it's not like booking a flight. You can't simply decide you want a child and then have one.'

'Well obviously,' she replied teasingly because he sounded so solemn.

'But one day, hopefully,' Fitz replied before his expression – and his tone – lifted again. 'Now, I don't know about you but I could do with a drink.'

CHAPTER 46

ON THE MORNING OF their birthday, every year at school and every year since they'd moved into the flat, Stella and Billie would open their presents together. This was normally in Stella's room, on her bed (even if there was a boyfriend in it), because Stella had usually overdone it the night before and Billie would wake her with a cup of tea and tell her that she shouldn't waste their birthday by sleeping through it.

This year, Stella was the one who woke early because she had a long list of worries. Had she ordered enough sausages? Would everyone like Fitz? Would her parents even show up? Would Harold and Marjorie get on? Most importantly, would Billie be able to manage?

After half an hour of mulling these thoughts over, she told herself to get up. Today, she would take her present for Billie through to her room with a cup of tea instead of vice versa.

Stella pulled a jumper over her pyjamas, made for the kitchen and, a few minutes later, quietly whispered outside Billie's door, 'Can I come in?'

Pushing it open with her shoulder, she grinned at the sight: Billie sitting up in Jez's Arsenal beanie; Jez asleep beside her.

'Is it too early?'

'Nah, come sit on this side,' Billie said quietly, crossing her legs under the duvet to make space for Stella. 'Thanks, love,' she added as she lowered the mug to her bedside table. 'And happy birthday.'

'Happy birthday right back,' Stella said, settling herself at the end of the bed, holding her present for Billie in her lap.

Jez opened one eye. 'Am I having a nightmare or is Stella on our bed?'

'Good morning, Jeremy, and thank you for your kind birthday wishes.' But Stella smiled as she said it because the passive-aggressive squabbling that used to exist between them had been replaced by something else. Stella wasn't sure she'd call it *friendship* exactly. But it was a much easier, more gentle teasing, almost as if they were siblings.

Jez stretched his arms over his head. 'Happy birthday to the two women in my life.' Sitting up, he kissed Billie on the cheek. 'You feeling all right?'

'Mmm, good. Better this morning. No headache.'

Stella squinted as she tried to work out if Billie was fibbing.

'What?'

'You definitely OK for tonight? We don't have to do it. We can just have your parents over and sit on the sofa and eat cake.'

Helen and Bob Martin were catching the 12.43 train from Harrogate to London, Stella knew, because they'd individually texted her multiple times not only about the journey, but also about what Tube line they should take from Paddington to their hotel, about downloading Uber to their phones, about Bob bringing his own cans of ale to the party and about what time they should arrive at the flat with the parkin. But she could cancel everyone else if she had to.

Billie looked solemnly from Stella to Jez. 'Right, will you both promise me something?'

'What?' they replied in union.

'That you don't ask me that question one more time today. I'm so bored of it! I'm so bored of you looking at me as if I'm an invalid! I'm fed up of you two whispering about me!'

'We haven't been whispering about yo—' started Stella.

'Rubbish. You're the worst whisperers. I can hear you from here, about how much I've eaten or whether I've drunk enough water. I know it's meant in the best possible way but just… enough. For today. No fussing, no whispering. I'm fine.'

'Jeez, turning thirty-three has made you really cranky,' Jez joked.

'Right? We try to organise a party and this is all the thanks we get?'

Billie smiled. 'I love you both. I just want today to be normal.'

'Oh well, in that case, if you want it to be *normal*, I presume you don't want your present?' Stella held up her present – bulky and soft, and wrapped in green paper.

'No, I definitely do want that because otherwise you can't have this,' Billie said before leaning down and pulling another wrapped in red tissue paper from underneath the bed.

'You first,' Stella instructed, handing hers over.

Billie opened her card. This was another ritual: they both looked for the very silliest cards they could find to make one another laugh, except this year, Stella hadn't bought a silly card. Instead, she'd ordered one with a photo of her and Billie on it, grinning at the camera in their uniform, taken during their first year at school.

Happy birthday to my best and oldest friend. I feel luckier than ever that you took pity on me that day you found me crying in the boiler room when we were 11, and thank you for being there for ALL the tears since. You are the kindest, most selfless, most thoughtful and supportive person I know and I love you very much xxxxx

Billie looked up. 'Thanks, Stell. You've absolutely ruined the tradition.'

'Didn't think this was the year for cards about penises or gin,' she replied with a shrug.

Opening the present, Billie found a cashmere dressing gown, as soft as cotton wool. Having remembered Sam's advice about fabrics, Stella had visited a boutique on Marylebone High Street that sold silk pyjamas and silk bed sheets along with thick cashmere dressing gowns in soothing colours: cream, light grey, pale pink, caramel. She chose the caramel one in the end, figuring it would go with Billie's freckles and that it was the least likely colour to show up stains.

'This is too nice!' Billie said in awe, holding the dressing gown up before clutching it to her chest.

'One of these days you're going to have to get dressed properly but, until then, I figured this might be comfortable.'

'Reckon I'd look decent in that,' said Jez, stretching out a hand to feel it.

'Wrapping it around your hairy man body? I don't think so. Where did you find it, Stell?'

'A shop near work. It was Sam's idea actually. He said something about soft fabrics for anyone having treatment. Sorry! I know we're not supposed to mention that today but I feel bad taking *all* the credit.'

'Well, thank you both,' Billie said before grinning across the bed. 'And Sam's idea, huh? How did that come about?'

'I texted him. And it's not like *that*,' she added when Billie made a face. 'Anyway, I told you, he's bringing someone to the party.'

'Which one's Sam?' Jez asked through a yawn.

'The doctor, the one who Stella slept with just before she met Fitz.'

'And he's coming to the party tonight?'

'Yes.'

'Along with the arms dealer?'

'Fitz,' Stella told him sternly.

'So your friends and family are going to meet your new boyfriend…'

'Not boyfriend,' she shot back quickly, although she was worrying about what her mother might say to Fitz. Having briefly mentioned that he was coming to the party on the phone a few days earlier, Valerie had replied, 'Darling, how exciting! Perhaps you won't even *need* egg freezing.' If Stella caught a whisper of her mother mentioning egg freezing or grandchildren to Fitz that evening, she would have to leave Earth.

'OK, your friends and family are going to meet your new lover *and* your old lover at the same time?' went on Jez.

'Sam was not my lover. We only… hung out once. And he's bringing a date.'

Jez sighed. 'I think *I* might be too tired for this party.'

'Oi,' Billie said, stretching a leg to kick him under the duvet. 'Stell, your turn. Here you go.'

She handed over her present.

'Bill!' Stella said, having ripped off the paper. It was a red cashmere jersey with a white S on the front.

'In sync,' she replied, nodding. 'I think red's a good colour on you.'

'I love it, thank you.' Stella ran a hand across the wool before turning to Jez. 'What d'you get her?'

He tapped the side of his nose. 'Top secret.'

'Is that because it hasn't arrived yet?'

'No! It's because I want to save it for later.'

'Ooooh, mysterious,' Stella said before swinging her legs off the bed. 'But right, I should get ready for work.'

'Yeah, clear off,' said Jez, pulling the duvet over his shoulder and reaching an arm across Billie's lap. 'Leave us alone for a birthday shag.'

'Jeremy,' Stella said quickly, 'she may be strong enough for the party but I'm not sure she's strong enough for *that*.'

'I was joking!' he replied before looking up at Billie. 'It's the sight of you in my Gunners hat that really does it for me.'

'*Puke*,' Stella said, rolling her eyes before closing the door behind her. But she could hear them laughing from the other side, which was a very welcome sound.

CHAPTER 47

THAT EVENING, IT TOOK four trips and all of Nigel's ice from the corner shop to fill the bath before Stella slid the bottles of Prosecco into it, as gently as new-born babies. She'd blown up an entire packet of balloons and now her cheeks ached. She'd put a bowl of party poppers on the coffee table. She'd arranged a stack of paper plates, paper cups and napkins in the kitchen. But she was proudest of the bunting.

She'd strung this in zigzagging lines across the sitting room ceiling, quite low, so it might garrotte the taller guests. It wasn't plain bunting; a few days earlier, she'd discovered a website that printed personalised bunting, decorated with different photos.

Opening up Facebook, Stella had clicked through her old photos, saving various favourites of her and Billie through the years. She felt more sentimental and nostalgic for the past than she ever had on previous birthdays and wanted to look back. So there they were at teenage parties with illicit cigarettes between their fingers; drinking in London pubs before they turned eighteen; on sunny foreign balconies, holding beers with unpronounceable names and smiling underneath sunburned noses; at previous birthday parties in the flat, arms draped over one another on the balcony; the one taken when they were turning twelve, which she'd used for Billie's birthday card.

Stella emailed these to the website, who'd sent her twenty metres of multicoloured bunting printed with the pictures in under twenty-four hours, and now their little faces were fluttering and smiling, strung between the walls.

Various cards were lining the bookshelf; from Billie's parents, from a few schoolfriends and from Harold, who'd slipped one under the door that morning, signing it 'Harold Vincent' as if they wouldn't have known which Harold it was otherwise.

The room was further decorated by a hundred cream roses dotted around the room in various receptacles – one vase, one glass jug, an old mayonnaise jar, two pint glasses – which had arrived for Stella in the office that day, delivered by a sweating man who had to stretch his arms around the enormous bunch to stagger from his van to the Harley Street entrance like he was dropping off a Christmas tree. *'Happy Birthday Miss Shakespeare, see you later. Present then. FX',* said the accompanying card.

Marjorie had been so stunned by the size of the bouquet that she'd briefly stopped talking about what she was going to wear to the party when Stella reappeared, panting from the effort of carrying the flowers upstairs. 'We've… got… to… get… the… lift… fixed,' Stella had said through deep breaths, which Marjorie had ignored before resuming questions about the sort of shoes she should put on that night.

She stepped back and frowned at the bunches of balloons in every corner.

'Do you think they look like haemorrhoids?' she asked Jez, who she'd put to work in the kitchen, piercing the sausages and laying them on baking trays, ignoring his protest that he didn't like touching meat.

'I think that's a question for your doctor friend,' he shouted back.

'The balloons, idiot.'

Jez turned from the kitchen counter and squinted through the archway into the sitting room. 'No, it looks amazing. Even I'm willing to admit you've done a top job.'

'*Really?*'

'Really. Apart from on yourself. You're not wearing that, are you?'

Stella looked down as if surprised to find herself still in her work clothes. 'Shit, no. OK, I'm getting dressed. Shall I wake Bill?'

Jez glanced up at the kitchen clock. 'Yeah, I guess.'

She made her way to their bedroom door, before tapping gently on it. 'Bill? You ready?'

There was no answer, so she pushed it open to see Billie still in bed, asleep. Stella glanced down at her phone. Half an hour until people arrived. Maybe she should leave her until then, let her get as much rest as she could? But just as she stepped back to close the door, Billie stirred and smiled at her. 'Hey, love.'

'Hey, lazybones, how you doing?'

'I'm OK,' Billie replied sleepily. 'What time is it?'

'Half six.'

'Give me ten? Just need to put my party frock on.' Billie gestured towards her door, on the back of which hung the cashmere dressing gown.

In her own bedroom, Stella pulled on a short black dress and reapplied her make-up. She tugged her hair over her shoulder before returning to the sitting room and surveying the decorations.

For a moment, the effort seemed tragic: balloons, bunting and bowls of Twiglets, since they were Billie's favourite. In the kitchen, beside the sausages, was a pile of bread rolls, along with three different types of condiment: ketchup, French mustard, American mustard. But suddenly it seemed pathetic to think that any of this could distract them from Billie's condition. Anxiety clawed at Stella's chest. If this was all too much for Billie, it would be her fault. The party was going to be the most awkward social event since Henry VIII's sixth wedding, nobody knowing what to say, everyone tiptoeing around the topic of Billie's cancer, waiting for the right moment to excuse themselves and leave. Or, worse still, what if this was the last joint birthday party? What if th—

'Stell!'

She turned to see Billie wrapped in her new dressing gown, gazing up at the bunting. 'This looks incredible. Like a film set!'

'I wouldn't go that far.'

'Seriously, this place has never looked like this.' Billie leant forward to inspect the bunting. 'Oh my god, that one of us in Malia,' she said, shaking her head at a photo of them both in a Greek pole-dancing bar. Billie had one hand around the pole, and was leaning back, dropping her head behind her, her hair almost reaching her bottom.

'And this one!' Billie leant towards another, taken on their fourteenth birthday, of them sharing a milkshake in Pizza Express. 'You're ridiculous, thank you.'

She stepped forward for a hug and Stella felt how frail her shoulders were. She'd lost kilos since the start of her treatment. In the past couple of weeks, whenever Billie had emerged from her room dressed, Stella thought she'd looked like a small child whose parents had bought jeans and shirts that were several sizes too big.

'Do I look all right?' Billie pulled back and ran her fingers down the dressing gown.

'Total goddess,' Stella replied, using a falsely cheerful voice. 'Where's Jez gone?'

'In the bathroom, polluting it before everyone arrives.'

'Nice. OK, now we just need them to get here. Please, please, *please* can they get on,' Stella said, placing her palms together in prayer.

'Who?'

'Harold and Marjorie.'

'They will,' Billie said because she always assumed everyone would get on.

Stella jumped as there was a knock on the door and she opened it to find Harold, and Basil in a red bow tie.

'Ta-daaaaa!' he announced, holding up a platter.

Stella frowned. It was half a pineapple, hollowed out and refilled with brown gloop, surrounded by Ritz crackers.

'What *is* that?'

'This is my curry pineapple dip,' Harold said proudly. 'I found the recipe online and it was ever so easy. All I had to do was mix cream cheese, mustard and curry powder, oh, and the chutney. Mustn't forget the chutney, and then I cut out a few chunks of fruit and Bob's your uncle. Happy birthday,' he added, holding the platter even higher, as if it was a trophy.

This is going to be a disaster, Stella thought, all over again.

CHAPTER 48

HALF AN HOUR LATER, the flat felt gently chaotic.

Billie was sitting on the sofa, sandwiched between their school-friends Britt and Rose.

Three of Billie's colleagues were standing over the coffee table, looking nervously at Harold's pineapple dip.

Pandora and Andrew were on the balcony, telling Jez about their upcoming holiday to a Caribbean hotel, although Pandora kept nipping back inside to ring the babysitter and check Hubie was still asleep.

Harold and Marjorie were talking by the bookshelf, but Stella wasn't sure how well this was going. When Marjorie came through the door, Harold seemed startled and, to be honest, Stella didn't blame him. Her boss had dressed as if she'd been invited to a white tie ball: floor-length purple gown, grey curls leaping out behind a velvet hairband, red lipstick.

Marjorie had looked similarly alarmed at the sight of Harold and Basil. She'd been nervous of large dogs ever since an incident in a Clapham garden towards the beginning of her police career, when she'd been peering through someone's conservatory and was almost bitten by a Dalmatian. Still, Stella had forced them together, saying that since they were both former officers, they must have plenty in common.

Valerie Shakespeare had arrived alone and thrust a bag of expensive moisturiser at her daughter. 'Happy birthday, darling. It's made from snail mucus. Think of that lovely, dewy glow that snails have. Your father can't make it. He's on a site visit, he said.'

'Course he is,' Stella mumbled before putting the bag of snail mucus on the kitchen table.

Bob and Helen Martin were also there, having hidden the parkin in the kitchen.

As Stella passed by with an empty bottle of Prosecco, Valerie reached out and gripped her shoulder. 'Darling, where's this man of yours? Did you make him up?'

'He's on his way,' Stella hissed before the front door buzzer went again and she hurried to the intercom.

'Hello?'

'Happy birthday!' came Sam's voice.

She let him up and, less than a minute later, felt intense annoyance that she'd ever allowed him to bring a plus-one.

There should be a law, Stella decided right then and there, that no guest was allowed to come to a birthday party if they looked more glamorous than the person whose birthday it was. Just like at weddings where no guest was supposed to outdo the bride. Sam's plus-one was wearing a tight leather jumpsuit and she had the large, vulnerable eyes of a Disney princess, along with a mass of dark, shiny hair that cascaded down her back like a waterfall.

'Hello,' Sam said, grinning and reaching one arm around Stella for a hug. 'You don't look a day over twenty-one.'

'Careful.'

'All right, twenty-two.' He released her and lifted a gift bag. 'Brought our own dinner just in case.'

'Ha ha. And hi,' Stella said, turning to his date.

'Stella meet Maddy, Maddy meet Stella,' said Sam.

She leant forward to kiss her hello and begrudgingly noticed that her hair smelled good too, like marshmallow. 'Thank you for coming.'

Maddy smiled, revealing blindingly white teeth. 'Thanks for having us.'

Us, Stella thought. *Us*? Had she and Sam formed a band? How were they an 'us'? They'd only been dating for five seconds.

'Come in, and let me get you a drink.'

'Hang on, you have to open this first.' Sam held up the gift bag again and pulled out a present.

'Thanks. And I have to open it *now*?'

'Yep.' He nodded firmly.

Stella frowned with suspicion but took the present and unwrapped it to find an Italian recipe book.

It was beautiful, with thick, matt pages and photographs of multiple types of pasta – tubes of pasta with aubergine, covered with emerald-green leaves of basil; yellow ribbons of tagliatelle slick with olive oil and capers; spaghetti with mussels and lemon zest. Plus, an egg timer shaped like a penguin.

'No more kitchen accidents, OK?'

She laughed. 'Sure, thank you.'

'Can we come in?' said Maddy, flashing another dazzling smile at Stella.

'Yes, course, sorry,' Stella replied, standing aside to let them through.

Sam sniffed. 'Is something burn—'

'THE SAUSAGES,' she shrieked, before racing past various guests into the kitchen, where smoke was billowing around the oven door.

'How do I do it?' she groaned, pulling it open and coughing at another plume of smoke.

'Careful,' Sam said, having followed her. 'Look, let me.' He reached for the oven gloves and slid out the tray.

They frowned uncertainly at the contents. They were definitely still sausages, but Stella wasn't sure she'd want to put one anywhere near her mouth.

'We can eat these,' Sam insisted.

Stella raised an eyebrow.

'Sorry, sorry, anyway, drinks. Coming right up. Er…' She looked from the tray of sausages to Maddy.

'You go do drinks, I'll deal with this,' Sam said, waving at the smoke.

'All right. Beer or Prosecco?'

'Beer please.'

Stella returned to the bathroom for another bottle of Prosecco and a beer.

'Cool place,' said Maddy, hovering in the bathroom doorway. 'Is it all yours?'

'Er, yes, I'm very lucky. Where d'you live?'

'Battersea. Easy for the hospital.'

'Oh. You work there too?'

'Yeah, I'm a nurse in paediatrics. That's how Sammy and I met.'

Sammy?

'Had my eye on him for a while,' Maddy went on, with a tinkly giggle, 'but it was Harold who set us up.'

'Did he now?'

'Yeah, he's a sweetheart, isn't he? Right little matchmaker.' She paused and giggled again. 'Sammy said that's how you guys met?'

'How we met?' repeated Stella. She frowned at Maddy and tried to imagine dating her. On the plus side: waking up next to that curtain of hair. On the downside: that laugh.

'He said you met when he came over to watch the cricket here. Sammy loves his cricket,' Maddy added, rolling her eyes as they'd been married for several years and it was a habit she'd learned to live with.

'Umm, yep, that's it,' Stella said quickly. 'That's definitely how we met, on the stairs here, thanks to Harold and the cricket. Let's go back through.'

They returned to the living room, and Stella poured Maddy a glass of Prosecco before leaving her with Harold and scanning everyone else's glasses. Her phone buzzed: *Be there by 8 X*

Back in the kitchen, she held out the beer to Sam, who was fanning the air towards an open window.

'Thanks, Shakespeare.'

'Just hearing about how you and I met.'

He frowned.

'On the stairs here?' Stella grinned.

'Oh, yeah, sorry. Do you mind? Just figured it was easier.'

She laughed at his guilty face. 'No, course not. Right, if I do the buns, can you load them up?' She reached for a packet of rolls. 'Anyway, Maddy seems *great*.'

'Yeah, she's cool. Thanks for letting her come tonight. I hope it's not weird?' he asked as he speared a burned sausage with a fork.

'Why would it be weird?'

'You know. Because we…'

'*Did* it?'

'Yeah, exactly. But forget that. Old news. How are you? All OK?'

'Should I not be OK?'

'Just checking.'

'I'm not about to have another panic attack, if that's what you mean.'

'Hey, I'm being nice, Shakespeare. I don't know if you've ever heard of it? It's this weird form of behaviour where instead of feeling as if you have to be the cool girl at school, you say nice things to people.'

'And here I was, thinking nice was a biscuit.'

Sam speared another sausage. 'What I meant is that it's your birthday too, and I get that you want Billie to have a good time, and everyone else. But so should you.' He dropped the sausage into the bun Stella was holding.

'I am having a good time!' she insisted, laying the hot dog on a platter. 'I just…'

'What?'

She couldn't get her tongue around the words. 'What if…'

'Come on, cough up.'

'I don't want this to be the last one, the last party.'

'That's what you think?' he asked, turning to her.

She pressed her lips together before answering. 'It's what I'm scared of.'

'Listen to me,' Sam said, reaching toward Stella's arm before thinking better and retracting his hand. 'She's seen the best people, and she's exhausted now, but the end of the treatment schedule is the worst bit. Give it a few weeks.'

'What if it doesn't work?'

He shook his head. 'Everything's in her favour. And you can't live thinking "what if?" I don't mean to sound like a motivational Instagram post, but what if it all goes right? What if you two are still living here when you're little old ladies throwing a party sixty years from now?'

Stella managed a smile. 'It'll be kind of depressing if we're still *here* here, Jez shouting at me about the compost, me their third wheel.'

He laughed and dropped another sausage into a roll. 'Talking of which, where's that terrible boyfriend of yours?'

'Oi. And on his way. Although why does everyone keep saying he's my boyfr—'

She was interrupted by the sound of a loud bang outside.

'Fireworks!' said Stella, her head snapping up. 'Quick, that's enough rolls. We can finish them afterwards. Come on. EVERYBODY OUT!' she shouted into the living room. 'Bill, you warm enough? OK. Everyone got drinks? If you haven't got a drink, get one. Come on, out!'

She chivvied everyone towards the balcony, where they stood in a tight huddle: Billie at the front, wrapped in her dressing gown, flanked by Britt and Rose for support.

Stella retrieved her glass from the kitchen and hovered at the back of the gang, watching Maddy sidle up to Sam and rest her head on his shoulder. He, in turn, stretched his arm around her. He was so far from smug, Stella realised, as a rocket exploded into green ribbons above them. He was thoughtful and kind.

And funny. She hoped Maddy appreciated him. Although she'd need to have words with him about his pleather headboard. Although maybe she was the sort of woman who *liked* pleather headboards. The idea of this, of Maddy in Sam's bedroom, made Stella feel a small pinprick of jealousy before she told herself to stop being so absurd. She held up her glass and frowned. She'd had a few. That explained it.

As the last fireworks died away and the distant sound of applause rippled from the park, she announced that burned hot dogs were ready in the kitchen. And, finally, the buzzer went again.

'Come up!' Stella shouted into the intercom over the hubbub of noise, pressing the button with another surge of adrenalin at the idea of Fitz meeting them all.

CHAPTER 49

'HELLO, HELLO, EVERYONE, AND happy birthday,' said Fitz when he came through the door, waving like a politician walking on stage, before kissing Stella.

'I'll get you a drink,' she told him. 'Beer or Prosecco?'

Fitz winced. 'Can't bear Prosecco. Why don't I open this?' He retrieved a bottle of Champagne from his overnight bag.

'Sure,' she said, taking his overcoat, 'I'll just chuck this in my room and grab a glass.'

By the time Stella returned to the sitting room, Fitz had done a turn around it, introducing himself.

'Twin sister, surely? You cannot possibly have a 33-year-old daughter?' he'd told Valerie, who turned pink.

He told Marjorie how much he'd heard about her, dazzled Pandora by remembering Hubie's name, told Jez that *The Guardian* was 'the only newspaper worth reading' and then settled on the sofa arm and devoted his attention to Billie. 'My second-favourite birthday girl. You look radiant. How are you feeling?'

Stella decided to leave them to it, but eavesdropped anxiously as she circled the sitting room, refilling glasses. She so wanted them to get on, for Billie to like him. Yet within a few minutes, Fitz had charmed her, too, asking thoughtful questions about Billie's treatment instead of avoiding the subject like others had.

Even Jez seemed won over, and started quizzing Fitz about his time in the navy. And as he talked of parachuting over desert compounds in Iraq and storming boats off the Somali coast, others gravitated to the sofa to listen.

When Stella saw Helen and Sam in the kitchen loading the dishwasher, she went through and told them to stop.

Helen tutted. 'It's no bother, pet, especially not when I'm doing it with this strapping young lad.'

'I'll take the strapping but I'm not sure I can claim to be young,' Sam replied, grinning at Stella over the cutlery rack.

'I'm not sure about the strapping, either,' Stella joked.

Sam raised his eyebrows. 'Oh, that's weird, because I remember a time when you seemed to appre—'

'Helen, are you having a good time?' Stella interrupted.

'Yes, pet, as always.' Helen Martin was a short woman, as round as a teapot, with plump red cheeks and eyes that were always twinkling as if she'd just heard a very good joke. 'But do you know what I realised earlier?'

Stella shook her head.

'I haven't thanked you.'

'For what?'

'For looking after our girl all this time.'

'Oh,' Stella said quietly, embarrassed because she didn't believe she deserved it. 'I haven't done anything. It's Bill who's been amazing. And the doctors,' she said, mindful that Sam was still putting knives in the dishwasher.

'Nonsense. She'd have been lost without you, and Bob and I, well, we're very grateful.'

Stella glanced towards Billie and wished she could freeze time. Just for a moment. If she could pause this, now, when everyone was here and the flat was full of her best people, if they could stay like this for a while, that would be nice. It was one of those completely happy moments when everything felt right in the world and she wanted to bottle it.

Instead, she could only blink several times and smile at Helen. 'Thanks. But I think it's very late payback.'

'Payback?'

'Let's just say I owed Billie for years of… babysitting me.'

'You both have each other. That's the main thing. Now, do you think they're ready?' She looked from the cake to the crowd gathered around the sofa.

Stella nodded and Helen picked up a box of matches lying beside the parkin. 'He's ever so handsome, isn't he?' she went on.

'Mrs Martin, all this flirting,' said Sam behind them. 'You're a married woman.'

'Get away, you daft thing, I mean Stella's fancy man. And his lovely voice! So posh. Makes me think of James Bond.'

Stella laughed awkwardly, even more aware of Sam's presence. 'Er, yeah, he's a good one, I think.'

She glanced back into the sitting room, where Billie caught her eye and stuck her thumb up over the back of the sofa. 'He's great,' she mouthed.

'Right then, that'll do it,' said Helen, standing back from the cake to admire her handiwork: the light from the candles flickering on the cake's sweet, treacly exterior.

'Want a hand?' Sam offered from the sink.

'Go on then, put those muscles to good use.'

He carried it through as the small flames on the cake danced in the air. Behind him, Helen started singing 'Happy Birthday' and Stella moved to sit below Billie on the carpet, smiling bashfully at the circle around them.

Despite Stella's fears about Billie, and the absence of her dad, right there, right then, she was perfectly content, and when the singing stopped, she leant aside so she and Billie could blow out the candles together. Looking at one another, grinning, Stella felt a bolt of gratitude. Perhaps life was made by several great loves, not just the one?

After whooping and a smattering of applause, Helen cut chunks of cake and passed them around on paper plates. Someone fetched another bottle of Prosecco from the bath. Stella remained sitting on the carpet, her back against Fitz's leg as he told a story about a birthday party in Afghanistan where one soldier started a fight with another over who'd had a bigger piece of cake. 'And eventually I had to step in and separate them myself,' he said, running a hand through his hair. 'Cream all over the place. I looked like I'd been pied.'

Their laughter was interrupted by his phone, so Fitz stood and excused himself. 'Sorry, forgive me, it's my secretary. Never leaves me alone but we've got a very serious deal on.'

'Take it in my room,' Stella told him, before turning back to her friends.

'Stell, he's amazing!' said Rose as soon as he'd left the room.

'SO amazing,' added Billie.

'Jesus,' Britt sighed, gazing after him. 'Sorry, Stell, I know you're the one dating him but that man could parachute on top of me any time of the day.'

'Britt!'

'Come aboard, handsome navy seal. Or whatever he is. You need to give me a good *swabbing*.'

They snorted with laughter until Stella heard her name and turned to look behind her.

Sam and Maddy were hovering by the front door. 'So sorry, we've got to go,' he said. 'I'm on an early shift tomorrow.'

Stella jumped to her feet. 'Oh, right, course. But thank you for everything. Again.'

'Again?'

'He just always seems to be saving me,' Stella explained, looking at Maddy, who smiled and slipped her arm through Sam's.

'He's good at that, aren't you, babe?'

'You don't need saving but you're welcome. And happy birthday.' Sam stepped forward and hugged her.

'Thanks,' Stella mumbled into his chest, before stepping back and, more briefly, embracing Maddy. Good *god*, what did the woman wash her hair with?

'Pleasure to meet you,' Maddy squeaked, 'and thanks for having us.'

'No problem you… you… lovebirds,' Stella replied, scrunching her face into an exaggerated smile.

She let them out, but their departure reminded others of the time so they started stretching and murmuring about the Tube. Stella's mother told Andrew to order her a taxi because she was incapable of doing it herself; Billie stretched and yawned. Helen emerged from the kitchen, drying the Tupperware, saying that she and Bob would walk back to their hotel.

Fitz reappeared from his phone call just as Marjorie came back from the bathroom and said she should be off too.

'Oh no! But I hope you had a nice time talking to Harold?' Stella asked her.

'Who's Har— Oh, yes, I did,' she said with another nervous glance at Basil.

Jez announced he was taking Billie to bed, leaving just Fitz and Stella in the sitting room, surrounded by paper plates, the bunting overhead and Harold's congealing plate of pineapple curry dip.

'I'm sorry I was late,' Fitz told her as they sat on the sofa and he trailed his fingertips through her hair.

'That's OK. Everyone loved you. And what are you doing tomorrow? I thought maybe we could get up slowly, go get breakfast from the deli down the road, go for a walk?'

Fitz made an apologetic face. 'I'd love to, but I've got to fly back to the States.'

'Again?' Stella replied, failing to keep the disappointment from her voice.

'Afraid so. But listen, in better news, I have your present with me.'

He reached into his inside pocket and pulled out a thick cream envelope.

Stella took it with a quizzical look, then pushed her nail underneath the flap and pulled out two sheets of paper detailing an itinerary for a weekend in Paris.

'Two nights in the Georges V, which is my favourite hotel in the city, and very possibly the world. Dinner there on the Friday and in my favourite bistro on the Saturday, where they do the most exceptional veal you'll ever taste. We can do whatever we want during the day, although I insist that we spend at least thirty per cent of it in bed.' Fitz lifted his hand towards her face. 'I know I'm away a lot, but I've blocked this weekend off. Just you and me.'

Stella traced a finger across the itinerary before looking up. 'Just us in Paris. Thank you. This is the most romantic present anyone's ever given me.'

'I'm glad to hear it,' he replied before leaning forward to kiss her.

CHAPTER 50

STELLA WOKE THE NEXT morning with a dry mouth and a headache, but also the pleasant, heavy sensation of Fitz's arm over her stomach. She lay still for a few moments before rolling over and kissing him lightly on the cheek.

'Morning,' she whispered.

His eyes fluttered open. 'Hello,' he said, moving his fingers under the duvet to trace the curve of Stella's hip. 'I love waking up beside you.'

'Me too.'

'Although, what time is it?' Fitz pushed himself up on one arm and frowned at his watch. 'I should be going.'

'To the airport?'

'Mmmm,' he replied before reaching his arm over Stella to pull her on to her front. 'Although not before doing this.'

This, it turned out, meant straddling Stella, kissing down her neck and her back, before reaching between her legs, making her slippery. And just as she felt like she was about to melt, moaning into the pillow, Fitz pushed her thighs apart, moved himself on to her back and slid his erection inside her.

Stella could feel his breath on her back as he rocked, and

moved her hands to the headboard so she could push back against him, making Fitz moan louder, and she held on until he was close before letting herself go. He came seconds later, then lowered himself onto her back again, his fingers finding hers under the pillow. 'I want to wake up like this every day,' he murmured into her ear.

Stella smiled into the mattress. 'Me too. But we can in Paris.'

'We can in Paris. Although that's only two mornings.'

His tone was so sombre that Stella wriggled from underneath him to see his face. 'What are you saying?'

'Only that I wish I could see more of you.'

'You can. You can see as much of me as you like.'

He smiled and murmured a line in French. '*Qui vivra verra.*'

'What's that mean?'

'Time will tell. Or we will see, in other words.'

Stella smiled back and poked his chest. '*You* are very serious this morning.'

'Because I don't want to leave you. But I have to,' he said, turning onto his back and stretching.

Stella stayed in bed while he showered and watched him lazily as he dressed. 'Want a coffee?'

'I'll get one at the airport.'

'And when are you back?'

'By Friday, with any luck. I'll call.' He leant across the bed to kiss her, wafting toothpaste and aftershave.

'I'll come see you out.'

'Stay. Sleep.' Fitz brushed his mouth against Stella's again, picked up his bag and let himself out.

She woke again two hours later to the smell of coffee, and went through to the kitchen, where Jez was making toast and Billie was sitting on the bench in her new dressing gown.

'How are we all feeling?' Stella asked, yawning and sliding into a chair.

'Not bad,' Jez replied before glancing over his shoulder. 'Where's the arms dealer?'

'Gone. And I thought you made friends with him last night?'

'I did! I liked him. It's an affectionate nickname. Although I swear I've seen him round here before. Does he live in Notting Hill?'

Stella shook her head. 'Nope, doesn't have anywhere in London. That's why he stays in the hotel. Only his place in Paris.'

'Why Paris?'

'His mum lives there. And he grew up in France.'

'Course, you told me that. And weird. He must have a doppelganger.'

'I can't believe there can be *two* men that hot on the planet,' chipped in Billie. 'I loved him, Stell.'

Jez leant over them to put down a jar of Marmite and the butter. 'Two men that hot apart from me, you mean?'

'Goes without saying,' Billie replied, rubbing his arm.

Stella frowned, suddenly noticing how translucent Billie's skin was, how fragile she appeared besides Jez. 'Are you OK? Not too exhausted?'

She flicked her fingers in the air. 'I'll take it easy today. But don't worry about me, we have a lot to discuss. And we need to open these.' Billie nodded at the presents, pushed to the window end of the table.

'So… Fitz gave me his present last night.'

'I bet he did,' said Jez.

'What was it?' asked Billie.

'Trip to Paris,' she replied with a coy smile. 'Staying at this amazing hotel.'

Billie did a little clap. 'Romantic! When?'

'A weekend in December. So long as work doesn't get in the way, but he says he's blocked it off so…'

'Exciting. And I completely get it now.'

'Get what?'

'Why you're so taken by him. He's hot, he's funny, he made such an effort with everyone. He spent *ages* sitting next to me. And so interesting! Like, he's done so many interesting things. I really liked him, Stell.'

'Good, I'm glad.' Stella smiled with relief.

'Although I do love Sam,' Billie went on. 'As did Mum, my god, I've already had three messages from her about him this morning.'

'Saying what?'

'Just that he was such a nice lad, and so interesting, and helpful and… blah blah. I'm telling you, she's got a crush on him.'

Stella laughed. 'He was helpful last night. And I take it back about him being smug.'

'Sam's the doctor?' asked Jez, back at the kitchen counter.

'Yeah.'

'He was cool. And I liked his girlfriend.'

'*Maddy*.'

Billie scowled at Stella. 'Why are you saying it like that?'

'Like what? I just said her name.'

'Exactly. What's wrong with her? I thought she was cool.'

'And a definite ten,' added Jez. 'She could nurse me back to health anytime.'

Billie ignored him. 'She sat next to me for ages, talking about my treatment, asking if there was anything she could do and when was I next going into the hospital.'

'No no, she was cool. But… I dunno.'

'Here we go. Breakfast is served.' Jez dropped several slices of toast in front of them.

'What?' Billie challenged Stella.

'I'm not sure she's that… great.'

'Stell, she's a paediatric nurse!'

'It's just those teeth! And that hair! She seemed a bit… superficial. And did you hear her laugh? It was like someone stepping on a mouse. What?'

'Stella Shakespeare, I believe you're jealous.

'Of *her*? I am not.'

'You sure about that?'

'It's all right to feel jealous of others, Stella,' Jez teased. 'Especially ones who look like that.'

'Stop it!' Stella replied with a flash of annoyance. Course she wasn't jealous of Maddie. It was a silly suggestion. 'Jeremy, can you chuck me a piece of toast please?' Maybe she'd feel less hungover and irritable when she'd eaten.

'Hey, what happened between Harold and Marjorie?' Billie asked, tactfully deciding to change the subject.

Stella sighed. 'Not sure. I thought they'd have loads in common but whenever I looked over she was glaring at Basil like he'd attack her.'

'I washed up Harold's plate,' said Jez, nodding at a platter. 'The one that had that strange dip on it.'

'Thanks, I'll take it down later.'

'OK, but now presents!' said Billie, clapping her hands again before reaching for the pile at the end of the table.

'That was from Sam,' Stella said, nodding towards the Italian recipe book.

'Let's have a look,' said Billie, flicking back the front cover. 'Ahhh, cute inscription.'

Stella looked up from the Marmite jar. 'What inscription?'

'You haven't seen it?'

She shook her head.

'"Dear Calamity Jane",' started Billie, 'although he's crossed out "Jane" and written "Stella" above it.'

'Ha ha. What else does it say?'

'"Happy birthday, I thought I'd start you off with something basic, but it's also one of my favourites." And then he's written "Sam" and added a kiss. Well, well, well. That is *very* thoughtful.'

'It is,' Stella agreed.

'Do you think he's…'

'Mmmm?'

'Still into you?'

'No! He's got *Maddy* now, hasn't he?'

Billie rolled her eyes. 'Are you going to continue saying her name like that?

'Probably.'

'A doctor would be way too normal for you,' Jez added through a mouthful of toast.

'Thank you, Jeremy. OK, next present.'

They worked their way through the pile. Britt had bought Billie a pink beanie and Stella a pair of fingerless gloves. Rose had given them both novels. Billie's colleagues had clubbed together and bought her a large bottle of rose bath oil. Bob and Helen gave Billie a small gold bracelet with a bee charm on it, and Stella a pair of gold hoop earrings, which she told herself she mustn't lose like every other pair of earrings she'd ever had.

'Jez, what did you get her?' Stella asked once the pile had vanished.

When he didn't reply, she glanced up from her plate. 'What? Why are you looking at me like that?'

Stella frowned at Billie, who pinched her lips together and slowly raised her left hand from her lap to reveal a new ring: a diamond ring. Quite a small diamond ring, was Stella's first thought, but definitely a diamond ring.

'Oh my god, are you joking? No, obviously you're not joking. You guys, oh my god!' Stella repeated. Then she burst into tears.

Billie shifted along the bench towards her. 'Stell! That's not the reaction we were hoping for.'

Stella made a sobbing noise into her hands. It was the shock, she thought initially, but it wasn't just shock. Billie and Jez had been dating for seven years so their engagement was hardly a surprise. What she was also feeling, Stella realised as she wiped her nose with the back of her fingers, was an entirely pure form of happiness.

There had been plenty of moments during Jez and Billie's relationship when she'd been jealous of their closeness, of their uncomplicated relationship and devotion to one another because she couldn't find that herself. Plus, until very recently, Stella had found it baffling that her best friend could love someone she didn't like very much herself.

But since Billie's cancer diagnosis, her attitude towards their relationship had changed. It wasn't only that she'd watched Jez look after Billie – shop for her, put her to bed, lie with her on the sofa all weekend, fetch her water, fetch her tea, fetch her ice cubes to suck when she was hot after her chemotherapy sessions, make her laugh and repeatedly tell her she was beautiful. It was also that Stella only wanted good things for Billie, the very best things. The twinges of jealousy that she'd occasionally felt towards her best friend had vanished, and Stella was astonished to realise that she felt *grateful* to Jez for making Billie so happy.

'Sorry,' she said, wiping her cheeks. 'I'm just so happy for you both. When did you ask her, Jez?'

'Last night, bending down on my knee on the bedroom carpet. It was *very* romantic,' he joked.

'It was!' Billie said, her eyes shining, 'it really was. It was totally perfect.'

Stella burst into tears all over again.

CHAPTER 51

LATER THAT AFTERNOON, STELLA carried Harold's platter downstairs.

'Thank you so much for making it,' she said, handing it over. 'It was a big, er, hit.'

Harold's face lit up. 'Do you think so? I'm glad. It was a smashing party, thank you ever so much for having us. And isn't Sam's new girlfriend magic?'

'Are we saying girlfriend? I didn't think they'd been together that long?'

'No, I think they've been out a few times now.' Harold paused and shook his head. 'I don't know what labels you lot put on things. In my day it was stepping out. Mind you, in my day dinosaurs were roaming the planet. Cup of tea?'

'Sure, why not?' Stella replied with a sigh.

'You're suffering?' he asked as she trudged after him to his kitchen.

'Yes, but that's always the sign of a good party, isn't it, that you feel terrible the next day.'

'It was a good party,' Harold said firmly. He flicked the kettle on and Stella pulled out a kitchen chair.

'Did you, er, talk much to Marjorie?'

Harold had prepared himself for this question. He'd become aware, the previous evening, that Stella was trying to encourage him and that Marjorie lady together. Every time he'd started talking to someone else, Billie's charming parents, for example, or Maddy or Andrew, Stella had reappeared with a bottle and marched him back to Marjorie. And he had *tried* to talk to her, and even offered her some of his pineapple curry dip. But she hadn't seemed very keen, especially when Basil sniffed at her dress. And if he was very honest, she'd also been terrifyingly opinionated about everything: politics ('bad'); the weather ('horrendous'); dogs ('a menace'); the corruption of the police force ('woeful'); marriage ('a trap'); and the prime minister ('a con artist').

'I did. She was very, uh, lovely. Was that by any chance…?'

Stella looked up innocently.

'Was it what people these days call a set-up?'

'What if it was, Harold? You're a dashing single man. And Marjorie… well… she's single too. And you've got plenty in common.'

Harold's face spasmed as if he had indigestion.

'You were both in the police. And you're both about the same age.'

'I thought she was very interesting but I'm not sure there's any romance there,' he said as he carried two mugs to the table.

'OK, but what if I go into the office tomorrow and she's keen to go on a date? Or should I say is keen to *step* out with you?'

Harold made the indigestion face again.

'I'll keep you posted.'

'I did like Billie's parents,' he added more enthusiastically.

'Aren't they adorable? They got engaged, by the way. Billie and Jez.'

Harold's eyebrows leapt above his spectacles. 'Engaged?'

'Mmm, this morning.'

'What tremendous news! We need another party.'

'Maybe not quite yet,' said Stella as she felt another wave of hangover wash through her. She picked up her mug and blew over the top of it.

'And your young chap is very impressive.'

She smiled. 'He is, right?'

'He is. All those dashing tales. Quite the soldier. Although I didn't know that Sam had been in Afghanistan too. Did you?'

'No, how come? When?'

Harold slurped noisily at his tea. 'Went out as a volunteer, worked in a children's ward somewhere near Kandahar. But I don't think he likes to talk about it because of what he saw out there.'

'How do you know about it?'

'What?'

'If he doesn't talk about it?'

'Oh, I see. A nurse told me about it the other day when I was in. Not Maddy, a different one.' He slurped his tea again. 'He's a good man.'

'He is,' agreed Stella.

'Rushing over here when you had your funny turn, and helping out last night. He's the same at the hospital. Nothing is ever too much trouble. Do you know, last week, he went round the ward with a box of medals. Not real medals. They were biscuits he'd made, with little icing stars, but the kids loved them.'

'I bet.'

'I know he wasn't the one for you,' Harold went on, 'but I am glad he's met Maddy. Isn't she a peach? *Very* pretty, not that men my age are allowed to say those sorts of things any more. And you should see her at work. The kids simply worship her.'

'I'm sure,' Stella said, a touch wearily.

'It needed a little prodding, of course. And I had to cajole Sam because I got the impression he was keen on someone else.'

She looked up. 'Did you? Who?'

'No idea. He didn't say, but men can tell these things. He was pining. Anyway, I soon put him right, and told him that he was missing an absolute cracker right under his nose, and now look – everything's worked out perfectly.'

'Mmmm.'

'I do hope he and Maddy make a go of it. I have to say, I think she's wond—'

'Right, sorry, Harold, got to get back upstairs. My headache's kicking in,' Stella said, pressing her fingers to her temples. 'But thanks again, for bringing that dip.'

'Not at all. We felt very honoured to be there, didn't we, Basil?'

Basil thumped his tail in the dog bed.

CHAPTER 52

MARJORIE WASN'T IN THE office when Stella arrived the following morning, so she let herself in, made a coffee and was waiting for her ancient computer to sputter into life when her mobile rang.

'Are you there?' barked her boss.

'In the office? Yes,' Stella replied, confused, as if it was a trick question.

'I need you to lock up and come downstairs.'

'What? Why?'

'I'll explain when you're down here. You can drive, can't you?'

'Drive? A car?'

'No, a spaceship. *Yes*, a car.'

'Mmmhmm,' Stella murmured.

'I did ask you about driving when I interviewed you, if you remember?'

'It's all right, I can drive.' Stella didn't add that she hadn't been behind the wheel of a car for years. She'd passed her test as a teenager but moved to London after leaving school and never needed her own car.

'Terrific. Grab your coat and meet me outside. Make it snappy.'

Stella scalded her mouth on the coffee and hurried downstairs, where she found Marjorie on the pavement, leaning on a walking stick, having a loud discussion with a parking warden.

'You see? Here's my driver,' Marjorie declared, waving the walking stick at Stella.

The parking warden pointed at the tarmac. 'Madam, I'm afraid this is a double yellow line and I need to give yo—'

'Stella, go around the other side,' said Marjorie, collapsing into the passenger seat of a very old Volkswagen like a bag of porridge.

Stella did as she was told, opening the driver's door and climbing in while the parking warden continued protesting. 'Madam, I've taken down the number, you will receive a tick—'

'Go, Stella, go, quick,' hissed Marjorie.

'Where are the keys?'

'In the ignition. Chop-chop.'

Fumbling either side of the wheel, Stella found the keys, crunched into first gear, pressed the accelerator and immediately stalled.

'Are you trying to kill me?' Marjorie shrieked, steadying herself with a hand on the windscreen. 'Come along, we need to get going. Foot, clutch, into gear, accelerate.'

Stella swallowed. She'd forgotten about the clutch. She tried again, putting her foot down, moving the gear stick into first and more gently pressing the accelerator.

'There we go, that's more like it,' said Marjorie as they eased forwards.

Behind them, a black cab honked as Stella pulled into the traffic without indicating. 'Jesus!' she said, glancing in her mirror.

'Never mind him right now. Keep going!' instructed Marjorie, glancing over her shoulder. 'I think we lost that bossy little man.'

'Where are we going?' said Stella, braving second gear.

'Rakes.'

'*What?*'

'The hotel.'

'Yes, I know. I've stayed there.'

'Oh yes. With that tall man I met on Friday?'

'Fitz, yes.'

'How long have you been courting him again?'

'Nearly two months. Why?'

'No reason.'

'I don't know the way. And why can't you drive?'

'Bunion playing up. I shouldn't have worn heels on Friday evening but you said it was a party. Left here!'

Stella pulled off Harley Street. 'Sorry,' she muttered, feeling that she was being blamed for the bunion. 'Did you have nice time otherwise?'

'Keep going and take a left after that estate agents. And yes, I did, thank you. It was only when I woke on Saturday that my foot was throbbing like a boxer's nose. I wish I'd worn my boots, quite honestly. Left, that's it, and carry on until we hit Hyde Park corner. Careful of that cyclist!' she screeched as their wing mirror nearly clipped a man in Lycra who waved his fist in response. 'When was the last time you drove?'

'Few years ago,' Stella said lightly. It was a quad bike on holiday in Mykonos but Marjorie didn't need to know that.

'Straight down here, through those lights.'

'They're red.'

'They're not red, that's amber, and amber means you can carry on.'

Stella clamped her teeth together as she jumped the lights. This was like a bad action movie. 'Why are we going to Rakes, anyway?'

'Because our friend Mrs Bartholomew is going to be there today. She told her husband that she was having a *girls'* lunch in town.'

'You think she's meeting the man she's having an affair with?'

Marjorie waggled a finger at Stella. 'Never assume anything in this job. She might well be having lunch with friends or she might not. She might not be having an affair, and even if she is she might not be having an affair with a man.'

'So you're going to do what?'

'Sit outside and watch.'

'But it's not even ten a.m.'

'She might be early. You never know. Pays to be prepared. Take this left!' Marjorie barked, meaning that Stella had to pull across two lanes of traffic and was honked at by an irate bus driver.

Ten minutes later, her palms sweating, Stella pulled into Roland Gardens.

'There,' Marjorie hissed, pointing at a space opposite the hotel.

'I'm not sure I can park in tha—'

'Nonsense. Course you can. Come on, into reverse, back a bit, back a bit, back a bit further, that's it, straighten up. Forwards, and then wheel to the right. There we go. That'll do.'

Stella turned off the engine with relief. 'Right, what now? Shall I go back to the office?'

'No! I may need you to drive me again. You'll have to stay here with me while we wait for her.'

'OK,' Stella fell wearily back against her seat. Nobody seemed to sweat this much in movie car chases.

'Not *here*, in there.' Marjorie undid her seatbelt and jerked her thumb towards the back of the car where the seats were laid flat. 'In we get, come on.' She turned in her seat and, with all the elegance of an elephant doing the tango, squeezed herself through the front seats.

'Why?' Stella asked, leaning towards the window to avoid being buffeted by Marjorie's bottom.

'Tinted windows in the back so I can take pictures, and there's also this.' Her boss pulled a small black curtain across the car, which separated the front from the back. Then she drew it again and reappeared. 'So nosy parkers can't see us through the windscreen. Come along, haven't got all day. Need to be primed.'

'What about parking wardens?' Stella asked, reluctantly undoing her seatbelt and climbing through the narrow gap.

'Got a permit for this borough. We're fine here all day. And we might be all day, I warn you, that's why I have my Shewee.' Marjorie tapped a large black bag.

Stella groaned as she pulled herself through to the back of the car. Surely she wouldn't have to watch Marjorie wee in the back of an old Volkswagen? She'd ask for a pay rise if that happened.

CHAPTER 53

TWO HOURS LATER, MRS Bartholomew still hadn't appeared and Stella was desperate for the loo.

Marjorie's black bag hadn't just contained a camera, several camera lenses of various sizes, a back-up battery case for her phone *and* a yellow Shewee, but a flask of hot coffee, a bag of toffees, a packet of plain digestives, a large bag of crisps and a plastic carton of glazed donuts, covered with sprinkles. Between them, they'd drunk the coffee, eaten two donuts, half the digestives and several toffees, so not only did Stella need to pee, she also felt a bit sick.

Worse still, Marjorie had removed her trainers, claiming her bunion needed 'to air', so the car smelled of feet.

Numerous women who looked like Mrs Bartholomew – dark hair, pale skin, smartly dressed – had entered the hotel, ushered in by the uniformed doorman ('he's called Jozef,' Stella had told her boss, who grunted in reply), but when Marjorie focused her camera, it was clear they weren't the target.

She reached for another toffee. 'Did you like my neighbour?'

'What's that?' murmured Marjorie, squinting through the passenger window like an owl hunting for mice.

'My neighbour Harold. At the party. Did you like him?'

Marjorie cocked her head. 'I did like him. Less keen on the dog. But I don't think he's the man for me.'

Stella started to protest. 'I didn't say he wa—'

'Young Stella, you're good at many things but I could tell it was a set-up the moment I arrived.'

They fell silent for a few moments until Stella decided to brave another personal question. It was easier to talk to Marjorie side by side, in the gloom of the car, rather than face to face.

'Are you absolutely sure…' Stella started. 'Are you absolutely sure you don't want to find love again?'

'Not right now,' mumbled Marjorie, still staring ahead of her.

'No, but ever, I mean. Are you done with it?'

'For the time being. I'm a very busy woman.'

That sounded like an excuse to Stella. How could anyone be too busy to fall in love? Falling in love was the most glorious sensation in the world. Dementing at moments, true; she'd messaged Fitz that morning to say she missed him lying in bed beside her and he still hadn't replied. But there was a five-hour time difference between London and Washington, and he'd reply when he was awake. She just had to be patient. Now that Fitz had met her family and friends, it was like they'd progressed another level in the video game. And her day would be made better simply by hearing his voice. Nobody could be too busy for *that*.

'Life isn't completed when you get married, you know,' Marjorie went on. 'That's the problem with a vast number of clients.'

Stella pushed the toffee into her cheek with her tongue. 'What do you mean?'

Marjorie picked up her camera as a woman in a long red coat approached the revolving door. 'People expect too much from the person they married. They expect to be healed by that person, for that person to solve all their problems. They expect that other person to make them completely happy, and when they don't, bitterness can set in.'

'I don't expect to be *healed*, but—'

Marjorie tutted. 'No, that's not her either.'

'What's so wrong with wanting love, or looking out for it? Why are people called desperate and made to feel ashamed, when all they want is for someone to love them back?'

'There's nothing wrong with wanting or looking for love, so long as you're looking for it for the right reasons.' Marjorie lowered the lens and looked at Stella. 'And in the right places.'

'What do you mean, the right pla—'

'Shhhhh, hang on, look, I think that's our woman.'

Stella squinted through the window, where a woman in a pair of knee-high boots was trotting towards Jozef the doorman.

'Yes,' Marjorie said triumphantly, lens pressed against the glass, shutter clicking as she took several pictures in succession, 'that's our girl.'

Mrs Bartholomew vanished into the hotel.

'What now?' Stella asked.

'Now we wait.'

They waited in the car for just over another hour, by which point Stella needed to pee so badly her palms had started sweating. 'Marjorie? Do you think I could just nip out for two minutes? Literally two minutes. I know where the bathrooms are in the hotel, I could run in, run out and you'd barely notice I'd gone.'

'Not on your nelly, we've got to sit tight because we may need to move again. You need the bladder of a tin man in this job.'

Stella wanted to reply that they were tailing a 43-year-old architect, not a gang of bank robbers. Instead, she sighed, leant against the back window, reached for another toffee and looked at her phone screen. Blank. For a moment she missed Fitz so badly it was like a rip in her chest. It was nearly 9 a.m. in Washington now so he must be awake. Opening up their WhatsApp conversation, she quickly tapped out another message. *Miss you. Am on a mad job with Marjorie. Will explain later xxxx*

Half an hour later, Mrs Bartholomew appeared outside the hotel again, hand in hand with a tall man in a suit.

'Oh my god,' murmured Stella.

'There she is,' said Marjorie, taking photos. 'And there *he* is.'

Stella knelt forward and pressed her hands against the window. 'Oh my god, I'm going to be sick.'

'Now's not the moment, young Stella, but there's a sick bag in the black bag if you need,' Marjorie mumbled. 'Always be prepared, that's my motto.'

'What is he *doing* with her?'

'That's what poor Mr Bartholomew will wonder too, when I send him these pictures.'

'It's disgusting!' Stella shrieked, her voice strangely high-pitched.

'Indeed. You see all sorts of things in this line of work, I don't mind telling you. This is relatively tame compared to the time that I was in Switzerland, tailing a client who was supposedly out there for a board meeting. I pretended to be the hotel cleaner and let myself into their room only to find…'

Marjorie continued talking about Switzerland while snapping photos but Stella tuned out, staring through the window, mouth open, unable to compute exactly what she was watching. It didn't make sense. Why was he with her? How could he? And why on earth was his kissing her like *that*?

'But I mean… seriously?' she said eventually, finding words again. '*Dad?*'

'No time for personal calls either, young Stella.'

'No, Marjorie, that's my dad. There, with her.'

Marjorie turned her head to look at Stella with astonishment. 'Your father? With Mrs Bartholomew? *Your* father?'

Stella nodded dumbly and watched her father lower his head to kiss Mrs Bartholomew again, clasping her head with one hand while his other arm snaked around her back, bending her backwards as if in a dance move. Then she remembered what Mr Bartholomew had told her during that first phone call about his wife's extreme bikini wax and felt another wave of nausea.

'Can I open a window, Marjorie? I need some air.'

'Make it pavement side,' she instructed from behind her camera.

Marjorie carried on taking photos while Stella wound down the back window and lifted her mouth towards it like an abandoned dog. Should she get out? Confront him? What would she say? What was the right thing to do?

'It's so brazen,' she murmured, turning to look at the spectacle of her father kissing Mrs Bartholomew in the street again. 'Don't most people try and hide their affairs? Why would he do this here? In broad daylight?'

'Some people get complacent,' Marjorie mumbled. 'Who's going to see you on a Monday afternoon outside a hotel in

Kensington?' She lowered her camera and turned to Stella. 'I really am sorry.'

But Stella couldn't reply.

'In the end,' added her boss, 'it always comes down to human error. You can have two phones, change your passwords, say you're away on business, pay for dinners and hotels in cash, but there will be a moment that you slip up and forget all the subterfuge, and that's when you get caught.'

Marjorie paused. 'Same with murderers.'

CHAPTER 54

ONCE IAN SHAKESPEARE AND Perdita Bartholomew had stopped fondling one another and caught separate taxis from Rakes, Marjorie announced they didn't need to follow them. They knew who the man was, after all. She said she'd write up the case notes herself and update Mr Bartholomew.

'Thanks,' Stella murmured as she drove them back towards Harley Street, scattering cyclists as she changed lanes without indicating, leaving pedestrians shaking their heads at zebra crossings when she failed to stop for them.

She didn't know what to do. Tell her mother? Ring Andrew? Call her father? Say nothing and let the family continue to be as maladjusted as always? The image of her father wrapping his arms around Mrs Bartholomew like a hungry octopus kept reappearing in her head. She'd probably need to have therapy.

'What do I do?' she asked, striking her thumbpad against the steering wheel. 'Literally, what do I do?'

Marjorie considered the question. 'How long have they been married?'

'Nearly forty years.'

'Happily?'

'No. Never. Well, I don't know about never. They must have been happy at first, right? Everybody's happy at first.'

Marjorie waggled her head from side to side.

'I mean, I knew he'd had affairs,' Stella went on. 'There was this drama with our nanny, once. She was sent back to Australia.'

'Very common, affairs with the nanny. That's why many rich people choose nannies from Norland.'

'What?' Stella asked faintly as a bus honked at them.

'Norland. The nanny agency. Where the Royals get their nannies from. They make them wear terrifically ugly beige uniforms so the husbands don't want to sleep with them. The uniforms are effectively a form of contraception.'

'But seeing that so blatantly...' Stella continued. 'I feel like I should say something to Mum. Otherwise I'm in on it, on Dad's dirty little secret.'

'Young Stella, I cannot tell you what to do. But in my experience, it's better to be open about these things. Ignore them and they become festering sores. Think of it like this job. We can only do so much and then we present the evidence to the clients. After that, it's up to them to decide what to do. You can do the same with your mother.'

'Tell her, you mean?'

'Indeed. Present the evidence and she can choose what to do with it. Or, put it another way, if it was you, would you rather know?'

'Yes!'

'There you go, then. That's your answer. But remember that you don't necessarily know all the facts.'

'What d'you mean?'

'Mind that woman with the buggy. What I mean is this is a shock, a terrible shock, for which I'm very sorry. Here was I, thinking it might be useful for you to have some experience in the field, and we end up watching your father behave as if he's auditioning for a porno.'

'Marjorie...'

'Yes, yes, I'm getting to the point, which is you may not know all the facts but perhaps your mother does? Perhaps she knows about this, knows about your father's... acrobatics... and she loves him anyway? The heart is a strange, unpredictable muscle, young Stella, and all of ours are different. What's right for my heart, or for your heart, won't be right for another. Actually, what's right for my heart is being left undisturbed with a pepperoni extra hot. But that's by the by.'

Stella inhaled and held the breath in her chest. It *was* a shock. She'd never been close to her father. She wasn't even very sure if she liked him, although she had relied on his money for a while, she admitted. For far too long, to be honest. But still, it was her father with another woman and that was a bombshell.

It wasn't just a shock, Stella realised, as she drove through another red light; she could sense a kernel of anger growing inside her. For years she'd put up with her parents' interrogations on her own love life. When was she going to settle down? When was she going to find a boyfriend? They'd been banging on about marriage for years, pushing her to find someone – anyone would do for them by this point – when their own marriage was a sham. Even if her own mother *did* know about this affair, how dare she insinuate that her marriage was something to aspire to? They were living a lie and, worse still, they were trying to sell that lie to her.

'Men!' Stella said, exhaling.

'Indeed.'

'Although not all men,' Stella added, thinking of Fitz.

'A good number of them,' Marjorie replied darkly.

After taking ten minutes to park in a space long enough for several London buses, Stella hobbled gratefully to the office loo before returning to her desk and staring at her phone. Ring her mother now or leave it until later? But she would only obsess about it all afternoon if she left it, so she might as well do it now.

It rang six times, but just as Stella was about to give up, Valerie answered.

'Darling, I'm just heading off to bridge. Can I ring you afterwards?'

'Not really, no.'

'Go on then, but it'll have to be quick.' Valerie tutted down the phone. 'Where are my gloves?'

'I need to tell you something.'

'Go on,' her mother replied, clearly not listening. Stella could hear the opening and closing of drawers in her parents' bedroom. She imagined her there, all made-up and ready to go to bridge, standing in their vast bedroom, which overlooked the lawn in front of the Tudor house. She felt guilty for the chaos she was about to unleash. Then she thought of Marjorie's advice: if it was her, she'd want to know.

'It's something I saw today, and I wasn't sure whether to tell you, because obviously we never actually talk about anything in our family,' Stella gabbled, 'which is part of the problem.'

'Darling, I did say quick. Ah! Here they are.' The sound of a drawer closing.

'You know the lady I work for, the one I told you was a wig saleswoman?'

'Mmmm, I think so. I didn't talk to her at the party but I think I know the one you mean, the woman who looked like a mystic?'

'Yes, her,' Stella said with a sigh. 'She doesn't actually sell wigs. She wears some pretty weird ones bu—'

'Darling, I need to get in the car.'

'Yes, all right! The thing is, that woman, the one who doesn't sell wigs, she's a private detective who specialises in affairs, and today we saw Dad— *I* saw Dad, earlier, outside a hotel in London, with a woman. Kissing another woman.'

Valerie didn't reply.

'Mum? Are you OK?'

'What were you doing loitering outside a hotel?'

'Working with Marjorie! That's what I'm trying to tell you. We were parked outside, working for a client, and I saw Dad with this woman, *really* with her, I mean.'

'Stella, is that all?'

'What do you mean, "is that all"? Did you hear me? I said I saw Dad kissing another woman. And it wasn't any sort of kiss, Mum. It wasn't the way you'd kiss a friend, unless you were a pervert. It was… It was…' The vision of Stella's father kissing like an octopus swam before her again. 'It was *revolting*.'

Valerie sighed. 'Darling, honestly, if I had a pound for every time your father's fallen into bed with another woman, I'd be nearly as rich as him.'

'Are you joking? You've got to be joking?'

'He has the sexual appetite of a baboon during the mating

season so he takes it elsewhere. Fine by me. I'm not sure I like the sound of this job though, darling. It sounds awfully seedy.'

'Mum, I—'

'Marriage is all about what you're willing to put up with, Stella. Or sacrifice, perhaps I should say.'

'Why are you always telling me to do it, then?'

Valerie paused. 'Because that's what one *does*. The trouble with you, Stella, is that you've always been too romantic. I don't know where you got that from. It's not helpful, darling, to have such fanciful ideas about love. I know you're head over heels at the moment with that extremely attractive man, and that's all very well, but the romance doesn't last.'

'I'm so sorry for being idealistic, for having standards and morals! How can you stay with him, knowing this?'

'Darling, I have to go to bridge. Listen, why don't we have lunch and discuss it when I'm next in London? My treat.'

'Mum...'

'And not a word of this to your father, please. Or Andrew, for that matter. It would only upset him. OK, got to go, darling, bye.'

Stella slumped in her chair. Just when she thought her family couldn't get any more dysfunctional.

She glanced at the time. Nearly four. So, nearly eleven in Washington. Fitz would be in meetings, she guessed, but she wanted to hear his voice. *Can you call me when you get this?*

He called back half an hour later, sounding worried. 'Hi, you all right?'

'No, not really.'

He sighed. 'Stella, forgive me, I'm so sorry—'

'Dad's having an affair,' she blurted.

'Your *father*?'

It tumbled out of her: the car stakeout, the waiting with Marjorie, the moment that she saw her father appear outside the hotel with the architect.

Stella paused for breath, having finished, but Fitz's first reaction was to laugh. 'I'm impressed the old dog's got it in him.'

'Seriously?'

'No, obviously not,' Fitz replied, detecting her tone. 'It's appalling and he should be ashamed of himself.'

'Right? But when I called my mother...'

'You *told* her?'

'Yes, obviously. Why wouldn't I?'

Fitz exhaled down the phone. 'Because relationships are delicate...'

'Delicate?' she replied scornfully.

'Complicated, as I think I've said before. From the outside, it can be very hard to tell what's going on in it. How long have your parents been married?'

'Forty years.'

'Forty years, there we go. Your mother knows your father better than anyone else in the world. Perhaps she knows about this other woman.'

'Exactly, that's the thing. She *does* know about her,' said Stella before explaining her mother's remarks.

'Listen,' Fitz said. 'Other people's marriages are other people's marriages, and no marriage is the same. If this works for your parents, what's the problem?'

'That's what Marjorie said. But it's so sad! And depressing.'

'Your mother doesn't sound as if she's sad or depressed.'

'Deranged, perhaps.' Stella sighed. 'Maybe you're right. I just can't imagine living like that myself. But am I too idealistic?'

'No! You're a thoroughly, beautiful, enchanting woman and I wish I was there to look after you.'

She smiled down the phone. 'Thank you. So do I. How come you're so wise about all this?'

'All this?'

'Marriage. Relationships. Life!'

'I'm not that wise. I've made mistakes. I'm *still* making mistakes but, ah—' Fitz stopped abruptly.

'But?'

'Hopefully not many more. Now, I have a surprise that should cheer you up.'

'What? Tell me.'

'I can't tell you but I can show you when I'm back.'

'When is that?'

'Thursday, I'm hoping, so what about Friday? You free Friday evening?'

'For you, of course.'

Fitz gave her an address in Chelsea that Stella didn't recognise. 'A restaurant?'

'It's a surprise, so you'll have to wait and see. But I'd better go. I miss you.'

'Miss you too. But hang on, what were you going to apologise for?'

'Apologise?'

'Just now, before I told you about all this, you started saying sorry?'

'Oh that! That was only because I've been so rubbish at being in touch since I got here. I'm sorry. I've basically been in back-to-back meetings with the Yanks.'

'That's OK,' Stella said through a sigh. 'I guess we've both got other things going on right now. But see you on Friday, can't wait.'

'Me neither. And it'll all be fine, I promise.'

She hung up and googled the address he'd given her, which was for a random street in Chelsea and seemingly not a restaurant.

Stella tapped her fingers on the desk, counting off the days until Friday. Four. Just four days until she would see him and find out.

CHAPTER 55

IT WAS DARK BY the time Stella reached 72 Eaton Square on Friday evening, so she squinted at the address under the orange street light, her breath hanging in the air. It was one of London's most expensive roads, lined with cream-coloured houses, five floors high, with stucco pillars outside each one.

She glanced over her shoulder at the sound of a car slowing and saw Victor pull up.

'There she is,' Fitz said, stepping out of it. He opened his arms and Stella fell into them, more grateful than she'd felt before to see him.

'Hi,' she mumbled into his overcoat, inhaling him, pressing her cheek to his chest, reaching her arms beneath his to hug him closer.

'Hello,' he replied before tilting her face upwards, one hand under her chin, and kissing her. It was a kiss that took Stella aback with its gentleness, as if he was almost afraid to do it.

'You all right?' she asked, pulling back.

Fitz gazed down at her. 'I am. I just missed you.'

'Hey, I missed you too.'

At that, his solemnity seemed to break and he grinned. 'Come on, this is what I want to show you.'

'Have you bought a house?' Stella asked, her eyes narrowing with suspicion.

Fitz laughed. 'I'm sorry to disappoint you but I have not bought a house.'

'In that case, what are we doing out here? It's freezing.'

'What I have bought is a flat. Or an "apartment", as the estate agent described it.'

'You're kidding?'

'I'm not, come on,' he said, taking her hand before turning back to his car. 'Back shortly, Victor.'

'Of course, sir.'

Fitz pulled Stella up the stone steps to a large black front door and reached into his overcoat pocket to retrieve a set of keys. 'I warn you, it isn't furnished yet, and it needs a lick of paint. But I think, or I hope anyway, that you'll like it.'

In the hall was an old-fashioned lift with a metal grille that Fitz pulled across before it carried them to the top floor.

'Ready?' he asked, turning to grin at Stella once they'd left the lift and were standing in front of another door. Suddenly he looked like a five-year-old boy on Christmas Eve: eyes shining, a hyperactive energy rolling off him.

Stella nodded and Fitz opened the door.

The musty smell was the first thing that hit her.

But once Fitz flicked on a light, Stella felt overawed. Technically, it was a flat, but it was the grandest flat she'd ever seen. Even *with* the musty smell.

The door revealed an enormous hallway with a polished

wooden floor. To their left was a room so vast it looked like a ballroom, with four sets of French windows running along it, all of which opened to a balcony overlooking the square.

'It was owned by the same family for over sixty years,' Fitz said, 'but the dowager duchess just died so it came on the market.'

'It's unbeliev—'

'This way,' said Fitz, reaching for her hand. 'Sitting room… my office… I'm going to make this a gym,' he said as they passed various doors until the space opened out across both sides of the corridor into a huge kitchen: no furniture but ghostly white shapes on the wall where pictures used to hang, and a long marble counter above a strip of blue cupboards.

Fitz crouched to pull one open, revealing a fridge that contained a bottle of Champagne. 'I was hoping Charlie would do that. He was the agent.'

'I mean, Fitz, this is… this is mad. You've *bought* it?'

'I have.'

'How come?'

Fitz nudged the cork free with his thumb so it shot loudly towards the ceiling. 'Because…' he said, turning his attention back to Stella, 'I'm starting to tire of hotels. And I want, or at least I would like to spend more time with you.'

An enormous smile spread across her face, so enormous that Stella could hardly speak.

'Ah. No glasses. Oh well, here you go.'

Stella took the bottle and sipped, the bubbles making her nose sting. 'I would like that,' she told him shyly. 'I would love that. I can't believe it.'

She turned in a circle, taking in the size of the place again, the high ceilings, the tall windows that looked out across the London skyline, twinkling with distant lights. 'I like the hotel but this… this is something else. Or it will be once you have a sofa. And also,' she paused and exhaled dramatically, 'I'm not sure I want to hang out at Rakes much, given it seems to be my father's haunt of choice.'

'I understand that,' Fitz replied, taking the bottle from her.

Lowering it again, he wiped his mouth with the back of his hand and looked more serious. 'Stella, I have to tell you something.'

She frowned. 'What?'

He ran a hand through his curls, and Stella saw a pulse in the hollow of his throat.

'What is it?'

'You see, when I met you in September, I wasn't entirely honest…'

'So you *are* an arms dealer?'

Fitz made a noise of exasperation. 'No! I've told you. It's not that. It's something else.'

She stopped breathing. The intensity of his expression scared her. It felt as if she was standing on a trapdoor that was about to open. 'What?'

'I should have told you… I have tried to tell you… I've wanted to tell you…'

'Fitz, seriously, what is it?'

He inhaled so that his chest puffed upwards and then he held it, before smiling and letting his breath out. 'I should have told you… that my first name is Lysander.'

Stella burst out laughing. 'Is that it? I thought you were going to tell me you were going to prison or you had a secret family or something.' She shook her head. 'Lysander Fitzwilliam Montague. Jeez. I thought Stella Grace Shakespeare was bad.'

'Blame my mother.' Fitz put the bottle down and stepped forward to wrap his arms around her. 'And I'm not going to prison, not any time soon, I hope. But can we please, please put this arms dealer nonsense to bed? I'm not *that* immoral.'

'Sure.'

'Come on, there's something else I need to show you.'

Stella pulled her head back and grinned. 'Full of surprises today.'

'I am indeed. This way.' Fitz took her hand and led her to an empty room on the front side of the apartment, painted a pastel pink. Through one of the large windows, she could just see the Houses of Parliament in the distance. 'This was the duchess's bedroom, I'm told.'

'I can tell,' Stella said, grimacing at the salmon shade. 'Obviously you're going to keep it like this?'

'Well… what colour would you like it to be, if it was our bedroom?'

'*Our* bedroom?'

He nodded. 'If we are going to spend more time together, then I thought we needed somewhere to do it. It's… for the future.'

'Pink is fine,' she joked with a shrug before laughing, giddy at the entire evening. Fitz had bought a place; he'd talked of their bedroom. Stella couldn't believe anyone could ever feel so full with happiness.

He stepped forwards and lifted his fingers to her cheek. 'I really missed you.'

'Fitz, I'm right here.'

'I meant when I was in Washington.'

'Oh. Me too,' she whispered before pressing her mouth against his.

The kiss intensified as Fitz's hands pulled her shirt free from her trousers and started roaming underneath it.

She stopped and blinked at him. 'Here? Now?'

He nodded before putting his hands on Stella's shoulders and navigating her backwards until she was against the wall. Pressing his body against hers and lifting his palms to either side of her face, Fitz kissed her again, harder and harder, until her mouth felt swollen and he pushed her down to the dull beige carpet.

This feels different, Stella thought, as Fitz pulled her shirt over her arms. It felt more emotional. Sex with Fitz had always been intense from the very first time they'd slept together at the hotel. But there had also been a primal, almost animal compulsion to it, as if they were addicted to one another and their arms, legs, chest and fingers had to be pressed against the other's, as close as possible, like they were melding into one.

It was slower now, more considered. And, as Fitz kissed along Stella's collarbone and she ran her hands over his shoulders, they kept looking at one another, holding the other's stare. It felt like they were making a silent promise to one another, Stella realised. It wasn't just this apartment. It was more than that; it was an unspoken form of commitment.

It was also how Stella ended up with friction burns on her shoulder blades and bottom, which stung in the shower for the next week, although she smiled every time she stepped under the hot water. It had been worth it.

CHAPTER 56

JUST OVER A WEEK after she came home with carpet burns on her bottom, Stella took Billie to hospital for a blood test and her first check-up with the oncologist. It was a Monday morning and they were standing just inside the hospital's revolving entrance while Billie worked out which floor they needed. 'It's in an email somewhere.'

She was nervous, Stella could tell, because she'd barely spoken on the bus.

'It's going to be fine,' Stella reassured her, looking around at the place that had become almost as familiar to them both as the flat: the bright overhead lights; staff hurrying past in blue uniforms; the noise of a laundry trolley being wheeled over the grey municipal floor tiles.

'I know,' Billie replied quietly.

'He's going to tell you he's never seen anyone respond so well to treatment and declare that you're a medical miracle.'

Billie crossed her fingers and lifted them up with a small smile as Stella wondered how else to distract her. She tapped at her phone to reveal a picture of a model wearing a sheer lace bodysuit, erect nipples poking through it like bullets.

'Look. Do you think this is too much?'

Billie whispered quickly, 'Stell! Put it away, people will think we're looking at porn!'

Stella snorted. 'No they won't. Don't you think it's pretty?'

'For what? Are you joining the circus?'

'No! For Paris next weekend.'

'Oh, I see.' Billie frowned at the model. 'What do you wear it *with*?'

'Under a dress. Or by itself. It's got poppers in the crotch so you can ping it open.'

'Shhhhhhh!' hissed Billie before glancing back to her emails.

Stella slid her phone into her coat pocket. 'I'm going to order it. Paris, Bill! We're going to get a boat down the Seine, Fitz said.'

'You'll need more clothes for that. OK, found it, third floor.'

'Coffee? We've got time.'

Billie nodded, so Stella slipped one arm through hers and they walked towards the café.

She'd need several coffees that day, she suspected. Marjorie had already emailed that morning, asking if she could spend some time fixing the printer because she didn't want to pay for an engineer to come in, and it was a task Stella already knew would make her want to fling the printer from the third-floor window.

She saw them as they walked towards the coffee shop, although Stella noticed *her* at first because she was so elegant. Most women who are nearly six months pregnant waddle like hippos off to the watering hole, but not her. She was in leather trousers and ballet flats, her chestnut hair pulled back in a swishy ponytail, with a bump as neat as a football.

Stella was about to elbow Billie and point her out, make a joke about how different it would be when they were pregnant, when Stella fully intended to get fat and lie on the sofa in leggings all day. But then she noticed the man beside her, his arm around her shoulders.

They were standing on the other side of the escalators, inspecting a piece of paper. And when the pregnant woman mumbled something and looked up for reassurance, Fitz shook his head and replied, before brushing his lips against her hair.

Stella could hear Billie saying words beside her, but she couldn't process what those words were. And she couldn't have replied because she couldn't form any words. Her chest started constricting again, like it had in the kitchen that evening, as if someone was standing on her throat, and she started gasping for breath.

'Stell? Stella?'

Beside her, Billie reached for both arms and shook them. 'Stella? Stop it, you're freaking me out. Stella?'

She could only stare in their direction. They were still standing together, looking down at the piece of paper, except when the pregnant woman dropped her hand to her side, she could see it was a polaroid.

Billie followed her gaze. 'Right, OK. Stell? Stella? Come and sit here. Stella? Seriously, with me, come on, I've got you. Look, here.'

She kept hold of her hand and pulled Stella to a table outside the café, on the other side of the escalators.

'OK, come here, sit, breathe.'

'Did you see? They can't see us, can they? I didn't know… He never said…'

'They can't see us. Forget them. Sit and breathe. It's the shock. Just breathe. Oh, Sam, thank god you're here. I think it's another panic attack. Long story. No, it's only just started, so I made her sit down here.'

Stella, staring at her knees, became aware that Billie had moved and Sam was squatting in front of her.

'Stella, do you remember what I told you? In for five, out for five. Here, hold my hand, I'm going to count for you. One… two… three… four… five… OK, well done. Out for five. One… two… three… four… five.'

One of the benefits of having a panic attack in a hospital is that barely anybody notices. In the café that morning was a man in an eyepatch who'd accidentally used lavender oil instead of eye drops; a mother with a screaming eight-week baby who'd just had his injections; an elderly woman on a drip, and a small boy in a Superman costume with a bandage wrapped around his head, sharing a piece of cake with his father. Stella was the least of their worries.

Within two minutes of counting, Sam had Stella's breathing back under control, but as the initial shock subsided, she started crying.

'Billie?' he asked, standing up. 'Can you take over? I'm going to go and get her a tea.'

'Good plan.' Billie pulled out a chair. 'Stell, can you hear me?'

Stella nodded and watched a tear drop to the hospital tiles, then another and another as she gave in to the pain and let it rip through her. He was with someone else. Maybe married to her. And she was pregnant. 'He's with someone else,' she murmured. 'He's with someone else. How has this happened, Bill? How have I been this stupid?'

Briefly, Stella wondered whether it could be a relation. A sister? But nobody kissed their sister like that. And if they did, they should see a therapist.

'Oh my love, you haven't been stupid.'

'I have,' Stella replied through her tears, 'I have. It happens every time. I'm stupid every time. I'm so stupid, Bill. I'm so stupid.'

She kept repeating it until Billie leant over and clutched her. 'Shhhh, you're not. It'll be all right.'

Sam returned with two teas and Stella remained slumped over her knees while they spoke quietly.

'You go,' she heard Sam say, 'I'm not on duty for half an hour. Go. Don't miss your appointment. I'll stay here.'

Billie crouched. 'Stell, I'm going upstairs and then I'll come back and get you.'

Stella wiped her nose with the back of her hand. 'I'll come with you.'

'Uh-uh. Stay here, drink the tea.'

'Marjorie needs me to fix the printer,' Stella replied through a blocked nose.

'Forget the printer. Stay here with Sam, I'll be back.'

Sam sat and passed over the polystyrene cup. 'Three sugars in this. Knock it back, please.'

Stella sipped at the tea while Sam sat beside her. Occasionally she glanced up in case Fitz was near, but mostly she kept her head lowered. Slowly, her heart-rate calmed and breathing became easier. She drained the cup and sniffed, so Sam passed her a stack of paper napkins.

'How you doing?'

'Better, thank you.'

'You're very welcome.'

'I'm not keeping you from work?'

'Nah, I was just grabbing a coffee. My shift doesn't start until nine.'

'Did Billie tell you?'

'Tell me?'

'What happened?'

Sam shook his head. 'Nope.'

'You can probably guess,' Stella replied, wiping her cheekbone with the back of her hand.

'I have a vague idea,' Sam said with a sympathetic smile. 'Listen, I don't know very much about the heart...'

'You're a doctor!'

'OK, sure, I know that it's an organ with four chambers, a left and right ventricle and a left and right atrium and it pumps bloo—'

Stella made a gagging noise.

'What?'

'I'm squeamish.'

'OK, OK. What I meant is I don't necessarily know much about the *emotions* of the heart, but I do know that no man should make you feel like you've felt in the past couple of months.'

'You do know a bit about the heart then.'

'All right, I do, but I didn't want to boast.'

She laughed softly. 'Thanks.'

'For what?'

'Helping me. Again.'

'Hey, it's normally seven-year-olds who've swallowed pen

lids or broken their wrists. Nice to rescue an adult for a change, and a pretty amazing adult at that.'

Stella rolled her eyes, embarrassed, and suddenly became aware of how she must look. She sat up and pressed her fingers to her eyes.

'Who was it that said it'll be all right in the end, and if it's not all right then it's not the end?' Sam asked after a few moments.

Stella dropped her fingers. 'Not sure.'

'The Dalai Lama? He's always coming out with things like that.'

She laughed again. It was such a bad joke but he was trying to cheer her up.

'Only you, Shakespeare,' he went on, gently buffeting her shoulder with his own, 'could bring someone to hospital and end up needing more attention than the patient.'

Stella turned her head to smile ruefully at him and they held each other's gaze for a few moments. She'd got him so wrong. Sam wasn't a swaggerer or someone who needed to make a noise to demonstrate how brilliant or successful he was. He was quieter than that. He was, quietly, a wonderful human being.

'She's smiling!' said Billie, reappearing over them.

'Hello,' said Sam, leaping to his feet and holding out his chair. 'Check-up go well? Who did you see?'

'Dr Moylan? And think so. I'll get the results from my bloods today, apparently.'

'She's great. And well done. But listen, I should head upstairs. Those broken wrists won't heal themselves.' He dropped his hand to Stella's shoulder. 'The prognosis is that this one will live.'

Stella smiled up at him. 'Thanks.'

'Like I said, any time.'

He waved, made his way to the escalators and Billie sat. 'How are you now?'

'I've had better mornings, but at least the sugar from the tea's kicked in. Anyway, more importantly, was the check-up really OK?'

'Mmm. Although I'm confused about something.'

'Tell me, what is it?' Stella bit her lower lip, anxious that Billie had been given bad news.

'What I don't understand,' Billie replied as she watched Sam disappear up the escalator, 'is why you both look at each other in that way when *you* claim you don't even like him.'

'What way?'

'Like the scene in *The Lion King* where Simba falls in love with the girl lion.'

'Nala.'

'Exactly.'

'No we don't,' Stella insisted before blowing her nose noisily into a napkin. 'He's just… a friend. A very good friend.'

CHAPTER 57

WITHIN ONE AND A half minutes of Stella arriving at the office, Marjorie had worked out that something was up. The woman was like a truffle pig.

'Why do you look like that?' she asked, standing over her desk.

'Like what?' Stella replied, trying to hide her puffy eyes under her mane of hair.

'Like you've been chopping onions all night.'

'Er… I…'

'Is it that man?'

'Um, yeah, I, er…' Stella started crying at her desk and, between gulps of breath and loud blows into tissues that Marjorie kept passing her, regurgitated the story: the hospital, seeing Fitz, the pregnant woman, her panic attack.

Marjorie grunted when she'd finished. 'I thought as much. I heard him on the phone at your party.'

'*What?* When? Saying what?'

'When I came out of the bathroom. He was having a ding-dong with someone…'

'Ding-dong? Marjorie, wha—'

'All right, a row then. He said that he'd got caught up with work but would be home the following morning, which I thought was a pretty tall tale when he was at a birthday party. I suspected immediately. I've heard that tone before.'

'What tone?'

'The sort of tone that wayward husbands use on their wives. Wheedling.'

Stella frowned at her boss. 'Why didn't you tell me?'

'I didn't know for sure, and I didn't want to upset you until I did. But I'd made a mental note to do a bit more digging, and I would have done if you hadn't caught the little toerag this morning.'

'I feel so *stupid*,' Stella said with a sniff. 'It all makes sense now. The travelling, the hotel, and the times he didn't message me back. He was always quite guarded about his life but I thought he was just… private. Oh!' Stella's eyes flared. 'He often talked about Carol his secretary, but maybe Carol was his wife?'

'Very possibly,' Marjorie said solemnly.

'But I'm so confused, because… he met my family and friends… and took me around this new flat that he's supposedly just bought. He can't have faked that, can he?'

'Could he have got the keys from anyone else? Was there an agent with you?'

She shook her head. 'No, but there was Champagne in the fridge and… and…' Stella burst into tears again at the memory of the pink bedroom.

Marjorie passed her another tissue and waited for the sobs to subside.

'I'm sorry,' she said through her tears, 'this isn't professional. I need to fix the printer.'

'Pfffffft! I don't care about the printer. What I want to know is did he see you?'

'What?' Stella asked, wiping her face.

'At the hospital. Did the blighter see you?'

'No. At least… I don't think so.'

'And you've had no contact with him since?'

'No!' Stella wailed. 'What am I supposed to say? "Hey Fitz, quick question, do you have a pregnant wife?"'

'Definitely do not do that,' Marjorie warned with a dark expression. 'Because what I think we need to do is give him a taste of his own medicine.'

She looked up, alarmed. 'What do you mean?'

'I'm going to come up with a little plan. So, say nothing to him and in the meanti—'

'Marjorie, no. Please no. I never want to see him again.'

'Young Stella,' her boss replied, a note of steel in her voice. 'Do you remember when we first met?'

'Yes, outside that office. I'd just been sic— I'd just had a meeting and I came out to find you on the steps.'

'Exactly. And you told me exactly what that human walrus Clive Williams was wearing.'

She nodded.

'And then you came to work here, and within a few days you'd already persuaded a hotel to send you the hotel receipts *and* the address for those hair tongs, and we cracked the Winman case.'

Stella sniffed, feeling bashful.

'And do you recall going to that ghastly hotel and discovering that Mr Ferrari was not, in fact, sleeping with his secretary but was going to a piano bar every night to think about his daughter?'

'Mmmhmm.'

'What I'm saying is that I knew from the very beginning that you were made of tough stuff. And I don't think you're going to allow a man called Fitzwilliam Montague to get the better of you, are you?'

'Lysander Fitzwilliam Montague, actually. He told me, the other day, it's his first name.'

'Well, that's even worse.'

Stella managed to laugh, which made Marjorie swing her fist through the air.

'That's the spirit. Now, leave it with me and I'm going to come up with a course of action. And if he gets in touch with you, act normal. Or as normal as you can manage.'

Stella took a deep breath. She already regretted this plan.

CHAPTER 58

TWO DAYS LATER, STELLA and Billie were sitting on the sofa in the flat. It was nearly eight in the evening and there was a newly opened bottle of wine on the coffee table. Stella was drinking the wine; Billie was cradling a cup of camomile tea.

This had been the routine since Stella had found out about Fitz: she got up, went to work, tried to concentrate on work, went home, opened a bottle, discussed Fitz with Billie, finished the bottle, bed.

After a long day in the office, however, Stella had news.

'Do you want the full picture or just the top line?' Marjorie had asked that morning, She'd been digging into Lysander Fitzwilliam Montague and appeared from her office with the thunderous face of a headmistress who'd recently discovered a pupil smoking behind the science block. 'Full picture,' Stella had replied. Her upset was hardening into anger by this point, as well as a morbid curiosity.

'So… Marjorie told me what she'd discovered today,' Stella began, reaching for her wine glass. 'About Fitz.'

'What? Why didn't you text me?'

'It was too much for a message,' Stella went on, 'because it turns out… it turns out he *is* married, and she's called Céline and they live in this big house on Elgin Crescent.'

'Oh, Stell. How did Marjorie work that out?'

'Easy. She just looked him up on the electoral roll. And his wife was on it too, and their address.'

Billie sighed.

'And then she spent most of yesterday sitting outside it, and took some pictures, which I told her I didn't want to see. They've lived there fifteen years, she said.'

'*What?* I mean that's, like, half a mile from here. Less!'

'Yeah. I was thinking maybe that's why Jez recognised him.'

'Fuck, that's brazen, to be lying to you when you could have bumped into him at any moment. What? Why are you looking at me like that?'

'You swearing. It must be bad.'

'It is bad! Fucking bad!'

Stella laughed. 'But the thing is he definitely was away for a lot of it. Marjorie said his business is registered offshore so she couldn't get much on it, but he wasn't lying about its existence. She's got some contact in the navy press office who said Fitz definitely served before setting up his business, which this guy, Marjorie's friend, said he'd heard of. So I guess *some* of what he told me was true.'

'How does she get this stuff out of people?'

Stella shrugged. 'He owed her a favour, she said.'

'Still feels pretty risky to me,' said Billie. 'Living with his wife while dating someone else who lives three seconds away, even if he was away all the time. I'm sorry,' she said, shaking her head, 'I don't mean to be insensitive, I'm just so angry he's done this to you, Stell.'

Stella shrugged again and had another mouthful of wine.

'Do you know anything else about her?'

'About his wife? Not really. She's thirty-eight, apparently. But I should have guessed because there was this time, there was this time…' Stella said, her voice wobbling, 'when someone in his phonebook as "C" called him. She'd called him, like, four or five times and he said it was his secretary Carol! I just don't get how he could have lied and lied and been so convincing. I know I can be an idiot about some things, but it felt so real.'

Stella's head had been swimming with these thoughts for days. She kept going round in circles because she couldn't believe she'd got it so wrong with Fitz. He'd lied about almost everything, but there had been chemistry dancing between them like fireflies, and you couldn't fake that.

'Maybe he wanted it to be true?'

Stella turned to face her on the sofa. 'Do you think you can be in love with two people at the same time?'

Billie stuck out her lower lip while thinking. 'Not sure. You think that could be true with him?'

'I don't feel like I can be sure of anything any more. But it doesn't make sense. Like, I just don't believe he can have been lying all the time. Can he?'

'He *was* very charming,' Billie replied as if that explained it. 'And you know that expression "If he likes you, you'll know. If not, you'll be confused?"'

Stella nodded.

'You were confused quite a lot, Stell,' she said gently. 'Like when he didn't reply to your messages or he cancelled dinners last-minute.'

'I know, I *know*. I guess I just want to believe there was something, because otherwise the only explanation is that I was stupid and taken in and I…' She stopped. Maybe Marjorie was right about men being more trouble than they were worth. A week ago, she'd believed she was falling in love with Fitz. She thought he was upstanding and impressive. She'd tried to imagine what the rest of her life might have looked like with him.

A week on, she realised she barely knew him.

It wasn't just him. It was her father, too. His lying, his cheating. Stella thought back to the missed birthdays, the missed parents' evenings at school, the long gaps when her father had been away from home, supposedly on business, just like Fitz had presumably told his wife when he'd been with her. For Stella – previously so dreamy, so determined to meet her great love – it was a double betrayal.

'I'm sorry, Bill,' she said after yet another long sigh, 'I'm sorry to go on and on and on, given what you've been through. I know it's pathetic and self-pitying. It's just… I'm back here again.'

Billie nudged Stella's leg with her foot. 'Hey, stop. It's not pathetic. And what do you mean, "back here"?'

'On the sofa, with my good pal Mr Sauvignon Blanc, grumbling about some idiot.'

'I wouldn't be anywhere else. Well, maybe in the Bahamas. But in the absence of being there, I'm very happy to be here with you and Mr Blanc.'

'I love you,' Stella told her with a glum smile.

'Love you too. The only thing I'm worried about is this plan. Has Marjorie told you anything else?'

Stella shook her head. She'd asked Marjorie three or four times about the so-called plan, but her boss had instructed Stella to carry on as normal until everything was in order.

Fitz had called Stella twice since her discovery and been his normal, smooth self, saying that he missed her and that he couldn't wait for their trip to Paris that weekend. If Stella was quieter than usual on these calls, he didn't notice. He'd messaged too, but his messages were easier to handle since she could reply with a few words or emojis. His bravado astounded her: he texted about a restaurant booking near the Eiffel Tower; he texted saying he couldn't wait to wake up beside her; he texted suggesting they meet for a celebratory drink at St Pancras Station on Friday before catching the Eurostar.

'No idea. She's being very tight lipp—'

Stella was interrupted by a knock on their door and frowned since the intercom buzzer hadn't gone off.

'Must be Harold,' suggested Billie.

Stella got up and opened the door. It was Harold holding a parcel.

'Evening, you two. I hope I'm not interrupting?'

'No, we're just watching TV.'

'Only that this came for you earlier.' He handed Stella the parcel and then glanced over her shoulder. 'How are you feeling, Billie?'

She stuck her thumb in the air. 'Better, thanks, Harold. Treatment all done. Had my first check-up last week and the blood results were clear so… fingers crossed.'

'That's terrific news.'

Stella frowned down at the parcel. It was soft, and she couldn't remember ordering anything soft.

'All good with you, Harold?' she asked, using her fingernail to rip through the plastic.

'Tip-top, thank you. Basil and I went for a little potter along the river today, and then I made my first ever quiche, which wasn't a huge success, I have to say, but I think next time I need to use more butt— Stella? Goodness, are you all right? What's the matter?'

She'd opened the parcel and an item of black clothing had slithered to the floor: the lace bodysuit she'd ordered from hospital the morning she and Billie went for her check-up.

It was enough to set her off crying. 'Sorry, Harold, it's not your fault, it's just that I ordered this last week because I was supposed to be going to Paris this weekend with Fitz.'

She dangled the bodysuit in front of him.

'Gracious, yes, it looks very... French,' he replied nervously.

'But now we've broken up,' Stella continued through sobs, 'although that's not actually true. We haven't broken up yet because Marjorie has some sort of plan and says I have to keep quiet until it's happened. But I don't know what the plan is! And I don't know if I want to do it and, oh, it's just all such a mess.'

'Hang on, hang on,' said Harold, waving his hands in front of him. 'I'm losing track. What has happened with your chap and why is your boss involved?'

'Do you want a drink, Harold?' Billie asked from the sofa. She pointed at the wine bottle. 'Why don't you come in and sit down?'

'Only if it's not intruding?'

'It's not,' sniffed Stella. 'Come in and I'll explain.'

She fetched him a wine glass before filling it nearly to the brim, and explaining the events of the past week.

'Blimey-o-riley,' Harold said when she'd finished. 'I'm very sorry, Stella. What a palaver. If I got my hands on him I'd… well, I probably wouldn't be able to do much nowadays because he looks a strong lad. But I'd have words. And you don't have any idea what this plan is?'

Stella shook her head. 'No, Marjorie's being very secretive.'

Harold's forehead wrinkled further. He didn't think Stella's boss would do anything illegal. She was a former copper, after all. But he wasn't comfortable with Stella putting herself in a situation that might be dangerous. 'Why don't you give me her number,' he suggested, 'and I'll give her a bell. Sound her out. Would that be all right?'

Somewhere deep inside her, Stella felt a small spark of joy at this question. To her, it felt like the only good development of the past few days. If her heartbreak over Fitz could somehow fling Harold and Marjorie together, then good could come of it. She reached for her phone and read out Marjorie's number.

CHAPTER 59

THE PLAN WAS PUT into action that Friday afternoon, when Stella arrived at St Pancras wheeling her overnight case. After three hours of sifting through her wardrobe with Billie, she looked sensational: blonde hair falling over her leather jacket, tight black jeans, knee-high boots. Every man at the station, and a good number of women, wished they were taking her to Paris for the weekend. Harold's personal alarm was stowed in a side pocket in her handbag. 'A good idea in case things get dicey,' Marjorie had warned her the previous day.

'What do you mean, "dicey"?'

Marjorie had waggled her head from side to side. 'You never know with these scenarios. Better to be prepared.'

Stella had the distinct impression that her boss was enjoying this drama. As she pulled her suitcase towards the St Pancras Champagne Bar, her body vibrated with nervous energy.

Harold was also now involved in the plan, having contacted Marjorie, who'd decided it would be an excellent idea to have him and Basil nearby in case there was any trouble.

Although Harold felt sorry for Stella and her heartbreak, he was secretly quite pleased to be involved in an operation again. He'd never liked Fitz. Too smooth by half and he'd ascertained at Stella and Billie's birthday party that he didn't even like cricket. What sort of man was that?

Stella found two spare stools at the Champagne bar and sat, pulling her suitcase underneath her. It was a very public spot, underneath the station's vast Victorian glass ceiling, surrounded by other travellers. To her right was a woman engrossed in a paperback, picking at a smoked salmon sandwich. To her left were two portly, fifty-something ladies, several shopping bags scattered underneath their stools, who had nearly finished their bottle. She glanced through the bar to a table opposite, where Harold was sitting in a trilby, drinking coffee while Basil lay dutifully at his feet.

Stella quickly ordered her own glass of Champagne to steady herself.

'Off somewhere nice?' the waiter asked, pouring a generous glass for the attractive woman in front of him. He more often served balding businessmen on their way to engineering conferences in Sheffield.

'Paris,' Stella replied. She picked up the glass and took such an enormous mouthful that the bubbles scratched her throat.

The waiter winked. 'He's a lucky man.'

'I sure am,' said a loud voice, and Stella swivelled on her stool to see Fitz in a grey overcoat with a bag slung over his shoulder.

'Hi, darling,' he said, leaning forward to kiss her, although Stella moved her head so his mouth landed on her cheek, not her lips.

Her heart was now beating so hard she feared it might burst

from her chest, so she thought of what Sam had told her: breathe slowly, in and out, in and out, in and out. 'Hi,' she replied as calmly as she could.

'Excuse me, ladies,' said Fitz to the two middle-aged shoppers, swinging himself into the empty seat beside Stella.

'You don't have to excuse yourself to us,' one of the shoppers cooed, gazing at him appreciatively before they both dissolved into hysterics.

Fitz grinned at Stella before waving at the waiter and gesturing at her glass. 'Could I have the same, please? Or actually, no, let's make it a bottle.'

He laid his hand on Stella's thigh and leant in closer. 'You look breathtakingly beautiful. Truly. And I can't tell you how excited I am about the next two days. Two whole days with you all to myself. I'm a lucky man.'

Stella took another large swig as the fear grew in her chest. She had to do it. She had to get the words out of her mouth. 'What about your wife, though? Won't she mind that you're going away with another woman for the weekend?'

Fitz's mouth fell open like a codfish. 'My what?'

'Your wife. Take your hand off my thigh.'

Fitz snatched back his fingers as if he'd been burned. His eyes stared wildly at her for a few moments before he dropped his head. 'Stella, I'm so sorry.'

'You're *sorry*?'

He sighed into his lap before looking up. Fitz was a good actor, she had to hand it to him; he looked genuinely pained. 'Do you remember our first dinner? When I said I'd been married?'

'When you missed out the crucial detail that you're still married and about to have a baby? How could you do this? To me? To her? I presume Céline has no idea?'

His mouth fell open again. 'How did you find out th— Oh, of course. I presume that boss of yours had something to do with this?'

'It wasn't Marjorie who alerted me to the fact you've been lying to me, no. That was your own doing. I was at hospital with Billie last Friday, and I saw you, both of you.'

Fitz leant back in his chair. 'I'm sorry. That's not how I wan—' He stopped, his chest heaving up and down under his shirt. 'I did want to tell you.'

'You wanted to tell me? Don't you dare, don't you dare suggest, for one second, that you tried to do anything right. I was falling in *love* with you.'

'I'm sorry.'

'Stop saying that!'

'But I am. Stella, I'm sorry for hurting you. This was never my intention. But can you listen to me, because it's not as simple as it might seem. Céline...' He leant forward and put his hand on Stella's thigh again.

'Don't try and justify this, and don't touch me!'

'This is what I was trying to say to you before, about marriage,' he went on more urgently. 'People on the outside think it looks one way, but it's not necessarily like that on the inside, Stella. Please let me explain.'

She blinked at him. 'Go on, then.'

Fitz ran a hand through his hair. 'Where to begin? Jesus Christ.' He sighed again. 'We got married sixteen years ago. I was in the navy, away a lot, and it felt like the right thing to do. She...

Céline's parents were old friends of my mother's and everyone expected it.'

He glanced up to see Stella looking at him impassively.

'We got married, but as I said, I was away a lot so the relationship was difficult. And the more difficult our marriage became, the more I wanted to be away. It was a catch-22, you know?' He looked up again.

'I'm probably not going to be offering you much sympathy, Fit—'

'No, I understand. Hear me out. So I was away more and more, but she was desperate for children and for some reason it wasn't happening. We kept trying, and saw endless doctors, and specialists and counsellors, and fertility experts in London and Barcelona but nothing, just *nothing* worked. That's partly why I left the SBS, because I needed to pay for everything. And we did rounds and rounds of IVF but they didn't work either. And Céline had two miscarriages...' Fitz trailed off for a few moments. 'And eventually our relationship was, well, I started to think, even if we had a child, there would be nothing left of *us*, so what was the point?'

Stella bit her lip as she felt a small wisp of sympathy.

'But I couldn't tell her that because a baby was the only thing she could think about. And I couldn't leave her when she was so low and grieving because what sort of monster would that make me? So we kept going. Different doctors, different specialists, more IVF.' Fitz paused and reached for Stella's hands but she shook her head.

'It must have been around a year ago that I decided I couldn't do it any more, that our life together wasn't a life for either of us.

She *knew* this, so we started the conversation about going our own ways. Then she offered me a deal; one more go, one more round, and if that didn't work, we would separate, get divorced, move on.'

'And it worked?' Stella asked in a small voice. She wasn't sure whether to believe him. He sounded sincere but she'd made that mistake before.

Fitz nodded. 'It worked. I found out after we met. I'm sorry, Stella, I'm sorry that I haven't told you any of this before. But I met you and life was good again. The days when I could see you, those were the best days, because even though Céline is pregnant, she knows there's nothing left of us and she hates me for it. She blames me and…' He looked up and stared into the middle distance. 'I know I haven't been a saint, to you or her, but I want to make a new life with you. I knew that somehow in the pub that evening. That's why I didn't stay very long. I couldn't, it felt dangerous to stay around you when I knew I shouldn't. But I couldn't stop thinking about you, and then this happened, *we* happened, and that's why I've bought the flat, and if you can somehow forgi—'

'Were you actually travelling all those times or were you lying? Were you at home in Notting Hill? Was there even a deal in America?'

He shook his head quickly from side to side. 'Travelling for most of it, I swear. And there was a deal, *is* a deal, yes. There's nothing else I… misled you about.'

'Misled?' Stella snorted. He looked so different, suddenly. Weaker. So much less impressive. Fraudulent. And then her eyes slid to his overnight bag and she remembered something that had niggled at her, a clue in plain sight.

'When did you go there?' Stella asked, nodding at the luggage label on the bag. Sugar Beach. That's why the name was familiar. It was the St Lucia hotel that Andrew and Pandora were going to for Christmas with her family. As the date had drawn nearer, Pandora had barely stopped talking about it on the family WhatsApp group.

Fitz looked at the label and quickly back to her. 'Stella…'

'Was it since we've been seeing one another? With Céline?'

'We went at the end of September,' he admitted, 'because she was tired and needed a break.'

'A babymoon.'

'Stella…'

'You went on a babymoon with your wife while I was falling in love with you. Nice.'

'Stella, please don't use that word, it wasn't like tha—'

'Which word, babymoon or wife?'

Fitz reddened and shifted on his stool. 'Stella, plea—'

'Have there been others?' she asked suddenly.

'Others?'

'Other women, like me, while you've been married?'

'The odd indiscretion, perhaps, but nobody like you. What I told you before about being restless is true. I've always been restless. But not with you. I married who I thought I should marry, but now I—'

'And Carol. I presume she's another lie?'

He sighed. 'I do have a secretary! She's just, ah, not called that. She's called Edwina. Stella, look, I'm sorry that I did—'

'All the lies. How can you have behaved like this when you're going to be a father? The *constant* lying, Fitz. Is there anything you've told me that was true? I can't… I just can't…' She tailed off, too angry and hurt to find the rest of her sentence.

'You've got to forgive me,' Fitz pleaded.

'No, I don't. I can't forgive you for this. And I never, ever want to see or hear from you again. Get off me.'

'Stella, I need you.' He lifted his hand to her upper arm and gripped it. 'Listen, I should have told you months ago, and I've tried to but…'

'Stop it, Fitz! Let go of me.'

She tried to shrug off his hand but Fitz held on firmer, his fingers tightening around her arm. 'Stella, please, you're not listening. I'm trying to tell you tha—'

A few seconds later, a high-pitched noise cut through the hubbub of station noise, surprising several pigeons that had been roosting overhead and scattering them into the air; Stella had dropped her hand into her bag, fumbled in its side pocket and pulled the pin on her personal alarm.

It was late afternoon and the station was full of commuters heading home or venturing further afield on the Eurostar. Most froze at the ear-splitting noise and looked for the nearest exit, fearing a fire or a terror attack. Only those closest to Stella and Fitz saw what happened next.

Basil, hearing the alarm, started barking and straining at his lead, which was tucked around a chair leg. Harold had just taken a sip of his cappuccino, the remainder of which sloshed over his shirt as the chair lurched sideways. But once he'd realised what the commotion was, he jumped up too and was dragged around the bar by Basil to see Fitz leaning away from Stella, his palms in the air as if protesting his innocence.

'Get that dog away from me!' Fitz shouted as Basil sprang towards him.

Those sitting around the Champagne bar looked from Stella to the man glaring at her, and then the large Alsatian.

Seconds after that, ripples of laughter started spreading among them as a large, unkempt woman in a golf visor and a pair of combat boots strolled around the bar, handing out posters from a pile tucked under her arm.

'HAVE YOU SEEN THIS DOG?' the poster asked in large red capital letters. Underneath the letters was a close-up photo of an extremely attractive man – with blue eyes, a square jawline, and curled, dark hair.

The fifty-something ladies with their shopping bags took a poster from Marjorie and frowned. The one on the left squinted at Fitz. She elbowed her friend, nodded at Fitz and sniggered. 'Here, this is you, isn't it?'

There was a line under the photo of the attractive man: 'Answers to the name of Fitz. A very unfaithful creature. Warning: may hump your leg if you approach him.'

Having read it over their shoulder, Fitz howled with anger, snatched the paper and ripped it in two.

Unfortunately for him, Marjorie had printed a hundred copies (having bought a new colour printer especially for the job), and continued to circulate the bar, calmly handing them out as the waves of laughter became louder and people started pointing at Fitz.

He stared around him, weighing up what to do. But after another few seconds of humiliation, as the laughter grew and people started reaching for their phones to take videos of the scene, decided to scarper.

'You can believe this or not, but you weren't the only one who was falling in love,' he told Stella before picking up his overnight bag and heading for the escalator.

She replaced the pin in the personal alarm as tears ran down her cheeks.

The two ladies beside her exchanged knowing looks before shifting their stools closer.

'He's not worth it, sweetheart,' said one, rubbing her back.

'They never are,' added the other, with a sigh.

Harold, standing behind them, decided to stay quiet.

Marjorie joined a few minutes later, having handed out the last poster. 'Terrific teamwork, Harold and Basil. I haven't had that much fun since I followed my husband to karate. Now, my good man, let's have plenty more of that,' she ordered and the waiter slid another bottle of Champagne towards the gaggle standing around the bar, consoling Stella.

Marjorie poured herself a glass and lifted it into the air. 'To new beginnings,' she declared.

CHAPTER 60

'WHAT YOU UP TO this weekend?' Billie asked.

It was a week later, and she was sitting at the kitchen table while Stella chopped tomatoes. She was attempting a recipe from the book Sam had given her, although she'd forgotten to buy the garlic and the capers, so she'd just ordered them from a grocery app. Along with another bottle of wine and a grab bag of chocolate buttons because, frankly, she felt like she deserved it.

Knife in hand, Stella shrugged. 'Not much.'

It was just the two of them, since Jez was playing football, and it almost felt like old times, before Billie got ill. It was over a month from Billie's last chemotherapy session and there was a bowl of crisps on the table. In the sitting room, on the TV screen, was a paused reality show where men proposed to women they'd never met.

'You haven't heard from him?'

'Nope,' Stella said definitively, slicing straight through the middle of another tomato.

'Do you think he could have been…'

'What?'

Billie shrugged. 'Telling the truth? That it *was* more complicated than it seemed?'

'It doesn't matter if he was, does it? If you're technically still with your pregnant wife, how can you be seeing someone else, taking them away for weekends in Paris, buying apartments, making promises about their future?'

'You really think she doesn't know?'

'About me?' Stella stuck out her bottom lip. 'Not sure.'

Stella had thought about her own mother a lot in the past week. She knew about her husband's philandering but chose to turn a blind eye. Was that what marriage was, loving someone enough to forgive them straying? Or did people stay simply because they were afraid of what life might look like otherwise?

Stella was still hurting, still winded if she thought about Fitz for too long. But she was also starting to feel grateful that she'd found out early enough, only a few months into their relationship. Marjorie, ever tactful, had told her that she'd covered plenty of cases where men lived two entirely separate lives, with wives in one place and girlfriends somewhere else, and sometimes entire families that didn't know that the other existed.

'I don't know if she knows,' she murmured, staring at the chopping board. 'But I'm done with men for the moment.'

'What? *You?*'

'Me, exactly.'

'Stell, come on, that's like Snow White announcing she's taking up yoga and giving up on her prince.'

'Plot spoiler, Bill: there are no princes.'

'I can't believe you're going to let him do this to you.'

'Do what?' Stella demanded, spinning round.

'Make you less romantic. Take away that part of you.'

'It's not just him! It's all of them. It's my dad, and Miles, and

Callum and Nico before him. It's every man I've ever slept with,' she replied, throwing her hands into the air. 'Each one of them has made me sad in the end. I'm tired of it, Bill! I'm so tired. I've been searching and looking and getting hurt over and over again for what? It's like sticking my finger into a flame and expecting it not to hurt, but every time it does. Every time. And I can't do it any more.'

'It's not *every* man you've slept with.'

'Who then? Who among the ropey football stadium of men that I've ever slept with could be considered a stand-up guy?'

Billie gave her a knowing look across the table.

'Who?'

'You know who. Sam.'

Stella tutted. 'He's with *Maddy*.'

'He's not that into Maddy, I can tell.'

'How?'

'I told you before, the way he looked at you that day in hospital.'

She frowned. 'Which day?'

'The day that we saw the man whose name we're not going to mention again with his pregnant wife.'

'Oh.' Stella crouched to find a pan in the cupboard before turning back to face Billie. 'OK, I'll bite. How d'you think he looked at me?'

'As if you were the eighth wonder of the world.'

'He was just being nice.'

'He *is* nice. Talking of which, did Harold tell you about drinks next week?'

'What? No. What drinks?'

'Knocked on the door yesterday. He's so cute. He wants to

do something to celebrate us getting engaged, so said could we come over next Friday?'

'Just us guys?'

'I think… us and Sam maybe?'

'And *Maddy*?'

'Not sure.'

'Harold hasn't mentioned anything to me.'

'He told me to ask you, if you're free?'

'Hang on, let me just check my busy schedule,' Stella replied, pretending to open a diary in front of her. 'Yup, it says here I'm free until I die of old age.'

'You're not giving up being dramatic, then?'

'No, probably not that. Just anything to do with romance and sex. I need to charge my romantic batteries. And I keep thinking about what Harold told me a couple of months ago.'

'What?' Billie asked, frowning.

'That whoever you're with, you should believe that they're the best person in the room.'

'What room?'

'Any room. If you're with someone, you just have to know that they're the very best person in it. That's what Ellen told him when they first met. And you think that with Jez, right?'

Billie looked thoughtful for a moment. 'Yeah. He can be difficult, and argumentative. And he has questionable taste…' She paused to glance at the wall in the sitting room, hung with the Banksy portrait of a chimpanzee wearing a crown that he'd given her. 'But none of that matters because I love him. He's got the kindest heart, and he's supportive, and I know he'll look after me. So… yeah, I guess he would always be the best person in the room, for me. Although, if I had to decide between you and him…'

'I could take Jez in a fight.'

'You'd win.'

'Obviously,' said Stella before becoming more serious. 'See, that's what I want. I want to know that I'm with the best person for me. And until someone really great comes along, then…' she paused and sighed, 'I'm taking a break.'

'For how long?'

She shrugged.

Billie grinned. 'All right. But if you're very lucky, I'll put you next to one of Jez's cousins at the wedding.'

'Ha-ha. How's planning going?'

'OK, actually. Dad's still trying to save money by saying we can do it in the pub, but Mum's found this amazing place not far away and told him I'm their only child and he needs to stop being as tight as a badger's backside or she'll leave him.'

Stella laughed. That sounded like Bob and Helen.

'Can I show you pictures?'

'Of the place she's found? Yes please, show me immediately.'

If anyone else had asked whether they could show her the potential location for their wedding, Stella would have snatched their phone and thrown it in the bin. It was a measure of how much she loved Billie that she would tolerate a discussion about the size of wedding reception and how many canapés they needed per person.

'OK, so it's about ten minutes from Mum and Dad's,' rattled on Billie, 'and you can have dinner in the main house or they can put a marquee outside for as many peop—'

The door buzzer went.

'Hang on, delivery guy.' Stella wiped her hands on a tea towel and pressed the intercom button beside the front door. 'Good evening, Shakespeare Retirement Home. Who is it?'

'It's your food delivery,' came a confused voice.

'Thought so. Sorry, ignore my bad joke. First floor.' It was lazy but Stella didn't have the energy to go downstairs. She pressed the button to let him in and opened their door.

Beneath her, she heard Harold.

'Come on then, out we go,' he mumbled, presumably to Basil. 'Don't think it's too parky tonight. I'm not sure I need a coat. Oh, hello, young man.'

'Excuse me,' she heard the delivery man reply, 'but I'm looking for Stell—'

'I'm up here,' she shouted, 'thanks, Harold.'

'There you go,' Harold told him, 'up a floor.'

'Ta, mate.'

A few seconds later, a tall, lanky twenty-something in a black tracksuit bounded up the stairs and handed Stella a carrier bag. 'Here you go, should all be in there.'

'Thanks,' she replied, although he'd already turned to go and was bounding back downstairs.

Stella closed the door with her foot. 'Dinner coming right up, sort of.'

She tapped her phone when she reached the kitchen counter to see a message from Sam. *Hope you're all right, Shakespeare. Been thinking of you. I'm sorry I can't offer any medicine for this kind of thing but I believe that very high cholesterol foods and outstandingly bad television can help X*

'What is it?' Billie asked, noticing Stella's smile.

'Your friend Sam, just… checking in, asking how I am.'

She grinned at her phone as she tapped a reply. *Is that official advice, Dr Ansari? And thank you. I'm good. And apparently Harold's throwing a party next week so see you there? xxx*

Stella glanced up at Billie, who was looking at her with a told-you-so expression.

'Don't want to hear it,' she insisted. 'I know what you're going to say, but he's with *Maddy* and I'm…'

'Incredibly stubborn.'

'Well, yes, that. But also no, Bill. That moment passed with Sam and we're pals.'

Billie groaned. 'I just want you to find someone who's good enough, who deserves you. And when someone comes along who is, it's like you can't even see it.'

'I want to find that too, eventually, but what have I literally just said about taking a break from thinking about this? From obsessing about dating and love and finding some mystery man in Nisa? I'm bored of it. Now,' Stella said, turning back to the recipe book, 'how spicy do you want this because it says half a red chilli but I'm not sure that sounds enough.'

CHAPTER 61

INSTEAD OF LOOKING FOR her great love, Stella was going to concentrate on work. That week, Marjorie dropped an old camera on her desk.

'To fix?'

Marjorie tossed her head like an impatient horse. 'No! Not to fix. To practise with, in case I can't go out on surveillance one day.'

'For me?'

'Yes, why not? You've lasted a lot longer than all my other girls and you're good at this job. You seem to…' Marjorie waved a hand in the air, 'have a nose for it. And I was thinking, what about a few refresher driving lessons? On the company, of course.'

Since she'd never been told she was good at anything very much, Stella was touched. The camera was big and bulky but symbolic, and the driving lessons were probably a sensible idea. Marjorie wanted her to start taking on more serious jobs just as it was dawning on Stella that she didn't want to work anywhere else. She liked this job, and she *did* seem to have a knack for it. The accounts were now so up to date that Marjorie had even agreed to pay a handyman to fix the office doorbell.

In fact, after the Fitz debacle, Stella found she felt even more strongly that she wanted to keep working there. It wasn't just a job where she was slipped a few notes every Friday. She and Marjorie were doing important work. True, it wasn't saving children's lives at the hospital or putting news on the front page of *The Guardian*, but they were trying to help unhappy people become happy again. As Marjorie had previously said: they could only do their best, present their findings, and then it was up to the client to make their own judgement call.

Take Mr Bartholomew. After Marjorie sent him the report, detailing her findings and the photographs from outside Rakes, he'd cried down the phone. But two days after *that*, he'd emailed to say he was grateful. 'No longer do I feel as if I'm losing my marbles,' he wrote, 'so thank you very much again, to you and your whole team.'

Stella thought he might be a bit less grateful if he knew that Marjorie's team consisted of his wife's lover's daughter, but there was no reason he'd ever discover that.

'Another happy customer, young Stella,' Marjorie had shouted from her office before remembering the sensitivities of that case in particular and adding quickly that she'd type up the invoice.

'Anything else?' Stella asked, raising her eyebrows as she noticed Marjorie was still hovering by her desk.

'How are you feeling?'

'Fine, although I could do with another coffee if you want one?'

'I meant about the unpleasantness with that man.'

'Oh *him*. I'm OK.' Stella looked up at Marjorie. 'I've decided I'm going to concentrate on work for the time being and stop obsessing about romance.'

Marjorie nodded. 'Very sensible. If they aren't the delicious frosting on the cake, then why bother?'

Stella frowned, confused.

'What I mean to say is, you have everything, young Stella. Your independence, your wits, your entire life before you. And if a man comes along who happens to be the delicious frosting on that cake, then terrific. If he adds to your life, in other words, that's magnificent. But if not...' Marjorie's brow darkened, 'forget him!'

Stella grinned. Although she may not have consciously realised it, the other reason she liked the job was because Marjorie had become such a supportive figure, providing the kind of advice that she'd lacked almost her entire life. True, some of the advice was dubious (a few days earlier, Marjorie had insisted that people should only wash their hair once a month, which explained a *lot*), but plenty of the advice was wiser than that, and Stella was very grateful.

Valerie Shakespeare was less convinced by Stella's determination to focus on the job when they had dinner that evening in a fish restaurant in Chelsea. She'd come up to London for the day to see her plastic surgeon about her neck, and texted Stella that afternoon to suggest they 'talked'.

So far, they were on their main courses and Valerie had done most of the talking. Unlike Marjorie, she seemed incapable of recognising that her daughter had turned her life around.

'But how did you even *find* such a job, darling? It sounds like the sort of role you'd see advertised on a mucky postcard in a phone box.'

'As it happens, it was indirectly thanks to Dad,' Stella replied over her salmon. 'I had an interview at a law firm where some pervy friend of his works, and the interview was terrible…'

'Why?'

'Never mind,' Stella said quickly. 'But on the way out, I bumped into my boss.'

'The one in that frightful purple thing at your party?'

'Marjorie, exactly. She runs the agency. And I'm happy there. I'm good at it, Mum. For the first time ever, I'm doing something I enjoy.'

'Rootling around in other people's marriages,' her mother said doubtfully as she speared a piece of beetroot.

'Some people are grateful for the service, if you can imagine such a thing.'

Valerie tutted. 'Not this again. I've had a very nice life with your father, darling. He may not be perfect, but then nobody is.' She leant over the table and squinted at Stella's nose. 'Have you seen Angelika yet because she could do something about those pores.'

'No.'

'Darling, how are you going to hold on to that handsome man if you don't look after your skin?'

Stella stabbed a flake of salmon with her fork. 'I don't need to keep hold of him because I ended it.'

'What? Not *another* one? What was it this time?'

'His wife.'

'Oh dear,' Valerie replied as lightly as if she'd just dropped her napkin on the floor. 'I suppose you can't blame a man who looks like that. He was ever so handsome. But what are we going to do with you?' She dropped her voice to a whisper. 'Are you a lesbian, Stella?'

'Oh my god, no, I'm not. More's the pity. But honestly, Mum, what does it matter if you're not married by the time you're thirty?'

'You're thirty-three now,' Valerie replied reproachfully.

'Or thirty-three. Or forty-three. Or ninety-three? It doesn't matter!'

'No need to get so worked up, darling. All I'm saying is that I have occasionally wondered if you're in love with Billie.'

'I love Billie but I'm not in love with her. Is that acceptable?'

'I suppose it'll have to do. How is she?'

'Good. Stronger. Got another check-up in a few weeks. And she's engaged, actually.'

Valerie dropped her cutlery and clapped her hands together. 'Is she? Thank heavens one of you has some sense.'

'Mum! Enough! I'm not going to get married just for the sake of it…'

'Stella—'

'No, listen to me. I'm not going to get married just so you can tell your friends that your daughter is married. You might be OK with Dad's behaviour, that might be enough for you. But it isn't for me. I don't want that life, I want more. I want to be with someone who adds to my life, who doesn't take away from it. And until I find that, I'm perfectly all right by myself.'

Valerie Shakespeare fixed her daughter with a dubious look. 'If you say so, darling, but I do think the odd trip to the facialist might help.'

CHAPTER 62

'HELLO!' CRIED HAROLD WHEN he flung open his door that Friday evening. 'Good of you to come.'

'Good of you to have us,' Billie told him. She was clutching one bottle of Prosecco; Jez had a six-pack of beer and Stella was holding another Prosecco and a large bag of Doritos since she wasn't sure what Harold was planning to feed them.

'Excellent, excellent,' replied Harold, who was feeling nervous about this evening. He'd never thrown a party by himself; Ellen had organised them in the past. 'Why don't you three go through and I'll bring the drinks?'

They traipsed through to the sitting room in formation: Stella, Billie, Jez. Dusty Springfield was singing from the record player, and Basil immediately climbed onto the sofa to denote that it was his territory and nobody was allowed to sit there.

'Christ, someone's going to have to eat that,' Stella mumbled, dropping the Doritos on the table beside a bowl of pineapple curry dip.

'I'm not,' said Jez.

'Shhhh, stop it, you two. I'll have some,' said Billie, eyeing the pineapple as if it was an unexploded bomb.

'I'm not sure it'll help your recovery, Bill. It looks radioactive.'

'Shhhh,' Billie hissed at Stella again.

Stella had taken an unusually long time to get ready for a small drinks party in her elderly neighbour's flat. She'd washed her hair, used her special conditioner, tried on five different combinations of jeans and tops and spent at least twenty minutes on her eye make-up. It was a party for Billie and Jez, she'd told herself, while applying a third coat of mascara. Why shouldn't she look nice? It definitely, *absolutely* had nothing to do with Sam or Maddy.

Harold reappeared with a tray of drinks. 'Here we go, then. Fizz.'

Billie reached for the tray. 'Thanks, Harold, this really is very kind of you.'

'Not at all. I should be the one thanking you.'

'How come?' asked Stella.

Harold lifted his glass in the air. 'What I wanted to say was not only congratulations to you two. But to say I've very much enjoyed getting to know you all in the past few months. And I'm so very, *very* glad that you're on the mend, Billie.'

Stella raised her own glass, and as she looked from Harold to Billie and then Jez, felt a warmth spread across her chest. It *was* nice being in Harold's flat instead of the pub, searching for a man who would only disappoint her. Over the past four months, they seemed to have formed an unlikely gang: her, Billie, Jez, their elderly neighbour and his devoted Alsatian. A bit like the Famous Five, but with alcohol instead of ginger beer.

He was right, too. Billie had turned a corner. In the past week or so, Stella had noticed that her face seemed less translucent and her cheeks had turned pink again. She was eating more, too, and spending less time in bed. The spark that had dimmed not just in Billie's eyes but more deeply within her seemed to be reigniting, and Stella thought if that could just continue, if Billie could get better and better and better over the next few months, then she'd never beg or plead God for anything ever again.

The doorbell went.

'Terrific, that'll be Marjorie,' said Harold.

'Marjorie?' exclaimed Stella. 'She didn't say anything about coming. What's she doing here?'

'I'll let her in,' offered Jez, loping towards the door.

'I asked her,' Harold replied innocently, 'last week at St Pancras. Don't get any ideas, please, Stella. It's not a romantic assignation. But we got talking, and she says she might be able to offer me some work from time to time. The odd spot of business to keep me and Basil busy.'

'Well, that's… great news,' Stella said as Marjorie appeared in Harold's living room in another peculiar party outfit: crushed-velvet dress and combat boots.

'Evening, everyone,' she boomed. 'Hello, Basil, my new friend. Look, I've got something for you.' She slipped a hand into her dress pocket and pulled out a small piece of brown leather.

'What is it?' asked Stella.

'Biltong,' Marjorie replied as Basil took the piece of beef and climbed back on the sofa.

Harold returned from the kitchen with another glass and they stood in a small circle and congratulated Billie and Jez again before an awkward silence fell.

'Would anyone like a piece of pineapple?' He gestured at the plate. 'Marjorie?'

Stella felt it was like a dare that nobody wanted to take but Marjorie sounded genuinely enthusiastic. 'Try and stop me,' she said, picking up a cocktail stick and dragging a small chunk of pineapple through the curry sauce.

Billie broke next and reached for a piece. 'Yes please, *delicious*.'

Jez followed her, chewing and swallowing as quickly as he could. 'Mmmm. It's really… interesting.'

Stella shook her head. Her newfound selflessness didn't extend that far. 'Not for me, thanks. Where's Sam, Harold?'

'Sam?'

'Yeah. I thought you said, or Billie said, that he was invited tonight…' Stella trailed off as a look of confusion crossed Harold's face.

'No, he couldn't make it in the end.'

'Oh,' said Stella, surprised at a sinking feeling, like a balloon slowly deflating under her ribcage.

'He has a shift at the hospital.'

'Right.'

'And you're OK, Stella, after, well, everything?' Harold went on.

'After Fitz, you mean?'

He nodded.

'Yes. Fine, thank you. Absolutely fine but I've sworn off dating for the time being. No more men.'

Jez snorted.

'Thank you, Jeremy.'

'Just saying, I give it a week, tops.'

'You're wrong, actually. I'm off dating and going to concentrate on work,' Stella said, looking to Marjorie for approval.

'As I told you, quite right,' her boss replied with an approving nod.

'But what about that young chap?'

Stella frowned at Harold. 'What chap?'

'On the stairs the other night?'

'What night?'

Harold blinked behind his spectacles. 'I was going out with Basil, and just as we left a tall lad came up the stairs and asked for you.'

'What lad?' Stella was baffled. There hadn't been any strange men on the stairs looking for her recently. Not that she could recollect, anyway. She'd been in every night cooking for Bill— 'Harold, hang on, do you mean the delivery guy?'

'Er…'

'The guy who came over to drop off… I can't even remember… capers, I think.'

'And another bottle of wine,' chipped in Billie.

Harold looked confused. 'Er… a tall chap, I can remember that. And he had a carrier bag so I assumed he was coming over to see yo—'

Stella laughed. 'Harold, that was the Gorillaz delivery guy. He was about eleven years old, and he definitely, in no way, is my new love interest.'

'Oh,' Harold said with a troubled expression.

'What d'you mean "oh"?'

Harold swallowed. 'The thing is, I saw Sam at the hospital yesterday and he was asking after you, you know, as he always does, and I mentioned that I'd seen a chap here and I thought perhaps he was your new beau.'

'OK OK OK,' Stella said, shaking her head, 'let me get this straight. You told Sam that I had a new boyfriend...'

'I didn't say boyfriend,' Harold remonstrated, 'but perhaps your new fancy man.'

'OK, you told Sam that I had a new... fancy man... because you saw a delivery guy bringing capers...'

'And wine.'

'Fine, and wine. You told Sam that I was seeing someone because you saw a man in a tracksuit bringing capers and wine to the flat?'

'That's about the measure of it, yes,' Harold replied with a nod. 'And I thought Sam went rather quiet after that. I believe he has rather a soft spot for you.'

'But he's with Maddy!'

Harold cleared his throat. 'Ah, it turns out he's not with Maddy.'

Stella's eyes widened. 'What?'

'They're not stepping out any more. I don't know the exact details but I think it was all very amicable.'

'Hang on, so you're saying Sam isn't with Maddy, but he thinks that I'm with the delivery man?'

Harold looked briefly pained. 'I don't think Sam knows he's a delivery man because I didn't know that, obviously. But otherwise that's the long and short of it, yes.' He reached for the platter. 'Pineapple dip, anyone?'

Stella put her glass down on the coffee table. 'I've got to go.'

'*Now?*' said Billie. 'Where?'

'I have to see Sam and explain. I need him to know that I'm not seeing anyone, I need him to know it's all a big misunderstanding.' She pulled her phone from her back pocket and opened Uber.

'See?' chipped in Jez. 'Told you it wouldn't last. Not even a week.'

'I think he's on duty,' added Harold.

Stella shook her head. 'Doesn't matter. I'll wait. I need to explain.' She looked at her phone screen. 'Right, car's three minutes away. Bill, I haven't got keys but will you…'

'Let you in? Yes,' Billie replied, rolling her eyes. 'Go!'

CHAPTER 63

STELLA'S UBER DRIVER SEEMED to be competing for Slowest Driver of the Year Award. He crawled down Notting Hill Gate, crawled behind several buses and crawled down Gloucester Road so slowly that Stella dug her fingernails into the sponge seat to prevent herself from shouting 'GET ON WITH IT, I COULD WALK FASTER THAN THIS.'

She couldn't voice exactly why she had to see Sam. Like many strong emotions, she simply felt it. She had to explain to him that she wasn't going out with anyone and that Harold had made a mistake. The idea that he might think she'd moved on so quickly was *mortifying.*

'Shall I take the Boltons or go down to the Fulham Road?' the driver asked.

'Whatever's quickest!'

He turned into Onslow Gardens so slowly it was as if the car was running out of gas.

'Is there any chance we could go a bit faster?'

'All twenty round here now, love. Blame the mayor. I'm telling you, if I was the mayor, I wouldn't have carved up this patch of London like he has. The other day…'

He embarked on a traffic anecdote and Stella's thoughts returned to Sam. Almost as soon as Harold had mentioned that he wasn't coming to the party, she'd realised what an idiot she'd been. It was as if a curtain had been pulled back from behind Stella's eyes and sunlight had poured into her. For her, Sam was the best person in the room. Any room. But she'd only properly understood that in Harold's flat when Sam wasn't there, and it dawned on her that she missed him. She really missed him; sweet, supportive, generous, selfless Sam, who had a slightly dorky sense of humour, true, but who was endlessly, *endlessly* kind.

Obstacles along the way had caused complications, including Fitz, Maddy, and Stella's own obsession with what love would look like when it arrived. She'd thought it would be Fitz-shaped: a man in a sharp suit with a swagger who would sweep her up and consume her every thought. But she'd confused being in lust with being in love. Love didn't have to be hotels and fancy dinners and a man in a sharp suit. It didn't have to be a hundred cream roses on her birthday, crates of oysters or a weekend in Paris. Love could be less obvious and less ostentatious than that. Love could be a man in a doctor's coat with a blue lanyard around his neck, who'd always been there when she needed him.

'Do you want me to pull up here or cross to the other si—'

'Here!' screeched Stella, already scrabbling across the back seats to reach for the passenger door. 'Thanks!'

She ran for the revolving door so fast several onlookers moved quickly out of the way, assuming the poor manic blonde woman was racing in with a medical emergency. A kidney infection, perhaps? They could be very painful. Or an ill relative upstairs?

'What floor is the children's ward?' she shouted at a man behind the information desk.

'First,' he replied, giving her a sympathetic smile.

Stella ran for the escalators, ran up the escalators, through a pair of swinging doors decorated with cartoon jungle animals, and arrived at the next reception desk, panting even harder.

'Hello… I… need… to… see… Dr… Sam… Ansari,' she said between breaths.

A nurse with a very shiny head of black hair looked up from behind the counter.

'Stella,' said Maddy with a dazzling smile. 'Hello, what are you doing here?'

'Umm…'

Maddy's smile slipped and her Bambi eyes widened with concern. 'It's not Billie, is it?'

Stella shook her head. 'No, it's not Billie. I just…'

The smile returned. 'Good. You look so crazed I was worried there for a minute.'

'I need to speak to Sam about something.'

'Oh. Is it urgent?' asked Maddy in her singsong voice.

Stella considered this before answering. Would she go to hell if she said it was urgent when Sam might be discussing a small child's asthmatic lungs with his parents? 'No,' she admitted.

Maddy glanced at a clipboard on the desk. 'He's doing his rounds at the moment and we never know how long those are going to take. Want me to pass on a message?'

What would that message be? 'Hey, Sam, I've come to the hospital to tell you that my elderly neighbour was wrong, that I'm not dating who you think I am because he has the brains of a turnip, but that actually I've realised that I maybe quite like *you*. No worries if busy! Call me whenever!'

'It's OK, I'll just, er, text him and wait. Downstairs. I'll grab a coffee, thanks.'

'No problem,' Maddy replied.

Stella headed for the café, bought a coffee and sat at a spare table. *Hey, I'm at the hospital. No drama. I'm in the café. Could I talk to you when you have a moment?*

Click. Sent.

She laid her phone face-down on the table, too anxious to watch for a reply. On a table beside her was a thirty-something woman, doubled over her knees, her head bowed, dark hair cloaking her face. She was sitting beside a woman Stella assumed was her mother. The mother gently rubbed her daughter's back before lifting her hand and tucking a strand of hair behind her ear.

At another table, she watched an elderly man nudge a small square of shortbread towards an elderly woman.

Behind them was a woman breastfeeding a baby that could only have been a few days old.

Love didn't have to be loud, Stella thought again.

After a few minutes, she tilted her phone up to see the screen. Nothing from Sam but a string of messages from Billie.

You OK? What's happening?

I can't tell if I'm still queasy post treatment or because I've had to eat so much curried pineapple.

Keep me posted

Stella clicked out of WhatsApp but left her phone upwards this time. Five minutes ticked past, then another, and another, until

Stella had been sitting at the table for nearly an hour. The elderly couple were still there, hunched over their paper cups of tea, but she was the only other person in the café and she felt less brave as the adrenalin that had shot through her body in the Uber ebbed away.

What was she thinking, coming here? She had no idea what she was even going to say to Sam. This was insane. She should go home.

Stella stood and dropped her empty cup in the bin, then made for the main entrance. She'd go back, re-join the party and they could all laugh about her moment of madness. Jez would probably tease her for the rest of time but he coul—

'Stella?'

Just before she reached the revolving doors, she heard him.

Turning, she saw Sam striding towards her, his lanyard swinging across his chest. 'Hey, I got your message. What's up?'

Stella opened her mouth but no words came out. She'd had an hour to prepare for this. Longer, actually, if you included the world's slowest taxi ride. And here she was, struck dumb. As talkative as a traffic cone.

'Stella? You're not having another attack?' Sam's eyebrows drew together.

'No! No, nothing like that.'

'Billie's fine? Maddy mentioned that you'd been upstairs…'

'Yeah, no, she's good,' Stella said, wishing that she could trap her own head in the revolving door. This was excruciating. She was a moron.

'What is it?'

'Um… what it is… basically… OK, the thing is… I had to tell you that I'm not going out with that man.'

Sam frowned.

'The man who Harold told you about, the delivery man.'

'Stella, do you need to sit down?'

'No, no, I'm fine. What I'm trying to say is Harold got it wrong.'

'Got what wrong?'

'About the delivery man.'

'What delivery man?'

'Oh my god, we're going to spend the rest of our lives having this conversation. Listen, Harold told you he'd seen a man at my flat, yes?'

Sam nodded.

'And he said that he thought this was my new… fancy man, yes?'

He nodded again.

'Ignore Harold,' Stella said more forcefully. 'He got it wrong, he got confused. It was just a delivery guy. I'd ordered various ingredients, and wine, that I'd forgotten because, actually, I was cooking a recipe for Billie from the book you gave me.'

'Nice. Which one?'

'The one with the capers and the aubergine.'

'How was it?'

'Great, once I'd got everything I needed from the delivery man, who is absolutely not someone I'm seeing. Just to be clear.'

Sam's frown returned. 'Right, so you came here, to the hospital, on a Friday night, to tell me that you're not dating the Deliveroo guy.'

'It wasn't Deliveroo, but yes.'

Worry shadowed Sam's face. 'Okaaay. Look, Stella, are you definitely feeling all right?'

She nodded. 'I'm good. But there's something else I need to tell yo—'

'Do you want a glass of water?'

'Can you just let me get this out?'

'Sure.'

'So, also, Harold said that you and Maddy weren't, er, going out any more?'

Sam's eyes locked on Stella's and for a moment he said nothing. 'No,' he admitted finally. 'No, we're not. That wasn't really a thing. She's great. Really great. She's incredibly sweet, and the kids love her, and she's funny and clev—'

'Yeah, yeah, yeah, I get all that,' Stella interrupted.

'Oh, right. Sorry. No, we're not together.'

She bit her lip, unsure what to say next.

'Anything else?'

'No. I mean, yes! I just don't know how to say it.'

Sam smiled and jutted his chin towards her. 'Close your eyes.'

'What?'

'It's a trick I do with the kids when they can't tell me exactly where it hurts, I get them to describe it to me instead. Close your eyes.'

Stella closed her eyes. She didn't think it was possible to feel more idiotic than she did already, standing beside the revolving doors, her mouth trying to wrap itself around the right words – and yet now she did.

'What is it?' Sam asked gently.

Stella screwed her eyes more tightly closed, bracing herself for the embarrassment of her next sentence. 'I wanted to say… I wanted to tell you, really, that I've got a lot of things wrong, and I've been a moron. Like, a real moron. But the truth is… is I like you. Quite a lot, actually. You're the frosting on the cake, I think.'

'Huh? What cake?'

'Never mind,' Stella replied, scrunching her eyes tighter. She had to get the next sentence out. 'And the thing is, I don't know if you feel the same but I had to tell you, I wanted you to know, and if you wanted to go for a drink at some point, well, uh, that would be nice.'

'Are you asking me on a date, Shakespeare?'

She could hear him smiling.

'Maybe?' she replied tentatively, opening one eye to see Sam had stepped closer.

'Here,' he replied, still grinning, 'in the impossibly romantic setting of the Chelsea and Westminster Hospital?'

Stella nodded and realised that Sam was now so close she could see his individual eyelashes. So close she could reach out and put a hand on his chest. So close that he felt magnetic, like there was an invisible spool of cotton wrapped around them, pulling them together.

'Are you free now?' he asked.

'*Now* now?'

He shrugged. 'I know a place nearby that does great coffee.'

The corners of her lips twitched and she smiled. 'Yes, I'm free now.'

Sam leant forward, so close now that their noses were almost touching, and looked at her for a few seconds before pressing his mouth against hers.

A memory came back to Stella then; she remembered the feel of his lips from the first time they'd kissed in the pub that night, three months earlier. It was like every other kiss had been wrong, but this was very, *very* right. It was familiar; it was safe; it was everything she'd spent so long looking for.

But she also remembered something else and pulled her head back. 'Sorry, there's just one tiny problem.'

Sam frowned. 'What is it?'

'Can we talk about your pleather headboard?'

ACKNOWLEDGEMENTS

Right, line up everyone. There are an ENORMOUS number of people I need to thank for LOFL getting this far (a year and a half on, the title's abbreviation is still making me laugh. Tragic.). It's hugely unfair that the author gets to stick their name on a cover when it should the author's name along with roughly 472 others. Ok, I came up with the story, but it took a generous army of people to transform it from a draft on my laptop to the book that's now in your hands. Or on your Kindle or other eBook device. Other eBook devices are available, apparently.

So, to everyone at HQ Stories, my very wonderful publisher, thank you. Two tiny words hardly feel enough for all the work that has gone into this. Book five! I am beyond grateful for this, as is five-year-old Sophia who used to write stories in a Care Bear notebook. We are both chuffed to be working with the most industrious and ingenious team in the business. Thank you to my editor Katie Seaman, publicist Sian Baldwin, Janet Aspey and Becca Joyce in marketing; George Green in sales; Aisling Smyth and Zoe Shine in rights; Kate Oakley and Stephanie Heathcoate in design; Liz Hatherell for copyediting with such a sharp eye, and Charlotte Atyeo for proofreading. Plus, as always, Lisa Milton for all our discussions about foot spray.

To Becky Ritchie, super agent, wonder woman and my therapist this year even more than before, thank you for all your wisdom and dedication. Whenever I'm in a flap (quite often, poor Becky) I am always reassured by your calm and encouragement. You are a saint. Saint Becky, I bow before you.

To my family and pals. I'm a pain in the ass when I'm writing, I know. Writers are (mostly) deeply selfish, deeply neurotic, deeply insecure people and I am no exception. When I'm in the thick of a book, living on toast and seventy-three cups of tea a day, barely bothering to get dressed, I am in my own world with my characters. And while I quite like being in my own world, with my own characters (especially Harold, HOW I loved writing Harold), I'm grateful to you all for dragging me out of it every now and again. Especially Hols, the best of all friends and the most positive person I know. Thank you for putting up with me in all moods, and for all the animal memes. Also, thank you for taking me to hospital when I was halfway through writing this book, after I accidentally swallowed a mouthful of glycolic acid face toner one night. Long story, maybe I'll put it in a book one day.

Most of all, though, and I don't want to sound too sincere because I normally do jokes, but *most* of all thank you to our hospitals for their heroic work over the past three years. On top of accidentally drinking glycolic acid, I also got Covid halfway through writing this book, but I was lucky because all it meant, for me, was lying on the sofa for a couple of weeks watching *The Morning Show* (brilliant, worth watching for Jennifer Aniston's wardrobe alone). Although my gratitude to our health service isn't solely due to Covid. Hospitals have looked after my mum in recent years, along with my very dear much-missed friend, Vix. And a few summers ago, when I came down with appendicitis, I was wheeled from the hospital ward by a porter called Jesus ('You're in good hands!' he promised) who sang cheery songs to me all the way to the operating theatre because he could see I was crying. My awe of people like Jesus has doubled... tripled... QUADRUPLED in the past three years as they've battled with Covid on our behalf. And that goes for British hospitals and those around the world, which is why this book is dedicated to everyone who works in them. Thank you.

Read more funny and feel-good romantic comedies from Sophia Money-Coutts

You never forget the one that got away, do you?

Nell Mason is extremely happy with her life – or at least, that's what she tells herself. She's lucky to have a high-powered job as a lawyer, even if it does come with an eccentric set of billionaire divorce clients. And she's absolutely fine living with her sweet, if slightly dull, boyfriend Gus in their London flat where they have very sensible sex once (OK, sometimes twice) a week. She's definitely not stuck in a rut.

But when Nell bumps into childhood friend and first love Arthur Drummond who broke her heart fifteen years ago, she's more than a little shaken. The seemingly perfect life she's worked so hard for starts to feel, well, less perfect. Maybe Nell's been kidding herself all these years. Can she ever get over her first love?

He's perfect. . . on paper.

Florence Fairfax isn't lonely. She loves her job at the little bookshop in Chelsea and her beloved cat Marmalade keeps her company at night. She might have been single for quite a while – well, forever actually, if anyone's asking – but she's perfectly happy, thank you. And then Florence meets eccentric love coach Gwendolyn, and everything changes.

When Gwendolyn makes Florence write a wish list describing her perfect man, Florence refuses to take it seriously. Until, later that week, a handsome blond man asks for help in the bookshop.

Rory seems to fit the list perfectly. But is he 'the one', or simply too good to be true? Florence is about to find out that her criteria for Mr Right aren't as important as she thought – and that perhaps she's been looking for love in all the wrong places. . .

One first date.
One (not so) little mistake.

After eight years together, Lil Bailey thought she'd already found 'the one' – that is, until he dumped her for a blonde twenty-something colleague. So she does what any self-respecting singleton would do: swipes right, puts on her best bra and finds herself on a first date with a handsome mountaineer called Max. What's the worst that can happen?

Well it's pretty bad actually. First Max ghosts her and then, after weeing on a stick (but mostly her hands), a few weeks later Lil discovers she's pregnant. She's single, thirty-one and living in a thimble-sized flat in London, it's hardly the happily-ever-after she was looking for.

Lil's ready to do the baby-thing on her own – it can't be that hard, right? But she should probably tell Max, if she can track him down. Surely he's not that Max, the highly eligible, headline-grabbing son of Lord and Lady Rushbrooke, currently trekking up a mountain in South Asia? Oh, maybe he wasn't ignoring Lil after all. . .

Polly's not looking for 'the one', just the plus one. . .

Polly is fine. She's single, having sex (well, only twice last year), and stuck in a job writing about royal babies. So the chances of her finding a plus one to her best friend's summer wedding are looking worryingly slim.

But it's a New Year, a new leaf and all that, and Polly's given herself 365 days to get her s**t together. Her latest piece is on the infamous Jasper, Marquess of Milton, the last man she'd consider a plus one or 'the one'. After all, she's heard the stories, there's no way she'll succumb to his charms. . .